The Laestrygonians
The grim Poseidon y ⸺ *meet,*
Unless you have them in your own soul,
And your soul paints them before you.
  C. Cavafy, 'Ithaca'.

CURED MEAT

Memoirs of a Psychiatric Runaway

Polly Trope

ONEIROS BOOKS

To those I left behind

Cover Art by Sabrina Andresen
Cover Photography by Joe Palermo Noir
ISBN 10 : 1497590442
ISBN 13: 9781497590441

Contents

Enter: Through the Elephant Gate

In my dream, I am on a bus in London, my groceries are stolen. Annoyed, I go back, get new grocery shopping. Same thing, packed bus, uncanny loudspeaker announcements, someone playing hide and seek with me steals my groceries again. This time also my wallet. Am meant to report theft at the nearest police bureau, which is at King's Cross station. On the way there, start hearing my thief's voice again, still playing hide and seek. I start chasing him by the voice, although I never see him. Leads me to the back of the station, where I see a nice looking couple speaking Russian, playing in the sand by some overflowing bins. I decide to follow the Russian couple around rather than the thief, and to befriend them. Find the way to the police bureau, but once I get there, after a long walk through a subterranean lake resort full of shorn men in dresses on lounging chairs – some blue, some green – it turns out it's not a police bureau but an army brothel lap dancing supply shop selling mostly knickers and belly chains. A crowd of blonde lap dancers, who are half my size, rush in speaking in German, try to seduce me, and are hushed out by a man at the counter wearing a worn business suit and tie. I leave, escorted by an old English woman with short hair and glasses, who explains to me that the men in dresses are soldiers, some English, some German, those wearing blue the Germans, and the English, green. We are not allowed to speak. As we come out of the subterranean, I still have no wallet, but we are greeted by a small cohort of various people who, apparently, have also

[3]

been in the subterranean, and we will all be brought to the exit gate together as a chained group. The closer we get to King's Cross station entrance again, the more I hear the same thief's voice in between loud speaker announcements, again. At the station, it turns out I cannot take the bus anyway; it has been overtaken by giant beetles that have gone insane, growing larger and larger in the bus whilst flipping and turning in circles. I receive a scolding for having entered the subterranean domain, which no one is allowed to visit. Our little herd is led back into the middle of the King's Cross station lobby, where soon, everybody disperses into the crowd, and I am left standing alone in a cloud of passers-by and still on the lookout for my groceries, the thief, and my wallet. Two men twice my size turn up from the right; they are German and as I then realise, old school friends of mine. They lead me back to the overflowing bins in the back of the station, where the Russians are still playing in the sand. The English lady with the glasses, a man-woman with short hair, is also there. She takes me with her into a unisex toilet, which is filthy and slippery. I see a stair and begin to climb; it leads me to a large room, where I find many of my belongings. Infections drippings from the ceiling have made an awful puddle in my kitchen. I try to mop it up, but as I do so, the floor sucks up the drippings, the stain cannot be removed, and it turns rock hard, whereas the rest of the house seems to have somewhat soft, breathing and fluffy walls. A broken piano which I owned disappears while I look at it, but in the middle of the salon, a grand piano seems to have grown as a tree, and there are people dancing on it. I try to walk towards the piano, but start to sink into the floor. A trapeze swings by from above, which I grip and it drops me off by the same overflowing bin behind the station

[4]

again. The Russians are still there playing in the sand, and so is the old woman with short hair and glasses. She takes me back into the unisex toilet. Again, I go up to the space upstairs, but with the drippings from the ceiling and the soft floors, the house is just about to melt and to fall down on itself. I walk down a set of stairs to leave the house through the front door. At this point, I wake up.

One : Back in Ithaca

The Soul at Aulis

One afternoon, I woke up from a long sleep. I realised that I had been awake all the time, but life seemed suddenly to have transformed from a black and white photograph into a moving colour picture.

It was a grey life we lived, simple and harsh, every day waking up together in a single bed, two teenagers squashed against each other, getting bruised against a cold wall during the restless sleep this bare, narrow room with fading carpet and a small mirror and sink with separate water taps provided us with, on a twelfth floor in a Bermondsey tower.

I used to get up early, quietly, and first of all close our dirty window, and for a moment gaze over the flashlight-dotted view of London awaking in the half-light. Tower Bridge was just beneath the window, and, most days, a thin web of fog lay on the streets between houses as the eye followed down to a Canary Wharf glinting in the distance like gems of graphite detached out of what seemed an infinitely extending, grey and black horizon of reflecting quartz surfaces, cut through only by dark brown train tracks, and the eastward course of the Thames.

Getting dressed in stealth mode, I would walk down a long, sleepy corridor and into the ratty, greasy, hairy student halls kitchen, have tea and make croque monsieurs for my boyfriend, which I placed on the desk in the room for him to eat at lunchtime, before I left for the day. He'd sometimes wake up as I was about to leave, howl in despair and try to hold me back with tears in his eyes and ask anxiously when I would come back. The sight of him with his scruffy hair, circles under his eyes, and pale, emaciated face and of his body under the weather of eczemas, his front clouded by a kind of neurotic state of mind that mixed obsessions, rages, and great fears, always set my head on fire. What was I supposed to do with this boyfriend living illegally with me, who had turned out to be an abuser, lashing out at me in the room every day, and on top of that, he had become too ill to take his life in his own hands? I was just eighteen. His knees had swollen and made him unsteady on his feet. Everything was only getting worse since September, and it was January perhaps, or February now.

The loving and carefree, dreamed-of student life was rapidly turning into a reality more alike to a nightmare. Our daily life, full of angry explosions, physical fights, unease and fear of the future, was overcast by the damp clouds of poverty. Even so, we could share a tear or have a laugh together, and never got tired of telling each other stories of great expectations, inventing a bright future we were certain would eventually come. Because we had only very little money, we did not go out to see films together or rock concerts as we would have liked to, did not go to restaurants or cafes, didn't follow any fashions or drink alcohol, nor did we smoke cigarettes like we had done as young teenagers. Instead, we would sit on the bedspread together on weekends, and read books to each other. From my university library, I borrowed books that we could read together in this way, as we had similar taste. We read many Russian novels, French Enlightenment prose, the complete works of George Orwell, and we even got through Proust's *Recherche du temps perdu* in full, on those long nights

[8]

when autumn turned to winter in the twelfth floor window whilst getting intimately acquainted with Tesco's value product range, and also, he was ill with a mysterious mental derangement, and scared of other people, and scared of going outside.

If we got into a fight, as we did almost every night, the life and fire would come back to him. Once it started, he wouldn't stop hitting me in the face, twisting my arms and throwing me on the floor, kicking me in the stomach and threatening me with any sharp objects that may be there, and he would only stop when I started bashing my own face into the carpet. I would say 'I don't know how to change this situation either, it's not my fault' and cry, and inevitably then, he would start to cry as well, horrified at what was happening, and ask me to stop hurting myself. He would try to take me into his arms, but by then, it was my turn at being angry, and I would recoil from the love, I didn't want to be in his arms at all, then, rather, I felt like blowing myself up.

There was no space in this situation, no place to go to for either of us, we had no relatives in this city, no money to sit in a bar and talk to strangers, and there certainly was no spare room. We'd have to sit opposite one another for a while without speaking, and I would eventually go outside and throw up in the bathroom, because in that time I was bulimic, and he would have to wait.

I would then start working on my university essays, focusing in a way that all but physically removed me from the time and place, and he would not disturb, and go to bed, and call me before falling asleep, begging me at least to do my studying in the bed rather than at the desk. He would have liked to fall asleep together with me, and for me to come as close as I could get, to make up for the

[9]

many hours that he had to spend by himself in the room when I would be away at university, in the daytime.

As time moved forward, I understood better and better how he was slowly going more and more insane, and saw that I was going with him. When I say 'insane', I don't mean that in a way that I or anyone can really explain. I mean the astonishing way that irrational forces can take over someone's mind and start running their life whilst common sense just flies out the window. With hindsight, I know that I should not have stayed in the situation and should probably have called the police the very first time he hit me. But not only did I not know what to do and who to turn to, I also had, by way of response, begun to starve myself in a methodical way, and this eating disorder was insidiously weakening my ability to pull out. We were eighteen. The madness had begun much earlier – at sweet sixteen, in secondary school. It seemed an age away.

We had met in school, in Berlin. At sixteen, I wanted to become a pianist, and I had plans; but they just disappeared when I became particularly stressed at school, ran out of time to sleep, and started to neglect myself somewhat, failing to keep reasonably well groomed and harming myself, too. My results in school were always very good, which meant that my parents were happy for me to go out at night or do whatever else I pleased in my spare time. In my case, that was mostly to trawling the dank and crumbling east side of Berlin, which was still fairly new, uncharted grounds in ways, for western Berliners like me. In those years, as a teenager, I first got acquainted with lady vodka, street art slogans, arts collectives, and parties in midst the ruins of Berlin.

I collected my thoughts in growing piles of journals. Much

of that was, I'm sure, the usual teenage girl's journalling, but on top of that there also began to emerge descriptions of a more poetic sensitivity, relating to tiny things I saw in life's window that nobody else seemed to see or feel, and that I wanted to catch and stop on my pages for the day when they all would fall into place and make sense: the secrets of Berlin's dark and abandoned houses, the wasted trace of momentous times in history, the modernist symphony of a great city, the furious passion of music, the poetry of destruction.

We were reading great authors in the classroom, too, which weighed heavy on my mind all the time. I really loved words, and places and characters I read of in books often seemed to me as vivid and true as the real world I inhabited. The boldness and brazen morals of bohemian poets and writers seemed immediately enticing to me, and I soon felt at home in the country of literary imagination, painted in the evergreen flora of classic and modernist imagery, mediated through altered states of mind, voyeurism or alcoholism, and I honestly began to see new layers and new depths to what was happening around me every day. It's not that I glamorized reality, but I filtered and enhanced it.

I drank much vodka at a school prom when I was sixteen, then got stuck in the pipelines of sordid subways, and lingered on in dark stations, under iron bridges. As I looked over the dankly glistening river, nightmares of the sleepless type came to haunt me. I started thinking about writing my own stories, in the middle of the night, and I also thought it was the end of me. I would not have been surprised if I had died on one of those nights outside in the cold, inspecting the city and its nocturnal mores.

There was always, in those days, an atmosphere of

[11]

apocalypse hanging over our school, perhaps because the neighbourhood where it was located, a red light district near a traditionally gay neighbourhood, increasingly was crowded by street walkers and a washed-out army of narcotic faces, threatening to recruit new flesh from the pool of pupils. Syringes on the floor adorned the way to school and our teachers were pulling all the strings possible to make sure we knew we were living a tale of two cities and not allowed into that street's reality, only to the reality of our big and weighty books, Nobel prizes and ambassadors.

School days finished at about half five, when high booted, latex corseted, platinum-blonde-extensioned ladies were already standing in line waiting to be picked up by clients in dark, metallic cars. Fringing the scene, alcoholics on benches ending the day slowly with their dogs, were gazing at business suits, biker jackets, leather trousered crotches and nonchalant cigarettes flitting by, and I was very hungry for the lives of others. The canal, the ships, the parks, the junkies on benches, the bars, the women with babies, the people sitting in their cars waiting, the business suits out for lunch, all this life I couldn't be part of because of the long school days, the long hours of homework, the difficult equations and the dissertations about humanist ideas, and a perfect arrogance keeping me from lowering myself to the common people – there wasn't time for any of this, really. I was expecting something magical to happen, someone to emerge long haired and leather jacketed, and sweep me off my feet.

I walked around town, quite far sometimes, if there happened to be a gap in my timetable. Down a broad, burnt-out boulevard in Berlin one afternoon, I came to the

[12]

museum island, an island of neoclassical museum buildings upon the city canal. Inside them, Schliemann's loot is stored: ancient Greek gods of white marble, the altar of Pergamon, whole temples and market gates. From the outside, I gazed at the museums black with time, their walls full of withered alternative punk band posters, blinded windows, urban plants growing through the cracks, broken scaffoldings and overflowing waste containers all around.

Back in the 1990s, the place seemed abandoned for good. Improbable that the city's impoverished senate would ever produce the funds to restore the ruinous East side of Berlin in the wake of the Cold War. The museums had been closed for decades and war damage had been left gaping open on the buildings, like untreated wounds. The classical collections were mostly unavailable, although I could see, through the window, some Greek and Roman heads of philosophers.

I crossed a stone bridge over a little black water, small branch of a slow flowing, darkly glittering canal that ran past this fabled and sleepy island, formerly the home of Greek gods, now just a sinking utopia. Looking down into the dull darkness underneath my feet to see if I could catch my own reflection in the city canal, thinking it could carry me out of town, all the way into the pale green, dry and sandy plains of Brandenburg.

Along the opposite side ran a shadowed, crumbling colonnade and in the background I could hear trains hissing on old rails elevated on iron bridges, as they entered the station, which seemed like a giant-size, glass and iron bell jar placed upon a large and busy crossroads. Berlin-Friedrichstrasse, the lively thoroughfare, where all the noise once, not that long ago, had been paper boys, coaches and horses, and Prussian military parades, which we read about in school, in the old Prussian plays from the turn of the century. It was also, I thought, the same sort of time this grand museum complex was erected on the island. The train bridges, the museums, the big station, all that was still there, but modern man in modern fashions was rushing around the scene like children in a dead amusement park.

The falling, old-stately museum buildings were hugging in the cold, strangely asking for my attention. I felt their stealthy whisper in my bones, enigmatic like fairy tales the trees talk in – were they calling on me? I drew closer, and just as I stepped inside their blazing aura, leaving trains and clamour behind me, a crow, fanning with its wide and breezy wings, shot over my head and upwards to the right, into the clouds.

That century-old, unworldly, stone and iron corridor seemed to echo my sigh and carried it further, gave it a gigantic voice. I thought then that it could lift all the weight off Atlas' shoulders and unhinge the world and rearrange its meaning, melt down solid rock, turn houses into soap bubbles, evaporate and breathe life and kindness into train tracks, rails and station domes, to open the way for my soul running out into the light of grey dust, with the wings of desire.

That day, I had not yet known the frustration of wanting to find words for something that can't really be told. And I thought that revisiting the place could decode my mind's secret messages, and so, many times I revisited and meditated there, re-lived the day in dreams and deja-vus, often returned to the bridge and looked down at the black water, only to find again and again that it could never again be the same river. Only change remained, and I had to continue looking within myself to shine light upon the darkened landscape of my imagination.

And then, back to the school, to the west side, past Slumberland and the Metropol, Big Sexyland, Club Tropicana, sex toys and neon, fringed by old Benz's, and latex, latex and more latex in window displays, up the concrete stairs to the top floor where the sixthformers had a special smoking lounge in which creative types like me would sometimes exchange short stories or discuss other lofty topics. There was a roof terrace, too, back when smoking was legal at sixteen, which was where cool teachers mixed with cool students; someone was always playing Oasis or Bob Marley on the guitar, drumming, or singing Californication on that roof, looking over Berlin's horizon, then full of cranes, wondering how it could look so blue, so gentle and so silent from here, and turn to our slim acres of strawberries and marijuana.

The corner shop, run by a warm and mothering, umphy Berlin momma, was where we, the grey and overworked crowd of teenagers imperceptibly turned scholars, could enjoy becoming something more than pale faces bent over difficult books. Frieda, who made chocolate sandwiches for us all, baked croissants, made coffee in the morning and also sold vodka in small flasks, knew all the gossip and more, she could help us in our difficult decisions, such as whether or not to quit the lyceum and go for an 'easy' school when our grades were promising a kick-out. In this warm and friendly room, the line between teachers and students was somehow blurred and we would all be

[15]

standing next to each other, young and old, wrapped in cashmere coats and scarves, sharing a croissant or a cigarette, telling the teachers not to have whiskey this early, whilst they would tell us not to smoke so young. Rehearsing a last theorem before a maths test, one could still smile for a moment, look at the rotting school building with a sigh, maybe murmuring a witty quote by a great thinker about this mortal coil, walk through the door, nose in the air with the impeccable arrogance of elite schools, and find consolation about the disaster that it really was, in knowing that this here school was second to none in the whole of town.

Such was the shabby chic and fiercely laid back microcosm of my Berlin high school in the late 1990s and early '00s.

Jonathan was a new kid in our school that year. He had come straight from France, he was good-looking, and he had a leather jacket. He was pale already then, exhausted by the recent move to Germany following the long illness and death of his mother. He and his younger sister were living with their father, a musician, his second wife, and their small stepbrother. The living arrangements were less than ideal; the mother had originally divorced Jonathan's dad because he was beating her, and he was not much different with his second wife, then, and soon also Jonathan and his younger sister.

We hadn't known each other long, but things between us had got very serious very soon. I was at Jonathan's house having dinner with his family: his younger sister, his father, the father's second wife, and their little son. The small child was fidgety in his high

[16]

chair, his dad got angry and the kid didn't stop, so his father got up. Instantly, the kid was under the table, his father was holding a kitchen knife, shouting at the boy under the table and the sister said something like 'stop it dad' and there was silence. Then Jonathan got up and shouted at her, telling her to shut up because they were at risk of getting thrown out of the house. They ended up on the floor, she was screaming, biting. The wife said, 'guys, get up, what are you doing', whilst the father was just standing there with his knife, she said to him 'this is nuts, sit down', he sat down in his chair. We finished the dinner. The father said 'can I have more wine please', his wife said 'you shouldn't be drinking', so he went to a bar, we cleaned the kitchen, the wife was crying, and we all went to sleep. The next morning, his dad dropped the 'maybe I'll just shoot myself', nobody answered anything, Jonathan dropped a glass, it broke. His dad said 'you and your sister are moving out', his wife said 'come on you shouldn't say things you don't mean' his sister said 'really you're so selfish you're not even allowed to kick us out like that', he threw her against the door. Jonathan said 'I think we are going to move out' his dad said 'no, don't do that, my children, please…' his wife said 'well in any case we need to find an arrangement' my fiancé said 'our mother was his wife before you and we have a right to live here too' she said 'yes I know but you must follow the house rules you never help out' his sister said 'oi I never see you do any cleaning either, so how come this place is spotless' her father said 'listen I told you to do as she tells you, as if she were your real mother' the little boy said 'they're not her children are they?' - 'No' - 'what time is it? We have to go to the market. guys you keep wasting my time' - 'when are you paying the bills for the house move'

[17]

- 'dad I don't even have a bank account you said you get the money through that lawyer' - 'it is your job to talk to that lawyer I don't speak French' - 'I don't have her number' - 'I'm kicking you out and you're paying me back for everything'.

Jonathan and I just took the adventurous escape route and became a cute young couple, cruising the city's bars at night, and a new world opened up that was blue and shiny, in which nights began to glisten, and all things seemed possible. The joys of breakfast together in a cafe before school, getting drunk at night, wandering the steep cliffs close to coma, emptying our hearts and filling up on beautiful new thoughts and dreams of a different life. The future was near, it seemed like a pheasant over wheat fields to spread its wings and sail gently from the farther sky, from the clouds from whence it came, towards where we were standing and ready for it to land on our palms.

Of old Berlin, only one image stuck in my mind, of an accordion player in the dark, on the iron bridge over the canal. The water in the canals of Berlin is so black, it's almost oily, and it glistens at night, with the white lights. How desolate, and how full of hope, this creature in the dark, on an iron bridge, under the enormous train station, shoring its accordion against the might of trains and trains again, it was cold, the water was glistening, the bridge was iron, and stones on the bridge crackled under glum footsteps, under the singer's song and the accordion. The windows on the street were dark.

Old women's apartments that I knew were behind those windows, full of dated china, fur gloves and embroidered table napkins, black and white photographs of the beloved, the dead, and colour frames of those who are alive and

[18]

well, but hardly come for visits any more. Chipped cups and turquoise bathrooms, and that smell of life's evening, where stories don't matter any more, only the objects that stay in the house, these old-fashioned, crook-shaped, strangely solid products, oak chairs, velvet curtains on iron rings, porcelain flowers, octagonal amulets, copper clocks, indestructible kitchen pans, thick grey carpet floors and wallpaper, and drinking glasses with steel rim. Handmade dresses and socks in drawers, preciously kept letters from the front, and on the walls, oil-painted idylls and landscapes.

A sharp-edged melancholy rolled itself through my veins. I felt for the first time that I was not myself, but a bitter intruder, gatherer of stories. I had something in me that made people want to impress their stories on me and trust me with their memory. And so, often, I'm less of an acting character and more like a piece of wax being carved by the storyteller. I heard many stories of many people. But Jonathan's, I could not yet quite piece together, there were many blind spots.

Sometimes I could even remember a time that no-one now could tell a tale of, that time when the museums were built. In the age of empires, between famines, wars and industrialisation, German scholars started fiercely collecting, cataloguing, systematically arranging and organising the remains of the ancient world, numbering everything, classifying fragments and compiling large inventories, lists, producing collections of Latin inscriptions, or volumes of Greek poetry fragments. They were voluminous compilations of incomplete remains from ancient cultures, and many of the grand excavations that ended up bringing imperial loot to Berlin and London were initiated at just that time.

[19]

In the freezing winters, with sirens and trains roaring strident outside, when black trees, leafless, point their emaciated fingers erratically and poke the heavy snow clouds, between storms and hunger, automobiles and top hats, from within these museums, there was invented a golden land pieced together from the colourless scatter of long gone Greece so eagerly loved by the poets, that Greece that was so light-hearted, hot and sunny, full of ships and spices, comedy, tragedy and bitter war, wild religions and market-places, orators, philosophers, merchants and slaves.

With awe I wandered through the white sculpture galleries, past black and white photographs labelled with Prussian or Silesian-sounding names of people forgotten long since, of men and women on archaeological sites, next to reconstructed ancient gates and altars. Often I went right through the island on my train to school, peering into the mysterious windows to antiquity, always catching sight of the same white marble heads, the hermae of Socrates and Seneca, and clay pot fragments, 18th century paintings on the wall behind them.

The fragments, the irregular edges of broken jugs whose colour had evaporated, the quiet inside, and freezing cold Berlin outside with its iron rails and whining trains pulling past the island, seemed as a stone-set union and somehow from here, grew the memory of the Acropolis, light living, theatres, market places, and the Mediterranean sun. From outside, the museums seemed cyclopic monuments fallen from the sky. Bombed during the war, blackened with the rain, they were like wounded giants, withered debris of a departed spirit so different from our own. These museums perspired of two spirits that I did not know, the monster Germany and the monster Antiquity, here united by secret,

[20]

paradoxical bonds.

So it was this spirit, the twin spirit of Germany and Greece resuscitated through and in spite of the incredible, the positivist method of classificatory scholarship and archivalism, this giant inscription in time between Greece and Germany, young Germany, that land of high hopes and straight discipline, strange, yet strangely familiar to me by indirect, inarticulate particles, something painful, seemingly heavy and unattractive, but secretly, greater than armies and empires, deep knowledge to reach far into long-gone centuries, to stand in the stream that flows through the Bible, flows through Dante, flows through us. I had gained the power to be outside of time.

March, 2003
Museum walls turn away from the trains in horror with a screeching noise, the giants bend back at the sight of monstrous machines throbbing their way, fuming, expiring.
At rooftops we stand begging ourselves not to jump, with arms rowing to the surface of this madness, we shout from the bottom of all civilisation, please hear us who want to be saved and don't want to drown. Every word is a token brought back from the Underworld. But to tell the tale in full, that really is the hardest deed.
My memory is like a gentle giant, powerful but thick, looking to all sides, it lashes out at everything, but in vain, there is nothing but fog all around, thick fog between the fingers of my hands, and the heat of heartblood pulsing in my fingertips only reminds me that I'm alive, nothing more. Rails squeal to fill the station with the shrill noise of a world's end. The passengers on the platform look at each other and wonder if they've already faded to grey, or
[21]

if they can still drop their briefcases and run. Each year when nature makes ready to burst out in colours and shapes, and announces its passion, when trees stands in bloom splendid as if this were its last spring, I cannot stop my heart from breaking. Spring is breaking, the city is bursting, a thousand bleeding hearts are hunting all the people, they scream and cry, they crash and tear up, and the clouds in the sky press down as cotton in our ears to muffle the unbearable screaming.

The old central train station perched above the canals and the island, has often given me the grief of prolonged waiting times, and wrapped doubt around my head: that black water, why does it stare so dumb at me, when I've repeatedly invoked its demons? I know they are still there. That black water, why does it not answer? Black and glitzy, slowly it flows and passes over, no matter how many people have stood there before me and looked on it to no avail. But did I not hear a chime of fairy-tale worlds just inside that water lily filament? Just a twinkle, a chime, as of a glass bell hung at the end of a frail twig, ringing crystalline notes in the wet wind.

The site changed over the years and became pretty again with neat grass quads and whitened walls, the Greek gods do take visits again, now. But under all this splendour, on a slow fire, still burns my dark memory of blackened walls crumbling in the winter rain, the undying mystery of a place remains even though a little sand on the ground is changed and cheery visitors now flock all around. What then looked dull and falling apart today shines and glows, and yet there always is a whisper from the depths inside the walls, from the distant point just off the horizon, between black water and age-old cornerstones. And so it is that, hidden by leafy shadows and closed from the

[22]

*inside, memory wreathes about the place, lives on, sleeps
and sleepwalks, ambling through my dreams from time to
time, every year, like on days when we dream of the dead.*

One day, Jonathan read everything I'd ever written in my
journal books, got very angry about it, and told me to tear
them up, then we burnt everything. The day we trashed
and burnt my manuscripts, I was feeling ambivalent about
doing so, but thought I would forget about it and new
things would come to replace all of this anyhow.
A little after that, he started showing his true face,
punching me when we had fights, and becoming jealous of
my even speaking to my girlfriends in school or spending
time with my family. I got intimidated and shy and stopped
eating. I became very skinny and weak then already, and I
felt as if not just journals, but my whole self had been torn
and burnt, I felt strangely disembodied and as though my
mind was denied expression in order to destroy my life. I
stuck with him, at first, because he was the only person
who had read, and would know those books had been
written and that I had thought those thoughts. Later, I
realised he had misunderstood them mostly, and felt
hopeless, isolated and damaged. But there was no way
back, only forward. I made some drawings, but I was
never good at drawing. He confiscated them anyway, as
well as any new writing, and he insisted on reading any
letters I sent anybody, he also opened all the ones I
received. I thought I better destroy all of the letters his
sister had written to me, as they were private and
confessional, too.
There was a lot of destruction going on in those days.
Jonathan himself destroyed his dead mother's last letters to
him, cut up and burnt family albums. He trashed all the

books his mother had owned, we trashed all of my clothes that he didn't like, that were clothes from my life before I knew him. I gave up many friendships and lost touch with family at that time. We were fiercely exclusive to one another, and went out in the streets of Berlin at night wandering in our newly found sense of rebuilding ourselves from the ashes. Often, we got drunk together at first, but he passed out frequently and I found myself dragging him around a lot, into train stations for warmth, where he slept it off in my arms and I opened his gift, and also, I worried about the future. London, I had said. I wanted to study in London.

Here we were, in London, now. What a far cry was this brittle haired child, mongering grey hours of panic and despair, afraid to leave the house and scared of strangers, from the talented and fashionable young man he'd been when we first met.

I knew he'd be watching me disappear from the window as I got on my bike, waved at him, and made my way to university. During those mornings, I used to go up to the attics of the music department and practise the piano for an hour or two. Afterwards, whilst the janitors made their morning rounds, I'd wander about the university buildings, which I haunted like the ghost of silence, until my lecture schedule started, to which I never got even a minute early, so as to avoid conversation with classmates. They seemed all to be having a scrumptious and hyper-social first year at university, drinking past dignity and going out clubbing, dating, but I was far too broke to join them and also intensely preoccupied with my difficult relationship situation.

I'd sweep into lectures and out again as a flighty

apparition, in my boyfriend's sweaters, sit by myself and take notes about Virgil, Nestor's cup, or early evidence of the Greek alphabet, then rush to the library, and peruse bibliography lists, or sit in the church opposite university, where the blue glass threw incensed light over pious sculptures and a grand piano, which I was allowed to play if no-one was there.

Eventually, I'd always escape the stress of a day, get back on the bike, duck under the embarrassing looks, as in those days cycling in London was awfully unfashionable, and slip back into the house, run to the room where he would have been waiting for me all day. He would always be peering through the hole in the door, whenever the door went, with the calculating mind of a concierge listing every entrance, every exit, and so, he would always open the door for me without my even knocking, recognizing the sound of my steps, hush me in with a look of dismay at my long absence.

He'd be hungry, and ask that I cook something for us, which I'd then do, although the food was never great: Tesco's value pasta with cheese, carrots, or cabbage, plain yoghurt, scrambled eggs on toast, baked beans, lentils, potatoes, nothing fancy. After the meal, he'd pull disgusted faces and send me out to wash the plates, and when I came back, would be holding his stomach curled up on the bed in cramps, and ask me where I'd been so long.

Words would fail me at the sight every time, but I had to tell stories to him, it was important. I told of our hopes to make it to a better life, his eyes dim and furious, as he had forgotten everything that had come before we ended up in this little room with pale rose walls and an old brown carpet, stuffed with things we didn't need, his dead mother's furniture we'd brought there from France, piece by piece, over many Eurostar rides.

We were completely uncool, we didn't care at all. I wore his jeans and he wore my jumpers, which, incidentally, had been my father's before anyway. We didn't go out for drinks, I didn't have any dresses. We shared one bottle of 2-in-1 shampoo and one pot of nivea cream. By the end of each day we'd be screaming at each other, eventually, he'd get out of bed, just to shake and strangle me, slam me against the door and punch my stomach, pull my hair to break my neck, hold my mouth shut so no-one would hear me scream and cry, and I was afraid to hit him back, after he'd become so ill and so weak, and because I'd never been used to domestic violence before, and I was in denial, rather than muscling up a practical response. And now we were stuck in this situation.

Every day, for three quarters of a year. He had experienced a trauma in his past, and had become a case of paralytic anxiety, stir-crazy room pacing and wasting away in an obsession with putting things in order. I'd tell him stories, exhausted just like him, and invent his future, invent our hopes. I knew that he had lost the ability to see the light at the end of the tunnel, and I had to carry that light for him.

Every day, for an eternity, it seems. I myself began to feel more and more bleak, here, occupied with studying this subject – Classics – I had picked at random, in a country – England – I had not really known, cut off from my parents, and without much connection to the other students, who were partying, spending, and making friends whilst I was tied only to this guy who had become a child again in my arms, clueless, and a cruel child at that, ungrateful, without ears or eyes for my own grief in the situation.

I was clueless, too, and becoming in every way just as mad as he. This city was full of eyes that looked on me

[26]

malignantly, scorning my appearance of poverty, although I didn't deserve it. I just couldn't think, I only felt shame and the desire to disappear, and I was starving myself all the time and throwing up food that I sometimes shoplifted. It was pure misery. And yet, had I not once had such a great mind?

Gone somehow, dispersed, who knows to what fate. What he was doing all day long, while I was in school, I never knew. He said he looked out of the window, memorized car plates, watched people in windows, and listened to steps outside the door. I wanted him to go out and study like me, or failing that, to take a job, to meet some people and live a normal life. I started to teach him some English, but he wasn't learning. He was always rearranging the order of books on the shelves, dusting them, and putting everything into neat piles, looked out of the window and observing people and cars. These were compulsive behaviours that scared me, mingled with ever returning rage and violence turned against me, and the periodic re-emergence of broken story parts of how his mother had died, and who his mother had been.

It was a deranged kind of thinking that I did not know how to touch, how to heal. So I said nothing at all, made dinner, and told a story about how we would be happy in the future. But each week, he was only becoming a little bit more paranoid, and I, a little more used to it, in a strange parallelism. By the middle of spring, I knew the inside corridors of his thinking as well as my own, I knew the many snaps that could occur around the many bends of his mind which seemed teeming with angst and obscurity, oblique and menacing as the film set of *Dr. Caligari's Cabinet*.

He hadn't left the bedroom at all for many weeks, and

could no longer walk properly. I couldn't eat anything at all any more, throwing up every day. One time in a rage, he had thrown me off a chair so that I'd fallen with my hand on a sharp edge and needed stitches. That day, I kicked him out of my room in the middle of the night and told him to get lost for ever. How many times had I not already tried to tell him that? I wanted to break up! How many times did he stay, with the all-engluttoning argument that 'you may break up with me, but I don't break up with you, so, I'm staying' – and besides, he had the argument that without me, he was lost in a strange land, nowhere to go, no one to see.

In the morning after I had kicked him out, there he was in the middle of the street in the rain, waiting patiently for me to come out, he didn't see me coming, and when he did, bounced back, and then didn't move until I came to hug him and took him back home, he was sobbing, and so was I, and he had bronchitis on top of everything else.

He had tried calling home, and had it confirmed that he was no longer welcome in his father's family, and with that, not welcome anywhere except in my tiny home. I knew that something needed to change then, and that I should no longer listen to his wishes and grant them, but work for what I thought was best. He refused to see a psychologist, but I convinced him to start leaving the room and spend the days outside, even if it frightened him, to go for walks in the city, get some sunlight, and to see some things, to be amongst people, anything, rather than staying in my room on his own all the time while I was away in the day and making neat piles of everything over and over again.

He agreed, but was adamant we'd need to leave the house together and do so before the security warden came in at

[28]

5am. Thus it came about that we started to get up at 4.30am and to steal out of the building each day when it was still dark, slowly dawning. We walked around London until 9.30am. We walked out of the estate block through some of its smaller streets. Life here was visible: basketball sets for children, cars with stickers, chairs on the balconies, laundry on porches, bikes on balconies, a cat in some window, and from time to time, one or two windows were twinkling with the light of a television or a small bedside lamp. We walked slowly towards Elephant and Castle, through chestnut tree and platana tree avenues, and watched trees sprout, blossom and stretch their leaves over the new season. Birds woke up gradually around 5.30am and started singing and twittering loudly together for an unearthly and enchanting, transparent blue morning hour between night and day.

We always turned left past a small, triangular church with a slim and spiky bell tower by a fenced-in green and near a larger, less well-kept park with a rusty playground at the end of a run-down residential street.

Several large trash containers were at the entrance of the park, pieces of cardboard and broken furniture leaning against the containers, a disused sofa and dead fridge were planted in the landscape, and behind it in the middle of the park was a tall, cylindrical iron structure, rusty like the playground and tentatively fenced in by a broken fence. Discarded oil paintings, portraits, bad portraits of unknown people in flashy colours, were scattered about its base. At the back of the park, a small pavilion and a low concrete wall were covered in mural paintings in the slightly nauseating colours and style of occupational therapy art that discreetly adorns so many of Europe's train underpasses and municipal backsides. Weird place, I

[29]

thought, weird excrescence of human existence.

We sometimes saw dogs or foxes in this silent field shooting tall greens into the grey dawn as the season got warmer. At the end of the park, beyond the painted wall, were the backs of a row of Victorian houses. Small, narrow English family houses. In the windows, I could see the sleeping bathroom equipments, bottles of shampoo and Kleenex boxes, and small mirrors, placed on window sills and waiting for their owners. In the downstairs, there were sleeping paintings hanging on the walls, so silently closed without a viewer, without a party of tea-drinkers. There were armchairs in this sleeping air, too. They had sunken into themselves for the night and the morning where nobody would sit on them. And dull lamps hanging from the ceiling. Everything was sleeping, the cars, the chimneys, the park, where thawing fog was rising and sinking gently into the wet grass.

In the beginning, we couldn't walk more than twenty minutes at a time, we had to take breaks. His knees were bad, and I had a lot of bruises, was underweight and couldn't take the cold well. These eccentric morning walks were difficult at first, but eventually they restored some of the joy and happiness we had lost over the months before then. We stopped to stroke cats that we saw, explored city parks. The hours I had to be at university, I took him to spend either at the British Museum or the Tate Modern, where I would come and pick him up again in the afternoon and we would walk back to London Bridge at night along the Thames, zigzagging across bridges and contemplating buildings, reading blue plaques and discovering more of the city. We also joined the free film screenings that the film studies programme at my university was offering twice weekly, and we attended free

[30]

public lectures, too. All this new input seemed slowly to dissolve the obsessions and apparent paralysis of our situation until then, which I had diagnosed to be a sort of living limbo, if not hell, that had transformed my home into a grey zone verging on true insanity.

Since Jonathan had long quit his law degree in France and was living with me already, I decided for him that he should start a new degree, and I suggested History. He was open to the idea, but under no circumstances wanted to leave me even for a single day, so that he would have to study in London as well. This also implied learning English. I was despairing, but decided I had to stay in charge at this time, and began to teach him English in a crash course manner, sometimes repeating with him for four hours in a row, I would sit with him and take him through all the learning and preparations. I even went as far as writing his university application for him, initiating and replying to his correspondence in this matter, pretending to be him.

I had to fetch his e-mails anyway, as we did not have a home internet connection and in the early months, he never left the flat. I knew all of his passwords, everything. I used to paste his e-mails on to a memory stick, and also took some electronic newspapers on to it for him to read later. It seemed to me of prime importance that he should somehow stay in touch with the world of today and the real time of media, even if, as I could see all too well, his mind was stuck somewhere in his private past, and he refused with all he had to see or hear anything that was new, that was outside.

Once only in all this time, he received an e-mail from an old school friend. It was a girl I also used to like very much. We talked about her, and he thought of answering

[31]

her, started to tell me what to tell her, but in the end he could not think of any answer. He was sick, sick of it all, and I was not sick, maybe, but I had become speechless. This was not looking good, I thought. But I had no better idea. And this was forever. So I got us a place to live. We just moved to Soho then.

There are many things that happened in that year that I never thought worth the mention, dark and cruel things without dignity and honour, that were the truth even if the further one goes appearing to do well, the less likely anyone would believe that truth, and since it's in itself a hard truth to face, I carried on pretending not to see it, and today I regret not having spoken out about it earlier, because once I eventually got separated and far removed from all this, there was no space for discussing that kind of past, and it became a pointless tale of senselessness and waste.

Rainbow Dawns in Soho

And herewith, the story begins.

When we moved in at Frith Street in London's Soho, I was a student at University. I'd decided to read Classics in London, and I had brought my boyfriend, Jonathan, with me. We were happy. The house had been newly refurbished, everything was squeaky clean, bright and shiny.

Very soon though, it started falling apart. Black mould in the bathrooms, water was running through cheap glue, broken tiles, into the kitchen, where, first, all the wine glasses broke, countertop surfaces began to chip, and then, handles came loose from drawers and cupboard doors. Inside the walls, underneath the stairs, behind the skirting boards, it was teeming with rodents, who, well, how shall I say, took on a role far beyond the importance even the boldest animated movie would allow them. In fact, looking back, the unfailing rushed hushing that would happen imperceptibly, all the time, this diagonal darting across the floor of a barely visible grey spot disappearing into an indiscernible tiny hole in the wall, which I'd find myself looking at in disbelief then for a whole minute, those split second heartbeats at a sneaky little spot just outside of my sight field – that could be blamed for all the bad luck I have ever had. I began to wonder if I hadn't just imagined it, if I might be prey to delusions involving non-existent rodents.

As time went on, it became all too obvious that the mice were real. I could watch them with a mix of sympathy, disgust and curiosity as they comfortably walked over the cooker, warmed up by the toaster whilst nibbling on a crumb, played hide and seek underneath a fridge whilst we cooked a meal, rustled inside the trash cans and sped under the carpet if a human came too close. Every now and then perhaps a dead mouse would appear lying stretched out near the fridge, but there still were hundreds of live ones. With all that laying out poison that we did, one day, they all left, of their own accord and found somewhere better to live. Only a handful were left to emerge every now and then, far less boldly, in fact quite cautiously, lonely and lost in the sudden emptiness, perhaps suffering the same sort of existential doubts as I was, in this half-vacated no-man's land. I began to wonder sometimes if I hadn't just imagined them.

There would be something there, just in the far left of my sight, close to my foot, and perhaps I'd have done well to jump, but as soon as I looked down at my foot, there'd be nothing there. I began to see how I might be delusional.

But whether or not I was insane, it's only fair to say, the mice didn't do it. There were cracks in the façade, for a long while there had been, and if mice were running inside them like humans lost in corridors, that was only for negligence of these cracks to begin with.

Tempest rages of domestic violence, the year that lay behind us, those mental derailments in the face of brutality inside a doll house of poetry and romance, perhaps would have shaken and reduced to dust any house, but I refused to see this because I was happy, and all happy people are blind. It never occurred to me I was walking on the edge of ever steeper growing drops, only some hours in the day I knew that some day, there'd be nothing but black holes left here, and I guess I imagined it would be the day the mice

[34]

grew bigger than men and ate up the entire world. And I guess I figured, to think this, I must be insane.

Dana lived in the room above us. When we first met, she said that she was recently divorced, from a particularly status-obsessed guy and nightmare of a tyrannical husband who liked to show her around as his trophy wife, and next to whom she had to play 'little bitch perfect'. She explained that she had walked out of the marriage with some money for herself and was here to take a break and enjoy herself a bit. She wouldn't need a job, she said – she just wanted to take it easy for a while and come to terms with everything. Later, she added that she also had been to rehab. It didn't take long for Soho to take a hold of her again, and her money soon disappeared.

She was a smiley and sunny, stunning looking, stylish Indian woman who everyone in the house wanted to be friends with at the outset, but soon she became intensely self-absorbed, pacing with her arms crossed and muttering things to herself, hardly noticing us around her any more. Her room became dirty and messy, and often at night I would notice her putting everything outside her door, in the staircase, saying that she was tidying up looking for something, but actually she was more likely going round in pointless circles. She'd get stuck, opening and closing bags and boxes she'd already checked multiple times, repeating in an endless loop, and stop when she came across any familiar object amongst her stuff, such as an old photograph, a piece of jewellery that meant something, that touched her memory across an ether of heroin and confusion.

I could see her stop and muse, and a dark cloud would run over her face. Her feelings were so slow and laid bare that

I was able to follow them just from seeing her hands and her body posture, even though to me, these objects held no stories. At two or three in the morning, my usual bedtime, I would be on my way to the shower when she would be searching frantically for a mystery Burberry handbag and ask me if I had seen it.

We'd spend time, not saying much, sitting together at home in the daytime and drinking tea. Everyone else was working or sleeping, it was just us there. I guess our cultures were different, she was Indian, I was German, she was divorced, I was engaged, she was drowning, I was rising. With hindsight, I suppose she may have been the one who was rising. Come the spring of my final year of college, I was always feeling so low and deranged that I never could get out of bed before the late morning. Thus Dana and I saw quite a lot of each other, lounging on our kitchen sofa and letting it all pass us by.

We talked about bulimia. She told me that she had got over hers. I didn't want to let show that I had it, but wanted to know everything in detail, exactly how she had got out of it. Bulimia, for me, was a monster in the closet, a tentacular and inextricable jack-in-the-box that, once out, would spring to gigantic proportions and was only difficultly pushed back out of sight.

She said 'Oh, I just took it one day at a time' – I tried to picture it. That sentence made no sense to me at all. Looking at her, she was very skinny, perhaps owing to drugs, but maybe also anorexia. I didn't know what to say or not say, because the official protocol was that she was recovered and clean, but I would have had so many questions. One time she got emotional and said I was an angel, that she had told her mum about me and that her mum would like to meet me, if I would. Then it really impinged on me that she was in a very dark place. She always seemed to be walking, smiling, a handful, and I could follow what she was thinking, and imagine the breakage in her mind. It didn't frighten me. I guess I didn't know, at the time, that it is possible to discuss one's inner troubles with someone else, that it could be comforting, and that this is where sanity lay. I don't suppose I had ever heard of this, and thought that when it comes to the uncanny, the deranged and worrying thoughts and existential doubts, each is alone with their own.

Meanwhile, the other housemates were turning against her. She was not that popular with her chipped and dirty nails, stained shirts and sometimes bruised face, broken lip, a glowing portrait of misery from every angle. I told her to take her time. She gave house keys to Jamie, her dealer, a pretty rough, unkempt dude with ugly manners. He helped himself from our kitchen fridges and left dishes so dirty from his touch that one of the other housemates, who once saw him, refused to eat from those same plates ever again – so he and his wife, Katie, got themselves a whole new set of plates which they kept out of the kitchen and with that, the war on Dana was pretty much declared.

Dana for her part began to enter a truly dreadful state, and at one point she stayed in her room for three full days, during which the others thought of breaking into the room just to check that she was not dead. She wasn't. One day, or perhaps not just one, Jamie beat her up, and she was looking ghastly. After that, nothing new happened for a while, until we started noticing she was getting threats over the phone. Jamie and another man, with a comb stuck in his locks, came knocking on the front door so violently on a Saturday morning, they were going to break in. The street was full of people and Katie opened the kitchen window calling out to 'leave us alone or I'm calling the police', to no avail. Nobody listened, nobody stopped. These two continued knocking until the door gave in and Dana dragged herself downstairs and dealt with them somehow.

There was a family visit to Dana, her mother, uncle and brother had come, worried what was becoming of her, and tried to talk her into moving back home with them. Dana was not about to move back home. The mother was worried about bank statements and tried to get Dana to show her some, but Dana was too confused to produce any. Instead, she told her mum about a foursome, and showed her photos of herself that she wanted to send to some modelling agencies. Her mother was not impressed. They went upstairs to her room. Her brother wanted to get a glass of water in the kitchen, at which point Katie, who was just starting to prepare a meal, turned to him and asked 'do you take drugs too?' – He said no, and looked down. Katie delivered a rap about Dana's misbehaviour. 'They're dealing drugs and having her in the bath with the door open, she's got black nails and a black eye, she doesn't even bother to close the door when she pees and she's got a room that resembles a graveyard. She doesn't know what she's doing, she's wearing dirty clothes in layers and never washes and she's bringing in those men that bring diseases in here, she's confused and she hasn't a clue who we are', etc.

It was awkward. The poor little LSE student, quiet and polite, said nothing but 'I just wanted to get her this glass of water'. Katie would personally have brought Dana out of the house, but one night, Dana simply moved out. Without saying goodbye, she got her uncle to take all of her stuff into a van, at around one in the morning, they carried down a few boxes, then the two of them disappeared. The room she left was in such an unseemly state with dirty trails on the walls and stains all over the carpet, that no new tenant wanted it for a long time. It became a door for us to walk past quietly thinking back to her and if we did her wrong, until Frank came along, moved in, cleaned up, painted it, and still found drugs underneath the carpet when he was clearing up.

Frank was a tall and thin, long-haired man in his fifties and a cross-dresser. He first appeared together with his wife who helped him bring all his stuff over. She lived somewhere in the country, while he worked in London, and was going to be there only during the week and back in the country with his wife on the week-ends.
To be honest when I first met them, I didn't notice him as a cross-dresser, rather the seemed to me a bit hippie-like, cowboy boots and long and dangly sleeves. But apparently, I was the only one who had not picked up on it that those were women's clothes. I was disabused, at the latest, when I saw him heading out for the night in a red sequin dress. He explained that he was a singer and porn star, especially famous in Israel, and that he was living in England because he could not handle being recognized in the streets of Tel Aviv all the time and the screaming women had just got too much for him. I was tempted to say 'Oh, you're big in Japan', but that would have been in bad taste.
A few weeks on, two young girls moved in by Frank's side, one redhead and one blonde, and although they were not introduced, one mid-morning that I came out of my room there they were, the three of them in the living room, having cooked breakfast in underwear. Frank was wearing

[39]

a thong and over-knee boots, and the girls were wearing matching bra sets, a silk dressing gown was thrown over the back of a chair, a skull-shaped ashtray in the middle and some empty bottles of liquor and champagne; smeared make-up and handbags thrown across the sofa betrayed a long night spent.

Nobody was quite sure what the deal was, the girls stayed for a few weeks, then they left. Frank didn't really ever go back to the countryside to see his wife. Instead, he got into the vibe of going out clubbing in Soho. He'd dress up in drag, which seemed to come naturally, in a little black dress or a white lace number, diamond heels, red boots, or a leather mini skirt, perfect hair and make-up, long nails... and at my bedtime, around three in the morning, he'd be back in, we'd have a cup of tea, sit down and chat.

I'd gather my study papers and say good night, he'd say he was very tired. But it was difficult to have this conversation. You see, I was always drawn by the attraction of the gloss-rich nights, drunken derailments, the half-light and the half-world, I always understood the need for a glammy, outrageous disguise if someone were to voice their true feelings, and the need for some drugs and some companionship that would make one lose inhibition – and never was repelled by, or afraid of the creatures of the night. There was Frank in drag, there was I in my man's clothes, he looked like a diva, and I, like a wallflower. I knew he was assuming that I was judging him, but I wasn't. It never really bothered me that someone should have long nails, spiky belts or a funky haircut, or that they should have altered their minds for a while to complete their nightly carnival feeling. But back then, I was not one of them, I was perhaps awake through the night, but I wasn't out there wearing the shimmering dress

[40]

of some subculture tribe, I was just at home, looking out for them from the window, studying my ancient poetry and letting my spirit stray far, very far, back into the deepest waters, far deeper, harder and more broken than anything clothing fashion could convey. I may have had an open mind, but it was quiet and oblivious, busy writing essays, doing the housework, cooking our dinner and going off on walks to the far end of the city just quietly to see things, not to do them, and I guess I seemed square to most. So, Frank over that cup of tea was biting his nails gasping for a topic of conversation that could have suited me, he thought, all the time looking away in embarrassment, nervous about his appearance all of a sudden. After he had celebrated his dragness, and had it celebrated all night, with the telling scratches all over his back and a tear in his dress, wine on his bra – here he was, coming back to the weather and the topic of mice under the fridge, standard English and an interest in my studies but he didn't really know the secret that I knew, about poetry, that it's not boring books, that poetry in reality is the story of truly shocking things, even more so than what some kids want to celebrate in edgy night clubs. Ancient plays could be more raw, more frightening and more full of disaster and their poetry more evocative than even, if I may say so, the Velvet Underground.

Frank never spoke much to us, but I liked him. In fact, everyone liked him in the house, he was well-spoken and always friendly, it was only a case of some of us accepting his style. But we all knew that if anything, we were the ones who needed to adjust, not him – Soho really was home to people like Frank, and it belonged to them.

Next door from Frank there was Josh, a good-looking gay man in his twenties working at Selfridges Make-up department. He told me stories from his life, what had wounded him early on in his teens, that coming out in high school had been a disaster, after which he turned all Goth and never went to school again. Like many, he was into astrology and told me he was not surprised at all to hear I was a pisces – because I was so indecisive, so placid, creative and confused.

He told me I would do well to pursue my mystical side and began telling me scary tales of ghosts and witches that he'd seen before. I was not actually keen on those, but he insisted, and as he was a good story teller, I listened, placidly, as he would have said. But I found them difficult to believe and hard to see the point of, and it's not something I could really retell. All I can remember is this story: he was in a large warehouse, in the bathroom, which was on the top floor, very spacious and all but derelict. Looking at his face in the mirror, he suddenly saw, behind him in the mirror, rising from the toilet door, a ring of fire in the air behind his head. He turned around, but there was nothing there. He could only smell something burning and looked for the source of fire, but there was none, and there was no smoke, either. Worried that there might be a fire, he reported to the manager, who however could not smell or see anything. Josh in fact could hear the crackling of flames and was beginning to hear screams. The same day, he heard on the radio that exactly a hundred years prior to that, the warehouse had burnt down. Oh well.

Miumiu, as we ended up calling him – he himself wanted us to do so – introduced himself as Jonas. A young make-up artist from Sweden, well acquainted with the scintillating world of celebrities, full of New York vibe, he was obese, queenly gay, and wore his Swarowski belt over bright pink, XXL Ralph Lauren polos, and polished Jimmy Choo shoes, of which he had about fifty pairs.

His father, owner of a large warehouse in Sweden, well-established, wealthy and generous towards his family, didn't press Miumiu to work too hard whilst enjoying his youth in London's Soho. Miumiu had come there for the sole purpose of partying. He was 23 years old. When he moved in, he was helped by another man of about 40, who was to live with us for a few weeks. He too was from Sweden and a hairdresser, he worked in Sally's round the corner. Tall and thin, with hair dyed blonde just like Miumiu's. The boyfriend was interested mostly in Miumiu's money and was milking him. He made fun of him behind his back; unlike Katie, who told Miumiu right out that he wouldn't fit through the door at Starbuck's.

There was also Jens, a young and beautiful insouciant callboy who came to pick Miumiu up to go clubbing from time to time. Clubbing was all Miumiu did while he lived with us. He would go to the afternoon lounge, then a club, then the afterparty until the early morning. Partying on ecstasy like in the '90s should have been fun but I only ever saw him come home exhausted and sleep through the day, and in the late afternoon, make breakfast shots and cocktails for everyone, playing house music in the kitchen, it all seemed desperately vacuous to me. He would cook improbably large amounts of pasta, and talk to me while I was in the kitchen. Five servings of penne carbonara fit easily into his stomach and yet he had an immensely hollow soul. We had great laughs together, often, when he'd proudly tell me which celebrities he had done make-up for, but ultimately I was left with the impression that he was lost and lonely, trapped in a morbid body in a world where appearance was everything, the world of fashion

[43]

and beauty and the cruel world of London's gay scene. His body was full of tattoos at least, a particularly prominent one were the words 'Miu Miu' spelled right across his back. A living caricature of consumerism, he'd go on spending sprees at – of course – Miumiu, Prada, and H&M (because it's Swedish). Seen from outside he had the best life one could possibly have, every wish granted, but getting to know him in his home, he was a most unlucky child, beleaguered by unmet needs and frustrated desires.

Katie and her husband Salim completed the house share with an element of arrogance and pride. She had been educated at Oxford and knew about good bourgeois manners, and was working as a line manager in a big corporate firm, and in her spare time she was a foodie and loved to cook.
He was a few years younger and came from Tunisia. The two had met when Katie was on holiday in Tunisia and visited Salim's home in a small and backward village in the desert. They fell in love and got married right away with a traditional Tunisian ceremony. Katie told us about how, as the bride, she
was made to sit on a throne of pearls, wearing an elaborate and heavy, ravishing dress. When it dawned on them that Katie would have to return to England, they decided that Salim should come with her. He did not speak English, but he was to learn it. He did not know how to navigate the London jungle, but he was to learn it. Then, nothing worked out the way it was planned. Salim did not find a job. He had only recently managed to find work in a Tunisian hotel and restaurant. The job was boring to him, and he was becoming moody. I have this vivid memory of them sitting together and talking, on facing chairs by the

[44]

kitchen window, their knees touching and their profiles cut out against the bright night lights of the Soho street, two large glasses of red wine in the window sill and empty bottles lined up on the floor.

Katie, when drunk, could be hard to handle. She would have loud arguments and throw things around the flat or sulk like a little child. One night, the two of them had a hefty argument and Katie cursed and shouted, then walked out of the kitchen window with a meat knife in one hand and her wine glass in the other. She stepped along the balustrade on the outer façade, walked up to Jonathan and my window and sat before it, crying, her feet dangling over the café marquee. Jonathan spoke to her and finally convinced her to come back in, through our window, whilst I sat with Salim in the kitchen.

Their marriage didn't do very well, Salim told his family over the phone that he was unhappy in London, and they blamed it on Katie. Once Salim disappeared for a few weeks. Katie got worried and flew to Tunisia to look for him, but when she went to find the family, she was received very coldly, even Salim himself would not speak to her.

The family had organised a new wedding for Salim, which Katie was now disrupting. Salim came back to London with Katie. But he disappeared a second time and this time, Katie did not go to look for him, but became an even heavier drinker. These lives I saw lived and unfolding next to me seemed like so many threads unravelling and dissolving slowly, defying the human wish for things to fall into place, refusing to roll out happy endings.

June, 2005
On the second floor opposite, there's a small brothel which

[45]

mostly keeps the curtains drawn. On the first, a gay couple are living, seemingly careless of the fact that if they sit naked on the windowsill, I get a free viewing. And the third floor? That's always closed, it's quite dirty, and oftentimes when I look up to that window I see some pots of plants have been moved, the back of a photo-frame, and postit-notes of different colours come and go, migrate like souls, and in the green bottles, I can see the tide sink.

I don't know who lives there. But somehow, it is essential to know that he or she does change the arrangement in the window, it keeps the window alive. That window more than anything tells me that this day is different from yesterday. It's someone as lost and singular as myself up there. The window floats calmly over all the rest in mid-air, bitter-sweet and transitory as life itself, and it's canvassed with all that mild-minded melancholy that webs through all things quietly underwater as the filament of water lilies, and is yet so slight that it cannot be pulled and grasped.

Since I began writing, I have got better at it, but I have not found a resolution yet. Polishing an opaque surface, I reach for something inside a pool of mist, behind translucent clouds. Behind this stained glass window, something I could draw out from an endless rummage in uniform white cotton, something I could bring back to feel and discern the forms and colours of in the bright sunlight.

In a city that is not here..., the glittering, boozed-up, flashed and dazzled life, the tourists, tramps, the 'models', the barber shop and café windows. Life has a rhythm of its own.

In the mornings, Bar Italia alone still pulsing, reverberates rays and echoes of worlds gone by over night, marvellous trips and odysseys, sunk and foundered

[46]

with an awesome gargle. Italia never shuts, its eyes remain half open constantly. In the mornings, the cafés are cleaned, stocked and opened, as they eternally make ready for the eternal big night, one that cracks louder than destruction, life that explodes and ebbs every morning around 1am. Smiles, faces and dress codes, jokes, manners and violence so well rehearsed, by streams of men and women in fairytale glamour swallowed again every night in the abyss of self-indulgence, grim laughter and drunken confessions, and met by deference and servile complacency. This language is complex, but easy to learn. The other door goes out the back. To a court of no humanity, with only air conditioners blowing out hot particles, and water drains, and clatter from restaurant kitchens, staircase windows, and ghostly beats from inside some club. Nothing if not greasy dirt and waste air.

Red-brick chimneys indifferently crumbling along blackened walls, in their turn falling apart in disenchantment, broken windows replaced with planks, aluminium foil stuffed into cracks, rusty railings, trashed clothes and other useless objects, eroding iron stairs, dirty rooftops, from where the sky looks ever brown.

Bent antennae point nowhere, erratic, raking the clouds and the cotton, stretching into emptiness. Wild cats live here, feasting with the rats and mice, from bins and kitchens, through windows opaque for lack of cleaning, for lack of oxygen, for lack of space. This silent and soulless court with its ugliness lashes out blindly at whoever inspects the pollution. Nobody steps out here, though occasionally some doomed workers are sent down, or a lady hushes by her window, if it is not one of the men, and sometimes a chef smokes out the back. Their hands are old and sore.

[47]

Despair wells up from the backyard with its shafts, fans, garbage cans, and blackened windows with greyed curtains, and the eternal poor soul crouches there, even if elsewhere, shining streets glitter and splendid dresses do shine in the sunlight where polished cars flash up to the heavens, almost blinding us to our demons and lurking selves.

When pointlessly at night the windows light up with a grim twinkle over an inert wasteland, they watch on an abyss of mercantile carelessness, and numbness at the end of pain. So dark are the waters here that nobody can remember daylight, and humans creep, the star of hope long extinct, yet we all creep on forwards, we must.

I was working with a great professor of Greek drama, Peter. We would sit and read in his office, forgetting about life and its vicissitudes. There were shelves of books in the rear of the room, and many box files. Three tall and grand windows went out to the Strand, linden trees waving their hands from the outside, bending in the wind. There was a heavy oakwood and leather meeting table by the bookshelves, and a large desk by the windows, black and white photographs of jazzmen hanging over the fireplace, potted plants and rugs on the floor, a green desk lamp, leather armchairs, and the sweet smell of cigar smoke hanging in the air. It was an old-fashioned, palatial reception room that seemed to hang in between the corridors of university as a separate entity where time was an altogether different measure.

He would open old box files with archival materials about bygone theatre productions, and talk about Aristophanes with great excitement. His office was like a ship floating over the vagaries of life and over the sound of cars and motors, a privileged space for ideas about Greek drama.

After the second year exams, I had won some awards, and was getting ready to direct a student show at the theatre. Peter called me in for a first meeting, he congratulated me, and as a sort of initiation rite, offered a seat in his leather armchair, underneath an arching lamp, and tendered a cigar.
He was always smoking cigars, I was less used to them, but a fleeting apparition of a 1970s image of a young woman on a record cover, who was smoking a cigar and holding a cello between her legs, reminded me just in time that I could perhaps pull it off with poise. I hadn't had a whole cigar before that I could recall, the gesture succeeded in making me feel important, suddenly on a par with this formerly rather distant and arcane seeming man.
The palatial office suite I had become accustomed to admiring rather as a shy guest, was now open to me as a place to work in, the leather seats were for me to sit in and explain directions for a production of Aristophanes. The erudite and venerable Greek professor had suddenly taken on an air of being a producer in 1970s Hollywood, fully fledged with a cream suit, cigar, ring bound script in hand, and sweeping gestures of largesse.
We discussed things over cigars and, as the evening turned violet and darker, walked over from the Strand office with its warm and softening lights in flower lampshades, to the silk-and-gold, art deco lounge of Simpson's hotel, and ordering Kir Royals, we continued.

Over the course of that summer, Peter and I spent many afternoons on a stone bench opposite a round fountain in the Temple on the embankment side of Fleet Street, which,

[49]

as a particularly ancient part of London, was scenic in its own silent, dull and winding elegance. With our pub drinks and scripts before us, we never got tired of talking, planning, musing, pondering things. It seemed an unusual friendship, he was more than three times my age and had a highly appraised scholarly career to look back on, but in a random kind of privilege that I didn't quite understand, he gave me a feeling of particular appreciation and confidence, and I accepted his gift.

I got my own office, as the show's director, and, come the end of summer, I would have a team, and, of course, a cast of students under my direction; it was as yet unclear to me whether I would be accepted by the other students, because I didn't have much of social standing amongst them, but on the flipside, this could be my chance to become a little more popular.

The Greek play office was in a minuscule loft room at the top of the stairs at university, right opposite Deloitte and Goldman Sachs. I ended up spending many evenings and nights there and was reassured by the fact that the folks at Goldman & Co. were working just as late as me. My office space was so tiny, the only window it had took up the entire wall, I was in a kind of crystal ball, and also, the steep drop below the window always reminded me of suicide, although the atmosphere between antiquated computing equipment, yellowing posters and flyers of various expired Greek plays, astonishingly prolific costume cupboards and a filing cabinet full of old ticket stubs and relics of previous productions made it an instantly pleasing and fun place to sit in. The costume cupboard held untold marvels, between rhinestone tutus, frog outfits, and all manner of shields and helmets, parts of armour in all shades of gold, from the farcical to the tragic, crowns, masks, dusty wasp outfits, flowers, lion skin and clubs... The old theatre bills and sticky notes with the phone numbers of someone's crushes, old stage photographs and programme booklets, gave me a previously unknown sense of joy, and then, living in Soho, one was never very far from a stage. Often as I walked home through Drury Lane, Covent Garden and Soho, I eyed the venues and revues, theatres big and small, the slippery stages and the swanky ones, with a growing sense of affection and belonging.

I met another German on my course, Lizzie from Munich, a theatre enthusiast, a tall and blue-eyed, stylish woman on a bike with a messenger bag, a denim jacket and short, almost shaved, bleached hair, smart shoes and with a hint of punk in her appearance. We got on wonderfully right away and got started on long, very long philosophical conversations in a waterfront bar on those mild and slowly darkening London afternoons. Dropping the weight of the world, we'd first talk about where we had come from, then discuss the difficult and unhappy here and now, in the German way I knew well from Berlin, with a lot of cigarettes, a lot of vodka, and a touch of mal de siecle.

Also at university, I had met Andrea. I had not made myself very approachable during my first year and kept silent for most of the time, as I had some trouble with myself and my living situation, and was shy to socialise. I was trying to reveal as little as possible about myself to others, as the situation seemed to me an inexplicable cluster of disasters that few could sympathise with.

[51]

Andrea, from the outset, gave me the feeling that I could not pretend or lie to her, and showed genuine interest in me. She had a sympathetic, all too serious and proper, almost strict tone in her speech, and lively, intelligent eyes (behind a pair of glasses). I wanted to escape from her, because the truth scared me and I could not tell her anything but that, but neither could I tell her the truth. She never ceased being friendly to me and, in her gentle way, inquisitive, almost earnest with me. Slowly, after a year, we started getting to know each other. Chatting in the cafeteria from time to time, we shared a story or two about family. I met her boyfriend, she met mine, we had some movie nights together.

The summer I started directing, after exams at the Royal Horticultural Halls, we wandered around St. Billy's park and got drunk on cans of cider from the off-license shop and ate spring rolls on the grass. She told me that time, that her mother was very ill. I heard, suddenly, an echo of Jonathan's family story, and then, saw all the the blind spots in his story of a depressed, divorced mother, fighting breast cancer, alone, and of children left to fend their thorny and lonely, tearful way back into the other side of the broken home, as beggars, a tale of hatred-filled relatives, predatory persons eyeing inheritances, intent on milking the kids.

I looked at Andrea, this lovely, caring and intelligent petite girl with long brown hair and glasses sitting with me on the grass and gazing in a slightly drunken way at the junk food by our feet. This was, after all, the one who had seen me during a time when I behaved myself like a ghost.

Andrea spoke of arguments in the family, and of irrational and hurtful actions taken by various people, said that she didn't even want to visit her family. Again, I thought I

[52]

heard, from the other side of memory, Jonathan's bitter regrets for mean and immature words that he could never make up to his mother.

None of this was my own experience, but I thought I could foresee how Andrea would feel then, later, when the cancer would have taken all these choices and feelings from her. So I, with reluctance and a great fear of striking a wrong chord, spoke about some of Jonathan's distress (in a very veiled way), and advised her to fly home as soon as possible. I said she wouldn't forgive herself if she lost her mother without the chance to resolve those teenage arguments. And I thought I'd made a good case, she decided to book a plane for the next day.

She only made it in time for the funeral. She wrote me, from home, to say that her mother had died at the very moment of our conversation, during which she had shut off her mobile phone, which left me feeling almost as if I had personally taken her mother away from her.

After our conversation, I recalled, we had walked around Soho, bar-hopped, and she showed me music on her iPod, bands of her Hungarian friends who were playing a lot in Berlin at the time, I remember, at the Russian Disco, Kaffee Burger, and it was nice hearing music from back home. We switched to champagne, and laughed together, we laughed a lot.

Andrea and I had put in together for the Greek play, but she had had to pull out at first, in the light of the family situation. When she came back from Budapest, and the other students also arrived, the scripts were ready and marked up, we auditioned, had lots of meetings and socials with the cast and crew, the Greek play generally was just one big party, and even though I and everybody worked hard in rehearsals and in between, it was a time of smiles and laughs.

As for me, being the director of the student show had made me instantly the best known face in the department, and I also got myself a long and feminine brown suede coat from Oxfam, that made me feel at once bohemian and elegant, and somehow gave things a more self-assured, fashionable swing. It was my turn now strangely to try and look out for Andrea as we took our Greek poetry classes, which mostly were taught by Peter and happened around the seminar table in his grand office, attended only by Andrea, Lizzie and myself.

Meanwhile, our gleeful madhouse in Soho suffered a burglary. Some strangers came in and disturbed every order in the bedrooms, picking objects at random, opening all the doors, every single case or box, throwing disorder over our rooms, turning inside out the deepest privacy. They took with them almost nothing: bank statements, perhaps in the mistaken thought that they were somebody else's, and left other valuables untouched, helping themselves to a piece of cake instead.

There were no traces or fingerprints, no broken locks. The lock could easily opened with a credit card, but it seemed to some of us that someone might have come in using a key. All eyes fell on Dana – metaphorically, as she had already left – and on the fact that she had given keys to this obscure drug dealer Jamie, who had threatened her at the door before and in the streets, and had come to the room in her absence.

Everything could be explained, the Police said, explained, by drug abuse. All of this was looking to them like a classic case of a desperate drug burglary.

'You know, there are a lot of drug addicts hanging round the street corners over here. Drugs can change the way people think and make them dangerous and mad', the woman said. I could have guessed. Was that all? They could be numb now, and later in extreme agony, despairing to the blood, trembling, their minds suspended, like Dana herself, who could be seen erratic around the house in the middle of the night, wearing several coats and jumpers, in search of an alleged Burberry handbag, stacking chairs, desks, cushions, clothes, CDs, magazines, shopping bags, bottles of wine and water on her bed, piling boxes in front of her room. Most of the time she'd be met vacant-eyed, her hands contorted. The constant presence of her demons in our house made the work of the intruders also seem less deviant, indeed strangely familiar. We already had tacit acceptance of a drive beyond our grasp, silent apprehension of a different form of seriousness.

In Frank's room, the police asked who lived there, and Katie said 'Frank'.

'But… Someone must be living here with Frank', said the police lady, pointing at dresses and other women's clothes on the floor and over the chair.

'No, he's just a cross-dresser', Katie said.

'Oh', said the police woman.

She was visibly amused. Katie, on the other hand, was not, nor was Salim.

'Those guys are still wandering around our block, and they can see my face today', he said, 'but they are invisible to me. If I knew who they were... but I don't... That's an awful feeling. Every familiar and unfamiliar face on the street is now under suspicion'.

The inside had lapsed to incursion, the street had rushed into the house, like a wild torrent, the doors were kicked in, the locks broken by soft force of a discreet intruder, and the pocket that was behind the door truly emptied: the house just a brick mound, its spirit escaped into the open. That is how the big lines got blurred. These guys had poked open our bubbles of storytelling and private self, and let flat air from outside fill the void. Nobody must know Soho better than they do, but our signs and boundaries mean nothing to them, they do not read the symbol of a locked door, when they have had enough, they do not care about volatile spirits in floating apartments and secluded spheres. They know a horizon our eyes cannot see, beyond status-symbolism, a vision we cannot penetrate. Their thinking seems easy and tangible at first, yet is incomprehensible. We may call them marginal, but without knowing it, we are in their hands.

December, 2005
Finding ourselves in each other, our familiarity breeds our contempt. Silent, in the eye of a cyclone. Behind doors closed fast, we knew ourselves, we made long speeches, as if ever we could do something. Here we believed, blinking at the flying fragments all around us and beyond our reach, in the absence of sense. This interior, this storybox, so unfortunately floating over Soho, suspended above the fronts and the backs, places teeming with life and filth exhaling its past and its stories, countless stories, of old times and from a different England. These two cities break their waves at the walls, back and front, of Soho houses like ships. We are sleeping, eating and walking inside a wooden hollow, between foamy, roaring waves and sea-monsters.
In the floating apartments, even Paradise seems just one door away. In these half-lit halls, thoughts can stay

[56]

without action. They are open for ample articulation, here in the shared living room. Overlooking both the hidden and the displayed, every house hosts its dramas, dramas that happen to those stranded here. Absurd stories that find rest nowhere but in themselves and their own tales, reaching out far beyond this tight space and short time, to colour the walls and breathe life into the house, they are told into these rooms, spoken into this Soho address, but lived elsewhere, sometime, someplace, far from the party and the dump, far from this big bad city.

We do speak of the many things that are not here, fashion them for house mates we didn't know, our kindly brothers, against the sterile silence of partying masses and the forgotten dump. Re-enact all that ever was in our lives, as if we were in prison. Stories of wine and voyage, hatred and love, a travelman, an ancient family, hopes and disillusionments, drugged confessions, the chances we missed and the ones we took, bad dreams we had and rejections we suffered, happy days we spent, honeymoons and strip shows, and it goes on and on, until we tell of our own funeral.

Communicating vases, a pharmacy full of boxes and pots of spirits, where odours permeate, interpenetrate, and objects free of significance glide about as on a spider-web, through hidden corridors and cavities, alcoves, niches, where clouds of dust particles move in clusters, lean over parapets and jump into dark rivers, infernal channels, taking the wrong door, entering forbidden places, on defunct transfers, they make so many mistakes, they lapse adrift, aberrantly fall into loopholes, until not even one is left in its right place, where rigid chalk walls turn spongy and liquefy, the edifices melt, rushing down precipitously

[57]

with this glistening water.

Imagine the end of life, imagine, at last, the silence on this planet, Soho deserted, and inspect our burnt-out ruins, the streets you've often walked now carbonised, your courtyards dusty, and most of all, our houses, now cratered brick cubes with doors and windows gaping, forced in from all sides, where streams of air can move throughout, ventilate those Soho streets that once crammed life and urban waste where it was impossible to breathe, with hellholes drawing in and spitting out, endlessly, the sparkling fabric of never-ceasing life...

Who would have thought that we should become such carcasses, so empty, so torn inside, in the bloom of this golden life? In the guilt of post-post-modern life, men and women, lost explorers, greet each other fortuitously and under cover.

Particles encountered in the street, above all surfaces, beneath all languages, beyond all relations, inside ourselves as much as far-flung and outside of reach, it is these that push us to pile words and try to write. Consciousness is a formless inscrutable matter I am in vain investigating. I am searching, without sensation, seeking to mould this nebulous thing, into words, then structures, or stories, wondering what it is that I mould without seeing or feeling it. I search, and while I mould I search more, hoping to find freedom from moulding and return to wordless solitude.

I had many creative visions. The days arrived when we were going to have our dress rehearsal for the Aristophanes. With the help of my team, made up of Andrea, Lizzie, Peter, myself and a few other beautiful people, my vision had grown into something quite substantial. Painters, singers, actors, stylists and costume shoppers had been at work to make my idea happen, and it was looking really very exciting – beyond my dreams, beyond my abilities, beyond what I ever could have done alone. A lot of the time that final week in the theatre, I spent waiting for people to deliver things I could not do myself. I was waiting for the stage to be built and ready, waiting for technical setups, waiting for the actors to arrive, for crew members to emerge, testing equipment, checking the sound and checking the view, waiting for actors to be warmed-up, dressed and in their make-up, for the audience to get there, for the show to begin. There were many last-minute doubts and hangups, but we spent a whole week in the theatre together and eventually got everything ready, though nothing else could be dreamed of in that week, I was pretty much living in the theatre for a week, and yet I never quite knew what I had been spending my time doing, I only knew that I could not leave the theatre for a week.

It was hard even to get in a few breaks to send some e-mails, yet I had to e-mail: I had to organise my trip to America, as I had been invited by a great ivy league school to interview there for a graduate position. They were paying for my trip, even if I didn't think I would get in, I obviously wanted to get on a plane to New York, I had never been before.

That week by the theatre on the South Bank finished with a bang in the legendary pub across the theatre, a pub decorated with virgin Marys and catholic votives. At night, in a fairly drunk state, I walked up from the South bank to Soho, crossing over Blackfriars Bridge, walking past St Paul's cathedral and up the Strand, through Covent

Garden, into Soho, and into bed. I can't recall what I thought on those long walks, but I know for a fact that I was deliberately neglecting my relationship with Jonathan. Things were moving forward for me, and besides, they were, for him, too. He was doing his history degree at UCL and starting to thrive. I had come to know Jonathan's innermost thoughts, his secret fears, and the story of his life, but soothing his worries was nothing I could do any longer. Once I had got a taste of how I might make a career, in classical scholarship, or in the theatre, I never again wanted to let go of it in order to turn to private troubles.

Although the intensity of his troubles often moved me to tears, I never knew what to do about it, and so, without quite noticing it happening, I decided that I would not give his problems any more thought and let him face his demons all by himself in the future.

From that point on, things became very quiet between us. It was sad, immensely sad and destructive, but more smooth. I stayed out late every night, whilst he got up early in the morning. We closed ourselves off from each other, we became estranged; then, we got re-acquainted. Things worked out better that way for a few more months, neither of us ever mentioned it. It would have been too sad a thing to talk about. At some point, he voluntarily brought up in conversation that he was cheating. Great, I said. Keep going. Admitting the failure of this relationship would have destroyed even its last romantic, ideal relics.

I stepped out of my plane at a mid-morning Newark airport in New Jersey where I arrived somewhat clueless. I thought I was in New York. I had to get to Connecticut. I had been told to get there by Connecticut Limousine, I was mystified as to what that might be, and chuckled when I discovered it was a shabby minibus with darkened windows. But the staff were deadly serious about calling it a Limo.

We drove off on the big highways, past big Toys'R'Us and Walmarts, small towns flashing by on the sides, tower blocks and clapboard houses flitting by, until we got to a big hospital, science labs, orange rocks in the distance, and a flashy gothic sandstone fortress. This was the campus, I knew.

I asked to be dropped off, took my luggage and here I was now, standing underneath a large gate, all pale rose sandstone, and saw before me a sign on a door: 'Classics department: Take the elevator to the fourth floor'. That was lucky then, I thought to myself. I'm already in the right place.

I took the elevator up and stepped out into a yellow-lit space with conference posters and pigeon holes, just like my department back in London. It was reassuring. I kept checking that I still had my luggage, as I was beyond exhausted, and here in New England, it was only the early afternoon yet.

'Well, hello! Are you here for an interview?' said a lady in jeans and glasses opening a door.

'Yes, I am', I answered.

She was the secretary with whom I had already been e-mailing.

'It's nice to meet you', I said.

'Did you get here ok?', she asked.

'Yes, fine. Thank you for the directions...' – 'The professor is ready for you, and when you're done talking to him, you need to fill in some paperwork with me'.

It was an unexpectedly swift transition. The professor, a

[61]

Dutchman whose office seemed like a spaceship to be flying over gothic bell towers and spiky castles, told me in the first few minutes that I was their top choice, that they only wanted to meet me in person briefly, but I could still to take part in the two-day interviewing and selection process with the other twelve shortlisted candidates. He said he and the committee were hoping I would come to the school, although he understood I probably had other options. Then he told me about my job responsibilities, the undergraduates I would be teaching, and he said that in the ivies, undergraduates were very bright and teaching them would be a piece of cake. I accepted the offer. All this promised something entirely new coming my way, crushing the swamps of London with a bright and shiny, gigantic foot.

In the spring, the air was mild. No matter how happy, how lucky, how blessed, I was feeling low and out of touch. I must be insane, I repeated to myself. Maybe I am. Liz and I had become friends, she sometimes came to the house in Soho. We would walk from the Strand, through an early afternoon central London, full of business suits, workmen and caterers on their lunchtime errands, cross through Chinatown and buy rice noodles or oyster mushrooms. Then we went to the house in Soho, that house of sleepy eyes, where there was nobody home, put on a CD, and started chopping.

A big box of Marlboro tobacco towering on the kitchen counter, we were smoking the mandatory student roll-ups, one of the flatmates peeped in, said hello, we all had a chat. We made our stir-fry and got tipsy, went back out to the backstreets of Soho, bought funky clothes in a junk shop for a laugh, eyed the tattoo parlours and sat down in small cafés between haberdashery and record shops. We laughed a lot then.

On other days, I would walk around Soho, trawl slowly the old and withered streets meandering by sex shops, wholesale jewellers and a shabby small open vegetable market on Berwick Street, underneath neglected council housing blocks, around the corner from the NCP car park, which was a crack and heroin smoking hangout just off the supercheap strip club paradise with makeshift illegal brothels on all the house floors.

In the less populated, more neglected streets of Soho north of the Windmill strip club and west of Madame Jojo's cabaret club, were hidden away health centres for the homeless, sexual health clinics for addicts and sex workers, and strewn right between that were cards of pin-up boys on abandoned, run-in doors. So many buildings were vacant and had their windows boarded up, all that Raymond splendour in ruin, on the edges of Soho, between large redbrick buildings with hauling devices as of former warehouses, small printing and fashion businesses popping up here and there, photo studios, fashion retailers, costume hire and junk shops around, and maybe a few tourists who had strayed off the main path... it was pretty melancholic and burnt-out as a setting to be wandering in, but I was bound in its magic spells.

Somewhere off Dean Street, there was a Starbucks, where Liz and I sat down in purple velvet armchairs to discuss whatever it was that was always keeping us vivid and absorbed. With the mild air outside, I felt so fortunate to be sitting in this café with such a wonderful friend. There was a calm to it, after the storm in winter, a simplicity and freedom I did not want to give up, then. I wished then that this life would never stop and that this moment in time

[63]

could last forever, that I would forever have America to look forward to, and this beautiful present forever stay where it is.

On weekends, I sometimes went into a phone booth on Soho square to call home, and would have these long phone conversations with my mother whilst inevitably sampling all the sex cards one by one. Stuck all over the phone box were half-censored porno shots with telephone numbers and seedy sayings such as 'all services', 'no rush', 'hotel visit', 'I love my job', 'pre-op' written on them. I used to wonder, and never quite decide on the answer, whether or not if one rang those numbers one would get through to the actual girl on the picture or whether those were random ads.

My last month in London was a warm May. It was my last month living with Jonathan, our last month in Soho, last few days with friends who had become very dear. I was definitely leaving for America and felt that I should make this month especially relaxed. Jonathan and I did something we had never done until then, we went out together – for breakfast pancakes at Balans. We enjoyed it, sitting in the open windows, we watched the stream of Soho-people pass by us, ate our pancakes, and smiled at each other. Everything now was bitter-sweet and under-stated, swept under a bright and friendly surface.
This slow and extended farewell to Soho and to Jonathan, it was as if I were cheerfully swimming away from a sinking island in hot tropical water, and leaving behind a smiling life that I knew was poisoned and came with a cannibal cave underwater. Although I could already see the other shore, I was somehow tied to the scary island on a

[64]

leash.

The air was mild, café clatter beside the stream of grazing people on Old Compton Street made everything hip and fashionable, gay, colourful, and upstairs in the old pubs, old men were smoking, taking it easy in the morning, delivery boys rushing around with trolleys, men in suits on their way in and out of twenty pound shops were flying rainbow flags.

I was going to be a classical scholar – deadly deadpan, now. Peter and I had been talking so much about so many books over so many pints and cocktails, I had been reading and writing so much, now I was going to go to New England and meet the faces behind the books, and there wasn't anything else I needed to worry about. I won my last set of awards in London, and thus I had some money to go backpacking in central Europe over the summer, before I'd disappear to America and take some entirely new grounds.

I don't know what I was hungry for, the melancholy of old Europe which I wanted to suck in as much as I could before settling into the brave new world where everything would be order and beauty, comfort and gold would close me in, and from where I knew, a return would be difficult, now that I was slamming doors on Jonathan and everything else. So, I went travelling.

First to Athens. I travelled alone, and after what seemed a long and exhausting journey, when I was at last blinking on hot Syndagma square, where dogs were sleeping under olive-trees, I was impressed by the buildings, the upmarket shopping streets full of beautifully dressed people. I walked along, past high end fashion stores, and at the end, through a smoggy rift of houses, under the dirty blue sky, there it was, unobtrusive, looking familiar yet peculiar like something seen for the first time, the Acropolis.

It was floating all by itself, like the mare of a cloud in a hot summer sky, mild and dreamy, infinitely far remote. I gasped when I first saw it, I had not expected to be so surprised, I thought I'd seen it already, on so many pictures already. But it was a moment of awe and revelation. All I was thinking fell from me like a coat I could have dropped, and this image replaced it, ultra-familiar and at the same time strange and brand new. The old gods seemed to live again and flutter about the place. Old buildings, magnificent or spooky, seemed to steer clear of the road with its circus, like a backdrop to the actual events, sunken within themselves, with the melancholic reserve of certain old people. Rarely did I dream so much during the day, and so little at night as when I was in Greece.

July, 2006.
Went on the Budapest castle hill in a church and saw relics from close-up for the first time. Strange idea to present half a skull between gold and velvet ornaments under a lace mini-napkin, or fingers in an ebony miniature sarcophagus. Then I read a medieval Latin mass in a thousand-year-old book. Spent hours in the Liszt museum reading every letter, every invitation, every menu, every programme, book page, libretto excerpt, whatever there was on display. What a superstar he was. His pianos, his desk and his living room and bedroom. Suddenly the elusive ghost steps out of its tenebrous shed, the rushing world of music takes shape and substance, the man

[66]

emerges who knew how to balance, to model and confine incommensurable, exhaustive and delicate fantasy, without cutting it up.

Liszt is my piano hero. I want to be able to do what he could do with music, with writing. The way he cross-weaves themes, flies over them, underscores them, the way he works with repetition, the refinement and lightness, this sound that surrounds itself by a thin layer of glass, round and perfect as a crystal sphere, a world within a world, polished, dark and glossy, but clear-cut, but sharp, geometric, infinitesimal and glittering like a thousand small shards...

The train station waiting room, greenhouse hot, the beating sun out there. All round the walls runs a chain of immovable brown plastic chairs in stylish soviet '70s design. The floor is wood, the ambient smells of smoke and concrete dust, as there is a hole in the wall, a pale yellow wall. The light switches are authentic '70s as are the neon lights hanging from the ceiling, otherwise there is only a square clock for company here.

I'm waiting for the Eurocity to Berlin, my destination is Bratislava but the train goes on to Prague and Dresden, then Berlin – it must take 15 or 20 hours to reach Berlin, cutting through Europe like that... Berlin now seems at a distant remove, and the stations of that train journey a dream sequence of dark areas in memory and imagination, cities I know from hearsay, from history books, from their music, from famous names, from the soft flame in the eyes of people speaking to me of their faraway homes. Being in a train that never arrives, foreign voices lulling from each side in languages I can't make out.

[67]

Then, Poland. In order to get to Oswiecim, I didn't catch a tourist shuttle bus but took the train, which is slightly more expensive and less convenient, but it gives a better sense of place.

A young Polish couple was travelling, a mother with little son & grandmother. The lovely pale and wide faces of men and women seem to glow like moons as they get out packed lunches of meat stew and dumplings, cabbage and root vegetables.

It was 3am when I left. After visiting Auschwitz I tried to walk to Birkenau. The last bus to get there had left already, but it being only a 3km walk, I made my way there on foot. I got lost on the way, and landed up in some rural villages. I know about Italian village life, but the Polish farmers seem to be far less fortunate with soil, weather and plants. The earth must be mediocre, as the faded colour of sways of uncultivated land would suggest. Probably much like Brandenburg, which is very nearby, after all, and is just as barren and sandy.

Having given up on finding Birkenau I returned to the train station, but no more trains were going to Krakow, so I had until 11.30pm to kill so I tried again and found Birkenau, in the dark, with nobody there at all. Barbed wires and bad grass, the motorway crossing past, and just the word 'Judenrampe' on a withering memorial plate, it was like a hammer bursting all of my thoughts into pieces at once.

I suddenly became very scared, and ran back to the train station as fast as I could. There was a Swiss family there, waiting for the Vienna train, and various other stranded individuals. The train to Trzebinia seemed mysterious, maybe only by its lateness. At Trzebinia, I had an hour and a half to kill. Inside the waiting room, it smelled of a gas leak, so I went outside where I noticed the entire area must have been infested by some factory fumes so there was nothing I could do. The station was really in the middle of nowhere, if there was a city there, then certainly all its lights were out. Lights here in Poland have generally been off. In the ticket hall, there was another guy trying to read brochures, and a man in his 50s snoring over his suitcase and talking in his sleep, while the ticket officer behind her window was answering night-time calls and outside on the platform, cargo trains were passing through. At about 2a.m. the platform filled up with people, soon the train got in, it was packed. Most people were a little drunk, sleepy, or chatting away having a picknick, a small puppy in a cardboard box was howling and another dog somewhere on the train had noticed and started a barking conversation. Everyone laughed and talked.

As for Auschwitz itself, what a peculiar little brick village. Through its chimneys have passed thousands of men and women come from near and far, with all expectations but this one, in packed treks and transports, through strange and empty lands, real masses, crowds, voices, souls, families. How many stories they could have told. What a thought that somebody deliberately invented and engineered all this machinery of death. I tried to picture the people who had worked there, who saw and knew all about it, the ones who planned to carry it on. Now I knew good faith had to be an illusion. Bible tales and words like 'guilt' and 'punishment' belonged to an old order where the world still lulled itself in beliefs like the natural good of humankind. Or perhaps there never was such an old order, but I somehow had perhaps thought about believing that there might have been. The suffocating cellars in darkness, the impossible architecture of torture cells,

[69]

chimneys, crematoria, the little train, and certainly the worst of all were the euphemisms. It was a delayed and deep shock that I noticed only once I was so thoroughly chilled from within that it was too late to run away from contemplating it. The thoughts suddenly fall down on memory like a block of concrete, this fatal force from within that scatters even self-deception, and then this flashing, worrying, biting question, 'where has that evil gone today?' where will I meet it?

Two : My Personal Troy

Brave New England

I said goodbye to a lot of things and people. Served on the jury to appoint a new director for the next Greek play. The pubs, the streets, Liz's drunken flatmates in Dalston, everything fell flat now I knew I would not be living here any more. Jonathan was off with some Russian bombshell and working as a salesman. Good good, I thought. Just yesterday, it seems, I was hovering outside the library at midnight, studying and going mad about this impossible London life, walking up to Soho at three in the morning when all the noise was long gone quiet, quiet and depressing, but the house has ears, the house was floating as a silent archive of conversations and of lives, and its glassy, unrevealing window-eyes half-shut, guarding Soho's residents peaceful sleep.

August, 2006
Not now, not any more, now I'm a guest here, and a foreigner. Everything is dissolved into a cloud of smoke and ashes where I've lost the thread that could lead the way back. From this point onward, I'll have to walk alone, even without knowing the way – blindly, and I'll have to keep moving forward until things begin to look familiar again.
It's too late now to turn back. I wanted this, but there won't be a circus net if I fall, there won't even be an audience. And as for the rest... all these places I now come past aren't mine any more. I don't need them, and they declare they don't need me. I did visit Jonathan in his

[71]

new home, but he didn't want me there. I just wanted to say goodbye, because I know it's painful. It's painful for him, it's painful for me, but we can't stay together and this way, it is for the best. I wanted to have the time to make up and say goodbye. It didn't work. Then, the next day, we met for coffee by Somerset House, and suddenly we started crying so awfully, we decided to stay in touch. He cried, I cried, he said he hoped that I would be okay in America all by myself, I said sure, and then, suddenly, this escape to America filled me with deep fear about what might happen. I wanted to run away from it all. I really understood now that I was going out of this world and I wasn't keeping my ties with the old, and I didn't know what to expect. But I got on my plane, of course, and ordered a double vodka. 'Aw, you've had a bad day!', commented an American brat next to me – yes, actually, I have... I started making new friends. What else is there left for me to do now.

It was mid-August and I had a few days before the start of graduate school. It was hot and humid outside, I was constantly falling asleep in my room, so once I'd done the mandatory admin and sourced an IKEA to help me furnish my dormitory room, I thought it a good idea to explore the surroundings. On foot.

I walked a few hours westward, starting from the centre of town. First there were the fading limits of the city, a gas station, a long road of abandoned industry where the crazy weed grew. I crossed a small river, walked through some woods, past a few gated communities, into emptiness, then I came to a Latin village, where I stopped. I went into the supermarket, marvelled at their foods and products.

Thinking to myself it was all much more Spanish than I had imagined, I stayed in the shop for a while, bought two bottles of shampoo there, just as an excuse for being in the shop. I was in a new world of which I didn't know a thing, besides the mirage of Hollywood, Reuters, and corporate rock; but this place where I was now standing was, apparently, off the radars of any of these portrayals.

Coming out of the supermarket, it was beginning to become dark. Through the little row of houses on this gritty street, attempting to keep the appearance that I knew exactly where I was, I tried to sneak a peek into the dusty windows that seemed to have behind them South American used furniture shops. They had something of the colonial-style antiquarians one can still find in Brussels, displaying dark and polished wood tables, gold-handled chests, pearling lampshades, stuffed parrots, curvy cages, leather bound books and exotic dolls. But I didn't dare to enter, thinking that I might come too close to a melancholy that was in truth nothing to do with the post-colonial fascination, but was closer to the real thing, had more of a used dream emporium, akin to that fabled South American literature of magic and fairy tale, tinged with the wreckage of emigration.

Dreamscapes were pulsing in the momentarily caught reflection of my self in these shop windows, vague and barely known dreams that slept in the wood-inlaid cradles on the other side of the glass, with piles of broken toys I would have loved to bring to life, under dust in which I'd have loved to draw shapes, dreams I would have loved to dream, an old world I would have loved to find the compass to, perhaps right in this messy antique shop behind the dirty window. But it was getting dark, the yellow dust was curdling on the sidewalk, and I had only

[73]

arrived here by the accident of my shameless explorations, when really I was here for ivy laurels.

The shop owners, heavy-bellied and pipe smoking, were leaning in their doors, speaking in Spanish to young women in pink tank tops, who were curious and loud. Ola, me llamo Fernando, said one of three men in builders uniforms coming home from the long road, as I have, to the people on the East coast, apparently, a rather Hispanic complexion, which I only learnt much later – I only replied 'English, English', and then walked out of their village.

The hot and humid weather made me drowsy in the afternoons, in my modest dormitory room, where so far my only acquaintance was Nicola, a Romanian scholar of queer studies. She, however, thought my hiking out of town had been a really crazy idea to start with, so I was disappointed that probably she wouldn't come on any further exploration walks with me. I had also walked to IKEA, although that was clearly at the edge of town; it was a tiny small town, for god's sake, nothing was far...

I had taken the trip to America by myself, for the promise of a prestigious career via the ivy league, as much as to get away from the dead ends of my private life back in London. Winding up in a small town dormitory with hundreds of scientists from China, a Romanian house mate seemed pretty close to home news, and we soon became friends, smoking cigarettes in the back yard with a Canadian Britten scholar who had a faible for feather boas and the Elton John look, and a Mexican Milton scholar who with his greasy long hair and goatee could just as well have said he was a truck driver, exchanging vivid comments about our impressions of it all.

During the night, crickets and the heavy weight of clouds

[74]

pressing a sweaty atmosphere on to one's chest like cotton in an ear, I began to feel as I though were moving in a vacuum of absent-mindedness and the impossibility to share with anybody the life I'd had so far.

Soon, I discovered I was not alone with the feeling. A Gambian bio-engineer I met one evening in the elevator, said in between the doors, 'oh, life before we came here? it seems just like a dream, now, nobody can believe it. Nobody wants to know! It could even all be lies. You can say whatever... nobody cares, they all just care about this, this and how good they are'. I began to see that perhaps it wasn't only my fault for wanting to tell too many stories, but perhaps also a part of the place's spirit deliberately to ignore and obliterate stories from the outside – heartlessly so, sometimes.

This great, big ivy league school – so my entrance there began with a sweeping sense of isolation, and loss of identity. Certainly, I did attend many glamorous and ceremonious welcome dinners and welcome speeches. In fact, these social occasions were happening nearly every day, but they were so formal, and so star-studded with Nobel prize winners, top-level politicians, famous writers, film-makers or scholars calculated to impress us new kids, that they were almost always completely rigid and formal and all would be sitting along long tables in restaurants, starchy napkins in our laps, poking scallops or plantain, drinking iced water and trying to find a topic to keep us going.

I got used to the American way though, to the wooden and angular way of wrapping everything in grander rhetoric. By late October, my new German colleague and friend Nina and I were planning on what we jokingly referred to as 'an anthropological investigation', attending the Halloween midnight concert. In a 1930s concert hall, built as a meticulous imitation of a Renaissance arts temple with a trompe-l'oeil on its cupola, an enormous organ in the middle with the school's motto on a banner, on the multiple floors with wooden seats in a circle above the stage, in came stampeding and throbbing a mob of undergraduates in Ugg Boots and denim skirts, or, on the male side of things, baseball caps and baggy pants, screaming hysterically in an illicit alcohol rush, ecstatic in their often chubby flesh, fuelled by expressly hired animators telling them how and when to shout things, getting up and throwing about scarves and bottles.

The gig itself began, a symphonic mashup of popular tunes from Vivaldi to Snoop Dogg, conceived as the sound track to a cringy film about student ghostbusters. It provoked applauses at times which were to me completely mystifying, and screams at slides I couldn't see the punchline in: clearly, I was missing something; but so was Nina beside me. The show ended, again, to me rather mystifyingly on a slide reading a flashing 'Impossible Is Nothing'.

Only much later did I understand the Aleksey Vayner reference, and when I did, it was besides the point anyway. I hadn't been able to place the quotes, get any of the jokes, and many of the cues didn't really mean to me what they seemed obviously to mean to everyone else in the room. The conclusion of our anthropological field study had to be 'we don't get it'. Nina, who was a gentle-mannered, petite and neo-glam looking young scholar with an apparently perpetual smile of bemused disbelief in her eyes, was probably ready to tear it to pieces with me, but I was tired, so tired. I was exhausted, not just because of the

[76]

late hour, but because things weren't making sense to me, even though I was trying since two months to understand where I was, I was only getting more estranged and isolated. When I went home and to bed, I dreamt the first of these dreams of estrangement, that I was to get much better acquainted with over the months to come. There was nothing but a tunnel through blue-eyed clefts of glass skyscrapers and whispered voices in the board restaurant. I felt my pockets, to check I still had my passport, but then I forgot what I was even looking for. I came out of the water and saw how dirty I was. Then I stopped a newspaper boy on his bike, to ask for directions. Where is the nearest... nearest... what? I am... I am... oh, you don't know? I'm sorry. Should I call Germany? Would there be a hotel somewhere? Oh but... Who are all these people so suddenly circling around me as vultures? They weren't there before, were they? Are they planning to put me in prison forever? Are there some here that could understand my language? But words fail me and slowly I am taken by my arms and brought somewhere, I don't know where to, but oh! stop! a phone cabin! let me make just one call! But oh misery, I have no money, don't even know the currency, nor even know the number I want to call. I can barely keep my eyes open or make a sentence with this headache... Yet it seems this moment calls for immediate action...

I woke up, not knowing where I was, looking for a telephone. I was in a room full of bulky brown fitted furniture. No idea where I was. Could be Japan, could be Korea. Slowly I realized that I was in my own dorm room. New England. So I *did* get here. I looked out of the window.

December, 2006.

It is winter now. I have to go to the library, just as I did yesterday. Yesterday... what was yesterday? What is today's schedule? Why do I have this headache? Oh yes, I remember now. The schedule is, and the cause of everything is, I am depressed. In this daze of waking up, I had forgotten all about that. I was just about to be fine, and here it goes again, the bleak envelope to slip my soul into.

This dorm room is terrible, and outside are the now familiar red blocks of paper wall, that have fallen from the sky in all their ugliness and are too heavy to move. Faces, always the same faces, dust, always the dust, and I'll be stuck in this place for another four years. Everything is grand and arrogant, clean, outmeasured, people are full of nonsense, self-complimentary, self-satisfied, patting each other's shoulders. This is the New England winter, then. When I talk about Soho, nobody believes it, they tell me I'm making it up. Life before this, now, seems like it was just a dream.

Woke up here having no idea where I was, who I was, what I was supposed to do, who knew I was here, where my friends were. I felt tearful, sad, truly disarmed. There is nothing I can do except keep my back straight and keep walking through these rows of houses that were designed to be elevating and beautiful, privilege and nurture of the highly gifted, but, as I can see now, I'm not one of them.

I only can see loosely the floating and fragmented bits and pieces that were beginning to make sense and are pushed out again now, to the margins from which I had begun to draw them. Here, where they make a living from boxing and shelving things, none of what I think fits in anywhere, and it is as if I had not any thoughts at all. I've lost the

[78]

thread to my kite.

Campus was looking marvelous, the American autumn had been all that Hollywood promised. And even in the cold of winter, sunlight was bright, and the colours beautiful in the afternoon: pale rose sandstone towers on the old campus flooded in a rose and orange sunset, glowing like ignited sugar cubes over an absinthe of green quads with thin fog rising from it. Fluorescent grass, dying winter grass that was bending gently in a mild wet wind, which, with its gentle breeze, reminded me of home, brought me back in my mind to the cold of Berlin, when the winter mellows, and stones sing with the thaw drops of snow and ice.

Berlin. Hadn't I once already in Berlin felt the winged soul fly by me? I saw those black and shedding walls again in memory, as two old photographs now Berlin and the campus were melting into one image, and I remembered a weird afternoon when I saw a crow fly over the museum island and pondered about its meaning, over these sleeping giants in their mystery silence, and the treasures they conceal. The glistening tar, iron fences, dark doors, and this wet air ringing the bells of my old home stayed hanging in my mind for a moment like bed sheet ghosts in the attics of children's books, as my mind flicked back and forth between pictures of Berlin and pictures of this new land. Then they dissolved themselves of a sudden, as glitter dropping off a canvas, a curtain falling before a final scene, and then, I understood that it was all just stone. The stones were just stones, and nothing meant anything at all. No magic, no past times, no murmured whispers, only stones that blacken with time in the rain. I recognized the realization much as I would an unfriendly face in the street, and then walked around thinking of it for a long

[79]

time, thinking I could perhaps come up with an answer, but something like a long sorrow raised its voice, like a dead mermaid raising her head from the waters, frightful and unworldly, defaced and wreathed in seaweed, began a low lament, and left me in silence. I was unaccountably sad, and carried this defeat in me like a poison in the heart, or a bag of drugs in my stomach through an airport security – a dagger in my throat, an iron cross, for the war-scarred soul. And so I could not find peace of mind.

There had been yet another wine social. An older professor approached me, I knew his face from the internet, but he seemed more imposing now with his deep voice and absence of a smile, overweight stature and rough hair.
'So, where are you from?', he asked me, I said Germany.
He commented: 'A lot of people here would tell you they wish they were'.
To me that came as a bit of a surprise. I started to gesture towards a reply, but then it began to dawn on me where I really was now, in the deep of the kind of speech which later sets on textbook pages, complete with examples, theses and a touch of stately pomp. I had read, a long time ago as it now seemed in London, scholars' personal prefaces expressing thanks in edited volumes, describing talk series, greeting friends from afar through the printed page. I was deep in the darkest ivy, all-American, all calm, all exclusive. Surreal, I was hanging over the dinner table and my head was hanging down heavy with alcohol when I understood this and, looking on the oak furniture and gothic windows, tried to keep good posture.

'What are you working on?' – a question I had already got used to.

'Greek drama, and the history of scholarship', I said.

'As a German, ah, yes...'

'I'm certainly very interested in the old German philologists', I said, and it was even true.

'Ah', said the professor, 'Do you know, then, of the great Calder?'

'William Calder, and the Villa Mowitz?' I asked, point-scoring.

'Yes, exactly', he laughed. So, I smiled.

I began to talk a little – after all, it was a social. It was more of a poetic interest I had in the old German philologists, I was from Berlin myself and had practically by the knowledge of street names and museum island trawls become familiar with the names of those great bearded men whose black and white photographs mesmerized me.

I can now confirm they were obsessed and driven by a furious thirst when they built the grand classificatory systems that are still in use today and enjoyed by many scholars. They did more than is humanly possible. What had hit me the day I came back from Auschwitz, this poignant question of how and why technical advancement and civilized humanity, humanism, could become so estranged from each other – I was to ask, here, again.

If I think now how I ended up dying slowly in America before the eyes of all and they all say they didn't know or they didn't want to seem to be asking inappropriate questions, if they weren't of those who were plain prejudiced, I realise the differences between our cultures are such long shadows that I could never jump over them – the myth of the self-made man, the American dream and way of life, the wars, the ideal of a strong and healthful

[81]

leader, the militaristic society, that, I could not follow.

The Marines sent a request to our department if we could translate their motto into Latin, this request was sent to a general mailing list. One American student suggested a translation forthwith, adding that this was 'in gratitude toward people who take responsibility for the safety of us all and thereby make possible our lives of leisure'.
An English student wrote 'what's the Latin for toe curling bollocks?', in answer to which another American on the mailing list wrote 'Do you think there would be an America for you to come to study in if there were no armed forces? You may not like where and when the Marines are deployed, and you may not like their policy on sodomy, but the fact is that the Marines don't make those decisions. Politicians do'.
The next reply came, again, from a European, an Italian: 'I find the word sodomy over the top'.
An American, again: 'I'm an attorney (...) I was simply using the proper legal lingo'.
Somewhere down the line of the exchange was the advice: 'Write President Bush a nasty letter, if you like. Become an American citizen and vote for someone who you think will be a good commander-in-chief', before it was broken off by a prudent student taking charge of mellowing the tone by reminding us this was a scholarly mailing list, not one dedicated to the discussion of politics.
To me it was, much like the Halloween concert night, a time when my understanding of America and its people seemed to hit upon its ceiling, or one of its ceilings, and a low ceiling at that. Clearly all of the participating Americans in this conversation were pro-war and all of the Europeans were anti-war. There were concepts,

[82]

educations, common childhood experiences and cultural values at work here, obviously, that were entirely unfamiliar to me. Yes, and it seemed that this America that I'd walked into so trustingly imagining that at first sight it seemed much like what the television in Europe portrayed, this America that I thought I was already familiar with, because I spoke English, because I got around New York well enough, actually had in store for me as great an estrangement and cultural displacement as any place that is a ten-hour flight away, really will.

I'd had no hesitation to write about classicists in the States what I thought of the German scholars of the early 20th century, both were meticulous and accurate at the price of being unaware, they knew so much because they understood so little. There was an elective affinity, it made me uneasy.

I was caught in between wondering if I was living in a police state, a militaristic society, or if this was a totalitarian regime. Somehow from outside the U.S., I had got this idea of it being a free country, but then, I realised, none are so truly enslaved as those who deem themselves to be free. It was far too late now to pretend not to see an imperial machinery in action. If the world in my lifetime had not become so small, with airline traffic and the internet, I would not have known, would not have lived there.

In the stacks of the library, I found myself in an endless labyrinth of written words, dark, narrow, low-ceiling rows closely packed with books by the thousands, a maze of them, floor on floor, closed books—silenced books, and some of those I looked at had not been opened in forty, fifty, sixty years. I imagined them, how they had been waiting, in the 1980s, in the 1950s, in the 1920s even, gasping, throbbing, waiting; singular how these stacks brought to my head the thought of waste and of neglect. In this repository of cultural reflection in which, no doubt, every question could find its answer, but none was, no-one knew how to keep a tradition. Every day, I was facing flushes of deliberately obtuse people and policies, and I was thrown around like a ball of flames, never safe, never secure, and here in the heart of a place that could have nurtured lucid thinking and beautiful ideas, this seemed especially cruel.

December, 2006 (2)
Christmas vacation in Berlin. In the morning, a dream I once had came true. I used to dream that I would one day see this morning. Last night, Jonathan and I went for drinks in the Café Cinema with his sister, and the sister's boyfriend. At about one in the morning, the sister was hungry so she asked if we could get Pizza. J. decided he would go to bed and walked over to his apartment, I went to have pizza with them. After the pizza, they walked me home and I had a good night's sleep at Jonathan's, in the silent flat, he took one of the old Berlin apartments with high ceilings. This morning, we visited the Museum island together. It's newly opened. The 'Neues Museum' still is in refurbishment, I remember when the ruined site was open to the public, it was beautiful, J. and I had been to see it with all its half-erased, royal blue mural art, its damaged arches and columns. Today, when we crossed the bridge to the Museum island, I suddenly felt that my dreams had come true - the dream of this happiness. That I could find a lovely boyfriend, and kind friends, that we would all get

[84]

on, do things we enjoy together and discuss everything and anything through nights, have many long talks over wine, because there is wet gold in the spirits. We went for late lunch. As a joke, we wrote a postcard of the museum to our London address. The weather was wet and windy, charged with a cold, humidity-saturated breeze to call back the mind from all the cliffs it wandered.

On the balcony above the bar where we had our lunch, old ivy was growing, and the birds nesting in it were chirping, reminding of the spring that comes... not yet, but I can feel already the broken hearts that cry out when the snow is thawing, before the snow even falls.

Everything was so German. It was a quiet morning, and as I was walking toward my friends, I felt memories raining down on me like hail, and a strange joy that my dream had come true, but bitter, it was a very bitter joy, too.

I looked over to the Pergamon Museum, and to the train. Remembered how my heart used to become heavy with the view. When I saw the dream come true, I suddenly felt scared. The picture was perfect, only one thing wasn't the same any more: I wasn't. This was my dream finally come true, my picture, and yet in it, I was already like a shadow, like a cut-out silhouette. In my mind, I was already at a remove from the new experiences. I felt I had an actor's soul, everything was pretending and make-believe, I was present, but I wasn't there. Pulled all the threads and strung them together, but lost the whole fabric, just because I was so nervous, walking in air, in dreams and thoughts, I dropped it... The year is drawing to a close. What a year. It seems that not only the year, but a part of my self is ending. Whatever comes now will be new and unknown.

[85]

The Wooden Horse

What happened in America in the wake of my, how shall I say, emotional fall on a hard rock, struck me as dull and grey for a while. I continued in the same style as before, but I was becoming visibly weaker in my mind, I was finding it difficult to sleep, feeling low and deranged, often thinking I was in a kind of Truman Show, that everyone but me was fake, and that I was somehow the object of a really bad joke.

I began to recognize that coming to the Ivies had been a mistake, and half-heartedly tried to battle the persistent propaganda on campus that was claiming that this university was the best of them all, taking hold of the majority on campus, who were all sporting the school branded hoodies and polo shirts in a kind of naturally uniform fashion and who refused to hear about any other place being any good. The overwhelming success of this propaganda was partially working on me as well, making it really hard for me to decide in a rational way that I needed to get away from it. I was waking up often with mood swings, persecutory delusions, or the desire to jump in front of a car. Seeing as personally, I took the all-importance of who we were with a pinch of salt, of course then, I was not hugely popular around campus, I picked up my fair share of biting remarks and dirty looks, but I still thought, rather that than being one of these piglets, I am sure someone here is on my side, I just haven't found them yet.

I had burnt bridges with England and somehow still not found happiness, I had to find a way out of at least one thing, my eating disorders. They were like a bad rash. I went to look for counselling, and I somehow ended up in the university's mental hospital.

The day I turned up for a counselling session, my second one in fact after I had already been prescribed schizophrenia drugs as a trial, I wanted to talk about it all, I was ready. About the dim and dark angles of consciousness I was bruising my heart against, about the social difficulties of being the youngest in my year and my resistance to the system, the scepticism everybody seemed to look me over with, my problems from back home, even, the culture shock and my estranged feelings here and the isolation that was eating at me. This was all starting to drive me insane, I had thought I could be stronger than this, but I wasn't. I knew that now there was perhaps a danger of suicide, that's why I was trying to get help.

But the doctor spoke these ominous words 'You see, I really don't think it's safe for you to be all alone with yourself, and I think you should be in hospital'.

It came as a shock and my mind blanked, this information did not process. I should there and then have said 'no, no', laughed it off, and made proof of extensive perseverance and sanity skills somehow. He'd asked me this question: 'are you hearing voices?' and I suppose I said yes – because it sort of was the next best thing after 'I seem to be listening up for things that aren't there', which apparently did not fit in with anything he had on his diagnostic chart. For all that I had facetiously considered the possibility that I was clinically insane, I could never have explained all this that was bothering me to him, and consequently I had not; I'd hardly said anything at all, but even without my

[88]

mentioning the mice in England or the mad year with Jonathan, even without my mentioning anything at all except the tip of the iceberg that I was feeling low lows and my heart was about to burst, he'd already surmised I must be mad and signed me off to an involuntary commitment on an emergency certificate, I just had no idea.

I didn't even know that nowadays it is more correct to say 'psychiatric ward' than 'lunatic asylum', that most treatment nowadays is done in the home with chemical remedies rather than in hospitals and physical restraint; that hospitals are only for transitional moments, and also, I believed that for all my pathos, I did not quite fit the doom of lifelong confinement. This is what I was assuming of lunatic asylums, in my mind they harboured confusion worse than death and certainly my career as an academic would have been over, indeed my hopes as a fiancée, as a daughter, as a friend, as an artist. Everything would be over, then, if I was going to be put into one of those places. And that wasn't at all the point I was at. This much I knew, but didn't know I had just lost my credibility. So here I was sitting momentarily baffled and visualising chains and straitjackets, thinking this could not possibly be real. In the next few hours, I saw myself getting pushed through a variety of waiting rooms with a variety of conversational attendants, nurses, social workers, and a doctor with a messy desk who was very interested in my problems, and my work.

I outlined the history of classical scholarship to him, the nature of Greek tragedy, gave him summaries of the various extant plays and philosophical dialogues, and pointed out to him the difficulty of understanding ancient texts now that so few are left of them, what was the interest of scholarly methods, and I pointed out what kinds of misunderstandings had already been debunked about Antiquity. I commended Aristotle, about whom he was very interested to hear more, and about the meaning of a literary language. The ambulance only arrived hours later, together with the police, and I emerged, tied on a stretcher, escorted by security personnel, at the turquoise and beige themed, glass-walled psychiatric inpatient unit of my university's medical campus. I was given a high dose of olanzapine which did not delay in putting me to sleep, and didn't quite register that for some reason I was switched between several different psychiatric units over three or four days before I was well-placed on the unit for psychotic adults.

Once I'd realised where I was though, an uncanny feeling spread through my stomach, but the door had already been locked behind me, and I was well over the three day habeas corpus. So, I sat down on the bed and just let my mind go blank. It was going blank all the time, I had also been prescribed lithium in the meantime. What was I supposed to do now anyway? All I could think of was a cartoon of an old granny with green hands (salad fingers) living in an isolated house deep in a sad and barren countryside under dark clouds amidst dead trees, a disconcerting waterfall, with thin voice talking to imaginary characters on finger puppets. These were new grounds to me, never before travelled, entirely strange lands and an ethical vacuum where I didn't know how one was meant to behave.

I tried to remind myself that I was depressed and unwell, as the doctor had said, to see if I could somehow conjure up my madness that had again sunken into my subconscious mind, if I could act up to the expectations of pathos and craziness required of patients in a mental hospital, but as usual, those feelings I'd had were difficult ones to get a hold of and hard to express, flitting in and out of view and I was only annoyed that now I'd have to answer for them when they were already gone.

I was a little curious about who else I'd meet, having seen a crowd of swollen and dishevelled faces on my way in. But for the time being, I was far too overwhelmed by tiredness and side effects to go out and socialize. I'd been brought here without notice, without a chance to go home and pack, or to notify anyone, and didn't have any paper to write on. I asked for pen and paper. I was given some, I thanked the nurse, sat down on the bed and continued writing my diary from where I'd left off – that diary I keep of that stream of thoughts, that undercurrent that never left me through all the changes in my self, my surroundings – that never-ending story of those quiet shades and fickle tremors below a coat of mist.

The heating in my room (a four bed room) was turned on high, the windows hermetic, I didn't know anyone, wasn't looking to meet anyone, and I had nothing to do. So I lay on the bed cover and fell asleep until on the night pills were brought to me – major tranquillizers, mood stabilizers, painkillers, and anxiety medicines. Some things had been added to my medication regimen, I swallowed everything anyway and went back to sleep.

And then I guess that I never really woke up properly again until a few years later. But that week, when I was being shifted from one hospital unit to another, I was like a piece of dead wood carried by water, as if I'd dropped my own past as two heavy suitcases and was now walking on air. I was willing to agree that I'd done everything wrong

[91]

in my life and got myself into a very bad situation indeed, all by my own mistake. I was willing to learn how a normal person thinks, and lives. I had nothing to say. I was guessing that after this, I would not be able to go back to graduate school, that I would not see those colleagues again, nor my people in Europe, with whom I had burnt bridges anyway, and I guess I thought that if I ever got out, I'd spend the rest of my life shifting parcels into the back of a truck living in a small bedsit, detached from everything, wondering if I could some day collect the scraps of my old life to write a book like this one, although, being cut off like that, I would have no readers, all of my life would have been strangely irrelevant, shuffled back and forth over and over again between back doors and broken pavements – I rebelled against the thought, thinking, no, no, not I.

But the question 'What will happen to me?' was not an appropriate one here, either. They said 'you're going to the adult unit in the other wing'. Again, security patrols to carry me over. Off to a fresh start, they said 'we hope you'll socialize better on this unit'.

Socializing with your peers seemed to be mandatory. Here they were… the white faces, the striped gowns, the dishevelled hair, the wheelchairs, the screaming people, the crying, the muttering, and the mute, the thinker poses, the self-conversationalists, the enraged, the suicide survivors, the obese, the ravaged skins, the angry explosions, the pacing, the trembling, the twitching, the messy eaters.

I thought that my worries must be trifling in comparison to the damaged souls of those people whom I found inside this psychiatric ward, and I continued to think so when I was there, but once I got into conversation with the other patients, I found that they were just like myself and not particularly crazy. Only I didn't look like them yet, I was still slim and well groomed, and I was still working, and talking about my career, and my boyfriend, and my country.

Mental hospital... what an irony. Before I went, and I didn't know of course that that was where I was going, I had made a date for a movie with Nicola, my dorm neighbour from Romania, and for a coffee, the next day, with Laurie, this incredibly well-read and sparkling minded Joyce scholar from Italy I had met in a Proust and Joyce class. Covered in Japanese tattoos and dressed in kind of gothic style, but with red cowboy boots, long black hair and golden christian crosses on her inky skin, she looked completely original and I was very curious to get to know her. Since we had been in the seminar together, despite her perfect arrogance and self-assurance, we arranged for a coffee meet, and I could not wait to find out more about her, she had something of a rockstar about her, and she knew about literature unlike anyone else.

It was her, Laurie, and Brian, the gay Irish junior professor, who, aside from teaching a brilliant Joyce class, was also a novelist in his own right, that I had instantly declared as my new role models. In the maze of this whole uniformizing and debilitating ivy league school propaganda and self-satisfied, moneyed laziness, they stood out as scintillating, infinitely well-read and creative individuals whose conversation was gold dust to me.

But I, of course, had been stolen out of the life for a while, and into mental hospital, and yet, after a few days, we managed to have our coffee... in the mental hospital. At this point I should have known something was not right with my university's policies about psychiatric hospitalisations of students. I'd already met two other students on the unit. That made four of us. But, I thought, well if I'm crazy then so is she, definitely.

Here I was in the ward then, and here was Laurie. I'd instantly recognized her voice, saying 'Please, don't make me stay here, I have already wasted two days of my time and I have many things to do, I'm a scholar'.
In the circumstances, I found it an odd thing to be telling a nurse. At first, she was trying to hide from me. With only a vague awareness of the social taboo of mental illness and the clear understanding that it normally meant losing one's job, I understood why she was uneasy and thought it probably best if we would knowingly play hide and seek so that we could both return to graduate school later, as if it never happened. By then, I had had a visit from my dean to let me know I could return unless I voluntarily left my programme, I knew I would be going back. But the ward wasn't nearly spacious enough for hide and seek, there was too much time elapsing without the possibility to go outside, to read or do something, and avoiding one another there was impossible.
Reluctantly, we eventually had our cup of coffee. We had many cups of coffee – decaf, of course. She explained to me that she was on a hunger strike in order to lobby for her own release, because she felt that she had been unduly sectioned. I was very sleepy on my new drug regimen and only half-listening to her as she gave me lectures about resistance, tattoos, and Gandhi. The graduate school's humanities dean came to the ward again, a judge was summoned to decide on her case, and a small trial staged

within the ward, inside the glass-walled meeting room, she was released within three days, and after this, she began writing a Psychology paper about the injustice of American psychiatry and the systematic internment of intellectual minorities. The reason for her admission to the ward, apparently, had been homicidal ideation. She said it had been a misunderstanding, something she'd said in an argument but that was not meant seriously, but somehow she could not persuade the psychiatrists of the same.

February, 2007.
Something very strange happened: One of my colleagues is here, she arrived today. She was embarrassed that I, being here like her, now know that she has been here in mental hospital. We got talking a lot. In Italian. She said that in her opinion, the world had no meaning, but that one's body and its form undeniably were unique and undeniably existed. And that the starting point of any existential thought, if one is not religious, could be the form and the beauty of one's body. She then told me about tattoos. I don't grasp what she is saying about that. Too hard, too advanced in her thinking. She is a very prolific thinker. It is good to have her here. She is lovely. Almost like a family member to me now, in this very strange and scary place, so far from home.
Dear God, I am sorry, but there is total darkness. I'm in a bed. In a hospital. In a small town. In America. The lights are out. And from the corridor, I hear laughter of two American guys. They speak American. I now know that language is as far away from English as is Chinese. Another patient has an amputated leg; he was shot, and cocaine. And I'm taking medications. Just now it comes down on me, how much I don't belong here. How absurd

[95]

the situation is. Another guy has tried to commit suicide many times. Hanging, overdose. In the emptiness, in the vastness of American small towns that get no care, that sink in the hugeness of the world. Just now I remember dimly Carson McCullers, an American author I read years ago in school. The Ballad of the Sad Café. I think that was really what America is all about. It's not about any of what I thought, and I don't know where I am. And I don't know who I am. If I survive, I have to tell, to write the story of this long estrangement.

There's a piano here on the ward. Quite a worn old piano, and dirty, but it's a piano. It is snowing outside and I would like to see that, feel it. I can't leave this floor wing at all. Managed to get as far as opening a book and reading the first few lines. I had a play in my handbag when I was sent here, it was last week's class reading. Much as I would like to, I can't read it. There's this piano here, I played for fifteen minutes, perhaps. But this tension in my legs, I kind of have to keep moving around. At least I've done that bit of piano, I felt nearly normal then. Walking is difficult, I have vertigo and am a bit shaky. Medication side effects. I'm not feeling well, really not, I can't think properly. Close my eyes to all this weird stuff and keep going like everybody else is doing. These things I was thinking about, from Europe, nobody gets them anyway, and they're all just stories from the past I should forget now. There is no point, the situation is already ended, I wanted this. Some day I'll be able to tell what happened in a way that makes sense.

I began playing the piano on the ward as often as I could manage. I met Sebastian because he sat there listening to me. He asked me where I was from, I told him Germany.

[96]

He asked if had come to this town for the school, I said yes. He told me he had, too, from the Ukraine, and that he was a psychiatrist in training. You don't know how far away from home you are, until you meet someone from the Ukraine, and it feels like home. We smiled at each other as suddenly we had a lot more in common. I played Schumann, he played Tchaikovsky. He told me he had a band. I told him about the Russian disco in Berlin. He asked me about my impressions of the school. I told him I was surprised that it wasn't quite as outstanding as I thought it would have been after all the noise about it. He said he felt the same. He said he had thought, back in Kiev, that in America everything would be better, everything would be state-of-the-art, that there would be better outcomes, but that it wasn't that way. He said he thought the more modest means of his own country in medicine could do more than all the hype of the new drugs. I said I felt the same about my field of study, and that I thought nothing of the almost military tone of teaching here. He said of course, and 'this country has a lot to learn yet. Some things here are almost like in communist Russia'.

He said he had the blues. I had the blues, heaven knows I had the blues, I was in mental hospital. He asked me about that. I tried to explain it, but he cut me off: 'you need to get away from this place, trust me. You don't want to be on these drugs' - 'But I…' - 'no. Listen to me carefully. There are people in this hospital who can't help themselves. They need help, but nobody wants to give it to them. But you are not like these people. Look at you, how many things you've achieved. You play the piano beautifully, you've lived in London, you speak all these languages, you have done amazingly well at university. You should be able to help yourself, these doctors aren't going to. You are not crazy. Remember this. You are having a normal reaction to the surroundings. You shouldn't have accepted anyone tell you that you're nuts, because you're not. Everyone gets depressed sometimes'.

It made so much sense to me, I almost felt ashamed. It was what I thought. I looked around me, at the other patients, at the many mid-fifties women, at the ill-grown men, I heard them talking, and I knew I was in the wrong place. I knew that everything was wrong. But I knew I had just three days before been wanting to jump into a knife, and that I wasn't now, and I knew that I absolutely wanted to stick it out here and get this degree, even though the school was such a terrible, terribly bad joke, and I wasn't even the only one thinking it.

Everything was wrong. I was already on fifteen milligrams of zyprexa and I'd just got my first shots of Lithium, that had somehow been prescribed overnight, and I couldn't keep my eyes open. I wanted to cry, but it was impossible. There were no emotions left. When I sat down to write, I realised that I could not think, or write. I fell asleep. I wrote something, the next afternoon. I wrote that I should close my eyes and walk through the tunnel without stopping or turning around, and just keep walking. Until there would be light.

In the meantime there, I had met Jane from Australia, a pretty looking, gentle and quiet young woman with dark curly hair and midnight blue eyes. She was an artist who had moved to New England as her husband, a sociologist from Australia, had been invited to work at the university and, much like myself, not found it in him to refuse the offer. As it turns out, Jane and I both had the same psychiatrist back in the outpatient clinic, we were both on

[98]

the same medications, and we were both not very impressed.

I met Jane's husband, Mark, because he had asked to speak to me. He was a small, thin guitar guy, in skinny jeans and new-romantic style waistcoat and jacket, looking just a touch geeky with small glasses and a very short hair cut. I didn't know what he wanted to talk to me about, he only said to me 'I would like to ask you for a very big favour. I think it would be very, very good for my wife if she could be your friend and talk to you as someone who knows her situation. You seem really nice and she told me she is very fond of you. I would like to ask you if we could become friends. Would you like to be my friend? Please'.

I said but of course. We shook hands over it, hugged, he was awfully formal about it, went back to talk to his wife, and when he had left, Jane fell into my arms and thanked me. I told her she should talk to this Ukrainian guy. We all became friends, in those New England winter weeks spent pacing around in circles, in uniform gowns, all day around the locked unit. There were several violent scenes every day, and I didn't want to get too close to certain other patients. Jane and I also became friends with Johnny, who was only 18, but had been in there for so long they were just switching him around units as a favour to assuage his boredom.

I heard so many and such extraordinary tales and lives, and yet I can't remember anything now. I was too sedated. If people weren't sleeping, they were talking about their lives. I did, too. I told Mark, who yet was a perfect stranger, about my planned project of writing a book, which was by then pretty abandoned. He encouraged it, we exchanged views on Foucault, I talked about the Greeks, he told me about his band, and Jane showed some of her art.

I spoke a tiny bit to a friendly seeming man who was talking about alcohol and drug problems. He told me that his ex-girlfriend was using heroin and that it had been the reason they broke up, that he could not watch her inject, because everyone knew it meant you die, and that he thought he and his family could do better than that. He told me the story of how he lost his left foot. He'd been shot, gangrene followed, the leg from the knee down was amputated.

Amputated limbs was something I got used to fairly soon in America. At first it seemed unusual to me, it seemed a relic of the early twentieth century, but I learnt soon enough about the insurance system in America, and the class system.

He asked me, 'will you come and hang out with me on the green? I'll take you for lunch and we can just talk about stuff' – I said maybe. The green: a down and out place that students were advised to avoid under all circumstances, even though I never understood what could be so dangerous about it. When he suggested this as a meeting place, multiple possibilities flashed before my eyes: getting to know new people, better drugs, a relaxed time on the town, making so much more of my time in America than just growing hair in an ivory tower. I was hot and cold on these men from the psychiatric ward, many of them violent or involved in gun crimes, and I never ended up meeting up with anyone except the people who were also part of the university.

When Jane and I were both out of hospital, we went to dinner together when Mark's mother came on a visit, Jane

[100]

and I met for a few coffees in the daytime, until they both left.

I met with Sebastian, too. But those memories now are so dim, because of the medications, it is almost as if it happened in a former life. To an extent, that is even how I refer to it nowadays. If I ever think of it at all. And then, they just disappeared. That time in hospital, it wasn't her first stay, she had been prescribed a course of electroshock therapy, which I knew nothing about then. When she had had them, it seemed to have been horrific, so that a few weeks later, she and Mark left the United States for good.

And when Laurie and I met again, weeks later, I told her that my hospital stay had helped me and she thought that was nonsense. She wanted me to stop the drugs. The hospital stay had helped me get to sleep, I said. It's true that it also was leaving a bitter after-taste and an inarticulate shell-shock in its trail.

With time, I understood exactly what Laurie had meant, why others had fled the country, like Jane and her man, and Kim, and this young Korean student who had been admitted with me once, and that American undergraduate I used to see, who also disappeared.

In fact, it seemed that everyone who I could perhaps speak to, disappeared. And when I was back in graduate school and on my pills, under outpatient supervision, this psychiatric internment thing was impossible to mention. Everybody seemed to know, in fact because they were informed by the dean of the graduate school. But I could not talk it over with them, could I? Who were they? Weren't they the people at my work who had been the sceptic and judgemental ones to begin with, weren't they in perfect agreement with the idea that I was insane?

[101]

Laurie was staying, and talking, yes. But I found her hard to approach, she was so busy, so extravagant, and incredibly strong and bold. She had only one thing to say to me, "stop the drugs". But it wasn't as if I could pull a hunger strike like her. The clocks couldn't be turned back, and I was too sleepy to think.

I was trying to make sense there, in the solitary bubble of my dorm room by day, in some way, of what was happening to me amongst all these doctors. But it never made sense. It was always the same few questions, the same advice, week by week.

Have you had any suicidal thoughts?
No.
Really? (Flicks through a chart) Considering how you've been feeling and what you've been telling me so far, this surprises me...
(Silence).
Have you been hearing voices?
No.
Feeling paranoid?
No.
Have you been taking all your medication?
Yes.
All of it?
Yes.
Every day?
Yes.
How much medication have you got left?
I don't know, not much. I suppose for a few more days.
I'll send an order down to the pharmacy for two weeks worth of all four.

[102]

Thank you.

No problem.

Have you been cutting yourself?

Yes.

Where did you cut yourself?

My arm?

Can I see?

Yes… this here…

Yeah…hmm …do you actually feel it's safe for you to be out and about…? I mean, do you think you need to be in hospital?

No, not the hospital.

No?

No.

Why not?

(…)

Miss...?

Yes?

Are you sure you haven't had any suicidal thoughts?

Yes!

Yes?

Yes.

Final answer?

(Grins) Final answer.

What is it about the hospital that keeps you from agreeing to go?

Oh it's just… first of all it's not very pleasant to be there, but the main reason is the academics, I'm missing class and work and all those things, everything gets delayed…

I see. Well, call me if you change your mind, or if any of your symptoms get worse.

Yeah, okay.

And, remember, if you have to call out of hours or during

the week-end, urgent care is available 24 hours, do you know their number?

No.

I will write it down on this card.

Thank you.

You're welcome. Will you be able to call if you are feeling suicidal or if you cut?

Yes.

It's important.

Ok.

I will tell the doctor on call this weekend that you might call, and explain the situation to her, that will make things easier.

Right.

Shall we meet again on Monday at 8.30?

Ok, fine.

Have a good week-end.

Thank you, you too.

Bye now.

Bye.

November, 2007.

A new low point in this new existence. The sun is shining and everything smiles, but I cannot feel this, too slow, arrested in dim dreams, in dark fears, weird mental clutter, not made for anything sane. All just bits and pieces of a monster inside me that's been dying forever and still breathes, sometimes raises its head to moan then it goes down again, but I know it's always there. But it's been bombed at. Still waking. Under observation, somehow, I'm feeling, uncertain, waiting for change, trying to stay awake, but nothing comes to mind. Had some bad dreams until mid-afternoon. Dark waters, loudspeakers, sweat,

[104]

anxiety, nothing.
If this continues, I will miss my train, I know that. But I
don't mind that any more, that's the point. I don't care
about a success-crowned future more than I care about
floor wax. This world that means nothing to me now,
nothing at all, I don't even know why everybody else is
making themselves so busy... the talking willows spoke of
Midas' ears, the willows said the king had grown two
donkey ears, and spread the rumour, like fire in a desert.
A desert! What is there to burn in the desert?

Good morning. Please, have a seat.
Thank you.
How have you been?
Not too bad.
Oh?
No, it's been okay.
Have you had any suicidal thoughts?
No, not really.
What do you mean by 'not really'?
Ah no, it's nothing, only briefly.
What was that?
Oh I just... I mean, I was lying on my bed for a very long
time and then suddenly thought I might go to the drugstore
to get sleeping pills.
And then what?
What?
You mean you would get sleeping pills to kill yourself
with?
Yes.
You didn't do that?
No.
Did you take any steps towards doing it?

No, not really.

Did you check whether there was any medication in the house?

There isn't, I don't have anything. Because of this.

Good. Would you like to go to hospital, or do you think you need to be in hospital?

No. That really was just a passing thought.

But it was one with a plan of some detail.

Okay…

What is it about the hospital that keeps you from agreeing to go?

Oh it's just… it's not pleasant to be in there, and more importantly, I am missing class and work and things, everything gets delayed…

I see. Well, call me if you change your mind, or if any of your symptoms get worse.

Yeah, okay.

Are you happy with your medication?

I'm sleeping all the time. I can't bear this for longer. It has been several months I have been waiting for fatigue to subside, but it hasn't.

How much do you sleep?

I guess about fourteen hours at night, and then I'm still drowsy. I try every day to sleep less but it doesn't really work.

Do you mean that you try to get up and then you go back to sleep, is that what's happening?

Yes.

Mmh, I see. What time do you go to bed at night?

Midnight, one…

Why so late?

I just try to stay awake for as long as I can.

But if you're sleeping 12-14 hours, and you go to bed at

[106]

midnight, that would mean you wake up mid-afternoon…
Yes, often.
Try going to bed earlier and using an alarm clock.
Hmm… Zyprexa makes me very tired and I've gained a lot of weight.
Do you watch what you eat? In terms of calories, I mean…
Yes.
Do you exercise?
Not really.
Why not?
Find it hard, I haven't got much time in a day if I sleep so much, and I try to keep up with my academic work, it's a lot…
I understand. Perhaps we'll have to consider lowering your dose of zyprexa, though I wouldn't lower your dose just now, at the moment, but once things stabilise for you, or we might try switching to a different antipsychotic altogether.
Right. I can't go down on Zyprexa dose?
I wouldn't recommend it.
Ah…
Have you had any trouble with your thinking?
Trouble with my thinking?
I mean, what you just asked does not sound like you are very clear of mind, about your situation, you are having suicidal thoughts and you don't want to take your medication?
Just because of the side effects…
Ah.
Yes, well…
Have you been hearing voices?
No.
Feeling paranoid?

[107]

No. As I say, it's been a good week.
I'm glad you're feeling relatively well.
Thank you.
You're welcome. Let's meet again early next week.
Alright, thanks very much.
8.30am on Tuesday, can you do that?
Sure.
Great. Bye for now.
Bye.

December, 2007.
Each hour is a twin to its neighbours,
The world rises, I sink.
The end is not in sight,
But walk, walk and keep walking,
That will be the best.

All I have left is memory,
All that is coming is nothing,
So formless and meaningless,
What keeps me going?

Perhaps it is better not to know.

That optimistic life when I take pills, how real can that be
– it seems fake to me. If I can't bear the reality of things,
why do I bother drugging up. That only delays, doesn't
help, doesn't cure. I am ashamed for living a life of
artificial comfort. I should be able to live through life
without putting my mind to rest every day, over and over, it
feels awfully wrong and dirty, and yet, for the sake of
everybody, I'll do it again. Sell my mind to medicines,

surprise no-one, keep being around. Though I'm pressing suicide and nostalgia of dark thoughts I never finished thinking. If only so many things hadn't happened! If only I had never been born, it all would be so much simpler.

The sun's going down, I have accomplished nothing all day.

Well, there still is time. But I'm not ready. I never am. I will never be. Every thought is sucked into this vortex of 'it's not worth it, it's all so pointless', repeats itself every time I want to start something. How am I supposed to find a will if everything is like this? This dull, long life on yellow pills, oh help me, how ugly, giving myself something every day like this, living in a rubber-edge world, despite my instinct to rapidly destroy.

I can't concentrate. I am writing this, all the time turning away, I can't even imagine reading anything now. Last night was like this too. I was trying to write, but I couldn't finish my sentences. And now I want to say something, but can't. What do I want to say? I don't even know. I'll have to call the health centre. Tomorrow. Don't know what good it's going to do, but I'll call if nothing changes, whatever it is they do to me there, there's nothing else I can do now.

I wonder whether in the future, a true cure will be invented to this suffering. I cannot bear this feeling insensitively good, there's something deeply wrong below the surface, a wound far from healed. I feel my stomach failing, my heart crying about poison spreading through my veins, that desire in my chest, that desire to crack open, spill my guts, to have bleeding wounds, to feel intensely, as if pain would exempt me from thinking in circles. I want to cry and scream, shout and feel violence, I want to break out of this afternoon. Always, this same afternoon. I want to... And I can't do it... I can't do it.

[109]

Mild suicide urges, mild pain, why is there not more? Everything is buried below thick mist. I feel shattered, no energy, no appetite, everything is pointless. Should I call some care provider? Walk over to a grey building with turquoise tiled floors? Wear a striped gown and fishnet underwear? Have my blood pressure taken and be prescribed the same pills? And then what? There isn't any way out, is there. I can't sit still, I can't move, I can't stand, sit, or walk. I can't speak. Eat. Nothing. And why is everybody else going about their day fine? If I want to buy my last ticket I need to go out to the drugstore. Tylenol PM. I would have to deal with 'can I help you', I want to smash their faces. My hands are tied. I am so unbelievably trapped and I can't think. Anything.

Would you like to be in hospital?
No.
Why not?
It's going to be ages...
How do you know, I'm telling you it won't
Last time I was there, the same...
You've been before?
Yes.
So you know it's not a problem! Of course, nobody wants to go to hospital, but you have to realise you need it. It probably will be just one or two nights.
I will miss class.
But in this state you're in, you wont get anything done anyway, will you, you've said that yourself.
I still don't want to go there.
Ok, well, we have to call a psychiatrist to determine this.

Hi, nice to meet you, I'm Dr. the Second, I'm the

[110]

psychiatrist on call.

Hi.

So, I hear you've had a hard time with suicide, can you tell me again what happened?

It's just I'm spending all my time thinking of avoiding it and so I can't do much else.

And she's been cutting, you know?

Is that true?

Yes.

I think you could use some nice people who will help you.

Oh yes?

Great! You agree! So, you are going to hospital

What? I mean…

I'm glad you made this decision, it shows you're responsible. Very good. Good choice!

(…)

OK, let's call the ambulance.

-

Alright young lady, we're here.

I know.

Yeah.

Hey you know, I didn't want to come here. I don't want to go in there now. It's all just coming back to me, what it's like here. Can we go back?

(Takes hold of patient's arms) You got to see what you got too see, you have to be here, you can't go home.

I've been here before. It's no use… I see my future on this ward: Old ladies, fat, in slow despair, with thinning hair and faces, long lost smiles. I may avoid them, but here they are, my future, if I stay on this path, and what other path is there but to end it sooner? What is the point of prolonging this!

None of my business.

-
Hello, welcome!

Its ok, she's been cooperative.

Of course she has. So, who is this?

She's a student. She is a sophomore in college.

Actually no, I said that I was second year student, but that was in graduate school, not college. I'm actually a doctoral student. Not that it matters.

Yes it matters. You can't lie here. We need to know exactly who you are.

That's not what I meant.

So, let's look at this form... Oh! It's an emergency certificate... ambulance ride ok?

(Security nods)

Ok, let's get things going. We will search you now quickly, you have to take your clothes off and empty all your bags and pockets, hand in your belt and any lighters or contraband...

Ok, Ok, where do I do that?

Over there. Go, go and then you will be seen by an admissions officer.

Yes.
-

Right! Everything fine? Then you can sign here please.

What is this?

It's a voluntary admission form.

You have me down as voluntary? I am not, you know, I would rather be at home...

No, but the staff from the ambulance said you have been cooperative, which is great! So if you like, you may sign your voluntary admissions form right now. Just to say you understand this is what's best for you.

What's the deal if I don't sign?

[112]

Not much. You will still be treated the same. But it tends to speed things up if you are a voluntary patient, say you have any disputes, or you want to get a hearing with a judge to see if you can get discharged sooner, it might speed things up if you're voluntary.

A hearing with a judge?

You can do that either way, but there's no point to that. It's not really a good idea. We don't mess around with you here, you'll get first rate treatment, this is a really great facility with some fabulous staff and you won't need any lawyers.

Ah.

What is your problem? Are you signing or not?

Yes, sure, pass it over.

Thank you very much, that is lovely. Now, I'll explain everything you need to know, while you're here, and you'll be seen by a doctor this evening. Follow me.

-

Right, so I can see you have been here before. Welcome back. Settle in.

How long am I staying here?

Two to three weeks…

Oh, that's long! I thought it was going to be less than that.

No.

-

Good morning. How did you sleep?

Good, thanks.

How are you feeling?

Fine.

Alright. I'm bringing your morning medications. My name is Joan and I'm your nurse this morning.

Thank you… What's that yellow pill?

Which one?

[113]

This one. I've never seen that before, I don't think it's for me.

This is your medication, as prescribed.

Yes, but … what is that yellow pill?

Abilify, 5 or 10 mil.

What's that?

An antipsychotic.

Oh yes? But I already take zyprexa…

You'll have to talk to your doctor about this, I don't make these prescriptions, I'm only bringing them to you, this morning, look, you have this prescription, Abilify 5mg.

Ok… Who is my doctor?

You will meet him later when he makes his rounds.

So I will take this pill then, later.

No, you take it now.

Alright then. Will I get counselling?

You missed this morning's goal group because you slept so long.

Oh, I take zyprxa and it makes me very sleepy. I don't suppose I can get an alarm clock here?

No, no. You are here to relax. It doesn't matter if you make it to group therapy or not. You can still come to the anger management session this afternoon.

But I don't have much of an anger issue, you know?

Everybody here has anger issues. It would help, if you had a positive attitude towards improving yourself. This is for you.

January, 2008.
I can hardly see a thing! This new pill is bad, earlier on I was almost blind. They say it'll all come back shortly. I asked when, they told me not to worry and that everything

[114]

would be fine. That they don't want me to be blind and that it's only a side effect, which will clear. The doctor took a note of it and went through the routine of questions that are nothing to do with anything, such as, am I having any problems urinating, do I have stomach pains, head pains, whatever. I am not, I am having problems understanding what is going on. I really am not sure if suicide would not be more in point at this juncture in my life. I am not going to recover, not now. I may not be as crazy as I was. But I've nothing in return, only these very short days in between all this sleeping, and yet those few hours seem to stretch like so many long seconds. Time, which used to be all I gambled for, and against, time which I would try to trick into stretching wider by doing things faster and better, time, which used to be so important, has now turned into an unsightly silver-grey and leaden, oily fluid that's just oozing slowly as it seems to stagnate, but it's just getting thinner and lower.

I get a bit further away from the days when I was doing stuff, and I get a bit more sick in my body, with every day, and my mind is in a freeze not moving anywhere except shuffling back and forth in the constricted cube of a few paranoias, a few anxieties, a few depressions, and at the opening and at the ending of each day, the physical fight against sleep. I am in the process of becoming an idiot.

I don't know why I am being kept in the dark about so many things I don't understand, when I am not at all feeling well. All these people here, they all seem to agree with this doctor, about everything, there is no one who has a moment to explain it to me, though they all have time to give orders. They're all so fast, so fit, I look like a neglected piece of wax and cannot participate in this, even though all of this is my life, it's too hard for me to

[115]

comprehend, too complicated for me. When they ask me how my urination is, it always throws me, because I wonder why they don't ask me how my inner feelings are. And although, presumably, they can see I have become overweight since starting the drugs last year, they pretend not to see this. By next year, I will probably be obese like all the other people here.

Unfortunately they are driving me insane with this strange routine in this hermetically sealed box with perpetually darkened windows.

I want to kill myself. But if I said so, they would just yell 'Heureka' and tell me they knew I was crazy from the start and that is why I'm here, and that's why it's good that I'm here... But surely that can't be right.

So I can say nothing at all. I am trapped in a system. A system of silence and professional hide-and-seek, and locking files away. All these conversations are happening behind closed doors. Behind these doors I am alone and too drowsy, ill-informed, and insecure to counter their insidious arguments. Harsh discourse and perverse persuasion techniques alternate freely, I am being suspected of planning to do or think all kinds of things that I would never do. But they are putting ideas in my head. I keep hearing the echoes of this voice in my head, "any suicidal thoughts perhaps...?"

I have so little to push against this, so little, or nothing at all, and I won't get out of here alone, and I don't even understand why things came to this point, what causes all this ill will and misery, why I have broken the way I have, in my mind, and, most importantly, I don't know what else I could do, I have no idea how I could do it otherwise.

All I did here is talk. I could have lied start to finish, but

[116]

for what I said, I am here, where I am now, and I am marked for life. All I did is say what I thought! Words are not made for truth, truth is not made for words. Only in psychiatry one cannot go back on what one has said, even months or years later. I will never escape from whence words are the truth. And I don't like this life any more. I can't live any more.

For colleagues, strangers and friends, I've built my thin walls of a plausible character I might have, in the absence of emotional life. Alternative explanations, excuses and an invented personality for myself, well actually simply, I recite what I would have said a few years ago. What did I do this afternoon, I answer, I met a friend, went for a walk, read a book, did some shopping... but... I was at home watching the same music video over and over again. Twenty times, fifty times, three hundred times, and I still couldn't say what it is about because things slip my mind and it goes in an endless loop.

Most evenings, I stay near the computer because the screen keeps me awake, and write down what passes through my head, which is almost exclusively flies, fridge and corridor noises. This is how I know my mind is damaged because otherwise I would have more interesting ideas. I do not know what to do about my university papers this year, I cannot think anything new with this head. Contemplating self-plagiarizing old essays from London, marginally expanding them. Catastrophic.

Socially, I say things that I'm not sure are true any longer, but they are the only ones I can say; I say things that aren't true, pure and simple, hoping that I will believe them myself, such as that I know what is happening with this treatment and I am hopeful for my health. But the

[117]

truth, so simply, is: I know nothing. My emotions are absent. My character is dead. Hope is lost.

The future is not bleak, like they often rush to describe the thoughts of depressed people. The future is not going to come. I am stuck in an endlessly repeating present moment. I don't know why I am here. I don't know what any of this means, or how long it is for. I can't see anything coming.

There is nothing after this.

When I will have consumed the stuff of my old dreams, there will be nothing but white padded void indefinitely. This dreaded dim waiting room lethargy, zyprexa, and all somniferous plants will bow down deeper over me and darken the view little by little. If this could silence the raging voice within, it broke me so thoroughly and suspended my mind altogether. It could make still and even this blazing land of flames where black trees bow on flowing burnt earth. How to kill this unrelenting pain, hammering pain of which my body is the formless prison. It is like dying and not wanting to. The prisoners bang their heads like woodpecks against mute and pasty skin walls, everything is padded and soundproof here. It's like being stuck in a marsh, a warm and humid breeze of bad breath wheezing around my sinking head.

Now that I have exchanged all for nothing, there are no tears, because I don't remember who I was. From all sides, mutilated symbols crop up of thoughts left unsaid, and unfinished business: dark and shiny, they gather round, and they gleam, lost to touch, too far down under layers of antipsychotic snow.

Memories, like flowers in a spring field. Watch heads and

[118]

limbs grow leaden with evil flowers' poisonous dust, and bodies withering like autumn, as memory kills them. 'Meat-eating orchids forgive no-one just yet', Kurt Cobain said it so well.

How to cleave one's way through this darkness, this dense and unknown, inscrutable darkness ever so treacherously scintillating. Trees waver as stroking hands, black waters drown in themselves, forever in darkness, thick silence, and waiting room twilight! If I could see land, shiny cities, and firmament... But I feel the contortions and fits from neurological side effects, dyskinesia, tremors, Parkinson's disease or whatever this is. Last year I promised myself that if this would happen, I would stop the treatment. Now it has happened, but no chance of change. I can remember all too much hateful talk, indiscretion, reprimanding, threats, humiliations, disrespect, careless hurt in passing, derision, reproaches, accusations, abuse... what was it all for? I have pushed it to blackness with this pill here, but I know it, I know it will catch me in time or forever pollute my colourless sleep.

Oh good heavens, you, here, again?

Sebastian!

Hello. Playing piano in hospital, eh?

Yes, it is amazing that there is this piano here where there is absolutely nothing else to do, I am playing this Liszt piece...

Listen.

Yes?

I am really sorry, I never thought you'd be back in hospital. This makes me really sad. I thought when were here last time that you would leave and never come back, because you don't need this shit. Some people here

[119]

need help, but you should be able to help yourself.

Oh.

Listen, you … I can tell you are on their drugs. When we first met, you were so alive, and look at you now. Your eyes aren't even properly open.

Yes, I get tired, from Zyprexa…

You need to get away from this place and these doctors.

(…)

I am really sorry to see this has happened to you. You know, I'm not supposed to talk like this in this place, or to share private information, but, here is my number, call me, we will talk, okay?

Thank you!

Yes. I am so sorry. This is so depressing.

Oh it is fine.

No it is not fine at all, I saw you when you were on no medication, and now this… it really depresses me, you know you were so beautiful just a few months ago.

I know what you are saying.

I talk to you later.

Ok.

Peace.

Lovely fellow inmates. I thought of Sebastian more as an inmate than a doctor, to be honest. Richard, a balding man tending towards chubbiness under a spotlessly clean white t-shirt, with cheerful blue eyes. He told me that he had been on antipsychotic drugs since he was fifteen and was now forty-two, and that he had never agreed to be taking them. I asked why he hadn't undertaken to get away, but he got vague. He looked alright, a bit of a victim, with gentle voice. I told him I'd been on them a year and a half and was afraid of tardive dyskinesia, at which he laughed

[120]

and imitated the parkinsonian movements of TD, and said 'oh, come on, Zyprexa doesn't do that'.

One afternoon we were chatting in front of the nurses' station, he drew back my sleeve which he knew was hiding cuts, put his finger these and said 'I'm worried about your cutting yourself like that'. Did he mean, like doctors had done, to caress the surface expression of wordless nothingness? I was so taken by surprise at this indiscretion, which, in the psychiatric ward, is yet so common, along with shameless curiosity and comparison of sob-stories, but something about his touch felt particularly creepy.

'It's none of your business', I said.

'You're an intelligent individual, but you're having securities.'

'I'm having whats?'

'You have in-securities'

'I do?'

'Well, you can't stand straight and speak for yourself, can you?'

'I see...'

'Listen, before you go, will you leave me one of your socks, the ones that you're wearing now?'

'No.'

'But I want to smell it and get a whiff of you girl... and revel in you.'

'No way.'

'What about your undies?'

'Fuck off?'

'Ha ha. That was good!'

I'd had several long conversations with him before this, and for some reason, his neighbour, a run-down obese individual named Sonya, who was also on the ward, told

[121]

me 'that guy Richard you've been talking to. He's no good, he molests little children'.

I remembered then that when he introduced himself to me, one of the first things he'd told me was an unintelligible story which, I now saw, must have omitted something, and which ran as follows: 'I bought twenty gallons of vinegar. Because, you know, there's a playground opposite my block, and the kids playing there are getting infected from the sand. There are insects and bacteria in the sand, I want to kill them off with vinegar'.

That was weird, wasn't it. At the round table, Sonya declared to the ladies lunching in striped gowns: 'Richard is a menace to society. He doesn't want to take his medication. He should be in jail'.

I guess psychmeds aren't much different from prison, besides, he had been kept in the ward for six weeks already and the end was not in sight. Once we had got a little more acquainted, Richard said to me: 'you know, in this place, I don't want to get too precise about what happens with a pill after it gets into my mouth' – 'ah, yes' – 'don't tell anyone, will you?' – 'no, of course'… but his plan didn't work in the world of blood counts, supervision and room checks. One morning, serenely, he told me: 'what do you think of me? I mean, just tell me what is your impression?' The first thing I said was 'you're very gentle' – 'okay, stop! Stop it right there. You're breaking my heart you know, you are the gentle one… they're thinking of being less gentle with me' – 'what do you mean?' – 'injections. I'm getting injections'. I didn't know what to say. Somehow, when everybody, patients and doctors, was turning against him, I didn't really want to let him go. But after the sock-conversation, I started avoiding him, as much as these things go, in a claustrophobic wing

[122]

where staying in half-lit rooms is as infuriating as sitting on plastic chairs in clinical light, among broken characters carrying themselves in bizarre ways, and nurses, doctors, social workers and counsellors busying themselves, with a dead-serious look and the arrogance of the sane, or the compassion, but ultimately, there were two worlds here.

In any case, Richard was on Zyprexa and thus sleeping most of the time, which, I guess, was to my practical advantage, but whenever he emerged, he would present me with small letters or a card, with sweet words and his phone number. When finally I was discharged, I gathered my stuff very quickly, since I'd only had my handbag when I came, I was given, from the 'safe', my valuables, cigarettes and belt, I wanted to get out, but the nurse announced to the patients vegetating before the TV: 'Hey everyone! She's leaving!', and depressed fat ladies waved goodbye apathetically, schizophrenic jokers jumped up with gleaming eyes, and Richard came rushing to hug me and said nothing but 'thank you'.

I said nothing, smiled faintly and left, remembering what Dr. M. had told me shaking my hand when I was about to go, which was thank you, to which I'd said 'well, thank you', and he 'the best way of thanking us is by getting better', a lovely line that struck me so positivist and directly relying on causal progression, that once again I felt he and I were living in different worlds.

'Thank you' is rarely said meaningfully, but these two times, meaning there was, although I will never understand what Dr. M. was thanking me for. Perhaps the surprise that he said 'thank you' was what made it special.

And Richard? I thought I understood why he thanked me, but he had been telling so many lies. I never phoned him.

February, 2008.

I've been discharged, out of the blue. The medication switch is not completed. I don't think I am well enough to go back into life tomorrow morning. But of course, I have to be, for nothing in life would I want to have gone back even for a minute. I don't know why I was discharged, just yesterday they'd told me a date in five days' time. The shower rooms in the university dorm suddenly seem a bathing place of luxury and cleanliness. The hospital doctor, for some reason, arranged for me to get a paid cab home and asked me if it would be okay to send me home. Hell yeah but... he said he's booked me an appointment with Dr. S. tomorrow morning at eight, and handed me my prescriptions, which I can get at any pharmacy.

Here we are. Again. My dorm room, and it's just how I left it. Same mess, like I haven't been away. Those papers on the floor, normally I would have thrown them away as soon as I got home, but of course I never got home, and now I'm not even sure what they are. I had meant to bring back some library books and answer e-mails, suppose I don't need to bother now it's been too long. My socks I should have put away, and made my bed, washed the glasses, turned off my music, I suppose... And now what, is that so, I have to put myself back in here? Everything, I almost had forgotten already, that grey flooring and the dry wood-scented air in here. I thought I wouldn't see this again. It's only just coming back to me. The shower, my timetable, assignments, and people I need to go see. People I need to phone. And food wrappings – Dunkin' Donuts? I'll be eating this again, then. This is my room, like a glove, like an envelope. Dreadful twilight. What now, back to normal? I suppose... Ok, deep breath, this can be done. I will do this. This is my desk, I am supposed

[124]

to sit at it. And now? Window? Highway? Bookshelf? The books are closed. I will have to pick this up. God, help me. Life is in that green garden outside, behind the stained glass window, I just don't believe it. I do know it within, am afraid of breaking the window, and finding something else behind it, and then not to return, here I stay, in my grey twilight sinking room.

The stained glass window, my memory, hazy inertia, my memory, indolent as my inertia, and my inertia, heavy as memory. It'll be two years now soon since I first went on zyprexa and I still don't manage to stay awake. My inertia, this room I am in, this grey room. Unable to get myself out of this permanent, infinitely extending waiting room, out into paradise lost, paradise that is life, thought and action, paradise, magical garden, life out there, all I long for is return of a life that resembles life and not death. I'd take any hardships, humiliation, pains, any disappointment now, only to regain the ability to think and feel with purpose and to have a healthy person's ability to finish lines of thought, and to act with free will. This here is a Truman show with nothing in it, only a cheap backdrop, grey walls and dim silence, there are only a few movements in my head, whether or not I've felt suicidal in a week or not, my mind is paper thin, I go to sleep all the time, I am more dead than alive. How do you break out of lethargy? I am looking for life all around me, can't find it, everything that once mattered now is either blacked out or doesn't bother me, forgetting stretches of lived life to vast emptiness, uninterested and drowsy dim dizzy blurs, expanses of nothingness, and my soul made of white clay is immovable, heavy, would sink in thick sleep and resigns to existence without meaning and thought without imagination. Life must be existing even here and now. I just don't know how to find it. I am locked inside my own inertia. This life is nothing but a long death. Can't I end it now? Won't they stop it? Tell me that I should have rung them up, give me electroshocks so I forget about killing myself, too? What is the purpose of life? I don't know the answer to this any more. Life is in that green garden, outside, behind dull stained glass window. And I am inside here.

Hi, good to see you again. How are you feeling?
Fine.
So, tell me what happened, why you went to hospital two weeks ago.
Nothing, I was speaking to the social worker, I think his name is Morris, about suicide, and he thought it wasn't safe.
Did you think it was safe?
I don't know, I was feeling very depressed and I didn't know what to do.
Were you cutting yourself?
Yes, it was pretty bad.
Can I see?
Yes, this…
When did you do this?
Maybe… Friday?
And on Friday you felt suicidal?
Yeah, I guess, all at the same time, it was a bad week-end, I was just home thinking dark thoughts.
What do you mean?
Well, maybe, how I want to bang my head into every wall but I can't do it, feeling that everything is pointless, I can't see the future, I have made only mistakes in my life, the world is a terrible place, I don't want to be part of this, we

[126]

are all going to die anyway, I can't take it and I want to die, why am I still alive, well, you know, that kind of thoughts... dark, as I said and always turning in circles.
Do you think you were right?
Maybe, maybe not.
You were going to kill yourself?
I don't think so.
But you cut yourself?
Yes.
Why didn't you call?
I don't think I wanted any help, I wanted to die, you know!
But I did call, in the end, didn't I.
Yes, but it took you several days.
I just couldn't.
Were you feeling safe with yourself at the time, before you called?
No, not really.
If you feel unsafe, you have to call me or call urgent care out of hours, that was our agreement. I will have to send you back to hospital if you cannot keep it.
I know.
And now, do you still think those same things you thought two weeks ago?
No, not really. I'm more hopeful now. More awake.
I'm glad you called.
(…)
So, this hospital stay went well, then.
Yes.
Good.
And… Are you feeling suicidal… now?
No.
What's the hesitation?
(…)

[127]

There is no hesitation.
Will you be able to call again should things change for you, if you think you need to be back in hospital?
Yes.
Can I trust you this time?
Yes, you can.
Alright. Glad to see you back. Take care now, bye, see you soon.
Thank you, bye.

Hi, good morning.
Good morning.
Have a seat.
Thank you.
How have you been?
Pretty good.
Good... Your social worker has told me about an incident with a stranger a few days ago...
Yes...
Tell me what happened, again, please.
Oh, a man came on to me late at night in the street and asked me whether he could come with me to my room, and I took him there...
Why?
I don't know. I just couldn't think.
What did you think he wanted?
I don't know.
(...)
(...)
Are you feeling quite shaky?
Yes.
How come?

[128]

I don't know.

Are you afraid of something?

No!

Feeling paranoid?

No...

Are you nervous, or tense?

Maybe a little bit tense, could be.

Sit back in the chair. Take some deep breaths.

(...) I am sorry, I don't know what is happening here I can't control my movements...

Your legs are quivering left and right... is this the first time this happens?

Usually my back jerks and shoulders twitch, not my... head (try to hold my head with my hands and bend down over my knees with my head in my hands)

Sit back in the chair and breathe.

(...)

You are not breathing, are you?

I am.

I can't see you breathing. Relax.

...

Alright?

Yes

Can you get up?

Yes

Can you get up please and stretch out your arms? (...) You have a tremor, is that since we increased your lithium?

Yes

Oh, I see. And it is worse in the left hand than the right hand.

I know.

Is it bothering you?

There are some things I can't do.

[129]

Like what?

For example, eat with cutlery. I can't use a spoon, when I'm eating soup I always spill it everywhere. Or hold things up for longer, write with pen, drink from glass without using both hands...

If you can't eat with a spoon, that seems to me significant, isn't it bothersome?

Yes, of course.

If it is bothersome to you, I can prescribe something against this, but you would have to check with an internist whether it is suitable for you, as it is heart medicine. Do you have asthma or heart problems?

No.

Your tongue is trembling, do you notice that?

No...my head was quivering and I could not control it, could you see that?

Yes. Your shoulders, too. You remember, this is something we discussed in the beginning, when we discussed side effects of Zyprexa, it is tardive dyskinesia, and we will have to be very careful with this, it can be irreversible.

(Silence)

I will do a small test with you, could you bend over and touch your feet?

..

And get up please and stretch out your arms and touch your knees?

..

And your left foot?

..

and turn around and stretch your arms left and right?

..

and sit down, and place your hands on your knees?

..

[130]

No, I can't see any movements. We might have to repeat this test to see how you progress.

...

Anything else?

...

You look like you are thinking something.

No, I'm not thinking anything.

You're not thinking anything at all?

No.

- (nods)

I knew about tardive dyskinesia, and I knew it is irreversible, but I didn't know that this is what these twitches are, I was not worried about them.

It might not be TD. I think you and I are through now, do you think you can go home now or would you like someone to sit with you?

I'm going home.

Okay. Let's meet again on Monday, can you do 8.30am?

Yes.

Fine, see you then, bye for now.

Bye.

April, 2008.

Something has broken in me once for all, and in thirty years' time I will still be eating from the same bread as now, I will still be dim, drowsy and unmoved any time, I will still be feeding on ever fading memories of old good times, this will draw me down further and further, I am broken here, at this point, I am broken. There is no point in pursuing any of this. I don't see myself here any more, I don't know how this was possible, but to be sure, my mind has left me, my old sparkling mind, and what has left me also is good will and hope for improvement. But I have

[131]

come to realise, that was it for me. It used to seem endless and limitless. But it's vanished under waters too deep to find. I must have broken, not sure how and when, but now I am broken since too long and broken for good. This isn't going to change any more, I was hoping for so long but I have just been getting a little bit worse with every day, and a little more used to it, and so, I'm still here, time keeps ticking, but life is behind me, I will continue sinking, it doesn't matter, I understand now, this is the end of my life, and it will keep being the end until I die one day, that's all. This is the end.

I had a dream, in which I died. I was in a clinic which turned out to be a euthanasia clinic, a labyrinthine hospital, in a single room in a basement with windows to a green and blue jungle. There was Dr. M. from mental hospital, his traits were distorted but I still recognised him. In his hand was a brown coated, very small pill. To my great surprise, he said: 'if you want to commit suicide, you can do that, we have the pill for you. But before you take this pill, you must say goodbye to your mother. She's in the room adjacent, can I ask her in?' I couldn't be bothered, and fell asleep. I woke up, in a different room, with three or more people looking at me from above. I thought to myself 'this suicide action really is taking unexpected lengths. Now I have taken the infamous pill, now I am not dead – what is next?' But then I understood I was dead. I was sinking within my body like my body was sinking in the pillow, and drowning, daylight became scarce and the voices of figures above my head became indistinct and then silent.

I am glad I met Billy, the ever frantic, never sleeping

Englishman who asked me to pray for his septum. The first day I talked to him outside the Classics Faculty, where we both were trying to be doctoral students, I'd asked if he wanted to go for coffee, to which he replied: 'Sorry, I must rush off. I have to masturbate'. I smiled and let him go but he turned around and added: 'into my fridge!'

Some things could reach into my old self, remind me of who I used to be. Billy was great to be around, one of the few in my department who took time from their ambitious schedules to have a long chat over coffee, or a brief but sincere one over a cigarette. Initially, we bonded over having lived in Berlin, being in a long distance relationship ('that must mean masturbating like a thing possessed!'), having similar academic interests and a passion for creative writing, later, it was simply shared misery.

One day when we were walking arm in arm on the way to Au Bon Pain, a tall and thin black man in his mid-fifties in a powder blue suit stopped us, saying: 'Billy!' – 'Yes!' – 'Can you lend me some money?' – 'Yes. Will 200 bucks do?' – 'For the moment'… Billy went to an ATM and explained: 'This man saved my life, so, I owe him' – 'Yeah', Joe said, 'I'm black and even I don't walk at night in the place where he was walking. He's crazy'.

After he was gone, Billy told me some about the man's need for medical treatment, and gradually he told me them himself. One day it was cancer, a marrow transplant, or chemo; another day he was starving; one day he pulled open his shirt to show me where his pacemaker was; one day he pulled open his shirt to display surgery scars. The dreadful thing is that all of these stories were true; he was continually begging in the streets in order to make it to his next surgery appointment, or he knew, he would die. 'My life sucks so much', he was always saying. One day I was with some other friends, and as he walked past he pointed at me and said: 'You know what I call her? I call her the quiet one. She never says anything. But you're alright, all of you. My life sucks so much.'

Billy and I decided to visit David in the summer, at his parents' house in the middle of nowhere. David, the third in our trio, was Laurie's upstairs neighbour, an American, a fantastic scholar of sarcasm and the grotesque, a redhead in lumberjacks with nickel glasses and a wholesome, irate American soul, tremendous learning, and a lot of time for late night bars and smoke houses. Billy and I decided to get there by Greyhound from Chinatown, New York, to State College, PA, and then the rest by pick up truck, courtesy of Dave.

The Greyhound was running late and stopped a lot, so by the time we were in State College it was past midnight, and Dave had been waiting for us patiently. His parents' place was a gorgeous American clapboard house in the middle of nowhere between the trees, and he told us about having chopped some trees just that day. It was getting late, and since it was a warm summer's night, we took our drinks outside and chatted into the night, forgetting time, until we heard voices from the street. I saw that there were people but I didn't see them clearly in the dark, and Billy didn't see them at all. He said: 'I don't understand what these people are doing here in the middle of the night', and David said 'and I don't understand why they are naked' – 'they are naked? I MUST see that!' and he rushed through the garden and broke the fence in his ardent efforts to see what there was to see, but they were already too far away. Some time passed, the boys had fixed the fence and we had resumed our conversation, when one naked man re-emerged and shouted in our direction: 'Hey! Can I have a beer?'

We looked at each other before Billy shouted: 'Yes! Come on up here!' and Dave said 'Of course, what kind of beer?'

'Whatever it is that you have. Can I sit with you for a while?'

'Yes, yes.'

'So! My friends! What do you all think about existentialism?'

'Existentialism? Umm…'

'I've been reading Sarté', he said, and we raised our eyebrows.

'Sartré?' Dave asked.

'Yes! *Norscha...*'

'Do you mean *Nadja*?'

'*Nadja*?'

'Oh, you mean *Nausea*. You have been reading *Nausea* by Sartre.'

'Yes, *Nausea*'

'I was thinking of a book with a similar sounding title', Dave explained.

'How and when did you read *Nadja*?' I asked Dave.

'Oh, I don't know… it's a weird book, anyhow.'

'It's one of my favourite books!'

'So… what is this with you and existentialism? Is that why you're naked? Is this some kind of experiment? Are you on drugs?'

'No, no, I'm never on drugs. And besides, I'm not naked. I'm wearing a tie.'

The three of us frowned.

'Okay, yes, it was an experiment, if you like. Me and my friends feel that society is shutting up the human being too

[135]

much and getting us all thinking that everyone must be the same.'

'Ah-hah… And why are you doing that in the middle of the night, in the middle of nowhere?'

'You think I'm crazy, don't you?'

'No, just curious.'

'Anyhow, what are your names?'

'I'm David', David said.

Billy said: 'You can call me Darius'.

I was not asked. 'My name is Joe Smith', said the boy.

'Oh, really?'

'Yes, it's a very generic name, but it's always been my name, it has its advantages.'

'I see.'

I said to Billy: 'Darius, could you pass me the glass?' – 'Yes, Aspasia, here it is'.

Joe Smith then inquired: 'You're not going to tell anyone that I've been drinking, are you?'

'No, we're not. Why? How old are you?'

'Seventeen. How old are you?'

'I'm 24, Darius is 26, and Aspasia is 22' , Dave said.

'What do you guys do?'

'Wrong question. We're graduate students, at Harvard.'

'You're kidding! No, that can't be true!'

'Unfortunately, it is.'

We chatted about this and that, until he got up from the ground, put his naked body in the lamplight, and asked: 'So, what do you think about my looks? Not bad, this body, is it?'

Billy, with a sleazy gaze upward from the floor where he was sitting, said: 'It's wonderful. I can think of a lot of things you and I might do together, upstairs.'

'What?'

[136]

'Darius is gay, in case you hadn't noticed', David explained.

'You're not gay!', Joe Smith freaked out.

'Yes, I am, darling.'

'No, come on. I know what a gay guy looks like, and you don't look gay at all.'

'Well, I am.'

'Then I must be going. I really don't like what you just said there. It makes me feel uncomfortable. That's not fair. You shouldn't have said that...'

'Why, because you can't take it? Have a cigarette!'

'Ah, yes, why not'.

But... he was obviously trying out a lot of new things, since he didn't know how to light a cigarette.

'Are you in high school?'

'Yes, at Springfield High'

'Oh, really! My mother is a counsellor in that school. Her name is Anne'

'I know who that is, yes.'

'And... are you seeing any counsellor at the moment? Because I can set you up with my mother, if you like', Dave offered.

'No, no, no. You're thinking I should, right?'

'Not necessarily...'

'Listen guys, I have to go. You won't tell anyone about this, will you?'

'No, don't you worry...'

'Good night.'

After we'd been on our country trip through the American mountain gorges, Billy and I made our way back to New York. On the bus, he suggested I come along to a visit he had to pay to the artist Zina, in her studio, where she was

[137]

going to show us some of her work. I went with him. The studio was spacious and light as studios should be and we did all the requisite things such as conscientiously sampling her art, immersing in the regularly creative excitement accumulated over the years in this place. Zina was a long and thin woman with curly hair. Her paintings, when I first saw them, weren't that evocative to me, as they were geometric and enigmatic, rectangles arranged in asymmetric series, on enormous canvases. But as she spoke some more about them, and of how she had in mind a Proustian seaside afternoon for this one, a Christopher Street night for that one, I began to see.

Billy took us to the Regis, where we were joined by our friend Kyle, an American theologian who had already been friends with Billy back when they were both Oxford, in fact the two had been going out together. The Regis hotel, extravagant, lavish, like a golden aquarium, was from all angles curvy and ornamented, mirrored, reflecting, and most of all golden. It had something European, the Louis XV fireplaces, French mirrors, Champagne and all. We sat gleefully in midst all of this splendour and ate petits fours with tea and Champagne, then the three of us took a yellow cab to the house of an art collector, where there was more Champagne to be had with Billy' New York friends, a chic and extroverted, glamorous black tie party of designer dresses, fashion suits and cigars, shined with a pinch of cocaine and made even more surreal and beautiful by the glitzy, psychedelic art that was hanging, lying and standing everywhere.

After Champagne, we all went to a subterranean Italian restaurant and had very good food, although by the time we had finished our meal, I could not keep my eyes open, since I was sedated, always sedated. I had to get back to

[138]

the college town, as I was supposed to see the doctor at nine in the morning. Billy ushered me into a cab and asked me to give him a call when I was back. I thought that so sweet of him that I did.

By then, he was exasperated: 'It's a disaster! We're on a roof, the guy took an Ambien, everyone is totally dopey and talking utter nonsense. You're so lucky to be home, it's dreadful, just dreadful out here, and this thing is impossible to get out of.'

He was, I could still notice, trying not to make me feel bad about having had to leave early. I pictured them, and smiled to myself. I had long slipped back into that old black envelope of my life, as soon as I got home.

What can I do for you, is something bothering you?

I was wondering, actually, about my diagnosis.

Oh, certainly. I can tell you. But I'd like to have a proper sit-down with you about that, and since we're just getting to the end of our appointment, can we arrange for another time?

Yes…

Why, after all this time, do you ask me this now?

I have wondered about it for some time.

It struck me, when we were discussing the possibility of my having a chat with your boyfriend about your situation, that you didn't ask me then.

I know, I was so surprised at the time that you wouldn't let him talk to you.

It's for confidentiality reasons.

Yes, but I expressly gave my permission…

I know, and I said he could call me on the phone, but he didn't.

I know.

[139]

I don't know what I would have told him that you couldn't have told him already yourself.

Well, he is even more unclear on my situation than I am, and he would like to be of help.

What is unclear to you?

Mainly, how long I have to stay on Zyprexa, and in treatment more generally…

That depends how you do. Could be two years, could be ten.

Right.

But if you take your treatment seriously, as you do, the chances of getting better, are higher.

Ah.

Are you surprised?

No, of course not.

As for your diagnosis, let's make another appointment so I can tell you then.

Okay.

Can you come Thursday afternoon at 2?

Yes.

Great. See you then.

Thanks, bye.

And… I'm assuming… no suicidal thoughts?

No. No, it's been quite good recently.

I'm glad you're feeling relatively well.

Thanks! Alright, see you on Thursday.

See you Thursday, Bye.

Bye.

'Princess, spare some change?' Most of the time I give this lady one to two dollars, but then there are times when she says 'but today I need more than just two bucks' – mmmm… Fine. I often stop to talk to her, and among the

[140]

stories she told me is one about a boyfriend who beats her and got her pregnant last year but then she lost the baby. One day she showed me a hospital wristband and told me about back problems and a psychiatric evaluation: 'I know I'm mad, but not that mad!'

This went on for some time, until she invited me for tea at her house. I said I couldn't come but she insisted, then she said she would give me a present because I'd been 'so sweet'. I said there was no need for a present but she said: 'you'll like it, you'll see. Come here tomorrow at the same time'. The next day, I did not go as agreed. When I arrived later, she was still waiting.

'Where have you been? I had something for you, now it's gone' – 'Never mind' – 'No, no, you have to get it, it's really nice, it's just for you, because you're so special' – 'Wow' – 'Can you come back in ten minutes?' – 'What?' – 'Come back in ten minutes. Get out of here, now! Ten minutes, okay?' – 'Whatever' …

Ten minutes later, she produced a magnificent bouquet of white roses. 'For you!' – 'Oh no, I can't believe it' – 'Take it, it will look nice in your room' – 'Thank you, thank you so much'. She had not even bothered to remove the price tag, I saw it was a $30 bouquet, and thought of returning it to the Gourmet store where she must have stolen it, but then I thought hey.

The next day she asked: 'So! Want some more flowers?' – 'No, no, it's fine' – 'You saying you didn't like them or what?' – 'No they're wonderful, thank you so much' – 'Alright princess, got some change?' – sure…

In the summer, I was ordering soup at a diner, and a man behind me in the queue touched me on my shoulder. I turned around, thinking it was somebody I knew. It was

[141]

someone I'd met before, but where? I could not think. I looked at him blankly, as he did at me. He was in his fifties, wearing suit and bowtie, he looked somewhat disillusioned and dislodged, something of Jack Nicholson in his air, well groomed, stylish and in the company of a slightly younger, palsied lady in a wheelchair.

He said: 'Excuse me miss, but... don't we know each other?' – 'Yes, I know we've spoken before', I said, 'but help me out, where and when was that?'

'I feel the same as you', he confessed.

'Well...' – 'I don't know where I know you from, maybe I don't?'

'Probably not, then.'

'I'm sorry' – 'Not at all'.

I was sure we had met before, and under dramatic circumstances, too. But I just couldn't think. Who was this? I took my food and chose a table. Whilst eating, I remembered that I had seen him before in the mental hospital. He had been a patient there, on my second stay, he had been the first most prominent person visible on arrival, as he had been sitting at the table in a hospital gown with his head buried in his hands, all the hair dishevelled, and he was staying in that thinker pose all day and all night.

He had been one of the ones who did not speak. Like that girl Rachel, whom I only just remembered then. Rachel... She looked cool and interesting, she was stylish, but she never responded when I smiled or said hi to her. 'Does not respond to stimuli', as they were saying in that hospital, trying the cold water bucket technique on her, she remained motionless. Her arms had many cigarette burns on them. This man's name, I now remembered, was Philip, and in hospital he had, much like Rachel, looked like an interesting person, but he had not been responding to conversation. Sometimes, he had spoken out loud to himself. He never had bothered to get properly dressed, and he would only speak in the group sessions, where he would have systematically forgotten everything we had been told the previous day, and would ask the same questions over and over. He used not to trust the other patients in the ward, or their visitors; when I had arrived in mental hospital and seen him sitting at the table with his head in his hands, I imagined that he must be a distinguished lawyer or judge beyond his prime or something, the cliché of the towering mind that foundered, but when I heard him talk, I thought his speech was formless, unduly slipping into pettiness. Seeing him properly dressed and looking me straight in the face, now, I was quite impressed with the changes.

After I'd finished my meal, I went over to his table. 'I don't want to interrupt your lunch…' – 'you're not interrupting anything, we love to talk to you', the lady said with a glowing smile, so I turned to Philip: 'I know where we met: the north wing'. He shrank from his meatloaf and took a deep breath before replying: 'Oh, yes' - 'yes'. 'I'm sorry. How have you been since then?' – 'Not bad, you?' – 'Same' – 'So you live here?' – 'Yes' – 'Do you go to school here?' – 'Yes' – 'What are you majoring in?' – 'Classics' – 'What a wonderful idea! I like Demosthenes very much. There's a lot of things to learn in Classics' – 'There are. You know it. Well, I'm glad to see you're out of hospital. You look much better… Have a good day!' – 'Bye'.

A few weeks later, I ran into him outside the Thrift Store. Again, he saw me first. 'Can you remember? You and I were in hospital together, a while back' – 'So we were.

[143]

Your first name is Phil, right?' – 'Yes, and you are...? Listen, if you ever get bored, give me a call. I'll give you my number'. But he didn't. He asked me to write down mine on a piece of paper, and as usual I gave him a wrong number. Seeing the crowded state of the notebook he had tendered, my name was going to drown in the masses of paper, like my face, apparently, in the forest of his memory. He then said: 'I've seen you in this store before'. That could not have been true. I supposed he was referring to the time we met at the diner. 'Do you come here often? I come here all the time. I'm buying supplies for the homeless. I'm on a budget of forty dollars a day. They've worked very hard to get me down to this budget. I used to spend a lot more... I buy everything they can possibly need. It's never enough'.

His story, like so many stories in America, sounded phoney, and hollow. Perhaps it wasn't. It was hard to tell, when two sedated minds came together, we were both standing in front of one another, stammering our way through blocked pathways of memory and understanding, pathetic, completely pathetic.

When I returned from the summer vacation, Laurie had news: a new boyfriend. A writer. I should meet him. I should come to her new house for dinner. So I went. By then, I was utterly disfigured, inside and out, by the effects of the psychiatric drugs. I was nearly twice heavier, tremulous and out of balance, with bad eyesight, and a pervasive sense of despair had led me to neglect my grooming and hygiene quite dramatically.

Although I was ashamed of myself, I wanted to show my respects and honour her invitation. I had been on psychiatric medication for many months and become very unsightly, overweight, my skin was bad, my face swollen, my hair discoloured, and my conversation drowsy and monotonous. She knew that, but insisted I come for dinner. The man was not there yet, but was expected to arrive soon. We had a glass of wine, she told me what their sex life was like.

The doorbell rang. Ecce homo, she seemed to say. A calm, strong and youthful man in a spotless white t-shirt, a clean pair of jeans and tennis shoes appeared. He sat down, we chatted, had a cigarette on the balcony, then Laurie took me to one side and asked if I was up for a threesome. I said no thanks, but she insisted. I said that I couldn't, but we ended up in bed anyhow, although I pulled out midway, as I really wasn't able. Seeing that it wasn't going to happen, Laurie suggested we have a cup of tea, the three of us, before I left. So we had an awkward cup of tea, then I left.

I was too embarrassed to call Laurie again after this, but it being a small town, I ran into them a few times, either together or separately. Once they were looking to buy a house and things were looking pretty good for them. I was happy for her, because I still had this image in my mind of her on a stormy night in the year before, when she had knocked on my door whilst Nicola was hanging out with me there. She had had in one hand a bottle of Champagne and sushi in the other, kissed Nicola's hand, and said it was time to party, we started laughing and giggling and bitching and having a lovely girls' night in. Nicola left after a while, but Laurie stayed, and then burst into tears, telling me that her grandmother was on her deathbed and that to her, nothing was more like the real Italy than this grandmother, and that very few people understood the real Italy like myself, herself and the grandmother. She told me that her family had rejected her, that she hadn't met a man in her life, that she was almost thirty, that everything was difficult and… what was I to say? Nothing. She went back to her dorm room and sent me skype messages about Proust, Milton and other books.

There was an endearing wrinkled old man with a walking cane, dishevelled clothes, grey beard and a raucous voice, who was always rattling with a can filled with coins and tossing at anyone who came past him: 'Small change! Pennies! Anything!'
So that is exactly what I gave him: small change, pennies, anything. 'Anything' usually something like a sandwich from Subway or a chocolate bar. One day I didn't stop, he stopped me. 'Hey. I don't want your money this time. I just want to tell you something. You are one of the nicest people around here. You've got a fine attitude, how you carry yourself. Really, really nice' – 'That's very sweet of you to say' – 'I just wanted you to know. Don't let those bad people get at you' – 'No' – 'You take care, god bless' – 'bye'.
In the same street is another Subway 'restaurant'. One day I was eating there, a run-down blue-eyed angular guy with a red hat and a pretty dirty winter jacket sat at my table and asked for money because his 'ma had a stroke'. Of course. He wanted seven bucks, so I gave them to him, since I had never seen him before and thought he would not, like everyone else, remember my face and ask again. But he returned. He did not remember my face and told me the same story. I said 'sorry, I don't have change now' – 'Please…' – 'Okay, I'll go to the counter and make change. Seven bucks?' – 'Well, while you're at it, can you make it a ten?' – 'man…'
I saw him again a few times, but not very often, and he
[146]

never did remember me, even after longer chats. One night I was smoking outside the dorm. It was the middle of the night and he was roaming the streets. He stopped right next to me and the cigarette disposal and said 'excuse me miss, I just have to get to those cigarettes in there'. He lifted the upper part of the disposal and began fishing for half-smoked items. 'No, honestly, have some of mine' – 'no, those here are just as good. But I'll take one from you, if that's okay' – 'yes' – 'thank you, have a good night'.

These people on the streets mystified me. They seemed, like me, not to remember things properly. I knew that the way my thinking was, was not normal, that it was impaired and below the average. Only, I could not break out of it, because I was also always very tired. But I still was able to tell that the healthy people were able to think in ways I could not, but that I had been able to in the past. These people fringing the streets of town were more like myself, I thought I could see my future looming right there before me.

One woman with piercing eyes, wrapped in a fading, stiff camel coat, I bonded with especially. Before I had even seen her, I had heard her story: a former student at the Drama School, she had gone insane one day, and continued to haunt the streets of town ever since, delivering speeches at random to passers-by.
The first time I heard her, I was in the pub, and it was more like a terrible scream, fit for a huge stage, followed by a dramatic fall to the ground. It wasn't immediately clear whether it was all acted or genuine. She was thin with short hair, looking confused, dishevelled, and neglected. Once she got into conversation with me a little

[147]

and then delivered a kind of looney rap version of the Greek alphabet, before telling me about all the great and famous roles she'd played in her youth. It was in ways amusing, but mostly it was depressing, because I could see that what she was saying was probably true, and it seemed so undeserved that she should be ghosting around the streets like that. Sometimes her movements were fluid and gracious, more often they were unnatural and abrupt, almost as if she was having a fit in slow motion, and her tone of voice was following the same pattern.

Out of the blue, she said: 'I take Haldol and Seroquel, you know', and I was going to say oh really, I take Zyprexa and Lithium, but she had already turned her back and disappeared around the corner.

The next time I saw her, she showed me her hospice admission letter. 'I'm going on the 25th, I have ovarian cancer. I just wanted to say good bye to you'. I was saddened, and did not know what to say. The group of people I had been with were being carried further and further away from me, off to some tequila place. I was alone with her in the dark, and in that moment I wanted to tell her that we should sit down and talk some more, but she said she had to leave, she had a few more people to say goodbye to.

July, 2008.
Woke behind stained glass windows, went back to sleep, what difference does it make. I know everyone else is alive here, but not me. I only need this half-dim shade in my dorm room and to lie horizontal.
Circe turned me into fauna, it's what it is, tame, locked in, turning in circles. In a white soft padded ball of Zyprexa, Lithium, Propranolol, regular blood checks, constantly

[148]

*looking out for new symptoms, perhaps there might be a
medication change that would allow me to stay awake a
bit longer, but not for now, now this perfectly blind and
deaf universe has gone all silent, all the doors have
closed, and I don't know how to read books any more.*

*'Forsan et haec olim meminisse iuvabit', As the poet says.
It's the only thing I can think of to make this situation in
any way bearable: 'Maybe in the future we'll be glad to
remember even this today'. And after all, I'm in this
fantastic school, the place where it's all happening, I am
still part of that. How will I not, in the future, look back on
this with joy. But now, just now, I am scared to my bones,
afraid to leave this room, and full of guilt and tears and
screams that just won't come out, and I must stab myself to
feel anything at all. Where is that promised land, there
isn't one, am I not right? In what drug is death, twin
brother of sleep.*

*I must have broken. My mind is broken, somehow. I need
to understand that I have wasted what short lifetime I had.
From this day onward, nothing more is to come. What
happens now? Once I'd had it all, sure, I'd had a mind,
lively and complex, a wonderful mind, an avid interest in
life and a will to live in spite of everything, boundless
energy for work and love, but now, there is nothing.*

I was trying to tell Europe that I was very busy and
pretend everything was fine, just so nobody would realise
what was really happening. I didn't think I had much left
to go. I knew any change to the worse and I would end my
life, but treacherously, with every day I got worse I grew a
little more used to it. Sitting with Billy in the Bookworm
café terrace one afternoon outside in the cold, smoking,
him so similar to my former live self that I was almost

beginning to hope that I'd be allright again one day, I watched the light change, this bright and rose-streaked New England sky with its whipped, fast-racing clouds and darkest blues at night. It felt as if time and the ivy disaster had stopped for that afternoon, just whilst we were talking. Japanese tourists were walking around the campus and taking pictures of us as we were talking over our sugar cubes and Aristophanes. We spoke about Berlin, night clubs, about England, and the universities there, about the theatre and our favourite plays... I, repeating things I'd thought in former years, asking myself if I could ever make the transition back into the living present. For now, it all seemed glazed behind a museum display that I couldn't touch.

Pandora's Box

I failed at graduate school, didn't I, everyone knew I was sick. Technically I didn't fail, but, to go with the popular saying: that's academic. I did fail socially, emotionally, professionally, ideologically, at every level. My boss, the person in charge of carrying over my stipend, urged me to take leave of absence.

I was reluctant to, because I didn't believe that I could or would get better again, and I wanted to preserve my job. I knew that if I stepped down, that would only be the beginning of a slow downward ladder at the end of which lay only social exclusion, homelessness, confusion, and squalid death, on the road.

I didn't know how to explain to my parents that I needed to come back home. My mother arranged for me to see a neurologist in Berlin. When I arrived, she noticed my visibly ill health. I was clearly very ill, so at least at first I didn't have to argue to convince them that I needed help. My parents had a house in Berlin at the time, in which I would be allowed to live, although come the end of the summer vacation, they would head to their respective work places abroad. I was already foreseeing the time on medical leave I would spend there alone at their house, I would fall into an extended comatose state and, with no schedule and no people to see, fall into the infinite void until they would come back.

October, 2008.
Today, as yesterday, I do nothing but stare outside and smell the scents of autumn, the smell of dying leaves and breathing trees, the smell of crushed grass and red berries

on the bushes. The light is wonderful, sunny and cool. I wore my London coat, brown suede, it's still beautiful to me, even if it is falling apart, quite literally now. Putting it on is almost like wrapping in a cloak of old feelings, and to think that time hasn't really passed, like I would have wished. I knew, the day before leaving to America that something awful was going to happen. I should not have gone there. But now it is too late to turn back, too late to change. Now it is too late for anything, now I will die – slowly, in silence, and with a smile, but I will die, I'm already dying. It's over.

The coat is the best telling sign that the chemistry of time has worked its dim effects on me and everything around me. The coat is worn; it already was when Jonathan got it for me from Oxfam in Cambridge, many years ago. The coat is breaking from all the seams, the pockets are pierced, it's like a scarecrow, the arms are getting dislodged and the lining is torn, buttons are missing, the belt is fading. And still, I like to keep this coat in my wardrobe. Stitches everywhere have not prevented it from cracking, and even my last attempt at bringing it to a tailor for thorough repair has failed, the verdict: this thing is irreparable. Metaphorically speaking, my whole life is like that coat. It was gorgeous and gritty, now too shabby to be salvaged.

This strange little university town in America. The life from before is now disintegrated, dissolved, partly by my doing. But there is more. It was evil, I remember. I was already starting to go mad in London. Since I have been through American psychiatry, I have seen new grounds, I'm not the same that I was. My coat is like the person I once was, irretrievable, and grey nothing is coming to replace it.

I have been forgetting a lot. But I wrote down everything about Soho, bits and pieces of it, here and there this

[152]

journal, I have everything, so that I can keep the memory.
It doesn't interest anyone, anyway, only me. Everything
should be fine, a dark fear and the hopelessness of the
future are eating at me.

My mother invited me to Riga at Christmas time. Although I didn't care for it now, I remembered clearly that in the past I would have been keen to visit Riga, and pretended the same was still true.

Since some time already, I practised elaborate self-impersonation, because, in truth, there was only a frightening void within my self, emotional death and blanks. I didn't know how to handle this strange absence of self in any other way but to pretend that it was still live, a thinking and feeling person, even though I was nothing like it.

When I went to visit my mother in Latvia, I could not get out of bed, as usual. She appraised the seriousness of the situation, and when she next came to Berlin, marched into the neurologist's practice whose patient I then was, and bluntly requested an explanation for the horrible job he was doing on me. I wasn't there for the consultation, but it resulted in the plan for me to stop Zyprexa immediately.

There were no indications regarding how to stop psychiatric drugs, at the time. Zyprexa was still under patents and information on its long term effects, or on how to withdraw from it, was scant, non-existent, or hard to come by, and the doctor was not really in favour of my getting off it. Even so, I was so ill from Zyprexa, inside and out, that I was ready to take further heath risks and start the experiment of going off it cold turkey.

For a year after this change, a little less than a year perhaps, more like nine months, I was caught in a sort of antechamber of insanity. Having removed from my

[153]

bloodstream no less than a total of twelve daily doses of a cocktail of mind-altering, dulling, numbing, soporific agents, I experienced, at first, two weeks of their sly departure from my system. Feelings of life returned, and then, first insomnia, then severe insomnia, and then, *very* severe insomnia, for nearly a year. Slowly but surely, I developed hypomania, then mania, then severe mania, very severe mania...

I have very few memories of the time. I know it was spent in bits, in various places: Berlin and London, where I visited Andrea, Cambridge, where I spent time with Jonathan, in Bucharest, where I visited Nicola, Riga with my mother, Biarritz and San Sebastian, visiting Jonathan's family, Dublin, Athens and the Greek country on a late summer conference trip, Philadelphia, where I visited friends, and New York, where I walked into a tattoo place at two in the morning one confused and forlorn morning, and had my first scarification done on my hip, which took several hours and was so painful it succeeded in calming my mind down for a certain time on that day.

Lastly, in the fall, it was back to graduate school in New England, where things began to take a vaguely familiar appearance again.

In the nine months before I was reborn a new human being, so to speak, I slept little, and at odd hours. Often, I stayed awake for three or four days in a row, working through fears and memories, circling in spirit around uncanny images and strange meadows.

I lived alone, and if I could not be alone, I travelled, went for long walks by the wild side, underneath the bridges. In Berlin, I was often spending afternoons with Billy and his friend Ben, a middle-aged gay Englishman, psychiatrist-turned-novelist. The three of us continued the tradition we had started with Dave back in New England, of discussing

[154]

pieces of our own creative writing – like a literati club, in a New England cigar lounge each week, or in this case here, in a Berlin night time café.

On many nights we talked until we had nothing left to say, took a single deep breath and began to discuss our own funerals. Ben and Billy were also planning away enthusiastically my sly insertion into their favourite gay clubs in Berlin, for which I would be disguised as a lady-boy, or disguised as Marlene, or go as Marylin Manson. I died my hair black at the time, and as I was losing weight very quickly, bought a set of new clothes, all black. And as for the clothes I had been wearing in the time of my illness, I burnt them.

I remember coffee shop discussions with an eccentric in Cambridge, in the Costa coffee to which I would retreat by day and, in a daze with all the noise I had in my head, would sit paralysed by the dazzling speed of my own thinking, contorting my hands in front of me, forgetting to eat and drink until the evening came and the café shut.

One last and brutal, physical fight with Jonathan in his Cambridge dorm room, in which he grabbed me by my neck, pulled my hair and threw me against the wall to punch my face because I was waiting for him at the wrong gate, sealed the fate of our relationship.

He said I was embarrassing him, that I looked like a tramp, that I was wasting his time, that I was stupid, that I should go back on my meds, that I was on a roll, that he hoped I would kill myself, the usual sort of thing he had got accustomed to saying since I first had been sent to mental hospital. I told him the relationship was over, but he refused to hear me and still was planning on moving to America with me, come August.

I remember Champagne brunch in Golders Green with Andrea in the spring, losing my way in London's Soho,

[155]

and a forlorn walk at night on the sullen north bank of the Thames, fleeing the difficult company of Jonathan's sister and her boyfriend at their apartment in Notting Hill.

Here on that nocturnal walk down by the oily mud, I first conceived of the possibility that I might be, in truth, incurably mad, after all. That from now forth, a life of dishevelment and irrational, senseless walking on borderlines to the crackling sound of thin ice, would be in store for me, that I had a choice only between a state of incoherent, chipped and broken thinking and sudden showers of crass emotion, and the psychiatric nursing that made for a life without dignity, without volition. That I could perhaps get healthy again, as I had hoped and was still hoping somewhere deep down in my efforts to weather the storm of this cold turkey withdrawal from Zyprexa, that possibility began to look ever more remote and subjunctive, as my tempest of feelings continued and I, like Odysseus, seemed sailing away from Phaeacia full of false assurances.

Pandora's box was wide open and the winds blowing my little vessel before grim monsters of the sea, dubious visions, marvellous creatures, black vortices and harsh rains, floating islands and false graces. It was all skewed, I thought, I could barely hold on to my hope to regain sanity, and all around me, family, friends, acquaintances and even perfect strangers, one by one stepped down from supporting me, and began more and more to believe that I was a lost case.

That is why I wandered down alone by the north bank and threw stones, safe from the minefield of society. The sound of sirens and ambulances always made me run.

Society, I came to think, could not know the true horror of psychiatric internment, nor know the extent of suffering that lay hidden behind the content appearance of the

[156]

medicated. And society could not know of my determination to weather this storm; society, I thought, could not know the storm itself even, for the drugs were new, and hardly ever had anyone heard of patients leaving the regimen. Entering, oh yes. But leaving? Society could not know about the hospital. No-one had visited me there; few would have had the permission to, and of those few, no-one had had the courage—to see, and perhaps then having seen it, to question its methods.

And I, though drugged and placid as a fish in a round bowl, had seen more there than I could bear to tell. A lot of broken noses, four point restraints, electroshocks, injections, gratuitous violence, too. All society could see were people who once seemed crazy, be turned into quiet, inoffensive things, and I could not blame them for deciding, based on this, that the pills must be doing good. But I could not believe this any more, and yet, was entangled in a state of half-light in attempts to explain myself, against walls of ignorance and stern self-righteousness.

Everybody had good intentions, calling a doctor for me, always, the doctor. As my mental condition seemed arrested in an endlessly repeating loop of strange extremes, my own hope for myself began to falter at times. But, I thought, even if I should always be this erratic, deranged character swept over by a moment's impression, ducking the blind, yet scrutinising, eye of self-satisfied people, wandering wayward paths and hiding behind the margin of society, laughing stock of protruding bellies tucked in jacquard shirts, that would still be preferable to the living death promised by the mind doctors.

Oh, society! Poor, good old society. Especially the bourgeoisie – what a minefield, and what an unpleasant, judgemental bunch. Especially Jonathan, then my fiancé, and his sister, and her boyfriend, who were friends of mine. They were the most vocal believers that I was clinically insane, creating a sort of vipers' nest around me.

But although I did not feel this so clearly yet, I felt strong urges to get away from that circle of people. I walked around London, in nebulous dreams. The walls of houses whispered to me and paths and streets seemed to sink in an aqueous twinkle as of a tearful eye.

It was my teenage dream again, the iron and the crow. The houses could talk to me again, their crumbling bricks as the faces of wrinkled old women, their barred doors and wooden planks, broken windows, the dust inside them, semblance of decay to conceal the laughter, cries, shouts and knocks of life's many yesterdays. Shedding stardust on to tar and cabs, the air inside them was a sparkling, soulful matter that constantly regenerated itself in fine glitter.

I longed to find my rainbow's end, a ball of white flames, blue-golden petals spraying from its radiance, grave and triumphal. Like a moth, I wanted the light, always more light.

There was nothing I recognised now on Frith Street, transformed into effervescent light blue matter bulging toward me expansively. Bedford Square when I crossed it, eyed me so peacefully, in the sleepy silence of its elegant green. Softly guarding the space, midnight blue and gold-scattered, spectres lay over the shapes of all the walls and facades. The houses were throwing on me, like masks removed from an actor's face, the shapes of their fronts, and thrown onto me, their windows, their doors, like so many eyes, noses and mouths, changed expression, became flattened and serene. They were throwing their skins, draping them over me like a blue and golden tent, and by the time I had reached Gower Street, I seemed to be dragging in my trail a sumptuous and glittering, infinitely extending robe.

[158]

The magnificent red-carpet Senate House Library with its grand reading rooms exhaled whispers of a secret promised land that I knew I could find. A poetic and surreal garden, a dreamscape that I knew I had within me but that needed moulding and chiselling out of the formless depth of dull meditations, to be presented on a decorous platter.

Nothing could shake my belief that this was only some sort of psychotic fever as part of my withdrawing from the drugs, that eventually would wane. Sometimes, even I began to doubt it and saw open before me the great bleak chasm of a life without identity, with misplaced memories and disordered thoughts, stuck outside society, outside the walls of town and castle, with horror thinking back to the poets to whom this had happened and the kinds of poems they then wrote.

I decided, to be on the safe side, to keep my Sophocles to hand at all times. Even if things were to go awfully wrong, it was still preferable to the dead silence, chemical straitjacket, the silence of shame and a real disability within a framework of carers. That was under no circumstances the preferable option. So I continued to run. All the way around town on its margins, sometimes. There were people there, too.

Behind Southwark Bridge Road on a small square around a greasy spoon and a beheaded obelisk, surrounded by abandoned, scaffolded pubs, three red faces drinking cider, a white-bearded man with a bonnet, a girl in tracky bottoms, and a blue-eyed face in a half torn suit.
'We don't bite!' – 'Who said you do?'
The old guy told me histories of local buildings. Just behind me, he informed me, London's very first Jazz venue was falling apart, the Dover, that saw 'the great

Louis Armstrong himself and none other than late Billie Holiday', then moved on to dirty tales from his honeymoon.

The other man with invisible tears told me he'd lost a three year old son, was about to get inpatient, locked-unit alcoholism treatment, when he cries every night even though he has two lovely daughters, but he lives in a hostel.

'Here comes Andrew!'... Man of forty, much better groomed, less worn-out, Jack Daniels in hand, carrying a paper bag, now the conversation turned a bit odd: 'I used to be a photographer, before this' – 'oh yes?' – 'yeah, and I'm telling you, the way you're looking today, you should be on the catwalk' – 'yeah, really, you should' – 'Anyway, what do you do?' – 'Nothing' – 'haha! At least you're honest' – 'yeah but, normally, what do you do?' – 'Student' – 'ah really, what do you study?' – 'Classics' – 'what's that?' – 'Ancient Greek and Latin' – 'like the programme on TV, digging in ruins and stuff... archaeology?' – 'yes, exactly that' – 'wow, so cool, you're nice'.

Berlin's largest Super-
market, under heavy train
bridge, had not found
what I wanted, walked up
road adjacent. Years ago
wrote a story, a boy
watching pigeons here, empty-
eyed, on dirty
benches, called him, Alexis,
you haunt me You
are me down an empty
road, past silent

[160]

station swing doors, clients'
cars, homeless ambulance,
Heroin mobile, Hi, said one
from a folding chair ending
a day, Hi, turn by soup
kitchen, again under bridge. Here
bring hygiene donations, round
corner from Central Police.
Ministry entrance, old zoo,
park shopping internet
connections and tickets, German
pasts, of course, drunkards,
full circle. Rays through gates,
tripe of the edifice, airy
lockers, stone floors, two
neon-haired talking, not one
brow at vague hopes
to be asked, Who
are you. Then shops, Can
I help you – Out
again, loiter more,
on end on a train,
wake through tunnels, bombed-
out scapes, shelled long
years ago, overgrown
green, or twelve-floored,
burnt squatted, none of this
brings tranquil to bloom,
cannot forget I don't have
what I own, Alexis you
haunt, you are me down
an empty, I will be who
I wrote, since I write
as I am.

[161]

July, 2009.
Glance one moment, softly, through another's lens, world.
Hey stop you have a fucking great figure,
Turn round and smile, Thank you,
You too.
You think I'm attractive?
Sure,
don't you?
Never asked that directly.
Would you like to meet me on a date?
A date?
Yes.
But when?
Now, later, tomorrow, today...
I have to go.
Oh, just, then, stay five minutes. What is your name?

Five minutes, ten, twenty,
Light my eyes up,
I have to go, really,
I can see you would like to stay longer.
Yes, I would.
In his eyes are no pupils.
Do you have e-mail?
Yes.
Because I don't use the phone.
Hang on, I write it down for you
Do you have pen and paper,
I don't.
Hey,
Do you have a used ticket?

Old ticket, yes, here. Okay.
Excuse me,
Do you have a pen?

[162]

No.
Hey, wait!
Hi.
This is my friend Tom, Tom, this is Jo.

Stands off, keeps his dog,
Sits
On the floor, brushed off irony,
Do you really want
Do you really have
A pen?
Hello hello there young lady
Yes what is it?
Hey
I have a pen!
Write to me, I hope I see you again.
I wrote to him.
I went back to Zoo,
Wrote,
I wrote and wrote to him again.
He is gone,
Off the distant sweet smile,
Unkempt week-worn shirt unbuttoned on tan skin,
Broken nails, hair uncut,
Bright, friendly and open
Indestructible eyes,
But he's so incredibly gone.
Glance just for one moment softly,
Through another heart's glass,
World.

It was slowly that I found some access to society again, through the lower tiers, through the most basic interactions. I was afraid as of the greatest disease, of the middle class and its hypocrisy, scorn and falseness.

I got on my plane at the end of the year, back to America, back to graduate school. My father gave me a piece of his mind, at the airport, when he realised I had left the packing of my suitcases until the early morning just when I was about to get on my plane. I'd found a house to share with Dave from Pennsylvania, Laurie's upstairs neighbour. He was moving downstairs into Laurie's former flat, because Laurie had moved out, so David, Jonathan and I were actually going to move into Laurie's place.

I arrived, met the landlady downstairs, and later, Jonathan arrived as well. My mind was still ticking out of its cracks, since nearly a year now, and no sign of respite. I could not sleep nor stop the rush in my head at all, I was always busy, always restless, always overthinking and spluttering ideas in hot particles like a volcano, firing everything out at random and without rhyme or reason. Large amounts of alcohol, a tablet of valerian root every hour, a few Lorazepam each day, zopiclone at night and still, I felt restless, wide awake and fidgety as a fish in water. At the same time, I became addicted to Zopiclone and Lorazepam.

The withdrawal... yeah it's that hardcore. A year without sleeping. But for the time being, I am sure that on the long run it'll go back to normal, it has to. No human can be without sleep for this amount of time. In the end, I will find sleep, I'm sure. Patience.
Slight irony, I have arrived here, and the porch of this house looks down onto the court of a care home for the insane. Well then, it can remind me each day of what I'm running from.

[164]

Three : Lotus-Eaters, from New York to London

The Last Sunset

The first time I ever had a phone stolen was at a bar in a university town in New England. When I noticed it was missing, I left Jonathan and the group of friends I had been out with and walked back to the bar to inquire about the phone. The bar was already closed but the staff were still inside, so I knocked on the door and they let me in. We searched for the phone, but it was gone. The bar staff were friendly and offered me drinks and a burger. Somehow, at sunrise, by six in the morning, this bartender and I were still sitting there telling the story of life. In the middle of that, I had a panic attack. At the time I was taking benzos, as prescribed by the German neurologist. I had a bottle of Ativan in my handbag, and I got it out fairly often, I was used to it. But the guy seemed surprised, and asked me what was going on. I began explaining something, but he wasn't really listening. He pulled out a pill bottle and said: 'Would you like a Percocet?'
I asked what that was. He said they were calming and gentle, a bit like Ativan but without the tiring bit, they would help me cool down, take the edge off; so I took one. Soon I felt my anxieties falling away in an instant, slipping off like banana skin and I emerged, the fresh banana -- this was fantastic! And I looked at him, fair skin and watery blue eyes, smooth looking in his white button-down and clean jeans, there was something pale and polished about everything in his person. The conversation went on about his childhood in a small town, Connecticut, and by the time it was day again, we got in his car and drove up the hill into the woods, we sat and talked on the grass until

mid-afternoon. He got a phone call from the town's police station asking if he had seen any girl come to his bar last night. He said no. We were high and having fun. Jonathan, who had called the cops, was angry and upset. I was also angry at him. Why was he even with me in America?

In the weeks that followed, I started seeing the dude from the bar lots more often. Back in New England, after my year on medical break, just starting to enjoy life again, everything was new.

September, 2009.
I've travelled enough,
Tonight, this evening, I arrived.
This here is America
An anchor, a bar
And all things I've run past, or through,
Have flashed in circles and then sunk
To quiet,
Quiet bottom of lake,
Silent as the sediment.
I'm spilling, crawling,
Drama queen,
'Scarlet starlet and she's in my bed',
Queen of Hearts
Hearts? Whose?
Nothing.
This is the evening that forever
Will be light violet and soft beats,
And pretty faces, and good schools,
Far, far away from all I breathed in, or out,
Small things that I never got used to.
Instead of packing up and wishing further,
Let's stay and sink,
Smile, and cease fighting.
I was hungrier for life, so that I could tell

[166]

Stories to
You who
Never asked
For stories!
Oh well,
Someone's got to do it!
Got stuff?

Yes, and we went on a cruise off to a different town, it was autumn and the farmers' markets were looking rich and colourful, a small town celebration was playing some country music and it smelled of hot dogs and fried onion underneath red acorn and poplar leaves, we stood looking at an antiquarian display of old typewriters, historic postcards, and Americana, and he explained to me about the invention of the fork in France in the 16th century, and about domestic archaeology, which he was interested in. We spoke of everyday objects from various historical periods, a fairly unusual and lively conversation, as we browsed through cardboard boxes of daguerreotypes for sale at a market stall, and ran our fingers over the faded spines of second hand books. The daguerreotypes were, all of them, showing pictures of Persian rugs, he bought one. I bought two postcards showing the town at Christmas in 1936, kept them in my room by my mirror, for a good while. I flicked through a box of easy piano music, American popular songs from the 1960s, and stood amazed before the old typewriters and sewing machines. Then we got a hot dog and drove off to the sound of Cake in his pickup truck.

I was living, with Jonathan and Dave, in a second floor apartment with French doors, looking on a horseshoe of detached houses, in a black neighbourhood, the streets full of rusty cars, people were sitting outside on their porches smoking, and at evening time, children were playing ball games between the street posts. Many of the houses had neighbourhood watch panels in their windows, it was an unpretentious, relaxed little few streets to live on, not too far from the laundromat, Walgreens, close to Broadway and close to campus.

On the back side, behind our living room and kitchen, the balcony looking onto the courtyard of a drug rehab centre, and to the right, a group home for schizophrenics. Ironic, very ironic, I had thought to myself when first I moved in. I especially loved the big living room with a surreal curvy swooning chair and two red sofas in it, and I had stuck post cards all over the walls meticulously, it was now looking like our walls were a mega-collage, I was quite proud of it.

On the porch next door, one madman who very much reminded me of the late Marlon Brando was always sitting outside on the steps at sunset and asked me each day whether I was Dutch, and whether he could have a cigarett. My landlady, who lived in the downstairs apartment, was an umphy and heavy, retired black nurse, who lived alone with her lovable and overfed pitbull, told me that those guys were always asking for cigarettes because 'that's all they've got'. I just nodded politely. This was another baptism of fire: acquiescing to the prejudice about mental institutions. Could I really do that? I pretended not to understand, not to see. Who the hell was I?

One evening, I had been out doing percocets with my American boy, when I came back home to find Jonathan, I seemed finally to be tired. Here we were both, after eight years, and I was still running away from him, and he was always running after me, chasing me. When I got home that day, I was exhausted, looked at him, and said 'honey, don't you get it, it's over', sat down next to him, and then we both cried.

We cried a lot, about everything, together. We went to a rock music venue on the station road for a while, where he had already been hanging out on his own, daydrinking, brooding, about my deserting him in this way. I was not going back on what I said, that I could not be with him, and he had to accept it, now, or life was going to be hell – but as soon as I had said all this and seen just how sorry he was, I remembered the eight years that we had been together, how much we'd already got through together, how precious his laughter was to me and how deeply disturbing his sadness was to me, always had been…

Things, again, were starting to blur. By the time we got home, I was the one crying. It was an impossible situation. Both of us knew exactly what the other thought and felt, we were looking on our own past, our many arguments, our many fights, our many make-ups, and we could not believe what we saw, which is that now it was definitely over, dead, exhausted, without question now it was over, and it was too late here to apologise or to discuss future improvement. Love was dead.

We sat on the red sofa together, holding hands and crying, looking at our eight year long argument, from which there was now not even one small alley left unexplored and there still was no solution on the horizon. I felt sad, canals of rain were breaking dams inside me, I was feeling so trapped between two bad solutions, and so sorry for everything I had ever done, and everything I hadn't done. In these moments you can do nothing but suffer, nothing's all right, and you know that by tomorrow, the world will be torn up into pieces. The lull before the storm, in which you try one last time to consider everything and toughen up in a decision because you know that once the storm breaks out, your composure will let you down and you'll just need to pull through with what you are saying here, now, in this brief peace.

His eyes were in my eyes and my hands were in his hands and the blinds were shut, outside was bright and chilly, New England autumn sweeping red and brown leaves over asphalt and the air indoors scented with dry wood, dusty upholstery and a little ocean flair, I wondered if this roof couldn't just collapse on our heads at this precise moment, but we just sat there breathing quietly and listened to the clocks ticking.

We went to the cinema the next day, to see a fashion documentary, and then we also went for a burger in a dive near our house, he spent some more time reading learned journals in the library, whilst I was rushing about the place making a massive fool of myself.

He was showing no intention of leaving. He was requesting me to make payments of several tens of thousands from my bank account into one of his, as part of our splitting agreement. Even that, I did, although it had to be done over several days, I did it. And he maxed out one of my credit cards that I had given to him for emergencies. With hindsight, of course, I should not have made these money transfers, but he had found a good moment to request large sums from me, when I was in a state of mental confusion and in between nervous breakdowns, and I could not really say no.

Lapses. A lot happened in such a haze of drugs and emotions, so fast, and some scenes seemed to happen all over and over again, starting in the same way, ending with a different way, and I found it difficult to say just what came when. Some things became impossible to remember unless I attached them to a story line that I knew belonged to a different night altogether, and the 'why' of things eclipsed itself. Conversations, evenings, and single persons

[170]

seemed to hover as condensed clouds above and in between the fabric of real time.

Percocet, to which I became addicted very soon, wrought a sort of thickening memory loss in some of the moments in which I took pen to paper because I was afraid things that slipped my mind would be important to know later. But then, more often than not, I lost the pieces of paper I was writing on. I remembered only points in time, single scenes, with valleys of oblivion between them, and it's as if the great playwright of life had shuffled the papers a few times and story lines become illegible.

Now, there were only turning points of experience, always the same turning points, recollected with the fluency and skewed association of drugged consciousness, to help remember anything at all, let alone to remember correctly.

The night that Jonathan left, I had been away, floating on drugs for several days, and he had left many messages on my phone, long after it had run out of battery. I had given him a present of a new phone, I think he was happy about it – I had wanted to see him smile, and I knew he liked phones. But he had, that day, also understood my gesture, and very quietly asked me why I didn't love him any more. When I came to the house on that last evening, I knew, as soon as I entered and walked through the pitch black apartment, even in darkness, I sensed that the air was different, his things were missing, and as my eyes grew used to the darkness, the familiar silhouette of where his things used to be was gone, and I knew he had gone.

He rang my cell, at about four in the morning. He sounded like he was in an airport. So it had happened. Jonathan and I had split up. I noticed he had taken a couple of souvenirs, a condom and a g-string of mine, and left me a goodbye note on the desk, in German. That night on the phone, soon we were both screaming at each other, one last and awful time.

I yelled as loudly as I could, in French, in English, and in German, how much I hated him, how he had ruined my life, that I would never want to see him again. There was a great horror in my veins and panic spreading through me, as I ended the call by throwing the phone against the wall violently. Then, I started banging my head into the wall, the bed, I ran against the wall hoping to break a few bones just so I wouldn't feel this thing that was burning me alive. So, that was the ending, with a bang.

I tried to piece it all together, how it happened. I remembered a scene in a bathroom, like from a dream. I was in someone's bathroom, having a terrible argument on the phone with Jonathan. Over the years we had become very close, as well as having grown apart. This phone call was long and enraged with the desperation and hatred of the powerless, the blind heart in darkness. Bitter tears were rolling down my face, I was drained. I thought it was awful that we were phoning each other in America rather than speaking in person. He was ringing because he couldn't sleep, alone in the apartment that we thought we would share in some kind of happiness, and I, stuck in some dude's bathroom, who for some reason seemed perfectly familiar, as well as being, in reality, a perfect stranger. The phone call ended with a long silence, both of us were quietly crying.

It was a little like mental hospital that night, the feelings and the outcry, and the white bath. When I came out of the bath, about to sink into a deep darkness, American boy was waiting for me and handed me a blue pill with that gesture I knew from nurses somehow, and I took it with the grateful absorbance of one in need, there was no talking, I only took it and there was nothing more to be said about this, not even 'thank you'.

I knew then already that I was addicted. I couldn't have done anything without oxycontin any more, then. We lay on the couch and used razor blades, which by then I was carrying with me regularly. I put out cigarettes on my own arm for the first time and briefly felt something, then, again, nothing.

Later, I heard all of his messages in sequence, on my answer phone. It was a few days later, and I was unable to function. I called for some painkillers but there was no answer, so I thought of going to Walgreen's, perhaps to sneak some percocets off the pharmacist.

It became day, it became night, my mind was scattered like ashes in the wind but thankfully, Walgreen's is open 24 hours. I was so slow moving and thinking, that it took me until two in the morning, just to get up and going. I came back from Walgreens with a bunch of stuff I never needed. For the rest of the night, I prepared the class I was teaching in the morning and went straight in at nine. Once that was behind me, I went back to campus, lay in the sun and fell asleep. I woke up with a slight sunburn on my stomach under my t-shirt. I thought of going to Walgreen's. I was not sleeping at all, even now, taking many sleeping pills each day as well as percocets and vodka each day, and I started carrying a family size bottle of Tylenol-PM with me at all times, thinking that I might use it to kill myself with if ever I might feel unable to face the rest of it, as I went on my strange ways.

I felt broken down and could not get up, or sit down, or eat, I had to keep walking, to be on the move, to go places, expend energies, to use drugs, and I was also getting addicted to cutting myself with razor blades. The leaves were red on the ground in that fresh New England autumn wind and I walked and walked with my headphones on,

[173]

sometimes fast and sometimes slowly, and when I eventually came to my house again I didn't want to enter, and sat down across from it, waiting for my nerves to let me in. My neighbourhood, so quiet and melancholic, black and peaceful, poor and smiley, and my landlady had this cute chubby pitbull that reminded me of my own late dog. I was so depressed, it was unbearable and I thought I would go to New York and just never come back to anything or anyone.

First I had been the one leaving, trying to get away from Jonathan, but then he followed me, and when he had arrived at me, he started trying to get away from me, then I left the town, but we crossed paths again, by chance.

I went to the bar where I knew I could find him. My American lover, who would say things like 'good body' and call 'oh God' from his bed, wear sneakers and drive pick-up trucks into the wide and beautiful, this vast and gently weeping country.

I really began to fall in love with America and to feel that all that was strange to me could become a lovely and homely backdrop to my life. We talked about dead malls, and I thought I now understood the American songs I used to know in Europe a lot better, where the road tripping songs of the red hot chilli peppers were composed, and such.

This man's deep ocean eyes and fair skin, French mirrors in his apartment with sky high ceilings, antique chandeliers, music on the fireplace and light chains in the bedroom, stacks of magazines, family albums, hundreds of thousands in cash, in an old tomato conserve can – smooth, soft spoken and a touch crazy, collector of t-shirts, starchy white bed sheets, he gave me heroin and percocets, the whole thing is such a blur, all these beautiful moments drenched in Oxy were so precious yet so light that no doubt I had to forget them – like individual stars in the night sky. But he's got a cooler head than this, and in his clarity told me that I was too much drama for him.

One day things were too much drama even for myself, I was getting ready to run, prosecuted by demons and nothing seemed bearable at all any more. I wanted to walk all the way to the ocean, Latin American culture in the USA had me dreaming in November of the day of the dead and of the South, the South, the South.

My splintering heart, that ubiquitous desire I had to start travelling and to make it very, very far away from the here and now, got me gazing nostalgically at the barriers of the city and had me feeling slow on highways next to the cars passing by the hundreds, so many days I thought of just putting my head down and leave without even saying goodbye, and that day, I packed my tears tight in my chest and with clenched fists in my pockets started walking. South. I got stuck on the green, in the middle of town and was so entrenched with my demons and that paranoia, that I felt physically stuck to the ground and could not move forward.

I sat on a bench, wished I could be underneath it, imminently expecting either of two things: a black fury bird from hell to snatch me away to liquid skies through malign rays, or a dead serious cohort of paramedics with straitjackets and the ambulance that would take me back to that chilly place of torture and inquisition – the mental hospital. But neither happened and so I stayed stuck for a while in pain and fear and only hours later, or so it seems, I got up, and cried with my face against a tree.

Couldn't get myself much further than that tree, so at least, people would not see my face. I was both afraid of the demons, and the psychiatrists to which, inevitably, I'd be brought if someone found me like this. I had tried to ring a friend of mine, but he didn't pick it up. Later on, that friend told me to leave him alone with my drama, as he had enough of his own. Fair, fair. Jonathan had left, back to England and away from me. I tried calling somebody else. He told me to keep these thoughts to myself because they hurt and offend him. Perhaps this other friend at whose house I recently stayed over, a colleague of mine who had opened up to me about his rocky past, who I was so fond of, I called him my twin. He too, was busy. So… who?

The bar where I knew I could find the American friend. Could he perhaps sort me out with more Percocet. He asked how I was, and did I want to come over to his later on. Yes! I sat down in the bar and waited. I read there all evening. During the night, men poured their souls into my eyes. This must be when I accidentally took someone's keys in my handbag. We all did a drug designed like a star-shaped pill, and snorted Ritalin, felt so much better afterwards. We did some fucked-up things that made us chuckle later, and when I went home at last, instead of this messy paranoia, I just closed the door with a sigh and thought what a lovely country it was, how adorable and open-hearted its people, how smiley, warm and peaceful this charming small town, what an amazing place this university, and decided that I was satisfied and that I would stay in America forever, finish my studies, become a lecturer, have a baby, work for this same school, get a greencard, settle down, make nice friends, save up for a house, the full whack. Total liberation, this, knowing the journey and the destination. End of doubting, travelling, wandering, Europe is in the past, this is my new life.
The next day, same thing, I was falling over trying to fray a way through darkness, drawn to the ocean… I got there.

I made it to the ocean. I stayed there for a couple of hours, fell asleep on the grass. Some men were fishing something and there was a hot dog cart. The weather was balmy. I started feeling much better. Walked back into the town. Went to sit down in the bar. It wasn't very busy. My guy was there, spoke to me a little, not too long, I left for a while, came back in the evening, tried to read something. As I did so, waterfalls in darkness with blue-rayed glitter were rushing down from all around my view, an infernal aura pulled me along and beat me down a narrow, seemingly endless vortex from which I knew I would never come up or out to light again.

I could no longer read. Or see much. I had not eaten, or hardly, slept little and the days before been depressed enough it took a whole hour for me to walk home, and by the end I was in tears and behind my scarf and did not dare to go inside.

I eventually did, the next day was better again, but no sleeping, or hardly, and in the bar my friend wouldn't talk to me so I small talked at the bar. Waste of time. Went outside for a cigarette and the chef was just chatting to one of the waitresses there, they were bitching on about European women, thin girls, and drama queens – so, I suppose, indirectly, they were talking to me, weren't they… oh. I couldn't say much, could I. It occurred to me that perhaps my guy had wanted them to get this across to me, there is no other reason they'd have mentioned it, they hardly knew me – but when I went indoors, he came to sit down with me, he was very sweet and touched my legs under the table, as the Americans do, and gave me a ticket to New York. Two, actually – the ticket to New York, and the return. I thought I'd go, and thanked him, I thought I'd go and never come back, but for some reason stuck around a little longer. I tried to read my book and again felt the same black waterfalls, pain in my spine, which got

[177]

unbearable.

I then thought about everything for a few moments, and decided this is my chance, now or never. I got up from the table. I was going to leave, when I was actually more inclined to hide under the table and get sucked into a vacuum. But no, I'd have to hit the door, and a Friday night street, if I wanted to make that train. I was in a bad mood. I bowed to the bar owner by the stairs on my way out, and he said 'you're one of my sweethearts'. I said bye to my friend and when I got out the door noticed that I felt very, very drained. I had wet eyes, oddly. My friend was being sweet, but I was somehow falling within myself, I could hear the waters rushing, echoing as awesome male choirs in high churches, and again falling down on me as broken rocks and crashing planes from the sky, I felt oppressed under impending doom – it is now or never, I thought. I have no future and no past, and the present one unending crow's cry echoing through blue-lit streets whose grey-chiselled buildings are gently and imperceptibly wiggling in my back...
My friend had said 'see you soon' and when he saw my look, added 'maybe'. As I was walking down the street, I thought of turning back and giving back to him my return from NYC, but always felt trapped in my own movements, by the surprised frown and shrug I was already seeing on his face, were I to turn up in the same bar again on the same night; I could not figure out what I would tell him upon trading his ticket back, and yet, I could not bear the presence of this ticket in my wallet. I could not throw the ticket away; it had to be returned to its owner. The other possibility was that I might chuck the entire contents of my bag down a bridge into water, that would have been the only other option, and I could do so in New York.
I walked into a RiteAid to buy Motrin for my back pain. I

[178]

had very bad pain that I knew the pills in the bag would not have done enough for, even for the duration of just the train ride. But it was a lot of Motrin I'd have to take if I was planning on helping this pain with just Motrin. Over the counter drug overdose now seemed very unattractive as a suicide method, but I knew no better wished now I had a gun, but there was none.

The pharmacy entrance shop alarms were decorated with life size grey skeletons in transparent shrouds, wreathed in spider web veils, climbing from the shop alarms, ushering me in with mutilated hands full of blood and an effrontery-laden grin from pale faces with cavernous eyes. What an odd decoration of the entrance to a drug store, I thought to myself. Took it to be some macabre suicide joke, or if not that, then perhaps some drugstore manager's take on prescription medication abuse, but it crossed my mind that it would be an unusually excellent joke considering that commercial America is so utterly humourless, and I really wondered for a long time what the skeletons might be about. Eventually it crossed my mind that Halloween was coming up.

I tried to hide how many painkillers I was getting. I felt I had to hide it from myself most of all, because in my mind was forming a dark diving plan to jump down into the black water. I felt as though this time, everybody knew about it, and would want to stop me, and know I should be stopped, I fear – well, I get the pain medicine, along with some food, just for good measure, I walk out with my headphones, I eat pills, I eat granola bars, I eat chips, I drink diet soda, I walk up the highway and outside town, along dark houses and the varying shades of private company headquarters artificial lighting themes, there's no one here, I'm carrying a white shopping bag from RiteAid and my whole life is in my backpack. I would like to throw it all out, even as I skip from song to song on my iPod,

[179]

there is none I can listen to, or bear to hear, they all jab me and music that used to be very familiar to me, music I have brought with me from home, the music on my iPod, all now seems strange and hostile, I am lost, lost for good outside the boundaries of a small town, in a big country, which is dark to me, and full of only Walgreens and Burger Kings, car parks and neon lights, canvassed commercials, food waste, and it is so very cold.

After some time, I see train bridges and rails, and at the end of the road, the station. And water. Every song I switch to, the beginnings are so intensely beautiful and unique that I can't bear to pick one, cannot last through a whole one, and suddenly I have a big smile on my face. And then again a deep grimace, because I feel it again, how I am not capable of these nuances or of sustaining beauty, but I feel so shaken up, and cascades rush around, I'm thinking that I will not kill myself in New York, but then, thinking I can't see how to live on, I could see no way out, or around, and within I was all determined and was neither happy nor sad, just sure, and now I'm not?

Inside the station, three younger college students were just meeting up, they hugged and giggled and showed far too much love, sitting on the station bench and looking at them, it seemed as though I was in a glazed state and could no longer be part of that world that smiles.

The guy on the New York bound train who I decided to sit opposite, seemed about in the same mood as I was, and I thought this is perfect, so we won't need to small talk. I was writing some thought list of mine on some scrap of paper, mainly in order to record facts, because I was noticing that I was getting memory gaps, which is why I was trying to keep a list of events. They were all slipping my mind.

[180]

Eventually, he did start up a conversation. We talked about sadness, death, and drugs. By coincidence, we discovered we had a common friend in London, Florian – Florian who'd been in the Greek play with me, and whom I'd last seen in New York maybe a year back; I'd been in this haze of zyprexa and unable to speak with him properly, but knew he'd lived in New York that year I got sectioned, and then, I think, decided to go work on a farm in Montana, gone to Montana, and then complete radio silence. This boy on the train, now, was Florian's childhood friend, and indeed about to go up to Montana to visit Florian. So I wrote him a note to take with him.

For that night, train boy and I were inseparable. We talked, and talked, and talked. This conversation with a stranger on a train then was a godsent, it made a part of my life flash up before my eyes that I thought I'd irretrievably lost – hearing news about someone from my cast in London, who had gone to New York himself two years back and kind of vanished there, later evaded to the Northern States and disappeared there... when I'd just started to think I would have to forget Europe and my old life, in the swing of old school American immigration, to wipe the table clean, which the long process of loss of self with psychiatry had already begun to seal in me, painfully, it warmed my heart to hear that this stranger, this strangely tearful boy I'd only just met on the night train to New York, was about to go up to find my old study buddy. The joy! Meeting someone out here in America to whom I could talk about home and who not only believed my stories, but also knew the exact same people. It was too good to be true. He knew not only my friend but also his nice girlfriend, whom I knew, and had in fact seen them more recently than I had.

I asked if I could write a note to give him, to bring to our mutual friend. Then we talked, and talked, and talked, we got a drink first by Grand Central, then moved on to Brooklyn and when the night was over neither of us really wanted to leave, but we went on our ways as we had to, and so did my note to the dear old friend.

I went to see my tattoo artist on Chris Street for a scarification, then I went to get some 'first aid supplies', Dave came to pick me up that night and I tried to convince him to have his tattoo done, after I already had taken him shopping for a leather jacket and everyone was enjoying his scattered and scholarly, rough-and-ready look. We sat in the Brooklyn apartment and went on the roof in the morning. I was stretched out on my back feeling good in a little bedroom in Brooklyn and spent a day of calm. I was on the phone to Liz from London for a few hours, then took the train back to our campus flat in the afternoon. Upon arrival I found that the grocery store was closed. Dave had asked me to pick something up for him to eat on his return late at night.
So I went to Walgreen's. I was quite glad to find that they sell a good deal of things to eat there. Walgreens was rapidly evolving into a therapeutic island fulfilling all my needs. As for myself, I ate at burger king. It was somewhere on the same level as Walgreens and the dollar stores, plentiful, distracting, impersonal, and commercially familiar to me.

I went to Walgreen's in order to buy an afterpill and replace lost and ripped tights and underwear, but couldn't find any undies there, there so I just got the tights. My dress was short and it had been a bit embarrassing to walk all the way there so I ended up calling a taxi, a few steps down the road from the door I had just emerged from. Who knew what difference it makes to a woman to be

[182]

wearing transparent tights, as opposed to no tights – it makes all the difference in the world. It was two or three in the morning, again, and Walgreens was empty. I bought an armful of things that I didn't need, sleeping tablets, Tylenol PM, a second bottle, as by now I was thinking I might need two bottles to be really dead if I overdosed. I walked out and saw that the cab still there, and asked the cab driver if he could get me to anywhere for me to buy clothes. He said 'I think it's a bit late for that, but if you need a change of clothes why don't you ask me to drive you to your house'. I said that I didn't have time as I needed to go and meet a friend straightaway. It did not quite occur to me that his suggestion was really quite practical. I was dim spirited, and deep in a conundrum at that moment. Ultimately, I decided to ask him to get me to the green, I wanted to see if I could get more drugs. As soon as I arrived there and sat down on a bench, I barely had the time to rearrange my clothes, I got a phone call from the guys at the bar, so I walked over to them.

The guys, by now my new all-American, sneaker sporting, burger eating, oxy-popping gold chained gang of cruise buddies, noticed the lack of underwear, and loved it. The taking of the afterpill was postponed for another day. When I next woke up in someone's flat I was in unbearable withdrawal pains and on top of that it was already getting dark. No-one was there. I took the afterpill, I felt a bit sick. Then, the man came in with percocet for me, he went out again, and I went to meet him later that evening, there were more oxys. Before I did so, I went to the dollar store and got several pairs of new underpants and tights, I put them on at Starbuck's. I also thought of buying further useless, valueless things that I can't remember, hair accessories, nail varnish, that sort of thing. We started by getting drunk, and I drank a drink that had

[183]

been spiked, as I now think, and I blacked out completely.

Walgreens, Walgreens, Walgreens. The next day, I walked the long way from his house to our town's big Walgreen's, to get a bunch of herbal pills, cigarettes and not sure what else, it was a pointless, erratic and desperate visit. I stood waiting in line at the Pharmacy. I was going to need an afterpill all over again, now, after the spiked drink. The line was long and chairs were few, so I sat down on the floor. A man walked in my direction and past me with that look in his eyes I knew from mental hospital. I made a phone call to someone I knew would not answer, just to distract myself. The man sat down by the pharmacy waiting area and began talking about his experiences in the armed US forces, his post-traumatic stress, his ongoing employment with the military, throwing in all the names of psychopharmaceuticals, Xanax, money, Seroquel, suffering, Ativan, paranoia, Zyprexa, and depression. I sat with my back towards him, unable really to hear it, and yet, unable to walk away.

I had been summoned to speak to my dean, my senior academics, I assumed, had told her to deal with my case of mental absence. According to the dean, I ought to have gone on medical leave of absence for another year. I said it was not an option, so she advised I urgently see a psychiatrist at the university's clinic. I answered that the psychiatrist was not an option. Insisting, she persuaded me to make an appointment with the school's division of mental hygiene to discuss these options one more time. I told her there was no discussing things rationally with the staff over at the mental health clinic, or at least I tried to tell her this. She said she was sure I could work something out. I remembered this dean, she had visited me, uninvited, when I had been on the locked hospital unit, that time

[184]

when Laurie had showed up as well.

Dark and bitter sea storms were blowing thunder inland as I felt the system's poisonous tentacles caress my shoulder gently. I knew now what I was getting into, and would not walk forward blindly like before. I began to feel very afraid.

I had a very depressed tea and lunch at a Mexican restaurant. Looking at pictures of skulls announcing celebrations on the day of the dead, I started dreaming narcotic dreams of dry plains and glowing cities in South America, and I thought about walking away from my life again, reaching the ocean again, falling into it, never to see the light of day again. As I picked up my check, the waitress drew a smiley face on it. I wondered if she had noticed the black shadows in my face. It put me in an emotional mood all over again.

Dave and I had taken over Laurie's old flat and I was looking forward to meeting her again and telling her my news about having got off meds. Perhaps she could even advise me on how to proceed with the dean. Meeting Laurie, the girl with the many tattoos and outlandish theories, who wore sunglasses in the classroom and black lace shirts with golden crosses, all provocation and edgy glamour, had been a constant wonder to me. That time in mental hospital I had been so impressed by her efforts to extricate herself from there. She had gone on hunger strike, and insisted on her right to have a judge hearing. She was her own lawyer, and managed to convince. I remembered clearly how the nurse had come to her with pills in a paper cup, and Laurie politely said no thank you, enough times for it to work.

This, now, was nearly three years ago, I had let pills run me down very far down the line. I wanted to tell Laurie this year that I had finally done it, and that I knew now

[185]

how right she had been, and to get her Champagne. I had already seen her briefly once in the street, but she had been evasive and rushed, so we could not speak properly. When I ran into her one afternoon at the library, I made a point of greeting her again, properly.

It turned out that she could not remember me. I felt put down at first. She said something like 'Forgive me, but I have lost my memory. Did we meet before? I don't know who you are'.

It startled me, but I knew immediately. I asked her if she had had electroshock therapy.

She nodded, looking up quietly: 'yes'.

'I am so sorry', I said. 'It's ok', was the gentle and withdrawn reply.

'Where was it done?'

'Here'.

It was surreal, and the odd moment of me knowing her and our common past, but her not knowing me, was bringing me to a never before travelled land of confusion and fear.

'Did you agree to do this?'

'No. It was done against my will"

'But…'

'Don't be upset. I have recently been readmitted to the programme. I am working on Billy Joyce'.

'I know, Laurie'.

'Oh, you know?'

'Yes. How are you today?'

'I'm fine, thank you. I'm great'.

Looking at her, I tried all I could to believe this was not actually happening. The mixture of pills she would have been on, and that she had forgotten much about her own life, was turning her into a walking zombie.

[186]

'When did you have your ECT?'
'Last February'.
'It's October now. You still don't remember stuff?'
'No, not yet'.
'You know, I have this other friend, Jane, whom you met. She also had it, and she said she has been able to get some of her memories back'.
I didn't actually know how Jane was. But the wild and bleak look in her eyes was breaking my heart.
I was standing there, caught in the headlights, tears started to shoot into my eyes. She said: 'Excuse me, I've never met you, but I think you look very depressed. You may want some help from a psychiatrist'.
'Really, you think so?', I said tilting my head.
'Yes, I have a really great psychiatrist, he is so talented, he saved my life'.

As she started to praise her psychiatrist, I looked at her appearance again. She used to have very long black hair, but that had been cut off, and she was now also overweight. I remembered her fasting and hunger striking, remembered her unbroken will. Her long hair, that she used to flick back and forth, always used to remind me of wild horses. Partly because I'd been embarrassed of the state I was in all that time, and because I was awkward about the bygone threesome situation, I had not kept in touch with her as well as I otherwise would have done.
I tried to play out in my mind how it could have happened, in the time that I was away, but found it impossible to visualize. As the new state of affairs was starting to sink in like a dagger plunged in through my throat, she started telling me how ashamed of her whole life up until this treatment she was, how grateful she was for her husband, her doctor, her family, and the school. And above all, the catholic church.

[187]

But, I remembered that, she was getting a lot of hate from her family when I first knew her. She hated psychiatry. She was critical of all sorts of academics here. And she was notorious for her wacko theories about the origin of the world, a theory that is nothing to do with Catholicism. She asked me whether I was catholic. 'I am Italian like you, don't you remember?' - 'you are Italian?' - 'yes, so I know about Catholicism' – 'I am Italian, too' – 'I know' – 'Really?' – 'Yes' – 'I'm sorry if I did anything horrible to you' – 'not at all' - 'do you go to church?' - 'No' - 'you should' - 'do you remember my name?' - 'no' – So I told her my name.

'Oh, my husband told me about you. I kissed you once?' 'Yes'.

I got excited. Now we were getting somewhere.

'I am so sorry, and ashamed of myself. I don't do this sort of thing any more'.

'Why, I kissed you too, and I still love you like before. You don't need to apologise'.

'I was a horrible, horrible person, and I am sorry for all I did to you, it was because… I had a manic episode'.

'I know how you were. And now, I am sorry you are having such a bad time'.

She knew what I meant. I looked into her eyes. She nodded weakly and looked away. I hugged her, she stayed in my arms. I felt I was almost going to cry. She didn't know me, but I knew her, and she was crying in my arms – the arms of a stranger, from her point of view. I was seeing before me the hospital, the nurses with their stern faces, between milk glass windows and the clanging of surgical instruments, blue arrows pointing to 'ECT' downstairs and all the highly alarmed doors, the loud speaker announcements and the dead faces of rebelling patients coming back in a wheelchair, not talking much.

[188]

I said to her: 'I'm going to leave town. I'm glad that I saw you; I've been looking for you. I wanted to say... goodbye to you. I have decided to leave America'.
'Why? Are you crazy? Here we are in paradise!'
'Paradise?'
'Yes! Look!'
'Well, I don't want to go back on psychmeds'
'Psychmeds? Do you take antidepressants?'
'No, same shit I was always on, zyprexa. Well, you know antipsychotics...
'Antipsychotics?'
'Yes they're bad, aren't they...'
'Take Geodon, it is the lightest of them all, I recommend it'.
'Ah, I guess here they like to use zyprexa or Abilify'.
'Abilify, I am on that'
'Oh... I thought it was not so bad when I took it, it is kind of weak, isn't it...'
'Why are you going to see the doctor?'
'The dean was saying I should go. I will go, but for one visit only. Then I'm out of here'.
'Why don't you just talk? Go to counselling and talk. Just talk! Say whatever, make them happy, just talk. Don't take pills, and don't do ECT... don't do it'.
'No, I don't think I can. I will go back to Europe'.
'But what will you do?'

I could halfway recognize the girl I'd known. She seemed as if her soul had been taken out of her self, her eyes so curiously gleaming in their emerald colours, all bottle green and diamonds. I thought I was looking her directly in the soul as much as I was seeing nothing. I used to be afraid of what she might say next, afraid and a bit excited. Now I wished I had magic skills and that I could somehow

[189]

draw her brilliance up from wherever it had been buried. Her facial expression was strangely motionless, as was her tone of voice and her whole body. She who used to jump over fences and talk with her hands, flip back her hair and cross her legs over and over... It was ghostly, as if someone had pressed the off switch.

Is this what inner stillness is? I thought so of myself, formerly on zyprexa, but it isn't quite that... it is withdrawal of life, it is waking lethargy, I have no word for it. Forgetfulness of the present, capture in the present without future or past...she was present without being there. I thought of Zeno's paradox, Achilles and the tortoise : Laurie was the faster runner, but it would take her an infinite time to overtake me. I marvelled at the speed of her life. I was going to burst out crying momentarily and quickly said goodbye, ran outside and already on the way through the cafeteria could not stop my tears, sobbing on my way up the stairs, as I ran through the library gates. Upstairs, I tried to walk in a straight line, but soon had to sit down, a few steps from the library in the grass. The longer I stayed there, the harder it became to get back up, so I cried and cried. I have been crying ever since.

I didn't really know who would understand the tragedy of this, except for a particular acquaintance, a lawyer specializing in psychiatric rights advocacy. I was on the phone to him, sobbing, telling him this story. He tried to impress upon me that the same might happen to me, and that, if I was to see a psychiatrist as my dean had asked me to, my attitude was going to get me in the biggest trouble. I said that in that case I would simply not make the appointment, and he reminded me I could be taken against my will. I blew all of this off and hung up, walked into

Classics, still crying, barging into a party of colleagues. An art historian with whom I happened to have shared the elevator on the way, asked if I was okay, and I said no. I said I was very confused and upset, and he offered to have a drink together at the cigar lounge and talk about it all.

A second lawyer I spoke to later told me that involuntary electroshocks were legal and that the procedure itself was up and coming again after it had been banished in the 1980s. One of its main proponents was, apparently, a doctor from our university's psychiatry department, a very sweet looking old man with a white moustache and round glasses I had often seen around the hospital. He believed electroshocks were therapeutic, safe and useful. Responsibility goes to... Nobody, as Odysseus told the Cyclops.

I suddenly felt very afraid of each face in the neighbourhood that got vindicated for seeing Laurie like this now, so docile, submissive and innocuous. A lot of people hated her for her provocative style and daring thinking, and many envied that she was glamorous, academically brilliant, independent, an angry young woman, stylish, and very beautiful... I lived in her former flat, I could not even walk up the stairs any more, as if someone had hacked an axe into my stomach.
Everyone always hated her, and now she has been stopped. She will never get to do any of the things she was dreaming to do with her life, those dreams are forgotten or drenched in this new self-deprecating rhetoric impressed upon her by all those who hated her before, and she would have no new dreams.

Laurie says she is alive and well. And yet admits placidly that she knows she is not and cries in my arms, now the

[191]

arms of a stranger, she doesn't care being in the hands of others then – She, humbler and more brave than anyone in the whole world. Though she survives, she is dead, and that whoever is happy now, is happy about a crime. These are all terribly confusing things and terribly difficult to explain, and the worst is that they're real and surrounded by secrecy and taboo. I have a feeling as if a poisonous snake inside my stomach is swelling, biting into my lungs, I am sick with this hypocrisy and can't be told not to care, this was my friend and my inspiration, and if more people had looked beyond the surface, they might have loved her more too, because she was wonderful, giving, and ever so sweet. I'm leaving now, and won't return.

When I woke up, I checked for e-mails, I had written to several of my friends. The first I opened, began : 'I remember Laurie, she was…' and already, I again started screaming out in fear, banging my head against walls and thinking, I hope nobody sees me, and nobody tipped me off, I hope no psychiatric ambulance stops by here now. *Surrounded only by smiling grimaces, this is fake-land. I cannot breathe now in this town, in this house. I could do it for a while—come by the Tylenol sections in Walgreen's, long pharmacy lines, the new England autumn wind, as in the smell of Purell, the opacity of glaceau vitamin water, the improbable muffin sizes in coffee shops, the looks of fed-up schoolchildren in the street down by the park. But I can't continue now.*
I am majorly confused and grieved, it's probably fair to say I'm deranged. I've been throwing things against the wall, screaming at my walls, hitting the walls, hitting the furniture, banging my head, destroying everything I own, in between feeling scared, helpless, it's as if a howling wolf pack in my heart has been let loose.
I'm unaccountably slow at doing the simplest things, then

[192]

again, stop in the middle of what I'm doing, erratic...
Thinking, thinking hard about these very hard things,
coming to conclusions, doubting them... But I know. I
know one thing at least: there is now no way I can see a
psychiatrist to tell them I'm sane, on Monday. I probably
can't even get up on time for Monday morning class.
They'll be phoning, and e-mailing after me. The gossip
has already spread. I've already talked about this over
drinks with a couple people. They don't understand, they
don't want to understand. They want me to see the doctor.
And so, I must leave before Monday.

Nicola's e-mail was:
I know e-mails have trouble conveying tone, but I'm
absolutely in tears and freaking out about your own safety
right now.
I recognized Laurie with stupor from your story. I cannot
believe that this happened to her. She was alive, quirky,
brilliant, and laughed in the face of authority and stupid
regulations, and I remember everything, her story with the
hunger strike, everything. I remember her getting terribly
drunk in your room, force feeding me sushi and kissing my
hand. I remember her red cowboy boots and how I
defended her from the silly boys who wanted her skin on a
stick because she was loud and peed in the men's
bathroom. Why, why...

From Andrea:
My advice is LEAVE. If your lawyer friend is right about
even a small risk (and from what you say it doesn't sound
like a small risk), you need to preserve yourself. She
admitted, it was done against her will. These are evil
bastards and you should not dignify them with your
presence at their tawdry institution. This is too high a
price to pay for a degree, for access to their resources.

They don't get to decide for you.

When you were on Zyprexa, I couldn't find you. It was temporary, because they're just drugs, but ECT is forever. But it was still so difficult to see; it was like deep, deep underwater. I don't know what I'd do if I saw you buried forever.

From Sebastian:

What can I tell you...? I would run away. In fact, I did run away, even though I was on the other side of the barricade. But I could see how easily one might switch sides if he's not conforming. And of course I didn't want to be part of this crap.

I said goodbye to a lot of people, at the bar. They were darlings, the tall girl whose name I forget but who is stunningly beautiful and the Mexican hip hop fan, and most people I'd hung out with. I also wish my guy had handed me back a long poem I wrote at his flat once, not really a poem, but a long outpour, one day I had fallen sunken on the ground at his place.

I threw away everything that I had ever bought at Walgreen's. I threw away pretty much everything I'd ever bought in America. I left some of the things I owned for my friends. With my trash bags that also contained most of my clothes, my everyday and my school stuff, I filled the entire trash can outside our house and filled one more. I didn't know I'd had so much stuff in my room until I was carrying it all to disposal. What a load of junk it all was, my assembled life. All that junk from Walgreen's I got rid of, and then I lit candles screaming, guess those had come from Walgreen's too. Dave would have to remove, when he would be back from New York. At the end of the night they had all fully burnt down.

[194]

Streaming London's Labyrinth

October or November, 2009.

I arrived in London a few days ago and am sitting in the Soho bar I used to live around the corner from. I got the local newspaper – the West End Extra – to look for work and a place to live. Staying with Andrea, who has been wonderful putting me up and all, but it just so happens that she's moving back to Budapest in a couple weeks. I walked past the house on Frith Street where we used to live, it used to fill me with nostalgia and old feelings, but now it seems glazed over by steam and ozone, not that vivid any more.

I might be OK, it's been a few days of continuous crying. Oddly, I seem to have gone missing for 24 hours after I was supposed to arrive, Andrea was waiting for me and got worried, but I can't recall anything happening at all. What is certain is that my wallet has been stolen so I am cashless. Andrea has lent me a little money. She is an angel. My former professor, Peter, whom I went to see, has a new office. I was hours late to our agreed meeting time, but he made all the time for me, listened to everything, he's such a star. He even sorted me out with a small job at the Royal Academy. There's an opera project there where they want some guest lectures about the Electra myth, which will be great for me to do. I ought to renew my membership at the Hellenic Society and get a British Library card. There's a paper about Metamorphosis I have been asked to write for a conference volume, I can now get on with that. And I have a few commissioned translations from Wiley, I can continue freelancing, at least it's income on the short term.

I'm glad to be sitting in this bar now, glad to be in

London. Stranded and a little sad, but the general pace of life in London will help me get moving again soon, I hope. Life was going so fast, I couldn't see the seconds tick, and now, everything is in slow motion. Soho again, but this time I'm up, and I'm out, all alone, and pretty wasted.

There is no money in the bank, no safety net, and I'm falling backwards and upwards into the stars. My heart is an astronaut. I'm not sure what will come now: there is no plan.

I went to see a friend and his band at the Gibson studios. We went to the pub later. The barman, I don't know why, I just fancied being with him. This time I didn't even lose any phone, I just waited until the pub closed, went outside, then went back to the door after about half an hour, looked through the glass and smiled at him. I lit a cigarette outside the door. He opened the door himself, with the words: 'The pub is now closed, you can smoke indoors'.

He asked what I was drinking, I asked for double vodka, neat. Once he was done closing off, we went to bar Italia. He seemed pale and low, like someone who had known sunnier days.

I don't know what exactly had drawn me to him, perhaps his tall, strong appearance. I was talking to friends about my job in Classics and my recent arrival, and he was behind the counter at this old Orwell pub in Fitzrovia, taking part in the conversation as if we were all old friends.

He said his name was Ed – this apparition of a man, balancing two pint glasses as if he was about to juggle, leaning back with a sarcastic and self-sorry grin, tall and strong in a trashy surf boy t-shirt, and his eyes were lively and mischievous. I instantly knew that I wanted him. I sat there, leaning over Sophocles. He took great interest in the

[196]

handwritten Ajax translations I was stuffing away in my handbag in order to talk to him, in fact he read them through like an expert in the middle of the night, deep in some basement night club where we later ended up. He started talking about his own dreams for the future. As he was a trained lawyer, he was thinking about studying in detail the legal history of the seventeenth century. I asked him more about that, and as he sketched the subject in a few sentences, I began to think our conversations could become much longer, perhaps even never ending.

We walked up from Fitzrovia to Bloomsbury, stopped by a design shop window to look at furniture, small-talking about types of designs we liked. He looked up at the houses, pointing out Poseidons on Victorian façades. Then we discussed the style and rendering of Greek and Roman Gods in architecture as we walked underneath chunky and nervy victorian Poseidones, Britanniae, and Hercules. Another night, our topic was Napoleon, as he eagerly explained to me on a stroll down Greek Street all the details of the battle at Waterloo and the strategic mechanics of the use of local farms as military bases. Another time, upstairs the O-bar bar, it was Herodotus we talked of. I had access, in my mind, to learned memories of all sorts, and could have carried on talking for nights and days on end.

The waiter in Bar Italia, when he saw me, asked me where I had been all this time. I frowned, unsure as to what he meant, until it crossed my mind that he might have recognized me from years ago when I had lived on Frith street. We established that yes, he used to see me pass by the bar every afternoon.

'America', I said, 'I was in America, New York, New York.'

'Oh! Wow', he said, 'What is New York like? It is my

dream to go there one day...'

Ed was leaning back and listening in. I said that, well, in London, you'd come and you'd keep your culture, and be a citizen of the country you're from, still. In New York, you would arrive there, and soon, you'd find yourself saying that you were a New Yorker, and then you would be a New Yorker. I liked Ed. He was like me, not surprised when things late at night got a bit surreal. He's of our little tribe, I knew that from the outset. Where everything is fine, and is surreal.

Enjoying some good old Italian football on television with a tiramisu before us, it was about four in the morning when he chatted up a drag diva at the table adjacent, middle aged femme fatale in a huge fur coat: 'Is that mink?'

'Yeah', said she, in an extended, lascivious manner, adding gratuitously, and for the shock value: 'I'd wear a coat of human skin if it was nice and warm, you know. I just haven't tried that yet'. Then, she deployed a long story of her family tree, explaining how she was a descendant the Russian Tsar house, and a white Russian, and also offered a review of the entire royal family in England. Constantly throwing in 'and the worst of all is the Germans. I hate Germans!' with that unmistakeably pouty diva tone as only drag queens can pull it off.

I said to her: 'So, where do you think I am from?' - 'No idea, I cant pinpoint you'.

There was my sly man on the corner of Old Compton and Berwick Street, just as I'd walked around the block with difficulty as if that was some kind of risky balancing act, wrapped tightly in a long black coat, a scarf over my mouth, hoping to catch the underhand eye of a dealer. I knew it would happen, and, as predicted, it happened.

A middle-aged guy in hoodie emerged from the shade of

[198]

an alleyway, cleared his throat ominously and asked for a cigarette. I took my time getting it out, smiled and asked casually: 'So, what are you doing out here, this time of night?'

'Helping the needy', he said.

Bingo.

I mentioned oxys, and we soon got chatting, about New York, about hip hop, about life in London, comparisons between the two cities. He had two chubby pitbulls on a leash, and a walking cane in the other hand. We walked around arm in arm for a little while. He was enjoying himself having a random stroll, nodding at various people passing by, and introduced me to a small, older man in a blue cashmere coat and hat.

'This lady wants two balls', he said.

'Two balls?' the old man frowned at me, avuncular, Caribbean, whistling his astonishment. He turned around and pulled two cellophane wrapped balls out of his mouth, removed the outer wrapper and gave me the celluloid treasures.

'Two brown for the lady', he said. I slid two notes in his hand.

'If you want my opinion, try snorting them like cocaine', he said.

I went upstairs the O-bar, locked myself in the bathroom, then I sat down on the sofa with a vodka and red bull.

Memories shone like headlights, memories of times spent just above these floors, like a fish in a bowl, years ago in Soho when I could still see all the colours. Soho then was so beautiful to see, then, it was so colourful. I remembered a winter morning the snow had formed iridescent rainbows over these few, magical streets as they lay motionless in the silence of Sunday morning.

That shabby, heart-warming grocer's market on Berwick

Street, and the Italian fruit monger, who had reminded me of my Italian roots one day when he said to me in Italian: 'Do you want a half apple? Will you eat it with me?', and I said, in Italian, 'sure, how much do you want for half an apple?', and he said 'don't you worry, it's on me'.

It had taken me back all the way to my four year old self hearing church bells in my grandma's home village, with its cypress trees, its dry river in the summer, children playing with horses and riding bareback, and familial cemeteries in fields of brown grass, there, far away underneath the Alps, in the Italian North.

By chance, amongst the crowd of rush-hour shoppers on Oxford Street, I ran past Jonathan just outside Topshop – and I think he saw me as well. In the split second when he walked right through me, far too late to jump out of his way, I recognized his face. He was wearing an old leather jacket and looking very out of it. I thought about turning around or calling his name. I did not. Nor did he, either. I considered it. Everything was still red hot and just a few weeks old. If I had turned around that day, all this perhaps would have been just an eight week long lasting fight, in our long relationship, and we would have gone back to our usual tempestuous menagerie, in London, both of us, again. I thought about it, and kept walking straight ahead, into the nearest shop and up the stairs, where I stayed in hiding for a few minutes, my heart pounding.

Time went on, and I got sucked back to Soho like fish to the edge of their aquarium. I walked up and down Old Compton and Berwick Street with a glazed smile at all hours of the day and night, long after Ed had gone home. Life now was not only practically, but also conceptually, a maze. I had many softly glittering memories from that brief and surreal American fall that had passed by me, tears day by day, drinking at night, and still this gigantic sleeplessness, and a restless extroversion.

I was a rustling waterfall that could not stop talking about what had happened in America, turning the events around in my mind whilst I was circling and spiralling down Soho. Every stranger at the bar who talked to me would have to listen to me telling them what I had seen happen, and even if I had told it a hundred times already, it was too much to disentangle, and gave me shudders and creeps.

Imperceptibly, I chromed all the colours of my clothes to black on black, matte shining black biker jackets, jeans, studded belts, dark metal studs, patent leather boots and a black rose on my lapel, looking like some sort of a failed rock star dying of drink and drugs.

The fruits of my confusion wasted in the cold. Doors closed on me, venues shut and opened like the eyes of children, I just kept skipping to the next best open door at random. It seemed an endless parade of chandeliered bars, dark rayed with blue, neon light glows.

I met many people on those nights that I sat supine on the O-bar's deep leather couches, gazing into disco balls between silk lined walls, dreaming that I was blowing soap bubbles before me, and in every bubble was an enormous, all-encompassing glinting dark night with the howling wolves of the soul, black horses, evil kings and queens from old fairy tales, and mirrors leading to infinity. Somewhere in those scenes was I, chasing shadows, in the sinking castle of addiction.

A trio of young soldiers just back from Afghanistan sat down with me one night to tell me about their feelings of disappointment upon their return home, they felt often insulted by the anti-war voices which made their great sacrifices seem pointless, reminding me that it was a matter of life and death. They didn't say much about the actual war, but everything in their demeanour, in their way of speaking, seemed brutalized and shell shocked, as if their minds and hearts were bomb sites. We were the same sort of age, but our lives had gone so differently, and a great gulf of violent experiences lay between us.

A boy and a girl in hipsterish outfits were bouncing around the bar and taking pictures of themselves with everyone there with disposable cameras, posing as sex kittens, as pop stars, as hipsters. They were keen on getting to know me, we joked around, left the bar together and walked around in Soho as a trio infernale for the rest of that night.

I met more men, more women, always new people, at the O-bar bar, couples, groups of friends. I had a knack for getting easily welcomed into new situations, and there was a lot of conversation, I heard all about the lives of French tourists, Irish photographers, English writers, American film makers, Swedish musicians, Polish youths, Saudi students, Ghanan bankers, Swiss programmers, met their friends, their partners, swapped numbers with so many, got invited to their next birthday party... whoever it was, I kept finding conversation, stringing all of these pearls on a long necklace, a rosary of cheaply drunk and lonely hearts that seemed never to end.

I got friendly with the bar staff, too. There was a pretty faced, Italian tattoo addict, wearing a lot of black and looking neo-punk, and also, there was a short and sharp-eyed Englishman with sleeve tattoos, who had a witty sense of humour, who loved mixing drinks so much that he had done a degree in mixology, an expert at longdrinks and cocktails.

I particularly enjoyed meeting Gianna, a sultry Hungarian violinist with an impressive crown of golden curls springing and waving about her head all the time. She talked to me a lot over her counter, about her dreams of

[202]

becoming a painter and her artistic vision, a bright red and yellow, fiery, contrast-rich and carnal one. She had got all the supplies for oil painting, and was telling me on long evenings about her past loves, and life in streaming London.

Ed is not around anymore now, although he could be. It's killing me. It's not like when someone dies, falls extremely ill, moves to a place far away with the family, or if we fall out somehow and the matter is closed. Heaven knows I know when people don't talk to each other anymore, that it's bad news. And with this wonderful boy, no, this matter is not closed at all... he just stopped answering his phone. Plainly, everything is fine with him and plainly, he's just ignoring me. I may have given up trying to get his signal, but not given up the love and admiration. I cannot force anyone to come to me, but... I cannot stay still and pretend that I don't care, so this means I'm doing the unheard-of... running after a guy. In spirit. Holding up the good times, which consisted of only a handful of evenings.

I walked around blocks in search of Ed, three times, twenty times, the imagery of my mind dulled, turned in circles to nowhere, sunk in a moor of fog and confusion. London may be a large and densely crowded city, but I always have counted on running into people by chance fairly often so that I wouldn't necessarily need phone numbers or addresses to track a lost soulmate candidate. I was waiting for this to happen and somehow to run into the stunning Ed, inadvertently hovering around places and venues that I had heard him mention, but he never was around. Why didn't he call back, I felt rejected, but could find so many good reasons for this rejection that I didn't blame the nice guy.

The thought crossed my mind that I was in the process of

[203]

dying of heroin, and I looked like it, too. I was pale and thin, like an anaemic teenager. If I wanted to see people like him again, I could not present half dead and dressing up in glamorous disguises in order to give fine semblance to rotting bodies, and mask the death within... But it was very late to turn around.

Something in my memory was barred and my body turned into a doll-like mechanism with wheels and springs leading me wherever drug cravings took me, beyond good and evil, and this cold world wasn't mine any more. I wasn't sure whose, but when I saw from the corner of my vision, faces popping out of alleyways, hacked bits of memory as mutilated symbols cropping up through vapours, with my distorted perception of pain and feeling, sense and sensibility had gone out of the world just then. I slept for a bit at a table in Balans. With the brown, I could attenuate so much, make things so breathable and breezy. I don't know what it was but something was bluer, clearer, fears lifted, and I felt that there had come a big relief, a big forgetfulness, a swim in the river Lethe, one huge soap bubble of soft and pleasing shines. How baby blue and soothing was everything all of a sudden... all bodies white and soft, nothing angular to hurt your head against. Any part of the world could be paradise, with drugs like these.

This was London's Soho. I had lived here, before, like a fish in a dream, eyeing temptation and man's trespasses from the safety of a well watered bowl. Would I one day become what I once saw around me, the air I breathed for so long, and impersonate Dana, the befuddled addict?

November, 2009.
It seems that way now. I take her appearances. So here we are again, Soho, this time much is changed, I am one of them – I impersonate the life now that I was always so

[204]

hungry for. Did I come haunting at night streets that I knew in the daytime? My heart falls so heavy with every step, and I would like to escape. I don't recognize the person in the mirror, this paleness, and she is so skinny. I think right now I look really dead. I often find myself smiling for their cameras, thinking that maybe someone somewhere will see my face in months to come, as if it was the last time I could do that. What's to come, I don't know.

On a mild December night, in my usual smoothing daze, I saw opposite me a middle aged couple sharing champagne and with a bouquet of red roses on the table and making out looking very in love. The lady was a stunning blonde with red lipstick in a transparent red blouse, no bra. The man in suit and loosened tie, briefly got up to use the bathroom. I took the opportunity to compliment the woman on what a lovely sight they were, together. I didn't expect the reply 'oh, maybe you'd like to come down with us for a drink at our hotel later then?'

When the man came back, she introduced us. 'My wife likes hot girls', he commented, and, 'are we going down then?' He went downstairs for a moment, re-emerged with a wrap of cocaine, and the three of us got on a tuktuk right to the Strand Palace hotel.

The lady took her blouse off. 'You're still dressed', the man commented to me, don't you want to take your things off? Meanwhile, the lady produced a bottle. 'I'm testing hotels across the country, it's my job', said the man. 'But it's nicer to have a beautiful lady here with me'.

We spent the rest of the night, the following day, another night, and a part of the next day, making out over and over again, sleeping sometimes, taking turns sleeping, talking about everything we possibly could think of. I had some poems in my handbag, and read them *Prufrock*, and Tennyson's *Lotus-Eaters*.

[205]

They had, miraculously, a pocket full of Tramadol, which helped me stay with them for the time. Room service brought us coffee after coffee, cake after cake. When I eventually got outside and on the street again, they were packing to get on their way to the next city. I sat down at McDonalds on the Strand, thinking I had just walked out of a dream. Then, I made my way up to Berwick Street, and walked around on the arm of the dealer, and sat down, awaiting more random people to turn up to take me on their random adventures.

December, 2009.
I think I am going to die before six months. This brown use of mine really fucked me. If I take it, I'll die in a few months, and if I don't I'd kill myself sooner, I cannot stay without it, now. Oh the first few nights that I was back from the States now seem light years away. A destruction in the soul and body has taken place, that is hard to fathom.
Today, I impersonate the freaks, our old house mates. I become Dana, I become Frank, I become the crazy people that don't see the boundaries. Liz had once said to me about Soho, 'that did not seem to be your world', and now I see it, perhaps, but I'm right here, phoning the dealer to come into the Balans café.
He sat down, I was having a coffee and writing these notes, under the eyes of French guys in suits, who thought I would not understand it if they spoke about me in French. They said the usual nonsense about the victims of society, how outrageous it was that people are dying in the streets, what a shame, oh, and oh, I heard them. They're looking at me with that curiosity of horror, that same look, I get the impression, people used to have on their faces when they came to see public executions in the old days. I'll give them a good show, no bother. Through the

[206]

window, as I was having a cigarette outside and waiting for my delivery, they couldn't stop looking at me, this skinny, faceless nobody under a conservative black cashmere coat. At least, I've sewn silver dragon flies on my coat.

I didn't want to use drugs today, but I couldn't stay still. My veins themselves seemed to be making the phone call to the dealer, aches were gnawing my bones, and the shakes just breaking me down, crying, cramping. This night of saying no to drugs, will have ended here.

I walked in circles so long in search of the poetry place that by the time I'd given up searching and tried to enter a pub, they told me sorry, ten minutes we've stopped serving. What was that? The Crown, Beers and Ales, Wines and Spirits, right by the British Museum. Great. That Poetry Place Café I was looking for... I lost the plot around Seven Dials, like when in past years I couldn't find my shortcuts that I used to take, I lost orientation. It was Sunday night. I walked along Long Acre three times. Past the high street clothes shops, and round the back, by the formal menswear stores, hat shop, around the corner, on to Covent Garden, same old Vintage Gallery, street fashion stores in my back, and all of them closed. At the end of it all, the Masonic Lodge, three times I walked towards it, three times I did not walk all the way down, though I thought to cross Kingsway and walk over to Chancery Lane – it was reassuring, down from the British Museum, that those red brick buildings hadn't changed, red, like incensed, gigantic sugar cubes fallen from the sky, here they are. Here was the Russian bar, O-Zone, closed, unfortunately – 10pm on a Sunday night. Liz from Munich had been here in London briefly, and we'd had tea and champagne there on one of these bitter-sweet nights of old friend reunions.

[207]

I wanted a place to sit and think, not like my usual hangout between the chandeliers and mirrors on Old Compton, Wardour or Berwick Street, certainly not the Balans Café or Bar Italia, where my face was all too familiar. I wanted a quiet place, a new piece of paper, where I could write a paragraph or two.

I really don't think that I can make it back from here. Had two overdose accidents already and I don't feel good either on, or off the brown. Taking it kills me, but I can't live without it. I never thought this would happen to me, but I feel very ill, and I know that I'm dying. I'm really skinny now and never feel any pain. I don't feel good on drugs any more. Sometimes, I feel nauseous and get sweaty palms when I have taken a bit too much brown, my heart races and I can get completely paralysed. I need to shoot a ball four times a day, and it doesn't make me happy. I wasn't always like this. Been digging my own grave, without knowing it. My skin is so white now, it's verging on the blue.
The whole point of my leaving New England was because I wanted to survive and salvage my situation. And now I'm dying, my story with me, my grand plan. Nothing. Pretty awful ending, isn't it.

I made friends with an Irishman, who lived in an occupied house in Brixton and had a wondrous existence of frequent travel to mysterious destinations, whence he would return with photos of unearthly scenes and stories with wicked twists of insane proportion. There was an Alice-in-Wonderland, surreal and almost magical style to his mysterious prose writings that would pop up on blogs or magazines, and his life seemed like a work of conceptual underground art. We talked about a lot, we shared a lot, down to the last cellophane wrapped croissant. He introduced me to a French legendary singer who, like himself, had been living a life of surfing couches and living in the sphere of gift for gift and favour for favour economy. They were both a similar age, both had been young in the 1980s.

When Sandra and I first met on chalky frozen Brick Lane, she was standing on the corner in a big fur coat, leather gloves, fishnets, dark red lips and a low hat covering her face.

She had with her, for me, a bag of shoes in my size that she had been given, and I had brought her a pair of shoes, too, that I had in my possession although they weren't my size. They would fit her, as we had established on facebook chat prior to meeting up. We were both really happy with the deal.

We went for a cappuccino in a red velvet curtained bar. She sat there on the upholstered gold and purple couches, ladylike and regal, a black lace veil hanging down before her eyes, glossy nail varnish, playing with the coffee spoon. We talked in French, about the scene in Paris, the scene in London, and Berlin. We discussed Brel and Baudelaire, the art of bohemian living, in between those red curtains. I felt warm and dazed, and wrapped in magic here, and in the evening, I followed her to a gig, where she recited erotic poems, and sang old hits from her '80s successes, then presented small paintings she had been making.

About my studies and passion for antiquity, she had said, to my surprise, 'Ancient Greek! How original of you to choose that... nobody else does that. It's a great idea for a profession. You can do a lot of wonderful things, you're very young, you know'.

On the cold pavement along Brick Lane, I told her casually about my drug problem. I knew death was coming, in the near future, a fait accompli almost, and I wasn't even squeamish about it. She told me about addicts she had known, ways they had found to deal with the issue. That you'd have to be very rich to keep going and stay alive, that I would, like I said, most probably die if I didn't do something about it.

It was the first time I'd had the privilege of getting practical advice. Usually if I mentioned my drug habit, I heard only that I was going to die, and people didn't want to stand by that, or be my friends any more. Sandra offered to introduce me to someone who could take me to NA meetings, a singer. I texted him back and forth; a few weeks later, I was ready to meet him and had coffee with him in Hackney.

He was Greek, so we talked about Greece, ancient Greece. And about poetry, and song and music, and eventually, got around to the topic of drugs – and I began to retell all the darker moments of my life. He said he could take me to the NA, but I didn't join yet, not until some months later. My first and last candle-lit NA meeting in a disused church where emotional outpours similar to my own thinking and feelings came around from every member of the circle, showed me that it was possible after all to cure oneself of dependency. All these people had already done the impressive feat, now I knew it was possible. I remembered that I had, in the past, been greatly appraised for my literary work on Greek drama, that I could do more, given the right circumstances. I was determined to create these circumstances again. It was like a card castle, that fell. Let me try and build it all up again, I thought.

I noticed the extent of the damage one mid-morning on a bus through the city of London, the stressed and dressed crowd in suits and black coats was spreading the eminence of the brave new world I had fallen from grace with. Opposite me stood a man with white hair, beige coat and red tie, whom I was about to offer a seat, but it struck me that he smiled at me as if we had met before. His face was sunny and relaxed, leather briefcase balanced over polished shoes, standing head to head with a young blonde woman with pointy shoes and a reptile leather bag, looking moody. I suddenly realized how down-and-out I must be looking to everyone on this bus, with my non-straightened hair and far from sporting pastel button-down and discreet make-up. I rather had scabby arms and paint on my jeans, a ripped shirt, and American basketball shoes. Wearing shades in the grey London daylight, blurring out their voices with headphones, I thought to myself: 'these people here are aspirin-takers', and 'I've used too many hard drugs'.

I had got on the bus not knowing where it was going. But then of course I didn't know where I was going, so it makes a good match. The bus wasn't going anywhere near my house, but then, I didn't have a house, a home. All I wanted was to push my time before me. I couldn't face the pain, ever since I knew there was this island of the lotus flowers floating before my reach all the time I wanted to score again and again. I knew I would in time detach myself, if I didn't die along the way like shipwrecked sailors. I was just beginning to see the social rift I'd have to jump. I would have to build bridges over the awkward frown of the bourgeoisie. If I survived, my anger would be boundless, and I would shred to pieces the safety net of social judgment, and tear up a few frowns.

When Andrea phoned from Hungary, and I told her how I was, she suggested I visit her in Budapest over the Christmas holiday. I thought it could be my chance to get unstuck from my self-destructive behaviours, and I travelled spontaneously, shades on, cigarette in hand, with a relaxed feeling of rejoining a loved one for the winter holiday.

[211]

Christmas, Gatwick Airport

I think my pain is better. I've travelled too much, though, right now I'm on my way to Budapest, from London, and it seems to me this morning as though I'd woken from a deep and unwakable sleep that like death itself, tortures me in hell among strange and malevolent beasts and evil onlookers, destructive orders and strange noises drenched in a bloodstained dark red light that smells of decay and stale breath, spreading nausea and disheartening sweat. Relentlessly bad premonitions, and bad news upon bad news, are hushed from unknown loudspeakers.
It is just how I imagine the underworld, something post-virgilian and post-dantesque, and my own schizoid bouts, in essence, what I have described here roughly is the setting of my nightmares, a wordless and unhappy land that bulges underground in labyrinthine caverns, and that I must traverse in silence.

This same old country of devils, to which I often return during my sleep, has been creeping into my bloodstream by day. Lately, I have started sleeping a little more than since I came off zyprexa. I've felt trapped in this imagery even during daytime, felt its vibes against the gently breathing membranes of reality, more and more I could not believe the life and colours of the daylight world if I ever happened to be up in the hours of light, I could not have felt more estranged from the British red brick simplicity, smart casual clothes and standard English fragments in polite turns of phrase, echoed across the service sector. And of course, full-on sunlight onto myriad signs and posts prohibiting, warning or requesting or whatever, instructing the population in desirable
[212]

behaviour, patronizing the general public 'Please leave quietly', 'It is against the law to smoke on these premises', 'Wear your seatbelt at all times', 'considerate builder scheme', 'do not feed the birds', 'CCTV is in operation for your safety and security', 'queue starts here'...

I arrived in Budapest. I feel nauseous and my legs and arms, and back, and hips, and ribs, and hands, and fingers, feel as if every bone in them had been broken, and all my muscles drained of blood. I can move only with the greatest difficulty, my stomach is cramping up a lot and my skin is full of rashes. I find myself scratching it a lot, often absent-mindedly, a vague state of panic is constantly imbibing my mind.

I have eaten everything that I could lay my hands on and I'm still very thirsty. These Hungarian mornings, that are so full of cold, quiet, and the silent realization of just how alone I am, like a ragged rock on the sea, are getting a lot of hot air out of sight.

Where have they all gone, who wouldn't let me go, who were getting impatient with me so easily, these strangers I followed from purple velvet bars to their cream and white hotel rooms as if I really was a disposable toy... Scoring heroin, that grand and all-soothing glitter of dreamt worlds, I felt so warm and lucid in its narcotic embrace, but now I haven't got that, I just want to die. Now, holding myself, in my own embrace, I have to drag myself towards the window to look outside and admire the sunlight, and I have to use extreme effort to drag myself away again from those windows. I want to jump. I can't make two thoughts meet.

Again and again, I see those heart-tearing images flashing in and out of view: Laurie's scared and humble smile, the beautiful hair that is now cut, all the memories, one by one, in a long row of black pearls.

[213]

Some of the gaps in her story are filled in by my own experiences, which are almost identical to hers, and translated to her situation: doctors, cold and white, windowless, locked hospitals, bully nurses, constant sirens and scenes of violence and broken resistance, curses, screams, blood and broken noses on turquoise linoleum tiles, four point restraints, electric shocks, armed patrols, mouth checks, blood checks, and a thoroughgoing destruction of the mind.

Humiliation of the proud, disfigurement of the beautiful, dulling of the brilliant, breakage of the wild. Shocking.

I don't think I need heroin any more, but I'm chemically addicted to it. I am trying to fight the pains of withdrawal in my knees and stomach. It does feel like all my bones are broken, and I'm harming myself a lot, to divert the feelings of pain.

I have not gone far enough yet to cover and soak in peace that great pain. I nearly froze to death in the streets once during an accidental overdose. I wish I could put my body through even more extreme pains so as to forget about that other stuff.

It's half past nine in the morning, I have been up for a while, woke from a confusing dream with a dirty feeling, and went to the kitchen. I had a terrible stomach ache because since I've got off h I've been eating with no end. And it seems I've put my back out. Everything hurts.

As I looked out of Andrea's window, I felt the swathes of broken gazes of fat, swollen, middle-aged patients in the American hospitals stab me from within. And I felt that this practice of shutting them down on antipsychotics had already come so far it would be impossible to stop this now. Impossible to stop the all-covering wave of silence and lethargy, and what am I doing here so wide awake, restored to life from the shock.

[214]

Sebastian had tried to wake me, often, before it got too late. Laurie herself had tried to wake me up. She'd tried it right in hospital, and tried it more. Now, she has been through ECT and is never ever coming back. The girl is alive and yet already buried, and she is buried forever. I can't draw her out of here. I walked in the dark, in the rain, in Soho and East London, falling over often and contorting my joints, scratching walls. Laurie isn't going to come back again ever, nor is she dead.

Oh well, this heroin use of mine, I don't mind it of course but it changed my whole life planning like no more future no more job no more nothing, just drugs and getting the money in for that, and the pain of cravings, withdrawal, swiftly remedied, in an endless loop.

I felt awful at first when I cut myself off drugs, I imagine it like birth, when they cut the cord on the baby. Then, I felt ok for a while, and suddenly my feelings went deeper and deeper backward, like in a spiral they seemed to go from bad to worse and even worse, so painful that I couldn't hear what people were saying, just wanting to tear my lungs out and wishing my stomach was gone. That pain I felt then showed me just how terrible the whole situation was.

I had sleeping tablets with me, I took a good few and fell asleep, and when I woke up I just had water and more sleeping pills. I think I slept for a whole night, day, night and a day, with only short hours of grey wanderings in dressing gown, ascertaining where I am, in Budapest, and the streets are snowy and frozen over. Tried to get up, several times but fell back asleep.

With this exhaustion aided by sleeping tablets, I had broken through the wall of my grand insomnia. A whole

[215]

year, practically, had gone by since I had stopped zyprexa and now only I was able to sleep again. Now, by contrast, I was exceedingly tired all the time. Waking up, I was feeling like suicide, feeling ravaged, stabbed to death, and lonesome... there is a special silence in those last few seconds before you kill yourself, and some kind of sudden doubt about what if there is an afterlife, after all? And then you know, even if it just got really bad, you're not a quitter, you're a survivor. I am terribly tempted to jump out of this window. In the sub-zero of a foreign country, isn't that simple, in the snow.

Some days I remember doing nothing but lying around in drifting coma, outside in the cold, but it seemed to me that I was on a beach in the sun.

Not so long ago, after I had overdosed on some codeine and found myself breathless in the cold someplace in North London, I thought of only one thing: '...not to faint now ...'.

Death never comes at a convenient time. I was so flippant about it all, but when it was near, I tried to trick it into going away again. I panicked, when I realised that I couldn't breathe any more because my lungs seemed to be paralysed, and my heart was going crazy, racing, flattening, pumping, stopping. My hands got sweaty and cold as I lay on the ice, I knew that if I fainted I could freeze to death. There was nothing I could do now, except focusing on the practical part of survival and hope my strength wouldn't fail me all the way through. I tried not to panic, and I tried to breathe, and it was good.

It took a couple of hours to get down from this, for the rest, the trip home, I was just trying to get better, breathe regularly, and when I came home I was exhausted, lay down and chilled out in the dark, in my usual untidy, situationist room. I was lying on my back, breathing in and out, thinking nothing, if not "wow, the world is beautiful".

[216]

The vodka levels went down to dry in my room, the wine I had, and I bought more, more, more codeine, Nurofen Plus from the pharmacy counter, I don't even want to know how many packets I got through in just a few days, using cold water extraction like a professional tramp.

Anyhow I'm moving in with Gianna from the O-Bar, we want to buy a piano. If I can manage and lay off drugs, I think I can get some kind of job. I have been saying yes to all jobs that came up, ended up being able to do none almost, slowly but surely drowned in vodka and opiums, and staring into the lights at the o-bar, and this spectral obsession with the lovely Ed. If I could get off to a fresh start in my life...

I met the fantastic Mr. Raymond on the internet whilst browsing e-bay for pianos. An ad had come up for a Bechstein grand costing £300. A page opened up with an impressively long scroll of text about some stranger's romance gone by in the 1960s, presumably a love story from the seller of this piano himself. There was mention of a red Maseratti, moped rides to the English seaside, pin-up girls and shaking the hand of the Red Baron. There were videos of vintage flying planes, photos of the original woman Mercedes, and talk of blondes walking in and out of the Ritz Hotel where Ray, the writer of this love story, had once been a pianist, just like his father before him. There was talk of his girl's hair, which blew in the wind as they raced to the beach on a vespa in the summer.

The Bechstein itself was described in high notes of praise and Liberace glamour, the story of its travels traced from Germany at the turn of the century, its first owner in Berlin, and its subsequent transportations around the continent all the way to England into the hands of Ray at a piano auction in the 1990s on Red Lion Square.

[217]

There were photos of a lonely old and ornamented grand piano painted burgundy red all over, silver streaks over maple wood and shots of its gorgeously carved note stand, legs and re-stringed, overhauled, gold plaited interior.

There were videos of a headless pianist in a white suit and tie playing ragtimes on it in between shots of cloudy landscapes, footage of world war two and a parade of old erotica. Then, the headless pianist got up and started speaking with a fake foreign accent about the Bechstein, as if it were a woman, and commenting that the hardest thing about selling this piano was the decision to do so, and that no bid less than 80,000 would be acceptable, aforementioned 300 pounds being for the delivery.

I looked at it all with amazement and wrote this seller a note on e-bay, saying that although I could not afford the piano, I had very much appreciated the presentation. I soon received a sweet and effusive response beginning with 'My dear baby', rambling on at some length, as well, talking about these same people from the Ritz and the old love story, as if I knew them, too. We kept writing to each other, a concentrated sequence of facetious and sometimes serious messages, until I dropped.

He said that he was a piano dealer, and had many more pianos to sell, and that he was living on the English countryside on a large farm he had recently bought to store his pianos and run a piano workshop. I had mentioned that I wanted to buy a piano, but couldn't afford his ones. I explained that I wanted to get an old piano for my flatmates and myself, that we were an artist flat share, and wanted a piano to mess around with in the lounge, an old piano that we could symbolically open up and prepare new sound waves with tin foil and plastic wrap between the strings, dress it up, and make short films... He said that I should just come to his house and see what he had: a white Steinway, a black Broadwood, a white Blüthner, an American Steinway, all sorts. So, one day in January I got on a train to Grantham, Lincolnshire, where he said he would pick me up with his golden Merc. When I arrived and stood on the station hill, there wasn't anyone there.

After a little while, when everyone else had long left, a red and gold sprayed, 1970s model 3-door Mercedes came up the hill and out stepped, in burgundy velvet jacket, white trousers and polished shoes, bleached hair, pink blusher on his cheeks, clown eyebrows and manliner, pink shirt and golden tie...

'I thought it couldn't be anyone but you'.

As he ushered me into his car, on to a sheepskin seat, announcing an eighty mile drive, he waved plastic bags of charity shopping at me : 'I got you some fancy dresses and shoes. Look at these fantastic golden sandals. I wasn't too sure what size you were but I think this will fit you. I discovered you can buy all these clothes, a dime a dozen in the charity shops' – 'yes, you can. By the way, is there no public transport at all to get from here to your place?' I was thinking, what if I want to leave later in case he's horrible and won't want to drive me?
'I don't know! I guess there must be, but I just always drive'.
'Sound good, so, this is Lincolnshire then, is it?'
'Yes, the country from where back in the 1600s the founding fathers first went to America...'

We decided to get sandwich lunch in a Grantham hotel first, a very beautiful, old fashioned hotel with waitresses

[219]

in white aprons and paintings of hunting scenes on the walls. We ate traditional roast beef and horseradish sandwiches with our tea, then drove to Boston, which, I realised, was a small and run-down village in England not all too well helped by the recession.

'What is it like for you to be living here as an eccentric, in a small depressed village like this, you must be the main talking point around here?'

'No, not really', he answered. 'I've only just moved here a couple of years ago, and I always keep my curtains drawn. Nobody knows what I do indoors. For all I know they don't even know that I play the piano. They would be talking so much, wouldn't they, if they knew...'

Alarm bells were faintly ringing in my head about how sound this stranger was, but I thought, well, it would be silly, wouldn't it, now that I have come all this way, to pull out of this now. Let's go into it, let's see this farm, let's see what he's got there.

He parked his red and gold Mercedes around the back and showed me, behind the farm, his red Maseratti, an old Chrysler and an enormous caravan that he also owned. We entered through the front garden and passed by an awfully kitsch mini-fountain adorned with a green and red Christmas light chains, which he seemed to be particularly proud of.

'Beautiful, isn't it', he turned to me.

'Sure is, uh-huh'.

The curtains were drawn indeed. In the hallway, two white grand pianos stood back to back, a black and cream Steinway in the corner, and an oak Blüthner stood just in the front, opposite a black and red upright with battle scenes painted upon its panels.

[220]

A few lids of grands were leaning up against the wall and an ivory keyboard stood vertically, with what looked like a blue, gold-buttoned, brass band jacket hung across it.

In the kitchen stood the red, silver and maple wood majestic Bechstein from e-bay, along with a terrific concert grand Steinway. In another back room, probably the former stables, he had put a red carpet and a small stage, upon which stood a beige lacquered baby grand looking down on to a mid-century black grand, whose lid had a butterfly wing painted on it, packed closely opposite a couple of other baby grands jammed next to each other and protected underneath some large cloths.

In the third room, the 'art room', there were paints, brushes, and pieces of yet another grand piano that was being painted gold and white.

Like a child in wonderland, I went around admiring all the pianos in detail. The grand pianos sometimes had artwork on their inner lids, that would pop up as a surprise when the piano was opened. One of the white ones I opened, had an inner lid painted simply in bright red, lacquer polished like a mirror. The black and silver Bluthner had the image of a blonde woman with stars in her hair, painted upon its inner lid. It also had 'Steinway' stuck in golden stick-on letters right where it should say 'Blüthner'. The other white piano had 'Polanski' and photographs of the girl Mercedes sprayed on one of the boards.

The butterfly wing piano was called 'Schmetterling'. There were pieces of other pianos, and bits of Liberace-style stage costumes, scattered everywhere.

The upright with battle scenes, he explained, was representing the battle of Trafalgar. One piano had a poem written in gold paint inside the lid, and another Steinway, which was half-black half vanilla, lined with silver, and it had a name. It was called 'Vanilla Skies'.

[221]

There was an old Clavinova in the corner and books about the house of Steinway and the life of Mozart on the shelves. Ray stepped toward one of the white pianos and whispered to me "this is the magic piano. Every time I play it, I compose something beautiful".

He took me upstairs. In his bedroom he flung open the doors of a massive wardrobe, full of white, gold, silver, tiger and leopard printed suits. There was also a red top hat, and a collection of flashy fur jackets. There were countless shiny polished shoes, heels, white hats, black hats, white gloves, and various biking equipment.

'They were my father's, and later they were mine. This jacket was worn by my father in 1963 when he was playing the requiem for a wedding in Westminster Abbey. Westminster Abbey, can you imagine?'
He told me his life and the life of his father as entertainers, how they used to live in a caravan, in hotels, play at lavish parties, and wear those glittering jackets and uniforms. He said that since his father had died, things for him had become quite lonely, and that he and his brother decided to buy this farm on which he was now living. The recession had been a harsh blow for him. He said that if he didn't sell a piano soon he would be quite broke, because he didn't have any good bank account, as he served up frozen fruit salad from Aldi and a home-made Curry.

He showed me the charity shop clothes he had bought for me, leopard prints were particularly prominent. He asked me if I had brought along stockings like he asked. I said yes. He said show me how you play. So we went back downstairs and I played bits of Beethoven to him, bits of Schumann's Carnival. Part of a Liszt Rhapsody.
He gave me an old biker jacket of his, which he said he

had grown out of since he had acquired a belly. We started filming as I got into the various costumes. He said that he would like to post them on his seller's website and he would give me commission.

We dusted pianos, shared some stories, made videos, until it was no longer possible to stay awake. He undressed, down to a pair of white lace underpants in front of me, and stood there in his skimpy lace and make-up, ready to jump into bed. I fell on the satin, rolled to one side and fell asleep. In the morning I went home. He gave me the biker jacket to take home as well as an American flag from the 1960s, a photo of his Chrysler, and an old violin, which I was keen to give to Gianna.

I went to a friend's comedy show, I had not seen him in ages. I went there in Ray's funky biker jacket. It was the time just after, when I was almost constantly smiling to myself, drinking sparkling water, so happy to have survived the drugs.

Four; Calypso in Mayfair

Shipwreck, Revisited

When I got kicked out of my flat, all my credit cards were overdrawn and the banks writing me threatening letters. Friends had closed their doors to me, some, as they later explained, because they foresaw my death, which frightened them, and others, because they had lost their trust in me since I'd become a drug addict.

I went to visit a friend, Sylvia, at her tattoo and piercing studio on Berwick Street. I had met her when I first arrived from New York and had got a row of dermal anchors in my back, alongside the top of my scarification. She stood arched over her reception counter, a girl of the same age as me, but already a successful businesswoman with a large and well located studio, smiling under her ultra-long false eyelashes and Amy Winehouse hair, leopard print and popstars tattooed on her shoulders, glamrock tattoos on her chest, prison tattoos on her hands, skin divers and small diamonds studding her entire self, a row of knuckles in her underarm, split tongue, and under-collarbone piercings peeping out from a fluffy pink playboy cardigan.

"I've just lost everything", I told her, "can I hang out here for a bit? I have to think about what to do"... She gave me a big hug, and a mug of tea. We chatted about everything, family worries, people we both knew, what we would like to do in the future, who we were. She jokingly said "I suppose you could have sex for money, you're very attractive..." and I said I didn't really know where to start that, but the idea seemed funky at the time.

I loved Sylvia, she was so youthful, yet so rich in character and experience, and her universe of urban jewels, body art and graphic motifs, tattoo artists, piercers and suspension lovers, graffiti, pop styles and fake furs, was like a hard pounding dream for guests to walk around in.

I was always magically entranced by the world she had created, and could trust always to find in her a sweet and relaxed, non-judgmental and welcoming friend with lots of quirky ideas and mischievous plans. We giggled a lot and concluded I had to go off on my strange ways and see what would happen, she gave me lots of good advice, and I was on the road again.

My credit cards may have been maxed out, but still, I had five pounds in my pocket. I deliberated whether it was worth trying to turn that into more or burn it on something silly like a drink, decided for the latter, and went to the usual place, the O-bar in Soho. I had become friendly with the bar staff to the point of moving in with Gianna – although right now, she had just told me to leave – but Gianna had moved on to Ronnie Scott's, and there was only Drew left that I knew, the Englishman with sleeve tattoos. We had often had long chats over his counter or nocturnal walks at the end of his shift, copying Ed's custom of superlate coffees at Bar Italia. Drew was always keen to hear my stories, he seemed to think I was a wandering book of surreal stories, and he enjoyed hearing me tell them. He had a high and crystal-clear laugh, and would share a story too.

Delightful as it all was, Drew couldn't do much to fix my rotten finances, and I had to move on. The night was starting to turn into day. I walked a pensive few rounds around Soho on a chilling morning in March, and at about 3 a.m., one of the drug dealers from the street corners approached me. My erstwhile drug dealer himself was just in jail, as I learnt, then. This man only knew me by sight. They all knew me by sight. Sometimes I had mused upon

[226]

it, that this second time for me in Soho, I was in the flesh of those I'd previously eyed from my silent window sill; copying their manners, becoming them. But a man was on the corner and talking to me. He asked me if I wanted anything, and how I was. I told him the truth, that I was not using any more.

'Congratulations, he replied, so you be hustling down here now?'

I was too tired for lies, and told him the truth again : I was doing nothing, hoping for something to happen – I knew it would. Hadn't I come looking for trouble, and hadn't I just found it. He suggested I help him with his business. He suggested we go around the clubs offering a joint package of charlie and blowjob.

'You do blowjobs, right?', he asked me.

'Sure', I said.

We started walking, small talking, 'but first of all you're going to give *me* one'.

Okay, I made a wild guess and named a price, he was agreeable on 40 pounds. In a Bloomsbury doorway, with a view on the British Museum, and trenchcoated couples tumbling by, inside of this blue and drunken, half-skewed hour that is 3 a.m. With that, I had some money in my pocket.

I lost that blowjob money just an hour later : the next person I met lost it for me at the casino. I had latched on to this next boy like a mollusc to a rock, walked next to this blond and blue-eyed youngster with dark frown, all night and all morning. We reached Parkside strolling over a dawning, glaring Oxford Street, sliding up and down Hyde Park corner, looking up to the Hilton when we came back through the green waving at equestrian police, looking nostalgically behind Jags and Ferraris, I slipped on a wet metal floor plate underneath a marble arch. He laughed, and said to me 'you and I have only just arrived, and now,

[227]

we'll make a brand new start of it.'

We had coffee in Leicester square. He disappeared in the Imperial Casino for a few minutes, I talked to the white gloved security man in his grey penguin jacket and top hat, who seemed younger than me, baby blue eyes shining out of a moon face with a naivete I could not quite explain. My guy re-emerged, just finishing a phone conversation in a language I couldn't understand. The door man bowed and nodded his urbane goodbyes, we smiled, walked up to Chinatown and into the West End through the parks all the way to Kensington.

Around the South Kensington tube station, we had Italian coffee and waited for alleged friends of this guy, who he said would soon show up for drinks. I looked right into the coffee cup of some Englishman who, I realised, I knew from the big screens, an actor; ageing, navy blue cashmere coat, designer glasses, reading his newspaper, hearing bytes of French from every side as we walked on.

As half-forgotten things, after such a long time spent in the dark night of drugs and a cold-blooded lifestyle, I noticed the window of Christie's. 'Oh, Christie's!' I said.

'What's that?' he asked.

I told him it was a famous art auction house, he said: 'it's good that you notice things around you. That way, you always know where you are, so you don't get lost that easily'.

Life had no end and no tomorrow, and I saw again, as half-forgotten things, the beauties and marvels of London : how beautiful Harrod's looked at sunset, a chain of lights tracing its architecture flashing up gradually.

Enclosed by monumental jewels, aspiration of a resting giant, here we were, a little couple of rascals throwing

[228]

their spirits up high as a diabolo, wading through the sky-high vestiges of that old Empire, the eye of the 19th century, with its imperial thoroughfares still broad and dreaming of battleships that sleep in the lulling breeze of great seas.

Awakening Londoners there were breathing a crisp, graphite-filtered morning breeze on Piccadilly, snobs waved their ties at little divas in plumy skirts, sharp suits, and starchy collars...

One hundred years later, the buildings are sombre, half-adorned with broken neon, discoloured curtains, rained-over canvases to advertise dated musicals, an awful dissonance of small businesses, here and there, flapping flyers, torn bills, porn card photos hissing on the floor like dead leaves in autumn.

March, 2010

Men and women greet each other under cover, a phrase I'd written once about London when I'd observed subliminal webs of knowing looks exchanged among strangers, I saw I had broken far into the core of this mystery. Men and women greet each other under cover. They really do. Amongst the millions that this city holds, on all your indeterminate routes, you become more and more sure of how to find a stranger who won't be such a stranger; and then, London is so densely populated, you know right away that you will never be alone. Lonely perhaps, but never alone, neighbours and brothers will always be arguing on the phone, shaving electrically or watching television when you want quiet, and there will always be everyone else's air vents to stain your kitchen window.

As we came back into Soho, I old him, my blue-eyed dark-angel-man: 'This house on Frith Street. I used to live here, you know. See how quiet the night is? I've always loved this about Soho, how quiet it gets when it sleeps.' There were no cars, no people, only paper foil circling in the wind on the pavement.

He was having a hectic few days, running through the city, never laughing, dodging all the fares and fees like a master trickster, popping in and out of casinos a lot, a little addicted to gambling perhaps.

We kept going in and out of the Piccadilly casinos, and I heard him speak on the phone in a language I not only didn't know, but couldn't recognize. At the poker table, everybody spoke it. Three guys, friends of his, I presumed, were sitting around playing cards and empty espresso cups in a red velveted interior, opposite a Japanese, insane-seeming man in suit and tie at 5a.m., I was the only woman. Everybody smiled at me and I, cloudy lemonade in hand, thought I had momentarily been catapulted back to my childhood in Italy, with these men here sitting so comfortably around their cards and coffees, it was like on a dry and sunny afternoon in my grandmother's village. Add only, perhaps, the grandiose lustres, the velvet-lined interior, the carved crystal glasses, the leather and glass polished, red-illumined cocktail bar shining behind palm trees like an oasis in the background.

I liked everyone, instantly. I sat down with my man, and since I didn't play, watched the game for a little while, then let my eyes wander – politely, discreetly, inostentatiously – to the four corners of the room, and saw, in the right side of my vision field, two leather-jacketed, white-collared men, sitting by themselves further back in a darker corner, doing a little business: a roll of money hastily pressed into the hand along the bench, against a small, gun-shaped black object in bubble wrap slipping

[230]

over a leg and into the inside pocket of the other's suit. Once the gun was packed away, I pretended only just to have turned in that direction – in the event that they had noticed my gleaning. A handshake, and two satisfied faces, caught my nonchalant eye, and, unsure as to whether I'd seen the deal and its object or not, they looked at me for a brief moment with uncertainty, but I smiled placidly, and so, they both kept the smile on their faces, rising up to meet me.

My guy was holding me, I leaned back, smiled. I didn't know how I felt such perfect trust in these people, why I'd come along this far in the first place, but now it was practically as if we'd always known each other. Everyone was smiling lightly, enjoying the game of poker, the thrills of it, cups of espresso, they talked with their hands and I felt returned to Italy for a sequence of a dream, as it seemed, the spectre of Mediterranean living seemed erect right here in London's dark and unworldly, subterranean paradise.

In an instant, I tried to remember all the finer and less brutal manners I had been brought up with by my international jetset parents and schools. Here, my knowledge of Italian suddenly became very useful, because the man, Louis, mentioned that he was Italian. So I said that I was as well. Once we started speaking Italian, it seemed to me that although he spoke it, it was clearly not his first language. So I asked him where exactly he came from, and he said Sicily. Althogh I had never been to Sicily, I was pretty sure it wasn't a Sicilian man I was looking at: with his blue eyes, strong cheekbones, and a brilliantined, black-loafered, black on black clothing style he looked rather more Ukrainian or Belarussian to me. On a second chance, only because I was curious, I asked again later over coffee and pancakes in Balans, 'what is your

[231]

first language?', he looked at me and said, dramatically, as if it were a secret: 'Albanian'.

'So you feel most at home speaking Albanian', I said, trying to do an encouraging smile. He, having apparently misheard 'so your home is Albania', blossomed a wide smile and started telling me with pride and stars in his eyes about the ancient mountains of his home land, the sea, the old trees and the beauty of his country.

'The only thing I know about Albanian culture...' I was going to talk about oral poetry and the research into it, on the Dalmatian coast, by a Homeric scholar of the early 20th century, but he cut me off, for the better, I assume.

'Ah, we have a culture, you have no idea! Beautiful, absolutely beautiful! Song, and poetry'... 'Yes, song, and poetry. I thought so', I thought to myself. And I also thought to myself, how very exciting now that I meet someone whose culture is still in touch with the ancient oral tradition of heroic song.

I did, in truth, find a strong sense of a code of honour, between all the men I subsequently met, as there was a clear-obscure ideal of what makes a brave man; there was the value of a beautiful, or a shameful way to die, or to live; rules for respectable living; things, I thought, that I was understanding through the textbooks on Homer more than anything, and once I had debated with myself whether or not this was a ridiculous comparison, and decided it was okay for me to try and use it in the absence of any other things that could allow me to make sense of what I saw, and heard here, I began to feel a little more familiar, and a little more secure in the interactions.

These thoughts were invisible to Louis, of course; still at that same table with the pancakes, I told him a little about myself, and said then what perhaps I shouldn't have, that I was alone in my life and without anyone to fall back on if something went wrong.

[232]

'Let's go for a walk', he suggested. 'I want to talk to you about something. And while I am speaking, can we agree that you don't interrupt me, you don't ask me any questions, you don't say anything, okay?'
'Okay', said I, and asked where we'd be going.
He said: 'No questions, remember?' – I laughed.
'Don't laugh. You'll be able to talk as much as you like afterwards. But for now, just keep your mouth shut for five minutes and listen to me, okay? Follow me, and listen. Because sometimes, five minutes can make a difference'.
OK...
'Come with me. I want to offer you something. Accept it from me, as a friend, I don't know you, but I see you are lovely and fresh, you don't have drugs in your eyes. You are very nice. You can just come with me, I will show you some places, you will make three, four, five, eight hundred, thousand, two thousand, every night. Don't be on the streets. I can get you into all the best places, nobody will touch you if you don't say so. If you don't like someone, you don't need to deal with them, and there will be lots of other girls doing the same thing, so you don't need to be embarrassed. They will be very nice. Some men make a lot of money, and they are so busy, they never have the time to relax. They are a little bit stuipd. They are rich but they drink, they do drugs, they party, they throw money out of the window, because in their head, they are messed up, and they have lost the compass. Lost it completely. But still, they are, all of them, rich businessmen, they are all very polite and very clean, not rude or bad to you. They are only lonely and confused. They will pay you, even just for a dance. They give all their money to you, and you, you know how to make money last, you do something nice with it, have a bit of fun, fix your situation. You can dance, which is the most beautiful thing a girl can do. You just dance. You do this

[233]

for as long as you feel is right, three months, six months...
until you want to do something else. I can show you the
places, and there will be nice girls, men walking in and
out, it's a business. The clients are real gentlemen and you
will use your manners. I noticed you have good manners.
Otherwise, I wouldn't have asked you. Everybody knows
me in the clubs and respects me. You can just go there and
say you are my girl. Nobody will ask you anything if you
say you are with me. Say you're my sister, my girlfriend,
ex-girlfriend, whatever you want. No-one will touch you.
Sometimes when a girl comes in out of nowhere, she gets
treated badly. But if I get you in, even like this, in shorts,
you'll be treated like the best from the beginning. What do
you say, yes or no?'
Yes.
Yes?
Yes.
Sure?
Yes.
You go with me?
Yes.
You are my girlfriend?
Yes.
Let's shake on it, and drink to that, I will introduce you to
some people now. Come!

Had I spoken the truth? I don't know. In my head, I was
twisting and turning all the possible risks and benefits of
this plan, evaluating possible disasters, the possibility that
the whole plan would come to nothing, compiling a list of
dangers to beware of, charting the likelihood of worst and
best outcomes on a dependency tree in my mind.
Eventually, I had reduced it to three possible outcomes:
either he would soon blow the whole thing off for any
given reason, or the scheme would go ahead and it would

[234]

be a complete disaster where he would pimp me out and work me impossible hours like I had often seen on news documentaries about human trafficking, or it would happen and he would leave me moderately in peace, with some possible ups and downs on the map.

I ruled out the possibility of gross and brutal things happening such as my getting shot or brutalized for running away, having an eye gouged out and such, on the basis that I was not an East European woman they had kidnapped and brought over with their own hands and money, but just some random girl they had met in London, thus an entirely replaceable bit of meat no-one would want to get their hands dirty killing. I did not quite realize that they all seemed to think that I was lying about being Italian, and that I was actually Romanian. They tried to get that "confession" out of me, but it couldn't be confessed, and they assumed I was homeless because I was on the run from some other crew of pimps.

Louis and I went to a phone box and picked up all the porn cards, phoned the numbers on them one after the other, but there was no response. We walked into a coffee shop, Louis said 'I'm looking for a person who is a regular customer here, his name is Tony'.

The girl behind the counter said she didn't know, but one slim and delicate, brilliantined customer in black riding jacket and velvet collar, turned around and said 'Tony? Tony?'

They looked at each other and said, nearly at the same time: 'Are you...?' – and then: 'yes', all three of us laughed, a conversation followed, he made some phone calls, and that night Louis took me to a basement flat in Mayfair. We were, both of us, pleased that it had worked. In fact we'd spent a whole two nights and days lurching around town and asking for auditions at the various strip

[235]

clubs, we'd even run into someone I knew from University, who recognized me, stopped me, and seemed inquisitive about what the hell was going on – I was in a micro mini dress then, wearing hold-ups and a leather jacket, you must know, and I did walk right next to someone looking like a pimp, which he was. I of course had been awfully embarrassed, as this wasn't the kind of adventure I'd have with my daytime person's face; but I have another face, and another heart, so dark and so cold, that lives its own life as I split my time. So I only told the young man on the bike, 'Actually we're late, I've got to go, we're going to meet some people at a nightclub, sorry, bye'.

It wasn't really a lie, although the good man probably took it to be some kind of ironic party disguise of mine, of ours; and in a way, it was a disguise; but a disguise that, somehow, was more about showing the truth than pretending fake facts, and because pretending fake facts was much closer to real life in the daytime, and nightly truths always adorned and fuzzed over with wine, and mares, and funky light: the outrageous reality worn with pride could just as well seem like a funky disguise. I was moving down circles.

I had been sitting at the club table with Louis and drinking grenadine and coconut, minty virgin cocktails, when a tall young man in white shirt came dancing my way smiling, said 'beautiful girl' and took me for a dance. I assumed he was a client. Louis wasn't paying attention, so I got up to dance. My dance partner, a banker from Argentina, living up to the cliché of the Latin lover, French-kissed me against a wall with a mouth all caipirihna, and touched me up through the dress, pulling it up improbably high, to the point of attracting looks.

An angry Louis came by asking what on earth I thought I

[236]

was doing, and I realised this drunken, embarrassing Latin lover was genuine. Louis and I left, arguing about what had happened. Louis was surprisingly pleasant to argue with. He didn't lose his temper disproportionately, and was able to avoid being pointlessly insulting to me even when he was angry, and he was happy to listen to me. We agreed that the whole thing had been a silly misunderstanding.

I wasn't being the solid me, I was being the nameless, the voiceless, the pretty face in a short dress, black lycra with diamante straps, and beneath the black fabrics, my pale, almost blue skin was glittery new snow. I was a silent, easy character, agile like a cat. Louis himself, who in the 48 hours that I'd known him had hardly once stopped running his hands over my features, stopping in corners to French kiss and send his hands along my back and stomach, into my underwear and into my lips, over and over again, couldn't resist sleeping with me. At his house (which, it turns out, wasn't really his but some nurse or doctor lady's flat in Denmark Hill, whom I only saw for a short moment before she disappeared again) we made love intensely and repeatedly, between showers, naps, and fried breakfast.

My life passed in revue before my eyes, I thought at times that I was dreaming, or on a sort of floating island, bathing in a warm breeze. I couldn't make sense of what was happening any more, I had only to forget about it all, the past, my fears, my sensitive and vulnerable soul, the poets, the roads of New York, the cigarette smoke in a Berlin bar, my sweet sixteen; all of the old life now, had to sink and disappear, as if it had all been a fabulously full and heavy laden ship that had ended up in a storm, a wreck, and sunk.

We were back on Leicester Square in the mid-morning and met with his friends, some of whom I remembered from the poker table. They had already started drinking and

[237]

cheered us on as we appeared. Now that I had locked away the old life, in order not to taint it with the brutish colours of a sex worker's blunt sensation, I found my own self curiously flat and vacuous, and began to develop an almost compulsive laughter, and comedic character traits.

I simply could not resist the temptation, at any moment, to crack jokes, and I convinced myself that laughing would help me cope. Having bought a change of underwear and a new jacket, I stuffed everything in my backpack. We walked; in the evening, we would knock on a basement door in Shepherd Market.

Gino let me in, a soft spoken, Asian kid in trackie bottoms, Snoopy t-shirt and highlighted hair, to a messy one bedroom flat with a bed in the living room as well, on which Dan was sitting, a young, tall male escort in hoodie, and with a scarred face, and on the couch by the game console and TV, a good-looking girl in jeans and t-shirt, with long brown hair, was lying comfortably stretching, watching MTV, talking on her phone, a pair of glittery stripper shoes thrown casually beneath the couch, biscuits on the coffee table.

He was sitting on a kitchen stool, offered me a seat. 'Do you understand English?'

'Yes, of course.'

'Okay, good. I'm Gino, I'm the boss here. So the prices are, half an hour is seventy pounds, and one hour is 140. Twenty minutes is 60. And we do half-half. Do you do any extra services?'

'Like what?'

'Oral without condom, anal sex, or kissing or whatever?'

'I do anal sex'.

'80 pounds tip, or you ask what you want, it's your business. If you need a shower, the bathroom is here. I will give you a towel'.

[238]

March, 2010.

Earlier on, I picked up a pill off the table, I read what it said on the back, 'Promethazine'. I asked Gino who was taking that here. He said that he was getting them from a doctor who was a client, whom he had convinced to prescribe them, as he could never sleep.

Had the first client, an octagenary in beige raincoat, who offered to be my sugar daddy, to take me shopping. We talked about movies and historical sites in Germany, and I said my favourite actor is Marlon Brando in A Streetcar Named Desire. *He asked 'what about* The Waterfront*' and I said, 'my dad has that jacket', then of course conversation turned towards Hitler, the Stasi, the 1980s in Italy, whatnot – he told me he used to be a spy before he retired. I joked 'So you are 007', he laughed. He said I wasn't like the others, offered for us to meet for tea at the Ritz, and then he would take me shopping. I said I already had everything I needed. He seemed surprised to hear that. We talked about pianos, too. We chatted for the full half hour, and he gave me a 90 pound tip, he threw it on the bed, some tens and twenties, and Gino also paid me £40 for the half hour. That was really easy money for a start.*

Louis came to pick me up again at three in the morning, we had breakfast at Balans, then went to stay at a hotel in King's Cross. In the afternoon I met Tony, the man in charge of a flat, and in the evening, was led to a basement apartment in Knightsbridge.

It was a Sunday night, business was quiet; the apartment had two majestic, silk and velvet draped bedrooms with tall, old mirrors and ornate wardrobes and inbuilt oak shelves, opening on to a back terrace with potted palm trees and a luscious living room with white sofas, a splendid white marble and gold-fauceted bathroom, and seemingly unending supplies of paper towels, baby oil and baby wipes, in the wardrobes.

A large bag full of sex toys – strap-ons of all sorts, whips, leashes, bondage tape etc. – was hidden away behind the sofa, another one containing outfits, nurse, school girl, police, choke masks, etc., was on the other side. Viagra pills (and now I finally knew who actually ever bought the Viagra pills that scammers don't tire of crowding everyone's box with) were in a gold and lapis lazuli vase on the fireplace, cocaine was in the kitchen under a loose piece of skirting board. All manner of phone chargers were in a white hat box on the shelf, and a large map of London before 1666 hung on the wall in the hallway. In one of the bedrooms hung a painting that I'll have found myself looking at an awful lot: a pointillist landscape, depicting the entrance of a vagina.

Six mobile phones, attached to six different porn cards in nearby phone booths, lay on the table and were ringing from time to time. A slim, tanned, pretty-faced blonde, was answering them in broken English.

One or two clients called in, she said they were her regulars, disappeared in the room with them for an hour, escorted them out afterwards with a friendly kiss on the cheek; it was a long, dark Sunday night in late March, and as she spent many hours of it shouting at someone over skype, in Romanian, I tried to rest myself or read.

She pointed to the couch and a blanket and said, 'if you're tired, you can sleep. There's not much going on tonight, Sundays here are always quiet. If a customer comes in, I'll wake you'.

She spoke Italian, and we talked a little; she said she was

[240]

twenty, she had been at the job for two years, that she was the girlfriend of one of the owners, that she was married to a policeman in Romania, that she was working five nights a week, sending money home, saving for a house, and for her retirement, when she would be twenty five, to start having kids. 'You don't know how many ugly things I have seen already in my life. But I say, everything in life, you have to try it, before you can say it's good or bad'. Well, certainly. I made myself comfortable and fell asleep.

When I woke up, she was in the arms of a short and stocky bald man puffing out smoke and smiling as he watched me wake up. 'Nice girl', he said to Louis, whom I now noticed sitting on the couch, too. I had never seen the bald man before, but was introduced to him as Tony's parner, Raffael, co-owner of this business. There was Tony, too, emptying a bottle of wine in the kitchen.
'How did you like it here?', he said,
'Pretty nice, thank you', I said.
'Would you like a job here? A regular day?' – 'Yes, sure' – 'Can you come every Sunday, and also, Saturday and Wednesday nights?' – 'Yes', I smiled.
He smiled and said 'okay. Thank you very much for coming tonight. If there is any problem, or any question, let me know. Let me give you my number'. We swapped numbers.

Louis, in the meantime, was getting ready to leave. He gestured for me to gather my things and come with him. We left, it was around 7a.m., and we slowly strolled to breakfast someplace in the West End. Then, we took a hotel. He asked me how much money I'd made so far, and if he could borrow it; saying that I wouldn't need it, if I went to work again in the morning.
I knew what was happening, I was getting pimped out.

[241]

Okay, so you caught me off my guard and I told you how much money I made, and now you want it all, I thought to myself. Right now, I cannot possibly leave. I'm alone in the hotel room with this pimp, he has my money, and I didn't have anything extra besides that what I gave him, and my old friends refuse to help me with money, because they think I will spend it on drugs. Besides, I cannot phone them, because my phone is out of credit and soon it will be out of battery, too. (I am tempted to throw it away. The phone was supposed to be for emergencies. Now is an emergency, but it doesn't work, because money is always king. Phones have never made anything safer for me, quite the opposite).

I still have no home. So this hotel, and this guy. I have to stick this out. I have to hide my money from him and others in the future. I will have a shower. A long shower. To relax, and to think about the a plan.

I was not perhaps the sort of frightened young girl from a small village in Lithuania these men were used to dealing with, whose reactions they were used to, nor was I quite as young as they seemed to suppose. Louis even quizzed me about why I wasn't in floods of tears, why I wasn't getting over-tired and nervous, why so relaxed.

I said nothing, and waited. I tried to sleep at work during shifts if it wasn't busy as much as possible, and to hide as much money as I could. I knew a little better than to call the police, I understood this was a well organized group, on good terms with the police, and if I tried to upset them either the police would have acted dumb or they would have come to me at a bad time. I knew this much. I had to find my own way out of this mess. Not out entirely: I did want the job and the money. But Louis had to go. I would have to use social skills, toughness, creativity, to save my own ass : everything.

[242]

But all this was yet to be mapped out and there were many dangers. I would have to use caution, intelligence and the good luck of a moment. Meanwhile, I was getting to know everyone.

There were habitually two madams, English ladies of a certain age, who spoke in strong Cockney and had had their entire bodies remodelled by plastic surgeons, were using botox, extensions, lashes, so that they looked deceptively much younger; they had infinite time for celebrity gossip, fashion magazines, and soaps on TV. With both of them, I talked through long nights. About their families, their children, both had mixed-race sons in prison, and girls in council houses, one with a four-year-old already; both had been depressed in their youth, and were on the disability allowance and housing benefit; neither was educated, one was bright, the other, not so much. They were both very friendly to me. The bright one, Joyce, had an infinitely extending vocabulary, it seemed, an excellent sense of humour, and quite a funky sense of style, I thought. She was perceptive, honest, and intelligent.

The other wasn't such an intellectual. Her speech was a little slurred, and she had trouble doing additions and substractions, one of her responsibilities as the madam, to be an accountant for the night. She was soft tempered, gentle, and generous, and yet somehow slow on the uptake and easy to fool, as she was hooked on Tramadol and charlie, which was shooting blisters through her brain. Her daughter, with the little girl, I met one night on the job, and with whom I stayed for some time as a paying guest, was even more dim.

The other lady, in any event, had managed to turn out one daughter who graduated in criminology, and one who became a hair stylist. With them, I talked for long

[243]

evenings, gleaned tips about the job, which I was learning, and heard all manner of things about the men in charge behind the scenes, and I began to crystallize in my mind the picture of who was who.

A French girl, tall, thin, red-cheeked, curly-haired, lipstick, gold earrings, and skimpy lace, was one of the first I met, and over cigarettes she told me she had studied geography, that she'd come to London and worked as a waitress initially, and had also somehow hooked up with a lad, who brought her here.

When she asked me if I, too, had an Albanian boyfriend, I said yes, she grinned, and said: 'At least you admit it. All the girls here, all of them, they all have an Albanian boyfriend. They don't want to say so. But I know they do. They all do'. She wouldn't say more.

The Ukrainian redhead, tall, green-eyed, black fishnets and heels, with this melancholy beauty that so many Caucasian physiognomies have, and who on top of this could spend seemingly neverending hours in front of the mirror doing her make-up and her hair, seemed to have such a boyfriend, too. She said he'd come with her from Canada, where she used to live, and brought her into this job in London; she wasn't proud, she said, ashamed in front of friends and family, that this was what she had become, a whore; she hoped she'd soon be able to get away.

Diana – a Polish blonde bombshell, only twenty-one, her voice as deep, and as smokey as Courtney Love's, only deeper, a broad-faced, wide-hipped lady with diamante where ever you looked, stilettos, wearing lycra and leather, and indeed smoking forty a day (like myself, at that time), had in her an irresistibly maternal, calming charm, and could produce the feeling of being full of Vodka only by her voice and her gently mumbled, reassuring words, 'Oh, darling, come, we'll have a nice time, handsome', etc. etc. She was a real diva, arriving every night with a designated

[244]

driver, courtesy of the client with whom she was living. She had a great sense of humour, and she'd spend a good hour cooking beetroot and sour cream soup in the brothel's kitchen for everyone to eat, nonchalantly slinging an apron over her red ruffled satin affair, stayups, and heels, or whatever she was wearing.

She wasn't as tongue tied as the other two; she was all the opposite, literally exploding with information, about herself, her boyfriend, her driver, who drove her to work and back every day; about her clients, her relationship with those ominous men; five years of London, Domino's pizza, All Bar One waitress, what have you, and one day, she tried the internet escort agencies, and somehow, another day, the brothels in London's basements, and she liked the money, and the life she could afford; it wasn't what she wanted to do for a living, but she wasn't very educated, so this was her only way to get quality of life... She was friends with the owners, and so was her boyfriend... Was he Albanian? No! Italian! She loved Italian men! She loved the food, too! And so it went on in an interminable flow, we laughed a lot, and we told us our stories as best we could, in the situation, interrupted by occasional client calls.

I'd had not many, but enough clients by a few days to feel comfortable enough in my shoes, when an older looking gentleman rang the bell. He knew the place. He walked straight down into the room and was standing in the middle of the room, in the red lamplight, his hat on the purple satin bedspread, when I, the third or fourth girl to be seen, came to greet him. I was quite good at greeting clients by then. I looked nice. From the sneaky erotica merchant who comes around brothels at night with a bag full of obscene goodies, I'd bought a black mini halterneck dress with a low back, which I wore with black thongs, patent leather stiletto shoes and hold-ups, I had long black

[245]

hair at the time, a slim figure with good breasts, and the more clients chose me, and complimented me, the more sure I grew that I really looked quite good, and my smile was ever more winning. The grey-haired gentleman, pinstripe suit, cashmere coat, cream shirt and grey tie, old briefcase, suede shoes, softly shimmering cufflinks, was keeping a stiff upper lip as I said hello, the light way, and so I was quite surprised that he chose me in the end.

I came back to the bedroom, meanwhile he was sitting on the bed. I enquired about the time he'd like to spend, took money for an hour, brought it to the front, and came back in saying something tacky like 'how are we doing in here, nice to meet you', lightly pressing my body against his and offering to take his shirt. I slipped it off him, gently, stroking his back a little, a cloud of cologne scent rose up. He got up to remove his jacket, produced a wrap of cocaine, and made some lines on the dresser. Removing more clothes, he offered me some charlie, which I declined with thanks, but he insisted. I had a couple of lines, he picked me up and placed me on the bed and started unwrapping his present, as it were, quite gently; he was kissing my hips, my stomach, and moved up to my chest, and lips. He looked me in the eyes and said 'you're simply enchanting', kissed my lips, rolled on his back and let me stroke him a little while, and I momentarily let my gaze linger on his hands; I took his hand, and found myself looking at a small golden ring, which had an insign on it. 'A wolf!' I said, desperate to get a conversation going, 'in fact, the she-wolf of the Roman Empire! How pretty! Something... et Avaritia – oh I can't read the beginning of the motto', he pulled away his hand. 'It's a family ring', he informed me. The voice was stern and formal again, now. 'My family is very well known in... Oh, um, well... I'm from Yorkshire'. I thought, and the coke also made me say, that I had a very dear friend from Yorkshire. 'He's also of

[246]

a big family. I guess you would know him in that case. Do you know … a young man, my age?'
'Don't know them', he said about the family, turning his gaze down as he shook his head, in a tone of voice that left everything ambivalent but reminded me this was thin ice.
'They must be Catholic?'
'Yes.'
'And what son is that?'
'Oh, he has many problems, he's gay, and that church, and that family, well, you know…' – 'oh, if you want to know about the Catholic church and the aristocracy in England! It's awful, god-awful! But, do read *Brideshead Revisited*. Have you read it before?'
'No, I haven't actually. I'll get a copy! I have time to read, these days, a lot of time to read...'
'Do you really?'
'Yes, in fact, at the moment, I…' and as he looked over at me, I suppose, in that very moment, I became a human being to him and ceased being a kind of plastic toy.
He sat up and looked me in the face, at the skin on my neck, and looked into my eyes, his hands folded in his lap; and I looked back into his, gently, and also inquisitively, and he adjusted his vision, from far to near, it seemed, to see me better, and briefly his gaze sank, and with it, his head, looking down on his own chest, wrinkled and white, he grabbed his shirt, started buttoning it down, leaned over to draw a line, and as he did so I helped him with the buttons; then we smiled at each other, and laughed.
'The paths of destiny are confused and discreet', I said. I could see that I'd struck a chord inside him, unintendedly, unexpectiedly. I was sorry, thinking that it must not be very nice to be an old man waking up to the reality that the woman you paid to take away your worries, turns around and puts you in a whole new position of shame. 'If you hadn't given me all this charlie, you know, I wouldn't have

[247]

talked so much. I'm sorry' – 'Oh, no, no. I think this is all terribly amusing. You're hilarious, and you're crazy, too'. – 'It's nice to meet you, you're a very nice man'. 'Really? Do you think so?' – 'yes' – 'I don't think I'm very nice. And I don't think anyone else thinks I am, either' – 'no?' – 'no'. – 'why?' – 'Oh I guess I've made some people angry, who... well. It's a long time ago, really' – 'oh?' even without the words to flesh it out, the story of a downward spiral in life, his life, had already told itself to me in these pained few words – 'you don't mind it, if I play around with your body for a bit? It's just such a temptation' – 'oh, please, that's what we're here for', again, we laughed.

After he left, I felt tearful and troubled. Impossible to explain. There was a lot of bad luck gathered here in this place, I realised. Bad luck masked and draped in the sheen of satin and diamonds, steeped in the glamour of provocation, indulgence, luxury and liberation, and I felt the warm and humid, plague-bringing wind blowing through these basement flats that smelled of air fresheners, durex oil, and sperm, as through a red-lit, mirrored maze underneath the ground.

I enjoyed the honesty, the simplicity with which everyone I met, presented themselves. After all, once you've already met in a brothel, what *do* you have to hide? Any social persona drops pretty much along with the clothes, and for a brief, stolen and secret time, all people are equal. Shame evaporates, and worries can be soothed, lifted, and dissolved, by lying on silky bedding in a haze of incense and perfumes, smoothing the line of an arched back, running hands over breasts, or tongues over neck lines, and letting soft lips and warm tongues search around for the infinity of orgasm, letting it in slowly, heightening the rush with cocaine, whiskey, or sparkling wine, letting the room

[248]

spin, looking into the glittery eyes of strangers, on the finely jewelled ears, glossy lips, beautiful breasts, flowing hair, in eternity holding a piece of warm, divinely finished flesh by the waist and moving in the moist dark... Is that the dream these men are chasing? I began to have fantasies of throwing acid all over my face.

March, 2010

I need to write some facts here in the notebook, things are going to slip my mind. It's late March in London, the night is ending, I'm sitting in a pizza parlour, the waiters are getting tired, the street is full of litter, couples are making themselves rare.

On Piccadilly Circus, underneath the lights, a street musician with a saxophone has got a few after-party people dancing to his music right there on the road. A terrific scene to watch, I would have snuck close to take a short film. But all of that calm observing of mine is out now. Instead, I'm sitting in a pizza shop around the corner, and what I will write now won't be in any way poetic. I have to be quick because it seems some people know my face here and I shouldn't be sitting here. I started making money three weeks ago as a mid- to high end hooker Park Lane and Hilton area. Already, I wish that I were dead. What I want to do now, is, I want to retroact some things I started, and give away all possessions I don't need, from storage, and live out of a suitcase again like I always have, that way I can move freely and I can see now I cannot live any other way. As of today, I'm dead to the world. It was a mistake to buy a piano, books, shelves, artwork, show props and sound equipment, clothes, costume bits, and the small heap of worthless things I own. I don't exist.

[249]

I'm afraid of any phone calls. I left Gino's flat without letting Louis know, and went into Café Nero at Green Park. I felt like hiding in the corner. I look awful. I feel I look awful. Been working Sunday night, Monday day, Monday night, Tuesday day, and slept when I could in the red light bedroom of the Shepherd Market apartment, that has got old semen all over the sheets, when I got up I did my make-up, that was all there was time for. Louis just wants all the money and is getting way unpleasant about it. There is just no way I am letting him over-work me and become so mentally exhausted that I end up handing over all the money. I am totally exhausted, that's true. But I have at least got the money in my pocket. I've been hiding it in the Sophocles text that's been lining the bottom of the bag all this time. Must bank it at the earliest, and hide the bank card. Louis tried to get the PIN off me for my bank of america credit card. He doesn't know I have HSBC as well. I must hide the card... in my sock, or something.

Can't stand the smell of me and everyone, would shave my head or soak it in bleach, because everything smells of air freshener, cigarette smoke, cheap perfume and rancid skin lotion. I don't like the feel of make-up foundation on my skin, hate everyone's looks, I want to talk to no-one, see no-one, but they just keep coming. This is a meltdown.

I did my stealy errands and went to a bar off Piccadilly, called Jewel, a sort of upgraded o-bar with bigger rooms, more mirrors, more white soft furnishings, bigger chandeliers, the whole thing even more glinty and lavish. Two guys chatted me up, one Croatian fair haired, burgundy waistcoated, bon-viveur character with glowing eyes and an uplifted tone of voice, and one slender, soft-spoken, shiny-shoed suit from Pakistan. They noticed my diamante, handgun-shaped belt buckle and the smaller guy said 'I have just decided you are cool enough to speak to my friend here', and we got into conversation, they were regulars at the Windmill club, we talked about that.

The smaller guy said I looked like I'd had a bad day, I said yes, and ended up explaining the whole problem to them. They said I was going out with a pimp, an Albanian at that, and I said yes. 'Don't mess with Albanian guys', was a phrase I'd heard a lot of times by now. But, I thought, I'd have to deal with this. Even if no strangers wanted to help me as a favour, and friends were out of reach, that was fine. I would bite the bullet and do it all by myself.

Meanwhile, we jokingly sat around a table with a chess board, they said they'd set me up to marry some millionaire, we planned this a little, it was fun, we saw the three of us starting a wonderful friendship and sharing a million, drank to that, and laughed a lot.

I left with the small guy. He led me to his parked car on Piccadilly which was a blue Porsche, and drove to his house in Borehamwood. It was a sort of live-in-office with several computers in the living room. He explained to me that he was an inventor and spent much of his time making inventions, for which people would come in and work at the many computers. A functional madman, I thought, what have we got here, this is excellent.

I spoke a little about mental hospital, Laurie, heroin and such things, we went to sleep, went for breakfast, he went to work, I spent the day in the town, bought some new clothes in a mall and new shoes with my cash from the Sophocles OCT, paid the rest into the bank, then went back to London and to work in the evening.

Louis was furious. Furious that I had escaped his grip, and

[251]

that I didn't have any money to give him. I didn't see the convenient moment yet, nor the plan of action, but I knew it was important for me to get him off my back soon. I knew no-one would help me, but I also knew that the situation simply could not stay like this, it was too cruel.

I started hiding cash, pretending business was slow. He got rather unbearable, not letting me get any sleep, making me work day and night, tell lies on his behalf, taking me on long walks, here, there, everywhere, in the hope that I would break down and cash out. Although I was exhausted both physically and mentally, I still wasn't done determining whether and how dangerous an individual he really was. I decided to wait a little longer and not to take any action, until I understood the dynamics of these half-worldly businesspeople a little better.

Eventually, he appeared in the basement flat during a work shift one mid-evening and said he wanted to talk to me, in private. I said that I had no secrets and was fine to talk to him in front of everyone else. He insisted on going outside, I insisted on staying indoors.
'You don't want a private chat with me' I said loudly in front of everyone. 'You only want cash, and you are ashamed to say so in front of other people. You know that you are not supposed to do that, and I don't want to see you any more'.
Dang, it was out. I knew I was playing roulette, but I'd had the time to get to know the girls a little, laugh with them, cook with them, and my hope was that in the situation, they would spontaneously take my side, if I showed courage myself, and he'd be outnumbered.

He got loud, violent, he jumped on me, punched my chest, I pushed him back violntly by the shoulder. The three
[252]

graces on the sofa were watching. I knew secretly that they were on my side as they got up and closed in on him, in a menacing circle.

Louis became even more angry, and tried to sack me from the job that he had got me. I said that we would have to wait for Tony to fire me. He made phone calls, gesticulating, and told me to leave immediately. I repeated that I would leave once the boss sacked me, if he did so, and that anyway, this wasn't the time and place for this discussion.

'It's a free country. I don't have to do what you say' – 'Yeah!', joined in the madam, and asked him to leave.

My phone rang, it was Gino. He knew all about this situation, and he was all on my side. He said that he'd known from the start that Louis was pimping me out, and that he was happy to have me in his flat. He said well done honey, you didn't lose your job here. If they kick you out there, you can come here, I give you a job any time'.

Louis, I didn't realise, heard everything and was in a rage. 'You know, you, you are nothing to me, nothing at all. I don't care about you. And because you are a woman, I can't do anything. But Gino, I'm going to cut his legs. And you'll see what will happen to you, you fucking bitch'. I laughed.

'Nervous?' he said, 'that's why people laugh, isn't it, when they're nervous! You're nervous, because you are wrong. You know you will be on the streets tomorrow again. And nobody will give you a job, because now everybody knows what a bitch you are'.

'Leave that for me to worry about', I said 'you won't see any more money from me. Get lost'.

He looked at me, grabbed my phone out of my hand, which I was absent-mindedly holding, and left, slamming the door.

[253]

'My phone! You idiot, that's my phone!', I shouted behind him, short of following him, but I was just happy that he left.

Just a few minutes later, the madam got a phone call from Tony, asking to speak to me. I didn't lose my job at all. Tony only told me that I shouldn't bring trouble to his business because it might turn away business, I said of course. Everyone offered me a place to stay, and offered contacts for me to get different jobs, in different flats. Diana and Tanya, the Romanian brunette, were busy with an all-night client doing a lot of cocaine, the Ukrainian redhead when she briefly stepped out said 'that looked and sounded awful, are you okay' and Diana, with umph, 'how stupid are you to let someone do this to you!' She was right.

Louis was standing by the exit when I came out of the shift. The madam had warned me of this; my money from the night, about 400 pounds, was in my tights, inside my boots. The four of us left together, past Louis, and I got into a black cab straightaway and went to Shepherd Market. Louis got into a cab as well, and had the driver follow me, but they lost us at a red light. For a few days, whenever I stepped out into the street, from anywhere, Louis emerged from the corner. He was constantly shadowing me. Money was piling up in my socks and I did not dare to go to the drugstore, bank or supermarket. I was homeless anyway, and so I lived in Gino's Mayfair apartment, available on day and night shifts, together with one other girl, a different one each day; Gino was often there, playing console games, and I never left, but only gave him money to buy takeaway for us. I only left the house if I had a shift at the other flat. Eventually, Louis caught up with me, around the back of the Hilton, and

[254]

apologized. After that, he left me in peace.

The Sunday before then, one of those long late winter nights when hardly a client called in, we'd all cooked dinner in the brothel kitchen together, a girls night in, it was when we'd got to know each other a little better and when I'd decided to make this bold move.
We'd talked about a lot of stuff, about school, which we had all quit somewhere down the line, about parents, about boyfriends, about life, about having babies, about not having babies, about London, about our countries, about our hobbies, about our lives, our dreams. It was awesome. Diana talked about her youth in Poland, being diagnosed diabetic, coming to London at sixteen. The Ukrainian girl talked about her youth in Canada, stylist college, ice skating, about her boyfriend, and her friends. I got to know everyone a bit better, and later I was not so sure about how happy they all were. But that day, these girls and I were joking and laughing, cooking dinner and watching DVDs, doing our make-up, discussing boyfriends we'd had, talking about our home countries, and thinking about what we'd all do when the difficult times would be over, and it was quite simply fabulous.

April, 2010.
Doing what I do is not very hard, but I have to look my best all the time, and I need to pay attention all the time, because although it all looks smooth and luxurious, there are many dangers lurking everywhere. Between kids like Louis giving me a headache, rogue clients, prima donna working girls and the constant threat of being mugged, raped or the place robbed at gunpoint by gangs... The best way to make sure I'm as safe as I can be is actually making sure the basic needs are met: getting enough sleep is key, avoiding drink and drugs, eating well, and keeping

[255]

a high standard of hygiene, wearing shoes, clothes and underwear that are breathable and comfortable. And looking pretty in the mirror is important, for the self-esteem. I feel that this situation is so dangerous that the smallest shortfall in attention span, memory, or body strength could prove fatal, so keeping on top of sleep and health is primordial now.

It's funny, but all this has made me feel very good lately. It's nice to be working in a fancy part of town where everything is well kept and swept, meeting lots of beautiful girls and gents in fine suits.

Being on this side of the barricade, now, I realise that even if, technically, I might be smarter than many people, in some ways I am scandalously dumb: in not realising the importance of social success and the power of money. Most people down here regret not having done well enough at school. I can't regret this, because that never was where I failed. My mistake was another, which here I find hard to pinpoint. Maybe it is, after all, genuine insanity, that fabled lack of judgment the schizophrenia doctors are always so keen to point out. But... if I was insane, I could not survive here. If I was insane, I could not resist the stress of this escort and brothel situation. I would be making all sorts of mistakes and precipitating my own destruction. But I must ask myself: how was this possible? How did I end up here, now... and what's to come?

I swam for my life after a big shipwreck, I would say. I never drowned, even through all the Skyllae and Charibdes, I continued.

Sometimes murmuring poems to myself that I know by heart, wishing to heaven I'd memorised more of them. For my sanity. Because this is where I realise how vacuous a consolation I find in rock and pop music.

'Endure, and save yourselves for better days to come.

[256]

Maybe one day we'll be proud to have lived through this'
(Verg.). 'Courage! he said, and pointed towards the land.
This mounting wave will roll us shoreward soon. In the
afternoon, they came into a land in which it seem'd always
afternoon' (Tenn.). 'These wet suns, in these wrathful
skies, to my mind have the charms, and the great mystery,
of your treacherous eyes, gleaming through their tears'
(Baudel.). 'Midnight shakes the memory as a madman
shakes a dead geranium' (T.S.E.).
And Billie Holiday : 'Lonely grief is hounding me, like a
lonely shadow hounding me. It's always there, just out of
sight, like a frightening dream on a lightening night.
Lonely wind cries out my name, sad as haunted music in
the rain.'
I said upon entering these places that I wouldn't do any
cocaine or drink alcohol with the clients, because I have
been going to NA, but eventually I started – because I was
told the stuff here is hardly pure. And that's true. It made
me wonder what these boys were all thinking they were
tripping on when they are taking it, because I only get a
stuffy nose from it. Still, I was ambivalent on it. But the
reason I did it with this one man I saw, wearing a family
ring with an embossed siglum and a motto in Latin
imprinted, which I recognized, and I wanted at all costs to
spend some time alone with this person. 'Your eyes are
enchanting', he told me. I can't remember now what we
spoke of, but the conversation reminded me of everything
that I used to know and now is vanished like a dream.

The Sirens

The nocturnal oasis I found underneath the streets of London was a bountyland of luxury apartments in basements of well-heeled areas, young girls in stockings and underwear sets, or fetishy outfits bought from a nighttime door to door salesman going around brothels selling sex shop goods. Viagra in a vase, snow in the kitchen drawer, whiskey and poppers in the fridge, and condoms in a fruit bowl. There were red-lit bedrooms with padded satin bedspreads, velvet runners, gold and silver embroidered rugs and canopies, silk curtains, and cupboards full of baby oil.

Watching the X-Factor all night on the television, or reading Vogue and Harper's Bazaar, we would sit there discussing hair and make-up, clothes, and celebrities all night long, every now and then interrupted by the phone call or appearance of one or several men in expensive suits, greeting them, doing them, showering, resting in the lounge again. I'd sleep much of the time, sometimes read. On occasion, getting a hot dress on and jumping in a cab to a hotel, if we got ordered there. Hotel visits were dangerous. You never knew what you might be walking into, but I found them a welcome change of scenery from the television and the long shifts.

Countless are the types I met, the things I saw. I got insights into the lives of many a rich and famous man. I got to know quite well the professional punters of Chelsea, knew all about their drug habits, their sexual ways, their work, their friends, their wives, their children, often their whole being.

[259]

There was Joel, stocky and tanned Englishman, the owner of a yacht club. He got his tan from where he ordinarily lived, Nice, but visited us every other Friday, staying the whole night. He liked role play, S&M, toys and kinky games, having several girls at once, drinking whiskey, and having a lot of charlie. He liked speaking to me in French, to tell me about a woman he once knew and loved, and over a few hours of whiskey and coke, he would bring himself to think that I was that woman, and I would play her, following his directions, wearing masks and dark capes...

He liked a game called play vampires, we would talk us into the scene and soon start to act and have sex as if I was that woman from the past. His erotic imagination was vast and reached into the extreme boundaries of pleasure and pain. Each time he was there, he would have in mind a new theme for the night. The theme about this woman he used to care about was a recurrent one, we all would act as her, and then, a few drinks and drugs later, things would get really hard core.

Once he showed up wanting us to pretend he was a painter me the nude. Another time, he wanted to be chained up. Every now and then, he would surprise me by saying to me in French: "I wish I knew you in real life" – "this *is* real life", I used to say, and he would shake his head with resignation.

Not everyone was as creative as Joel was. In fact, hardly anyone. Countless are the faces, countless are the stories I heard, had impressed on me as an innocuous and inconsequential, dumb young thing, a piece of furniture to witness happenings in beautiful mansions, rented hotel rooms, in cars, in shabby, broken pomp chic, velvet-lined establishments.

Louis, a small-town criminal, Tony, a London brothel

[260]

operator with serious front, a mortgage to pay for, Raffael, his partner, a hopeless player, Joyce, Pia, and Chantelle, sturdy English madams, Dan, male escort in search of himself, Isa, a freckly working girl, the octogenarian spy, an Arabic Viagra buyer, Victoria, elegant blonde with flawlessly perfect beauty, bordering on the ice cold appearance of a vogue model. Vanessa, a thirty-four year old, Moldovan long-standing pleasure lady with platinum blonde extensions to her bum and diamond heels, Diana, the no-nonsense Polish blonde bombshell, the Ukrainian redhead, a tanned sunshine of hearts on a business management course, a shorty with rough manners and kind heart, studying social sciences, who was scared to death that her family might hear what she did at night, the man with the she-wolf ring, Joel, the creative punter; Diana's boyfriend, an Italian alcoholic on the run from the police at home, pretty boy she had met on the job, his friend, a smooth cocaine dealer on a pizza delivery bike, his girlfriend, an Italian architect who built websites for escort services, a brown-suede-suited insurance company director with silk shirts and millimetre cut, who was ever on the brink of falling in love with any girl he spent hours with, a big, immensely-pinstripe clad Russian punter with sleep apnoea who would routinely fall asleep and wake up thinking it was his lovely girlfriend he was waking next to, an English forty-year old, slightly mentally retarded Chelsea good-for-nothing with curly hair, who would sit through hours sniffing Charlie and enquiring about the football, pairs and triads of Arabic cousins descended from a Knighstbridge joy ride in shiny sports cars, Essex boys in pairs, or alone, with Chelsea caps thinking they were doing something terribly obnoxious by phoning us, and even coming in, muttering disapproving things about the prices, a hilarious pair of forty-something boys who would call for myself and Jolene, every three to four weeks, to the

[261]

Copthorne or the Marble Arch Thistle, for foursome card games and cocaine shuffling, sometimes for guessing games or strip poker, and who were in a dubious colleague and/or friendship, and/or protégé relationship with one another. They claimed to be employed by a pub chain and to have meetings in London, during which one of them would unfailingly win large amounts of cash at the casino, which they then jointly spent on long sessions with us two; the two after-hour salesmen who brought dresses, stockings, pyjamas, and Viagra to the ladies, and menstrual sponges, a bon-vivant news CEO, also, a middle aged jazz drummer in flowery shirts and music-themed ties would turn up often, horn glasses, long-ish hair, exhaling the eccentricity of England through and through, a bestselling writer, a barrister, who had always stayed a bachelor and once invited me to his beautiful home in Ealing. It had an old weeping willow tree hanging melancholy over a pond and swimming pool, and gorgeous French mirrors, sculptures in the garden and a learned study room and library, where we sat on leather armchairs and talked about poems we knew.

There was a tiny, child-like Romanian blue-eyed blonde, wearing pale pink vests and fluffy fleeces in the brothels as she was perpetually falling asleep, homeless most of the time, a bit like myself when I had first started. She was under so much stress that she constantly would find herself confused, distraught, and stubborn, so she was often sacked from jobs, kicked out of places, beaten up by men she got involved with, or mugged on the streets. She was bright, though; I asked her to teach me a little Romanian once, and I could see that she knew how to teach.
Gino, one day, had come knocking on my apartment door with her, asking me to let her stay with me until she found a place, saying she had got herself kicked out of the

apartment in West Ken. At the time, she did not know any English, but we got by, with broken Romanian and a bit of giggling about incongruous situations.

After a while, she packed her suitcase, not to outstay her welcome. She had no place to go, and as she walked up the road looking like the rain, clutching wet cigarettes in her fingers full of gold rings and dragging her heavy case of girly stuff, I watched this young and pale, epileptic woman, little more than a child, disappear on the boulevard with anxious feelings of rage and powerlessness. I knew I was letting her go on to a road where she would encounter evil and destruction, maybe death.

It was a few weeks before she appeared in a flat again, unchanged, but speaking fluent English. I asked her if she had found a house, and she said yes, we swapped numbers again, as I had lost a phone in the meantime. Later, she disappeared again.

She had a friend, who was small and skinny just like her, and whom I once spent a Sunday night in a flat with, just the two of us. I was taking the phone calls that night, as this girl didn't understand English either, and there was no madam around. A client called first, and then came in, and chose her. They went to the bedroom, but soon she came running out with a frightened face saying she would not deal with him and went underneath a blanket on the sofa, in the far corner of the room.

I asked him what had happened, and he said he wanted to have anal sex. I said that if she wasn't happy with that, he just had to accept it. He said he wanted to have sex for free. I crossed my arms and told him he had come to the wrong place. He seemed menacing, and kept repeating he could do anything he wanted. I asked him to leave. He assaulted me, hitting me on the shoulder, so I grabbed my phone to call Tony, but he snatched it out from my hand, I grabbed his wrist, hissing 'Give that back to me, c**t. Who do you think you are?'

He punched me in the stomach, and said 'Where's the money?'

'What money?'

'Your money. What you have made tonight. I want it, and you better behave yourself'.

'There's no f***ing money, you idiot', I pretended.

He jumped toward my throat and I kicked his knee, he stumbled, I pushed him against the wall in the hallway and hurled abuse at him, the other girl joining in, and he left. Then, we took the money and went into the back garden with the phones, locking all the doors behind us in case he could somehow come back, and called Tony from the work phones. He came down right away, we split the money, and went home for the night.

Crude and brutish events happened in plenty, behind the scenes of the official business; places got raided at gunpoint, by groups of criminals, or by the police, every few weeks; and I was occasionally let in on a morsel of other lives, doing coke with 500 Euro notes in clubs after closing time, briefcases full of money, like in the movies. A seemingly unending stream of faces, like ghosts in the underworld, streamed by me, demanding attention, demanding their lives mean something.

The Moldovan blonde of the first Sunday, vain and beautiful, with high hopes of making a fortune; a tall, thirty-something brunette with beautiful features who had lost all illusions of the sort; a round of youngsters, friends of Diana's in charge of sticking cards in the phone booths, who lived all together in a small basement on Lillie road, where they drank Vodka in abundance and also organised a variety of store burglary jobs on demand; one of these boys' ex-girlfriend, Czech, dark brunette, ran her own flat in Gloucester Road, where I worked for a couple of weeks once and also lived in.

We talked as best we managed, about her seven year old son in Czechia, and her family problems. Then, there also was her other working girl employee, a sturdy, gentle-faced blonde and blue-eyed affair reminiscent of Ingrid Bergman, two Polish leather-jacketed and tattoo-covered biker friends of theirs on a visit from Manchester, an English hooded friend of theirs with piercing blue eyes and sympathetic voice, who kept two sweet mastiffs in a hopelessly over-furnished apartment that he owned in Earls Court, two Jamaican drug furnishers to the flat, who also liked to hang around and chat, and on occasion use our service, and tall Jamaican client who rocked up every once in a while in fine wool suit, golden cufflinks, and a leather briefcase, who would take lines until he reached a state of paranoia to barricade the room from the inside and stand listening by the door for steps, in his shorts, and who always paid for everything in Guernsey money; the tall French geographer lady, who once rocked up with her diamond chained boyfriend and a bottle of Champagne at my loft I then had, for a party where there was table dancing, wild shouting, and a lot of spraying of joy, until we got down to Jacques Brel; a big, sweating, Indian client who wouldn't grow tired of licking pussy for many hours when he'd already turned up at 4am and everyone wanted to go home; a tall, manly, East-Asian girl with glittering make-up, glittering dresses, sequins and gold and silver jewellery everywhere, very good at sensual massage, squinting her eyes laughing at Westerners; and a tall, feline black lady with perfect body, perfect silicone tits, supplementing her day job income, on a mission to have the perfect body.

[265]

With her it was that I first met Zach, a musician in the deep mist of sex, drugs, and rock'n'roll gone sour and soul-destroying. A little way into my grand decision to take cocaine with clients if it promised big bucks, in walked Zach, a slim man with deep and piercing blue eyes in a black, fur-lined coat, a bluesman's hat, black polished pointy boots, an American: there sat with cheeky grin on burgundy padded, tasselled satin sheets, taking a western-like drag off a Marlboro, what seemed to be a rock musician approaching the middle age, his posture twisted, speaking in a voice that arched angrily over the shades of self-loathing, sarcasm, slyness, hot temper, adrenaline, testosterone, and a feral addiction to pleasure. He asked me in first, later to be joined by the black girl. Asked to be walked over, tied down, whipped, squeezed and squashed, kicked with kinky heels, insulted by us as a carpet rug dog. As time ticked on, the drugs took a firmer hold of him, and he lay outstretched, turning and twisting, entering deeper and deeper into delusional states, whilst the air in the room thickened with the smoke of cigarettes tipped in cocaine on the glass table, whiskey vapours, and latex smells.

I felt more he needed kindness, and protection from himself – this icon-man, the great musician, hardcore superstar, the playboy, this actor of his own life, who had lost his way – and when he asked me to put out cigarettes on his balls, that, I could not do, nor could the other, he did so himself, giving this look that seemed to say 'see what I do for you, my queen'...

Then, he pulled out more cocaine from another pocket, prepared lines for us, cigarettes, dabbed some on his fingertip and once it was in the lung, not the time to exhale, he was asking for crack, or more cocaine, for phone numbers, for more of everything.

He made a habit of spending nights with me, we became a terrible pair. I could never know when I'd see him, but I was happy when he came in, and even through the aura of edgy and superlative masculinity, twistedness and recklessness, I could feel he had an open and friendly, lovable character. There was a truth to our kinky circus, our few words in that red room, a simple and natural honesty in this most bizarre outgrowth of civilization.

Sometimes, I thought with sadness that I had a dying man before me, and worried in my heart, for his health, and for his sanity. But I was not a real person. One evening, he asked to be accompanied to the cash point. He had a rotten swagger that but wanted a walking cane to be the ghost of Oscar Wilde.

'My mistress needs decent money', he told the banker in America, on the phone, 'raise my daily spending limit'.

Before we could get to the ATM, a credit card needed picking up in his car parked nearby, a scenic old Merc. Shuffling about papers on the car seat in search of the card, an AA Where-To-Find emerged from the pile and met my eye. I pointed at it. 'This. This is where you should be going now, Zach. Down here is no place for you. You are ruining your life. Is that really what you want? I am not blind, you know'.

He looked away, said nothing, and I smiled, and arm in arm we went around the corner to the Old Brompton Road and drew money under the twinkling lights of Harrod's. We crossed Raffael on the way, my overcoat barely covering the lace of the hold-ups. Zach didn't know, or notice, Raffael, so we acted as strangers, although I caught his knowing glance on the sly, and when we were back down, Zach looked about him and asked for more Whiskey, gave the madam a bright, accomplice smile, and then, we shut the door again behind us and the silk, and the tassels, all the smoked-out torture-den was starting again, like a dream of a red forest we walked in and out of, interrupted only by hourly knocks for money.

Two months, three months perhaps, in which I saw myself grow character traits, and a comfort with moral decay I'd never before dreamt of, until Zach disappeared. Had he run out of money? Had he died, possibly? Or was he gracing the blank rooms of any celebrity rehab, or away on business perhaps? I heard only on the grapevine, months later, that he had once returned to the flat emaciated, depressed, and stoned, and left early.

Other stories, other madmen took his place. And women. Another flat I lived in briefly, a shabby flat in West Ken, belonged to a tall, pale woman together with Gino after Shepherd's market had gone bust. An internet escort lady, student, dancer, whose mind was ever elsewhere, her English madam and house keeper from the World's End estate, a haggard and bitter affair; a young Lithuanian, innocent faced, pretty brunette with a penchant for little girl's things and pretty dresses with flowers, who talked about running in search of a children's home when her father was beating her with a belt; her friend, a slim, tall, Polish blonde party girl, who eternally had problems with boyfriends who gave her hard times, an Italian blonde escort lady in long black coat and green satin dress, who I met on a duo escort job to a hotel, who took me home to her escort flat in Gloucester Road, a beautiful apartment full of sex toys, which she called her 'golden prison', who ended up travelling to India and doing meditation every day and throwing philosophical poker parties in houses she ended up renting on fake references, and let them to others; the small man who Diana sent to my door once when I asked her to send me someone with white; who, she didn't tell me, was a much talked-about pimp, one of the last specimens of those who used to buy and sell girls on markets and mutilated them horribly if they caught

[268]

them running, back in the mid-1990s; a Lithuanian girl was telling us about them often, for she had been in those markets herself not so long ago, tall and staggering, with big blue eyes, always cracking jokes, talking in gypsy slang; there was a bleach-blonde, scarfaced Englishman, owner of many night clubs in London, who would come in from time to time in his broad-shouldered, silver-shining suits with pink shirts, and bring his girlfriend, a fair-haired young designer who liked going out without underwear.

The first time they showed up, they spent an hour with me, mostly initiated by the girl who was asking I go down on her, kiss her; she was very good-looking, her man was watching us quietly, wanking in the corner, and there was something a bit sad about him as he unwrapped charlie and got some lines ready; then we sat on the bed together, the three of us, half-dressed, scoring lines off each others bodies, talking about musicians and film stars.

The man ended up coming around to my house often, when he was out clubbing, he would give me a call and turn up with a few grams and wine, we would talk about the 1980s, when he was a synth-playing teenager, experimenting with radio waves and morse, and about the 1990s, when he was first a bar keeper, then manager, eventually, owner of various night clubs, about film and rock stars he had known and met, how he got the scars in his face, a brutal story involving a glass ashtray, and his first love, as a teenager; and there was a short, slim Transylvanian girl with curly blond hair, pearl necklaces and lace, who always reminded me of Marilyn Monroe, and who had a slight propensity to steal. I remember one time the curly-haired, Charlie-sweeping designer handbag salesman from Kensington High Street, Dylan, who would always try to pool a deal when the hours got long, trying leave a rolex or Gucci handbags instead of payment, alwas asking for credit from us with mixed results, managed to

[269]

win her over to grant him credit through the gift of a gold and snake leather handbag, and she, in turn, put the blame on me in the end when Tony wanted to collect the money and there wasn't enough.

Dylan was in the habit of coming down in the early evenings for a cup of tea in the brothel sitting and chit chat for an good hour or so, talking about how much he wanted to stop the drugs but couldn't, how tough business was even with designer handbags, moving his store every few months, to evade tax, and try to make friends with us girls. Once I casually was strolling, shopping on Kensington High Street, and noticed a window that caught my eye, maybe for a gold and snake skin handbag that seemed all too familiar, but I could not quite remember where I had seen a similar one. Eventually I remembered, and, working out it must be that punter's shop, I entered, ready to say hello, somewhat voyeuristic about the lives all these men led when they weren't high, drunk and tied to a fluffy bedpost.

He wasn't in, his clerk was sitting at a desk, smiled from underneath gold rimmed glasses, and so I said hello instead to a chihouaua curled up in an armchair at the front. About an hour later though, Dylan spotted me at a zebra crossing, in the car with his father, all black Volvo, black suits and designer shades. He introduced us, his father made a rude gesture, then off they whizzed.

He was the heaviest coke user I had ever seen and could easily get through ten or fifteen grams in a few hours. 'You're making a fool of yourself', I had told him once – as I'd got into the habit of telling some of these designer-suited, coked-up businessmen when they got too extravagant towards the later stages of their intoxication – 'if you ask for more now, you have already run out of cash, we are going to kick you out'.

He put his head down like a school boy after a formal

scolding, and for a moment had the clarity of mind to see he was lying outstretched on a heap of used and torn condoms, coke wraps and cigarette butts, the doors and windows barricaded from the inside with all the furniture he'd managed to move in his paranoia that someone might enter the room, watching porn on a small and green-filtering telly, bathed in cocaine that he'd rubbed all over his genitals, put in his mouth, his nose, on his face, and on my tits, my thighs, everywhere.

Merely the physical contact with him was getting me high. I had done the first two grams with him and then said I had had enough. But imperceptibly, I had ingested maybe five grams by the contact with skin and mucus, and I was having an overdose. I couldn't move any more, hardly breathe, my heartbeat had gone double, triple, and then flat; the doors were locked with furniture and Dylan gave no sign of tiring from rubbing cocaine on me. The madam was happily collecting money for me every hour but not bothering to stick her head in the room, and I prepared to die, that night, in the back bedroom of that sleazy basement.

I couldn't move or breathe well, but I was still conscious. It reminded me of a night on a Hampstead bus when all the stars came out and I nearly died of heroin. Staying awake was of the essence. I acted as if I had already passed out, although I had not. Dylan, sucking a white thumb, realised what had happened and started freaking out.

'Hey, come on, please, I'm sorry! Can you get up?' – but I didn't move. I heard him, but it was beyond me to do anything. I waited. We waited. He started pacing. Ten minutes, fifteen. I saw from the corner of my eye that he was pulling out his hair, crossing his arms, pacing back and forth, smoking. I felt hot and cold showers, sweat, and nausea fulminate all over me and eventually I got up, pale

[271]

and shaky and whispered 'but now you're going to let me out of here'. He nodded, and asked for a replacement girl, and I had a hot shower.

Some regular customers kept true to one girl, others didn't; some liked a little conversations, some liked a lot, some none at all; some men I only ever saw once; an old English horse dealer who smoked and placed his dark venous hands heavy on the glass table smoking a cigarette, then spent a silent and tender two hours with myself and a brazilian stocky lady in fishnets; a tall, wide, immensely endowed South African who wanted money back because he couldn't fit his dick in; a German finance economist, who sought me out in various places, for extreme hard core; a Nigerian economist, who visited me three or four times and talked at length about university, doctorates, the twists of fate, and the meaning of life; a Turkish-German prostitute who didn't grow tired of explaining that most men could be done by handjobs and it wasn't necessary often, to take the risk; a cheeky-smiled, emotional Romanian card boy with a missing tooth, another, who was talking about his time at the army and running from the army; an English bar manager, who experienced the transformation, in his eyes, of human toy into human being simply because I laughed at one of his jokes, and whom, it seems, the experience terminally turned away from visiting brothels, who offered me a job at his bar, which I took, for a time; but he then was keen on sex in the wine cellar, and quickly, keen on a relationship with me, which caused me to run; a pretty boy, posing as male escort, but in reality pimping out girls; an old-fashioned Neapolitan Mafioso, sunglasses and big belly, a pair of Russians who robbed brothels with guns at night; a mixed-race, cashmere-coated undercover police man coming to test the premises for drug dealing; an American art collector who

[272]

could not get enough and took me from the flat to his hotel; a redhead in the Dorchester, who called us in duo; a California oil trader, who left his Tiffany's wedding band on the dresser, which I picked up; a French tourist; many Saudi tourists, various sizes of belly; an English shy person on a self-improvement course; the landlord of the flat, who on a special deal, came down to see what was going on, couldn't believe his eyes, and had a hard time choosing a girl; an old man in West Kensington keen on licking pussy, claiming to have been a postman; a Russian in sunglasses keen on golden showers, who would always try to haggle the prices and get kicked out; a kind looking blonde Romanian girl in flowery dresses; a tall, slim Indian fellow with Beatle haircut who would often show up with lingerie he'd want us all to wear...

There were the crowd from the West End, a second floor apartment with two small and slightly shabby bedrooms, and a small living room where the backgammon game took pride of place on a small coffee table, and the couple, who owned and ran the business, played card games on the table, made espressos, and had a lively coming and going of friends who'd play, talk, and dance around whilst trying to strike friendly deals with either of the three half-naked girls in heels and dressing gowns invariably lounging in bathrobes on the sofas, of which on Tuesdays, I was always one. I went by various names, then; and in that place, which was as lively with friendly visits as it was with business, I somehow got into the role of 'the singer' and would give go-go girl style renditions of American Pie, Sam's Town, Paparazzi, mocking the X-factor, and the bemused, espresso-drinking loungers would clap the rhythm—except one bleach-blonde, skeletally skinny Hungarian student, who was a metalhead, and had no nerve for anything but Motorhead. There was also a

[273]

chubby blonde receptioinist who was pregnant and requesting massages from the girls, making fruit salad, and offering beer on the house to clients. The most beautiful woman of that apartment was a fair haired, blue eyed stunner with a dreamy face and a jaw-dropping, tanned body that seemed just cut out of a Vegas bill, in babydoll dresses and diamante bracelets. She was working six shifts a week with her mother in the know, at only nineteen, and sometimes we would try to persuade her to go back to school. The West End flat wasn't as spacious, nor as lavishly furnished as the Chelsea ones, but the couple who ran it prided themselves on employing only very beautiful girls. A tired face, flabby bottom, dull hair or bad outfit could never last in this place. There, I met a Romanian ginger blonde with a doll face and perfect features, who wore luxuriant red and black satin and lace sets and her figure seemed just made for erotic lingerie, which she wore with amazing grace.

At the Park Lane Hilton, a businessman had phoned for me to come up, I seemed to have arrived at a party, as there were two Asian ladies already in the room, they were watching seedy films on the screen, champagne and strawberries were ordered, and we sat around the table, the four of us, naked, talking about English horses, estates, and hilly counties.

The porters of a few Park Lane hotels, I'd been told, were in some sort of cahoots with the card boys. I was sent as a duo escort with a Vogue-top-model-like beauty to meet two brothers, who, I later heard, had a bet as to who would come first, which they communicated to each other using their hotel room phone. A client once came down who looked like an old seaman, with erotic mermaid tattoos; he left, saying he'd get money and I guessed that he wouldn't be back, that he was one of those we called 'wankers' who walk in, look at the girls, and leave, pretending to go out for cash. He returned, an hour later, by the time we were two girls, a dark-skinned, Hungarian shorty and I, he was over the moon to find this and stayed with us both for an hour, enjoying what seemed to him an hour of undeserved bliss straight out of heaven.

A twenty-something Polish butler in livery, good looking and skilled in bed, came down variously to find me, a greying, camel-coated Italian restaurant keeper, whose 'whore virginity' I took, and who seemed to treat the whole affair like a girlfriend experience, came down regularly to see me, an Arabic chef, who liked to have long conversations about books and the spirit of the desert, who often left without even having had sex, became regulars; a French finance lawyer with dark curly hair, stiff collars and cigars, who deemed himself very good in bed, took a special liking to me; as did a French lawyer in jacquard shirts with hair combed back, who was a bit nerdy, and often tried to strike up small talk, which tended to end early when he couldn't fathom how I could have dared to enter this kind of business, when I was tempted to throw the same back at him, but offered the explanation 'I like sex, and I like money, so this is not the worst option', at which he grinned.

As time went by, he kept on commenting that I must be getting very rich; but he reminded me that I was not. I was rather getting addicted to cash and spending. Sometimes, to make myself feel better after an awful night, which was pretty much every night, I would get a cab home, shower, and after a few gallons of herbal tea sleep a few more hours. Waking up, at about one or two in the afternoon, I would go out shopping, getting myself gifts and taking myself to dinner in fancy places. I didn't have anyone to love me, but I had myself. Later, I remembered what Ray had said, that when you feel cheap in yourself is when you

[275]

cover yourself in gold the most.

So I switched to treating my friends to meals and drinks more. My neighbours, an East European couple, became dear friends soon. The man was a heavy drinker, a metalhead and rock'n'roll bass player about the same age as me, with long black hair and tattoos, and we could easily drink a bottle and smoke two packs between 9pm and 3am; once Diana came to my house with a small group of friends when he was just sitting there, and we had an impromptu, wild and decadent topless dancing party with blowjobs, whiskey and coke.

Florian came back to London from the States, dishevelled, impoverished, and heavily addicted to crack. He moved to a squat, carrying in him that very same chill and restlessness, the howling wolves of the soul, that I had known on my return from America.

Percocets, heroin, crack... and in the middle of all this, Homer. Tipping ashes into an ashtray made from an old beer can, in an abandoned Hackney estate he was then squatting, the howling wolves of our hearts broke loose one night as we talked about it all, of the chills and the cold roads. When we talked about the *Odyssey*, we only spoke of shipwrecks.

'Shipwrecked', he said, 'that is how I feel.'

'Yes', I said, 'I know. We had to lose our companions and our men, and our arms, and our ships, fight the roaring sea, with its monsters. We have to be heroes in those times'.

He looked up, suddenly remembering the old Homeric verses.

'Some die trying', he said. 'Do you have a gun? I want to shoot myself.'

We washed ourselves with a bucket and sponge, as there was no shower, and wore woolen hats at night, as there

[276]

was no heating, cuddling together under the blanket to sleep.

In the afternoon, as I was coming down to a basement flat, lifting the iron latch to the gate, walking down and noticing no lights, seeing as I was the first to get there, reaching for the key in the hiding place, turning on lights and cameras, I stopped for a moment and began to murmur lines of a poem I would later write, I am the hook at which you hang your clothes, your false truths, your soul, as it were fish, I'm an old hook the garments tear and fall, I let them fall, all, those many coats you hung, those many souls that dangled...

It was the quiet moments in the cab that were the most poignant for me. When I would be sent for, to go to the Hilton, or the Copthorne, or the Dorchester, the Savoy, or the Thistle, and walk out on to Cromwell road, cocktail dress and heels in perfect make-up, condoms and phone in my handbag, with a name, room number and a cell phone number scribbled on a scrap clenched in my hand, hire a black cab outside Harrod's, sit by myself for a few minutes in the dark back bench, looking out at these well-lit, well-heeled evenings happening outside, and walk graciously through the wallet-wielding crowd, through revolving doors, on red carpets, or marble steps, through a maze of mirrors and champagne flutes, stained shirts and loosened ties, curly heads supine in red satin, in which I seemed just like another one of them, but somehow was another, I began to think that it really could not be known who was who under these black tied and cocktail dressed chess figures, and I began to feel the dull pulse of desperation, lost in the wheels of an infernal machine.

May, 2010

[277]

Born from the foam, Aphrodite,
The girl in the mirror opened her towel
In a shell on green waters,
The line of her waist and dark eyes, still as stone.
Foam blisters down
White marble baths
Golden drains, golden jail
Dreams out the window.
I rise from my nightmares
Sweat on the couch, snow on the glass -
They keep the curtains always shut.
The foam of all days dried and bubbled
A shape in the sand, a dead mermaid that sank.

Urban spring sprouts cherry blossom fenced in spearpoint
iron, nacre sun on white facades, birds twittering and
curved magnolia leaves hang heavy on grand pavements,
between Ritz Hotel sparks, black cab fumes in crowded
winds, foxes on the curb and low sweet littered sunsets in
the park. In this city without rain, I'm a leftover from
yesterday, in a basement on a couch.
If I could, I'd close a huge black lid over myself again, the
bell jar that Baudelaire and Sylvia Plath so poetically
described. That cruel springtime melancholy is here, with
blackest bitterness.

Story lines began to thicken into intrigues, between two
gentlemen who shared a suite at either the Copthorne or
the Marble Arch Thistle every few weeks, and who called
for me in duo with a sophisticated, busty and pretty faced
little Albanian brunette. One was a little older, and
married, in his mid-forties perhaps, the other was in his
thirties, and still single. We would meet them, sit down
and play games such as guessing games around the hotel
table. The guys would ask us to get undressed gradually,

[278]

and they would take turns at playing with either of us, sometimes in separate rooms and sometimes on the same bed, and there would be girl on girl action, too. Charlie would be lying on the tables, and be swept up, in a weird dynamic, as both men, who were colleagues (or so they claimed) would try to hide from one another that they were using it. They would get into arguments about who paid whom, and about who used more; the older guy especially was in constant fear that he was less liked by 'the girls'. As a married man, he thought he could do everything but have sex with us, whereas the younger guy, also by character, I guess, wanted to have that most of all especially.

One night, walking out with the older guy, Gerald, who was looking good in a sharp suit of a brown, gold-reflecting colour as we walked through the lobby, we ran into a lady in pencil dress standing with a small group of people he apparently knew, the lady waved and stopped us. He introduced me to her as 'his good friend'. She, drunk enough, seemed to buy it. In a tacit communication with the guy, we followed the usual script for party small talk for a couple of minutes before he came up with 'I'm terribly sorry, Mandy, my wife is waiting for us in the car', everyone nodded, and we left.

In a darker alley on the way to a cash point, we made out a little, and he suggested: 'why don't we, you and I, just go somewhere else, I know a much nicer place where we can go', and turned a corner, rang a bell on a black, unmarked door, and after a short wait a lady in business suit buzzed it open, sitting at what seemed a reception desk in the front lobby by a broad staircase.

I noticed the beautifully ornate hand rail, then stucco on the wall, friezes, trompe-l'oeil on a ceiling with a gorgeous, Louis XV rotunda. The colours were blue and sand, aquatic and calming, and the floors were marble chess boards, and mosaic. There were mosaics on the

[279]

walls, too, and gold plated ironwork in windows, pompous, ancient door handles, French mirrors. I was at first so overcome by the unexpected beauty and grandeur of the interior, that seemed to come close to a museum or historic house, smelling of rich mahagony and leather, that I walked up the stairs in fresh marvel, examining the paintings on the wall, Greco-Roman mythology, 18th century fresco pieces interspersed with moist patches that seemed like erasures.

I didn't take notice, at first, that the man seemed perfectly at home as he put on some lights on the first floor, poured two martinis into tall glasses and set them by a beautifully arranged fruit bowl on a small lionfooted table. We were in what seemed a regal, purple velvet-curtained lounge with pale silk arabesque wall paper and a gold lined chaise and couch set, under an opulent chandelier softly swinging its crystals, sometimes catching rays of the street, sending them through mirrors, reflecting lights erratically, like a dance of fireflies. I walked into the living room, looked out through tall and ancient balcony doors, on to a nocturnal square, as Gerald was calling from the room adjacent, a burgundy room with a high, richly cushioned and canopied bed, on which he was sitting, turning on covert lights to give the room a light and shade of pale rose. With dim flicker, a yellow lamp shade turned itself on next to the bed and stood there in the half-light, like a buttercup at dusk.

I was mesmerized by the high ceilings with stucco and frescoes, the place's ornaments, its fabrics, its cherubs and griffins, the Empire furnishings, burnished wood, and lines of old poems were flying through my mind. I was temporarily in the time of art and not counting minutes on my watch, but the guy's phone rang.

It was the other two, around the corner still in the hotel,

demanding for us to return. He told them to meet us at Little Portland Street, and the two of us went outside to greet them. They arrived in a cab, perhaps having misjudged the distance; and with them was a slim blonde in a sirenic green dress with raspberry lips and pearl jewellery. We mounted to the living room, when asked what they were drinking, the blonde demanded champagne, which was duly popped and poured into a Venetian glass set.

'I'm worth five million pounds', spat the blonde, resting on the couch, legs crossed, and that statement sat in the room for a good moment before Gerald asked, 'how do you know Matt and Jolene?', meaning his colleague and my escort friend.

'Oh, you guys know each other?' said the blonde, scrutinizing the round incredulously.

'Yes, we do. Of course we do. How did you just come in with them, I thought you were a friend of Matt's or something', Gerald said.

'Oh, no', said the woman, I was just out with my friends and couldn't find them, but I found these people standing on the road, it's 3a.m., you know, so I tagged along, they seemed cool'

'Right, well, I'm terribly sorry, but after you've had your glass of champagne, I'm going to ask you to leave, because this is a kind of private party'.

'Oh, in that case, I'll party with you all right'.

The four of us were exchanging awkward looks, and nobody knew what anybody else was thinking. She might call the police on us if we were rude to her, she was a stranger and shouldn't be allowed to work out, nor either us inadvertently to give away, that we were escorts and they were clients. Alex, the younger man, was at first quite keen on the idea of having a third girl there but when he

[281]

saw she wasn't popular with his older colleague, he was ready to force her out rudely; Gerald, noticing this, wanted to avoid that happening; she would have to leave at the earliest possible, none the less happy with her brief visit.

Gerald got up and asked her to come outside with him for a moment as he needed to tell her something. A quarter of an hour later, he was back, alone. 'All done, Matt, why on earth did you bring a stranger up here?'

'Come on, she was fine' – 'I need a drink', said the other, and we began a game around the table.

'I'm going to ask a question', said Gerald, 'and whoever can answer it, gets this fifty pounds. Ready?'

We nodded.

'When did World War Two take place?'

I rummaged around in my head for the ending date. Was it May 8th? May 9th? No-one else was coming up with contributions. 'September third, 1939, to some time in May, 1945', I said.

'Any other calls?', he asked.

'1917?' Jolene offered.

'No idea man', said Alex.

'You win fifty pounds. I'm impressed. But now I have a question you won't be able to answer. What's the capital of New York State?'

'Albany', I said, instantly.

Everybody looked at me in bewilderment, especially Gerald – Alex and Jolene were looking at us both in a kind of befuzzlement as to what on earth we were on about.

'You're quite intelligent, aren't you?' said the younger man to me.

'I know a few things', said I.

'Alright, we're not playing this game any more. You just know all the answers'.

We sat around, we got undressed, we got complimented on

[282]

our tits, touched, pooled between partners, until it got late, money ran out, and together with Jolene, I left.

We left in separate cabs, it was around six in the morning, and I got out of my cab at Earl's Court to pick up a few groceries before I went home. Off the Earls Court road, I ran into Diana, the Polish blonde bombshell, with her boyfriend Marco. By then, the three of us had something of a history together. This was perhaps four, five months after I had started the job and I was living near Barons Court, long after the time of surfing the couches of just about every brothel in town, and after the one-month stopover in a West Kensington loft undergoing construction works.

Diana and her man had, shortly after putting me up for a few nights some months before this, lost their housing themselves, and after I had let go of the tiny blonde Gino had brought me, Diana and Marco were knocking on my doors.
They were on the road, so I put them up. Diana and I were working girls, but she was adamant that none of her money could be given to Marco, that he should find a job himself. Having failed to do so, or rather, having got sacked often for drinking on the job, Marco had given up the search and was a cute, pot-smoking Neapolitan crying body wasting away through Whiskey bottles on my floor for a week.

I was barely moved in; the loft that the landlord, a hyperactive, shouty Indian who seemed to own half of West Kensington, had put me up at whilst I waited for my new studio, had two large bedrooms with some remnants of Argos furniture, an expiring bathroom and kitchen, access to the roof and a lovely view on the district line train tracks, although scaffoldings were blocking some of

[283]

the view. An old piano that I had bought on eBay for small change stood in a corner and I had picked up my book boxes from the storage with a friend, lined them up on the piano and on a long wall board.

The wardrobe was filling with bling-bling new clothes I had begun to buy as my solvency increased; studded, sequinny and leather jackets, designer jeans and cool sneakers, pretty boots, jewellery, watches, satin tracky bottoms, juicy couture; and I was stocking up on equipment like wonderful headphones, a new ipod, and rapidly changing phones as I was now used to muggings. In the fridge, I kept my growing supplies of high quality make-up, fragrance collection and and beauty products – it was the time when everything I owned was brand new, as I had, for a long time, had less than nothing.

Diana made plenty of money, too, and there was never really a shortage of anything, we went on spending sprees together and to parties and got Marco all the whiskey, beer and pot he wanted. Diana was secretly addicted to cocaine, always scoring in the bath, injecting herself, because she had diabetes, too. I tried not to think of this too often, because I really loved her. She was almost always drunk, injecting, and she was so very ill. I knew she was on death row. The whole thing we were doing, seemed a big decadence den, and they both were out of control, having loud fights every day, shouting, crying, having sex in public, smoking pot, spilling drink...

Diana had in mind that Marco would become a male escort, and had a photo shooting lined up for him, but he wasn't too keen. He was saying he couldn't live with the thought of cheating on her so routinely. She pointed out that she was doing just that, and that she wouldn't even be jealous, that instead, it would put them on the same level. He became tearful, doubtful; as a result, sitting on my bed,

[284]

she made a suggestion: 'I'll show you, and you will feel, that it's different. Fuck her' – she pointed at me – 'and I will watch'.

He protested, 'no, no, I don't want to... No offence, but you must understand...'

'Do it!' she shouted.

There was a pause, during which she looked at me, and said: 'You don't mind, do you?'

I said nothing, shaking my head in disbelief. He began to cry, then called my name and fell into my arms in despair.

Soon, his pants got bigger and a few minutes later, we were all whirling about the sheets in a naked threesome at noontime. It seemed that all was well, the idea of him becoming an escort was abandoned, and we all said how much we enjoyed our threesome.

But in the night, Diana and I were sitting in the lounge of a brothel, he phoned her up and said he was about to jump out of the window. Diana got angry with him. 'You're such an idiot, why do you want to do that, are you crazy? Do you think *my* life is easy? Do you think I do all this for fun? I also want things to change, but right now, this is how it is. Don't be such an asshole and kill yourself'...

She hung up and told me what had happened. I got worried, and phoned him up again, too. He was still on the roof and crying. 'I'm a homeless bum, my girlfriend is a whore, I don't have a job, I don't have a penny, what do you think this life is like, I'm going to finish myself off right here and now', he sobbed.

'Oh, Marco, think about your mother, how sad she would be, and think about us all, how we would miss you', but he was angry and emotional, and hung up. In the morning, we found him sleeping peacefully in my bed.

I had been homeless, surfing brothel couches for a few

weeks, and my first own place now, this very large, but run-down and partly dysfunctional loft apartment, seemed to be cramped up with girls in crisis, first the Romanian skinny blonde, and now, this out-of-control couple. I myself was extremely stressed, exhausted by the long homelessness, and migraine was beginning to creep into my life. I was in urgent need of a relaxing and quiet place to sleep and be. So I decided to move into a hotel.

I chose a modest but comfortable, West London hotel near my house. I told the receptionist who checked me in, the story of what happened. He took pity on me and let me stay at a cheaper rate. Marco and Diana soon got the message and found a new place for themselves. Later, I lost their contact, because my phone was stolen again.

The morning I ran into them after my job in the lavish house, at the off license store on Earls Court Road, was at least three months after all this madness. Now, they were sharing a small apartment in the area, and asked me to come upstairs for a drink.

I was ambivalent. On the one hand, I was happy to see them and keen to catch up. On the other hand, I feared that things might happen which we might later regret. I knew well Diana liked me, and I also really liked Diana. I thought back fondly of the crazy summer that lay behind us, our coffees in Soho, giggly shopping trips, afternoons in the park and Polish vodka parties in brothels, with her friends. We had developed an instant sympathy and a giggly bond when we had first met, and then, we also shared a dead serious and dark streak, as hookers, there was a lot of compassion for each other's difficulties in life, understood through a kind of identification with each other's feelings. Somehow we could meet in the middle and give each other gentle love and embraces.

Marco was jealous, although he liked me too, sitting on brothel couches surrounded by girls in sexy underwear, but he had great Catholic guilt. He had joined in, that once, but it hadn't really gone well for him.

So when I met them together and they asked me upstairs, an anxiety that something awful might happen overcame me. They could see what I was thinking. They said we would be good, and just have a drink. Marco was drunk already, and fell into bed right away. Diana and I were on the couch talking, and then we started kissing. Marco staggered in half asleep on the way to the toilet, and dropped his pants to an erect penis. I looked at him, and her, eager to carry on, and pretended suddenly to have to go, and left.

I was at home cleaning up a little, it was nine in the morning. Diana rang my cell, and I picked it up with a dark premonition.

'He cut his wrists, there's blood everywhere, he is crazy, he killed himself', she stuttered.

'You have to call the ambulance. He is probably not dead. Call an ambulance, now', I said.

'No, I already called the ambulance, they already took him away. He's okay', she said.

'Which hospital did they take him to?'

'I don't know. They just took him away'.

There was a pause.

'Are you okay? Do you want me to come over?'

'Yes, please, if you can'.

I went back over to her house. We cleaned up the blood, and tried to figure out what hospital he was at, we called a few, eventually we located it.

'We should go there and see him', I said.

We talked about suicide a little, that we all, really, were

[287]

dreaming to do it, but that it just wasn't right for someone to go ahead. Life was going to get better and much of it was beautiful already. Perhaps that for him, it would have had to get better earlier than this. But we didn't talk much. It was a tragic morning and there wasn't much to say about it. We went to sleep, cuddled together like little children.

Again, I avoided them for a few weeks. As my phones got stolen so often, I also lost her contact again, but got to her again through a card boy, who let me know she had opened a flat in Gloucester Road. It was winter by then, and I was on my way out from sex work.
I went to see her at her new flat, a vibrant, crowded place with cooking, table dancing and communal crack smoking, just in time to catch the night they were celebrating her engagement to Marco.
As they came back from dinner, she wore a diamond solitaire ring, and we sat on the bed, she, Marco, and a beautiful redhead escort with aquamarine eyes, the drug delivery boy, and I, smoking crack out of a coca cola bottle, and they announced they would be moving to Italy, as she was pregnant.

That morning, although again, I didn't have an apartment, I left the flat early, around 7a.m., and went for a walk in Kensington Gardens. I wasn't happy to have smoked crack, my first time, and I needed some time to think.
It was a misty dawn in early December, a setter dog that someone was walking came bouncing my way, and the silhouette of a long coat in wellies, under a large umbrella, came walking behind the dog.
I looked at the front of houses overlooking the Park with their elegant facades, their net curtains, their occasional balcony flower pots, and the street lamps flickering, about to go out. How much decay is beneath this city, I thought.

[288]

How much filth, how much smeary filth plastered in diamante and thick eyeliner, drenched in the poignant half-light of smoke, whiskey, coke, and cheap perfume.

I found myself a bedsit just a few days after this, and met Diana one last time for pizza in Earl's Court the day before she left for Italy. Marco's family, I heard, would give them an apartment, and he would work in the family business whilst Diana would be staying at home and get health treatment, have her baby, and they would live there for a while, until they'd fancy another shore. We cried a little, but both knew it was for the best, when we said goodbye.

Raymond asked me to come back for some more piano video folly, that he really needed me to do so for his business and that unless something changed he was 'finished', and that he thought I could help him a great deal with the advertising, so I went.

He showed me his bank statements, he was full of debt, and in his view, that didn't matter because he didn't believe the interest rates were real. At least, whenever he got cash payments for pianos, he could live on the cash. I suggested he make an inventory of his entire showman's wardrobe and his pop culture memorabilia, and place it for sale on e-bay, like the pianos.

The next time he asked me to come and see him, I cancelled a few times, eventually he decided to make videos at the piano himself, and since I wouldn't show up, he would impersonate me. He availed himself of a woman's wig, put on the charity shop dresses he had found the day we first; and from there, his drag fantasies sprang to a garden of bounty that seemed to have no end. He soon developed a youtube character with myriad, iridescent facettes and a range of moods and outfits, flourishing in the role, starring and reviving his whole closet of magical,

[289]

Liberace-style attire, improvising away, a joy to behold.

My meetings with Raymond, and seeing the depressed village he lived in, more than anything else gave the word 'recession' a meaning and tangible form. If Raymond had gone crazy all the way, if he had always been an eccentric, no-one represented as well as he the destruction wrought by the economic downturn that year.

His phone line had been disconnected, all the bank accounts were overdrawn and no steps were taken to address this. He just had to count pennies, eat frozen food from the low cost supermarkets, and wait for arts jobs to afford him a living again. Increasingly reluctant to part with any possessions, he ended up selling nothing, working nowhere, continuously hoarding, dusting and polishing his rhinestone treasures, his three antiquated cars, his scooters, and his pianos, crafting himself his very own, lively and glittering fake gold imaginarium.

My bedsit, and quitting sex work, weren't really attached to having found a better job, it was only that I had reached the point of not being able to bear it any longer. I had intended it as a temporary solution from the outset, and ended up staying in the half world from March til November. Steady cocaine use had given me migraines, and then, ultimately, this wasn't a life. One morning that I had walked out of a shift, I stood in the middle of the road and started crying.

November, 2010
I look quite good, now. I mean, I look well-adjusted, conservative, boring, healthy, normal... whatever. I look stable, like I'm a married woman or something. Not like a homeless hooker, mental hospital rescapee, drug addict, artist or poet. Nobody would think anything is wrong with me. I feel that a lot is wrong, but the last thing I need is for

[290]

my appearance to let strangers know about it.

I walked past the Crossbones graveyard in Southwark, that erstwhile dumping place for dead hookers, now a shrine with ribbons, pictures, totems and letters, wondering if some of my friends are dead already. I have left, and saved no-one, because saving myself was hard enough... to think that they all are still down there, answering the phones, cleaning up the kitchen, scared of police raids, pushing tough clients at each other, doing their make-up by the mirror, swapping clothes, trying on new earrings, straightening each other's hair, moisturising their legs, moaning about stingy customers...

Every now and then, though not often, I felt this dreadful blues sensation. Once at night, in a black cab to the Park Lane Hotel, as the taxi came past a school, I looked at my shoe, my stocking, the dress, and the hands in my lap, and thought to myself 'Gosh, is that what we were promised then – why I always did so well in school – to entertain the dicks I always considered scum?'

They all looked at me sitting down on a burgundy satin bedspread in amber light, in their navy suits and camel coats, cufflinks and pinned ties, greying hair and bulging wallets. They looked at me, unsure where to begin in the conversation. And I looked at them, trying to figure out what they'd want.

The hardest thing is not really the smooth operating of a decent day-to-day, it's the sudden curtain falls, flashbacks, side pokes, a familiar-sounding accent. The knowledge that my past sleeps, quietly sunken tucked under my ribs and breathes evenly like a bubble, like a cloud.

How deep blue at 5am the night hangs like a blanket covering my head, and how deep blue my feelings get then. What, all these things have happened, and I'm still around? So here I am sitting before the pyre of an awful past, a king in purple gown, a crown weighs me into my

[291]

throne, with golden fork and golden knife, and on the table before me a high piled heap, the rusty pieces that on my battles with the sea, when I was wielding my powers – my magic sword, yeah – those rusty pieces I saw along the side, never knew what they were, the arms of dead dolls, perhaps, the tusks of a mammoth?

Springs of a seesaw, empty food cans, old rubber tyres, what was all that? It's all on a heap before me now, round table, white napkin, and this time there is no escape, this time I can't move, the jester's grinning by the door. These are the cries of those I left dying on the way, these are women, men, in hospitals, hundreds of them. Begging in the streets, dying on the streets, these are the people I laughed with and who I have had to leave. People I've left where I found them, in dark holes I went through, left them there, I know they still are, prostitutes, little girls and little boys, stranded, homeless, half-dead junkies that everybody steals from.

But it seems I forgot to eat this dish, and they won't excuse me at the theatre, the tears I spill before it on a silver plate, the blows I send it, only make this gleeful society laugh, and laugh again.

I am going to have to think of it somehow, and make it disappear. It obscures my view, it obscures everything, and everyone's laughing. I will perhaps never find the solution. Since the day I left America, time did not really move on, seasons don't mean a thing, I can't explain how, but when I got back up, no matter how much I've done, my mind froze that day as if I'd become two, and as if one of me had moved forward whilst the other had not. I let a part of me float on an outward journey through storms and battles and gave it the gift of laughter, sent it to run, fall and rise over and over again, to endure always. I only ever saw the light of my soul's half moon, but the other half is freezing

[292]

in darkness.

I had lived a long tale, and emerged to a London that had barely changed. Soho, like Venice, eternally sinking, was still crumbling in its half-worldly glory like before. The old man on the road with little plastic-wrapped balls of heroin in the back of his mouth still walking around pulling strings, the phone booths still full of porn cards, Philoctetes is still screaming. All the world's a burning house. From time to time, when I open a philology journal, I come across black and white photographs of German classicists. It reminds me of Berlin, strolls underneath the Pergamon altar, round about the museum island. The tears of all things rain outside my window, my hands are folded, the world is sinking. I will just wait here.

I managed to see the charming Ed again, and the romance rekindled, but it confused me. An old friend from Berlin told me not to worry, that in cities, people can meet again and again, and be very happy when they meet, even if they never really stamp big declarations or get into the domesticity of a married life. A love to kill for, secret and passionate, like an affair.

I changed phone number, moved house, left no address. Gino had said this to me: 'If you want to leave this job, the day you do it, you do it. From then on, do never turn around again. You have to forget everything you saw and heard here, and never come back. Otherwise, you will be stuck in it forever. Every time you don't have money, you'll think about doing this again. You must say one day that you're finished, and never think of this again' – he was right. Orpheus already knew that. If you were lucky to return from the underworld, at least have the decency not to turn around.

[293]

Five: Atlas of London

A Bedsit for Heracles

I cut the cord, and jumped into a new anonymity, and rented a bedsitting flat in Shepherd's Bush. It was a time of economic downturn. I had not taken that into account necessarily. I had saved up a few months' worth of money. But I wanted to work, the money would run out. Things had to be put back in order, that had been the idea from the start, to live to continue.

The great bubble that had been London when I had just got my brand new B.A. five years ago, where they waved graduate traineeships and paid internships at me with my fancy 1.1, had certainly burst.

People with humanities degrees were huddling around cheap estates growing ever pricier, on ever smaller spaces together either in the pride of the artsy and starving, or without that pride, at the job centers, staying in sipping Morrisson's cola, or working manual jobs and smoking weed on benches, on Shepherd's Bush Green, where I then lived, as for those who had been disallowed by the job center, they were down and out. Money shops were flourishing, and Notting Hill and Portobello were following Bayswater and Paddington in a phase of transition and aggression where new poverty was visible. Strip joints in Soho closed down, as did many small businesses, big chain stores and market giants came down, swathes of people were sacked.

Trade with Germany was the new business trend, as I found out when I walked through the doors of recruitment agencies. My best quality, now, was that I spoke German. My first job was to be selling English shirts to German shop chains, and then, speaking to telecom clients in

Germany. It was really only in places like Knightsbridge that things seemed to continue with ease—with such ease as venal love could afford you, anyway. And this wasn't Knightsbridge.

The last night I had seen Ed, nearly a year prior and in the midst of my travels through the opiatic Soho, we had gone to see a drag queen karaoke show at Madame Jojo's. After the show, a hilarious affair with golden sequins, tassels, false lashes and 1980s smash hits, we had been to a night club. We sat on precious French armchairs and drank tequila, I on his lap, and he held me happily, after which we made out on the streets by the lamp posts, walked in circles around Soho in a happy daze until morning. Then, on the weekend, we went for dinner, and after dinner, to his apartment. Some very quick and embarrassed sex had happened, after which he immediately got dressed again. For a few hours, we lay there watching TV. After that, radio silence.

November, 2010.
Ed told me meet him at the Hilton. Alright, I get it, so he's got a woman. But I've not seen him so bold before. He was the one to ask, that was a first – so far I had been the one asking. I'd not seen him so smooth before. My Hilton visiting skills are great, just great. Now, the situation has turned over. Now he wants me, now I want him less. I caught him lying twice. Small, tiny, insignificant lies, but why does a man lie?
In his defense, I have lied to him as well.
It takes a certain kind of energy to be with a man who is lying, cheating, and to be genuine and emotionally honest nonetheless. But that is something I have got terribly good at now: putting true feeling into a false setting. It's as a curse, to be forever in between things, never to arrive, if

there is no destination, to be in perpetual transition. I will
always want to find the real Ed, look for him everywhere I
go...

With these frothy thoughts in mind and in the kitchen of my new Shepherd's Bush flat, I accidentally cut my thumb whilst attempting to open a pack of marzipan with a rather sharp knife, in fact a meat knife I had originally bought as a prop, it was that big. Now in my kitchen, it slipped on my hand and cut all the way into my bone.

I thought it all terribly scenic, in the night, in the new place I had just moved into, a worn and run-down, mouse-gnawed, sticky stained linoleum kitchen floor, thick layers of dust on the staircase windows, and a rainbow of grey shades of carpet on the stairs. Something of a horror movie scenario came to mind when I looked at myself standing there barefoot in this squalid kitchen, in my silk nightie, remnant of the escort life, large meat knife in hand, blood drippings everywhere.

I had felt a nerve or two twang and the tip of my thumb go numb, and assessed that now the damage was done, it was irreversible. I washed the wound with witchhazel, made a few kitchen roll pressure bandages until the bleeding stopped, sprayed disinfectant everywhere, and wrapped the whole thing up in gauze.

Ed saw it the next night and urged me to visit A&E.

Here I was then, in the waiting room of Charing Cross Hospital, at two in the morning after Ed had gone home. The wait was long, although I was the only patient, and I was pacing in the hall.

An unkempt black man came in walking barefoot in his shorts and wearing a hospital gown, in the company of two black police officers, one female, one male. He was wearing a hospital wristband and gesticulating vividly, and

[297]

I thought I recognized a psychiatric type scene. But I wanted to look away.

The police were not particularly impressed by the scenario but annoyed as it seemed to have been going on at great length already. Their conversation was approximately this: 'I have nothing at all, no family, no friends, no home, no job, and this is not my country. I am bipolar, I get depressed, I get so upset and my life is so hard, they give me pills in that hospital, but I'm telling you the pills are not working, and I want to leave, but there is nowhere I can go, nobody wants to help me, I don't know anybody, I'm ill, I'm homeless, it's cold, and I don't know what to do any more, I'm tired of life and I have tried everything but I've run out of options and I don't want to live any more and I want you to let me go'.

'I don't know about that, said the police woman, but you need to put some clothes on. These are your clothes, put them on and leave, you can go anywhere you like, just not without clothes'.

'I don't want to put no clothes on, I don't own these clothes, I don't have any clothes, I want to leave like this!'

'You must put these clothes on, or someone else is going to pick you up again and bring you right back here, and we have better things to do with our time, and by the sounds of it you've got a lot to do as well, so just get on with it, get dressed and go'.

'No, I don't want to get dressed, I'm just fine, I'm sick and I don't know where to go, and I don't know what to do with my life any more, I am tired of life'.

'But you're not going to solve any of these questions this time of night, so make up your mind...'

'But I am bipolar and these pills are not working...'

'Well get out of that hospital gown and put some proper clothes on, and some shoes, you can't walk in the streets like this, and if you don't go back to hospital, you can't

[298]

just hang around here all night just to warm your ass up, this is a hospital, there's people here who need to use this room... Didn't you say you had an aunt in London?'
'I have no family whatsoever, they all reject me, they say they don't want me, that's why I'm in the streets, and I have nowhere to go, I'm alone, alone, alone, get it?'

Darn, that all sounds familiar. My memory was replaying so many lived moments from the farther past. I felt compelled to get up and leap to his defense, and at the same time, I felt paralysed. I wanted to rise to change the past, but... but... I couldn't do anything. I was just sitting there like an idiot whilst the situation unfolded. I was reminded of a thousand things I spent a lifetime trying to suppress from my memory.

My doctor appeared and said: 'See, even some free entertainment for you, isn't that charming?'
'It's nothing to joke about', I whispered.
The doctor lost his irritating smile, gave me a stern look and sighed: 'Mental hospitals are best stayed away from. If you aren't crazy when you go in, you sure will be, by the time you get out'
'I know. I once was s...'
'Sectioned?' he asked, 'why?'
'Oh', I said, 'that was long ago, back in America. Back in *America*', as if we were both octagenaries talking about the war.
I was stumbling on the lapse of time and saw myself again, in America, a young and frightened, sick pound of meat. Zyprexa, Risperdal, Lithium, Abilify... a rosary of curses.
'Did these medicines help you? It sounds like an impressive cocktail, and you are on none at all now?' said the doctor present in the room. All the doctors were beginning to blur together in my mind.

[299]

I said that I thought they had helped in the first few weeks but that after that I found it to be torture to be kept on them, and that in America the current view is that schizophrenia is life long and will only get worse with time. I had my misgivings about such a view, I thought it was chiefly the view of the drug industry, for financial reasons, and that the drug industry had great influence on the education of doctors in America. I believed recovery was always possible. I said I understood that perhaps, some people might be prone to paranoia than others in certain life situations, which apparently had been my case, but that it was not as bad as some said it was. In no way was it legitimate to surmise that a person with delusions was prone to committing crimes, this reasoning was far too rash, and too vague, given the state of research and understanding of the phenomenon. To lock someone up preventively on the basis that they might do harm broke the trust in a country's political integrity. America was going the way of totalitarianism and the police state, and, and, and... it all just flowed out of me.

He said 'Well! I don't really know what psychiatrists do. I never quite understood what they are always talking about'.

I said 'I think that's exactly the problem. Nobody knows. The fact is, there's nothing there to know. I have spent many hours reading psychiatry textbooks, I got them from the university library. I've read many medical books. Psychiatry is a vague science.'

He said 'That's interesting. By the way, since you have all that scarring on your arm, I'm just going to write down for the surgeons at the other hospital that the cut on your hand today is nothing to do with self-injury and that the mental stuff is all past history, in case they get confused and think you did that cut on purpose'.

I said thank you.

[300]

The looks of white and blue linoleum floors, or even worse, grey and turquoise linoleum tiles, brought me back to stages of my life that are better not spoken or thought about. Without intending to, I started musing upon the blue and white tiles of linoleum in the psychiatric ward in the States and felt that grey, twilight-lit feeling of all things uncanny spread through me. It came automatically to me to get up and start pacing around the room in circles. I was beginning to sense a true waterfall of bad memories. Physical surroundings, fixtures and hospital noises, brought so much back to me. I started remembering faces I'd forgotten, patients from that ward back in the U.S., and wondering how they might have been since then. I knew that I would never know, and another wave of ill omens and the fear of bad news surged up. I thought of everything, again. Individuals whose undoing I had had a better chance to see unfold before me, whom I had seen again, and witnessed film strips of their stories, and Laurie's story too, all this was still haunting me, in dreams at night and mares by day.

The surgery procedure itself didn't seem quite as unworldly, otherworldly as expected. I had about the liveliness of a hundred year old dragonfly pinned to a museum case. After all the worrying and nervous and childish crying was done with, there was again this darker, deeper, calm and quiet sadness that won't speak, won't move, won't say, only marches forth within me in a stately funerary pace with sombre face.
The anaesthetist, a sort of real-life sandman expanding his vocabulary of painlessness, slumber and relief, re-opened that never-ending thirst of addiction in me with his arsenal of quiet, melancholy, rest and dreamful ease. Also, the nurse came around with codeine. I tentatively asked not to

[301]

be given these, but took them home in the end. I took a couple at first, when they began to work, I took another two, and as the sensation rushed up, I took the whole packet.

February, 2011
450mg codeine and counting
One thing I know for sure, now, is that I can take as much as I like, there will never be more than promise in them. They never fulfil, but only taunt you into thinking that if you took just a little bit more, you might just make it to neverland. I see that these narcotics brought me to death's doorstep, that this was the only neverland I'd ever get to, and I'll never really see it.
The other shore, I imagined it to be gleaming and paradisiac, marvellous, a land of sugar and icing from the fairy tales, all dew and fresh water, green grass, a golden Elysium for dreaming daemons.
Once arrived at death's doorstep, the gate is anguishing, the country dark, the path thorny and sorrowful. Addiction to narcotics – to the twin of death – I cannot travel the road twice.

I know it to be a vain quest, for a handful of dust. Yet I'm falling again for those same cheap dreams, with an even mind to forget the moaning and the screaming of mortals, the pain of loved ones, that I heard again in this squalid ward behind old curtains shoved beneath a sign reading 'psych alarm', that crying, trembling and despairing of those I knew, that's followed me everywhere as the shadow of my dog and won't leave me alone.
It has plunged a dagger into my throat that cannot be choked out nor swallowed. Dust that scatters itself in the wind, and though I know it, I'm running after the butterflies, hugging a ghost, lest my shadowed world

[302]

would fall, the waves break, chance be distraught and I, dead.

It was an overdose. My head was spinning and everything went dark, I was fainting, sat down in a chair, sweating and nauseous. I was feeling so hot, I was ready to get naked on the floor just to cool – and remembered a time I did this with the old flatmates, who thereupon thought it was time to kick me out.

My breathing went shallow and my pulse flat, I waited for what seemed an eternity on this chair. Images pulled themselves up of a summer afternoon by the lake, lying supine on a small boat in the half-light.

For weeks after this accident, I had to stay at home in bed. The beautiful Ed came to pick me up from hospital on the night after surgery, when I'd woken up from anaesthesia. Friends came to cheer me up and took me for a full English, showed up with home baked sweets and DVDs. Ed came often to check on me.

Once I tried to leave the house alone but quickly noticed that I was falling into states of deep sleep on the bus, unable to get up, so I realised I was really unwell and couldn't go out. So I stayed in. My mood was unaccountably in the low lows, in the wake of the accident, which I thought could be explained by the added traumatic reminiscences in the hospital and the dent they made into my drug addiction recovery. Only much later did I discover that the abtibiotics I was taking were causing a rare mental side effect in me.

I was feeling suicidal, confused and spent two weeks in a half-waking, half-hallucinating state interspersed with strange sleep at all kinds of hours. I was dysfunctional and housebound, chained in the psychological dungeon of

[303]

penicillin psychosis and the vagaries of my access to codeine for weeks. I was able to conjure up everything, as a grand catharsis after which I imagined myself to be a sort of weeping Achilles, terribly angry with the world, one who was owed rewards but had been given only dishonour, who had fought bravely but received no welcome home. Doctors tentatively diagnosed chronic fatigue or exhaustion, and ordered some rest and relaxation, a prescription I was only too glad to follow.

I couldn't leave the house much, but there was time to play the piano at home. The weeks I couldn't use my left hand, I got on to a few piano pieces with particularly difficult right hand parts. I also knew that piano practise and the music had a restorative and energising effect on my mind. For the first time since all the heat of that immense chaos, I could rest, and think things over. I hadn't noticed it, but I was traumatised: I had the 'worrying disease'. Once a warrior, always a worrier – this would probably be the final hurdle I would have to jump, to conquer my own fears.

January, 2011.
Blame it on my fragile health that I started remembering things I normally don't and that make me fugitive and restless, and a very sad, un-worldly traveller. I still have no better idea as to what I should do when that sadness creeps up and alongside it, the pain of being alone with it, this experience I've had so many times when I did talk about it, that people will tell me I'm crazy and I must be making this up. No.
I've learnt to live with both of these – that things went the way they went, and that nobody wants to hear about it. The thing I've probably heard most of all is 'you need to move on'. In all appearance, that is exactly what I've

done. I've moved on to and from more things than ever, in the past year alone.

Even if I don't do much revisiting, my memories come to visit me all by themselves. As long as I stick to regular sleep and try to keep the schedule busy, I rarely get into the embarrassment of being destroyed by flashbacks. The arts are what really makes me happy, heals me, and helps me be true to myself. They are and are not a separate place from difficulties I have with life. Wondering if I really still am the same human being that I was. I remember clearly losing all sense of identity when I was sat in an armchair in a basement in Mayfair staring blankly at this other working girl stretched out on a sofa watching video clips, and behind me, a guy in tracky bottoms was weighing up grams of cocaine and wrapping them in lottery tickets.

That time in the blue Porsche, I was going to take the train back to London, but as I walked along the high street, it struck me that I might as well just stay there – it made no difference, I was not less or more lost in that city than in any other part of the world.

I've been running down levels of experience, running through worlds, whole scenarios of lifetimes, endless conversations to re-invent sense. A shadow hangs over me, sleeps by my side, rests in my heart. After all these things I've seen and done, how much noise I've tried to dub over my ever-repeating dull heartbeat that brings back Laurie's eyes to me as it were just yesterday – that one dull beat, that old, dull, deep beat and uncanny reverb.

I walked thorough town all afternoon and all evening. I walked in circles. I felt this undescribable thing that if I had the words for it, then perhaps I could begin to dissipate. I could refine the rawness, perhaps, give meaning to a lump of marble that weighs on my heart,

[305]

chisel out a temple from it like the ancient people of Syria had done in the rocky mountains. It's rain, warm rain, dripping from a heart that seems to be able to bleed ad infinitum, as I replay that old scene from the New England fall in my head, or as American reminiscences well up from the corner of a British hospital door – such as that girl Rachel, who looked just fine but refused to speak, bathed in her clothes and had cigarette burns all over, but all over her body, who really did not say a word for two weeks, whatever people did to her. A man, an old man, who was unable to walk, whom they kept in a single room apart from the rest, that none of the other patients was allowed to approach, guarded day and night and they would beat him with their belts when they fancied it, we'd hear his screams in the morning – but why that was, I will never know. There was Jane, who got carted off to ECT, there were all thes people pacing around the ward in their stained gowns with their arms crossed, and the constant scenes of fighting, screaming, and blood on the floors, people being strapped down to beds, injected, broken like sticks, and then, those awfully vacant visiting hours, when no-one would come, and the phone would ring, my boyfriend from Europe, but I would not be allowed to answer it. Why? Rules. Leaving him angry and tearful on the other end.

Everyone was twitchy, tremulous, most people couldn't eat without making a mess, I couldn't either, and every fifteen minutes, you'd be asked what you were thinking. The windows not only had no handles to open them, they were also milk glass and sealed. So there was no way of knowing what was going on outside, and if you got there by ambulance, like I did, there was no knowing where you were. The sign outside on the corridor said 'ECT', not a great help.

And that poor dear old man, a year later, a man who

[306]

would not speak a word and always sit with his head in his hands, that poor man, now I understand why he could not remember me when I ran into him at the diner, again and again. At the time I did not know, but now I see it, he had ECT too. He was wearing a suit, a bow tie, he knew Demosthenes, time and time again approaching me with 'excuse me, you look familiar', I'd introduce myself again each time, he'd tell me his name was Philip every time, I'd remind him where we met, and he'd shrink back with a look I then took for embarrassment but now I guess was terror.

Watching my own body blow up, my organs fail on by one, my eyesight drop and my hands, head, face and legs twich and tremble on me all day long, trying to carry on, to carry on, always – heaven knows I didn't make this up. Just that day when I had finally got off these drugs, when I was half recovered, when I had begun to realise what psychiatry really does, when I had gone back to America – just that day when I saw they'd done it to Laurie, but done it to her ten times worse than to anyone else, to leave no hope she'd ever come back to us – that look in her eyes, that vacant and aqueous as it was, drew a little crack all the way through my courage, I think that moment when she gave me that look was the moment my mind froze and when my body started doing things on my behalf while I was still stuck in that poignant minute.

I cried, I asked questions, I rushed out, through the alarms, through the cafeteria, by the door I was sobbing, I ran up the stair, thinking if I should go back and find her again downstairs, I was not sure, I looked back at the students on the quad, I didn't know where to go from there, it was late at night in mid-October, in New England.

The grass wasn't wet when I fell on it, so I stayed seated. Ten minutes, twenty minutes, and still no way I could make sense of this. Thirty minutes, I began to feel exhausted. I

[307]

lay down facing the wall. I stroked the wall, I stroked the grass. I tore grass out.

On certain days, some lack of sleep or a bad dream perhaps can bring me back in spirit to that awful night. I know, I never worked on making any sense of this. It hasn't started making any sense on its own. I refuse to become one of those who believe that something like this can ever make any sense. It always draws up again somehow, I'm always floating in it, sometimes I widen the limits to almost freedom, I see more of the old days, how they fell apart.

I worried all day and all night, my mind turned into a glass vitrine with shards everywhere, a place where everything is fragile, that sounded clangy, splinty, cutting, ever so slightly artificial and glaring as the robotic, post-human world: that's how my mind felt at that moment, shattered, fractured, traumatized and brittle; For a few days, I was able to dodge it, dub 'I'm fine' over it, and I was happy there, but since the knife accident and hospital odyssey, everything melted down to leave a London full of sleazy merchants, intransigent lenders and interest-takers, unkind manner, a city that often leaves me penniless, fast and vibrant as it is. The erosion of morals in this city moves with the grave slowness of stagnation, to those who are less liquid. But I've known it for years, mostly I embrace it but on occasion the chill of arrogance breaks me down as a little boat against great cliffs. So many accidents have happened – a chain of mistakes, scandalous to behold, and facing it all alone.

I was starting to be OK on my own, until Ed started to come around again. Then, I could not bear to see him leave, wouldn't feel like myself until he was back, and as

[308]

he's not the most frequent of people, ignores calls for days, often cancels at the last minute, in the back of my mind I keep remembering that once when he said 'see you soon' he left it six months. It's probably the greatest fear here, that every time, goodbye could be goodbye.

I can stay awake all night listening to his breathing in the loving embrace of darkness, replaying scenes and verses of the shadowed past. I'm repeating to myself those great lines of Rilke, 'Had I grown in a place where the days are light and the hours sleek, I would have made for you a grand celebration, and my hands now would not hold you as they sometimes do, so tight and fretful. I would have dared to waste you, you, the boundless present'.

It's a kind of magic. He is wonderful, yet difficult to reach, calm and independent, yet at the same time, inwardly wounded. Always ambivalent, the man who always leaves the door open and yet never speaks with full clarity.

Terrified to show weakness, unable to move in his armour of rehearsed male manners, he is painfully slow melting, defrosting. Much that I want to be closer to him and share a tear, I worry, again, that in the event that he did end up melting in my hands, so to speak, I would not only have won this chase, but also broken locks I had no business breaking. After all, I don't know what it is that is always troubling him.

I realised I would have to speak less, if I wanted to tune in to his repressed, hardly expressed communication. At the same time as I deplored his lack of grandiosity, his well tempered passion and the absence of poetic word choices that rang of a darkly glittering, bold and glowing inscape celebrated by poets, and of the intensity of real things. I found his manner to silence me, a rare thing in my life, I was unsure what I should say, insecure, and afraid to have

[309]

said wrong things.

The longer I mold myself into this form, the more our conversations take a sensitive and delicate bent, and the more I suffer from a host of questions I cannot find the answer to, about our relationship. I begin to see we may just never arrive at any point beyond these brief and blind encounters...

It was only an eastern promise, but Ed and I were keeping it. I had once run after him, stood in the middle of the road and watched him disappear in the crowd.

He returned, more domestic, more loving and caring. We were those lovers my friend had described, who, in a large city, meet again and again, are fond of each other, and still, don't stamp big declarations to live happily everafter. I knew all the things he liked, and he knew all about me. At Christmas, we went to the opera. I started going to the Chancery Lane library more often and would meet him for coffee during his work breaks from the offices on Fleet Street. We had walks in the Temple, occasional after work drinks, went to the movies, at the old vue theatre near my house, and when the spring came, more walks in Hyde Park, sex in the fields by Bayswater Road, West End shopping trips, lunch at burger kitchens, dinner on my birthday, and another Christmas in my bedsit, luxurious provisions scattered on my shabby couch.

My stockings and underwear sets from the brothel merchant, glittery dresses and high boots, were finding appreciation even after their time, and something always kept us going. We slept together in my screechy single bed, I had him in my mouth plenty of times.

He seemed to breathe more easily and start to smile, amused, when I played with his hair. Always keen on impromptu kissing in an alleyway, we laughed a lot

[310]

together, went to shows together, started swapping comments about people who were passing by as we were having our lunch, gave each other little gifts.

The relationship was constantly at risk of falling down from its tenuous bonds and scatter itself in the wind like ashes. I had a hard time acquainting myself with the truth that I'd met 'the one' but would have to leave him there, because obviously, things weren't moving forward, and there was a complication in the background that I knew nothing about, but knew there must be one.

All kinds of fears, worries, hopes, laughs, and always, again, this fragile happiness coupled with the expectation of a long winter of the soul on that dark day when it would be over, as I knew it would be. The wind, waves, and shadows of the past broke and faded in the rays of new lights, we were always on the go, doing something new. Often we made love as if it were the last time we ever saw each other, as in the old Billy Wilder movies, when the war is about to tear lovers apart, as if we were saying goodbye in the palace of tears. But it wasn't anything as dramatic, at all. It was just one of these extended urban flings, with true love thrown in.

June, 2011.

His eyes are like magic lanterns, where stories pass as clouds and shadows, as ghost horses, without a word. Sometimes when I am on top of him, and run my hands over that luscious skin of his I want to pick him up, untangle the seaweed, and unbind his laughter, to scatter the stars and the blossoms, to make him feel as easy and as simple as it could be, but those are only dreams. I've waited for him, for a long time.

I still am struggling with everything: with the odds, the sluggish volition, the vagueness, the weightless form of our relationship, which, at first, I thought could no longer

[311]

become a reality, but then slowly it took its flaky shape. Anxieties began to tear at my heart and left me stranded on a desert island to wonder if there would really be a morning.

I can revert to my silent, contemplating nature that, once not so long ago, had been broken violently and turned into a loud flow of speech, by the great disasters in my life. There will be no grand welcome home any more, for I'm too calm now to tell the tale, tell the stages of my journey, now that I perhaps could find a hearing with those to whom I would have loved to speak, back when Troy was burning. And as for revenge, the best revenge is living well.

If I packed my bags? If I left all this, if I dissolved this tiny little household of mine, my Billie Holiday and Stephane Grappelli records and the good old record player, my wardrobe with its many dazzling dresses, the midnight velvet bedspread, my funky crockery, the silver art nouveau mirror, the postcards of Marlene on the wall, the Perignan wine cooler? All this, and more, heavy to move away, but was only meant to create a comfort zone I was just passing through.
Now love, an uncertain, enigmatic love that doesn't make demands, is keeping me in a situation that could drive me crazy – the old Shepherd's Bush bedsit with the Italian director, the nutella man... Life smiles at me, now. Now that I'm friends again with all those who were in the old, the straight, the good life. I have to go to Berlin.

The man I love just happens not to love me, although he's keen to play. And this is when I know that I've arrived back in the safe and happy hemisphere of mundane worries, and can quote to myself that dialogue from a

[312]

Berlin film I forget, where a woman tells her neighbour: 'I think it's lovesickness', and the other replies: 'How wonderful'.

Ed had a fiancée, whom he had neglected to mention. Facebook, google and the iphone did all the dirty work of letting the women find out about each other without any agency of Ed's. She found out about me first, as she casually picked up his phone bill at their house, noticed a particular phone number being called rather a lot, and went through his iPhone. There, she read nearly a year's worth of Ed and my texts to each other. Since he had saved my number under my full name, she was able to google me. She gave me a call, too. But then, she didn't know what to tell me, and hung up when I picked up.

Eventually, an engagement announcement in the electronic version of the Sunday Times casually came my way via facebook. I tried to ring him that day, but there was no answer.

He, rather laxly, e-mailed a few days later to let me know he had been unable to communicate with me as the lady was watching his every move, and that even now it would be difficult, but that he had never intended to dump me and I shouldn't consider myself dumped, and that whether or not the engagement would lead to a marriage, was a whole different matter.

I asked him if we could meet one final time, we agreed on the steps of St. Paul's as a meeting place. It was a warm afternoon in early summer, I felt washed out by the thought that I was to separate myself definitively, and I couldn't really eat anything or drink much when we went to Starbuck's. I brought him a copy of *Prufrock*.

The world seemed to have unhinged itself, the great house of St. Paul's cathedral seemed to dangle off a ferris wheel, and the houses along Fleet Street seemed to wobble as an

[313]

old denture, the road suddenly bulging with bumps and arching into an abyss. We were both in rotten mood, didn't say much, and didn't reach any conclusion.

Just then, I received a call back from my old madam, would I do a replacement shift.

I did. The same girls were all still there, and we chatted all night long about hair, make-up, and celebrities. Even the same clients were still coming in, recognized me, asked me where I'd been. I made a lot of money that night. That splendid derision and grand resistance to all things romantic, that is so salutary to the broken-hearted, that careless and insensitive shower of cash and luxury, that clear laughter of relief that one can stop trying making romance work and put one's emotions behind oneself, the liberty to judge from appearances, all this came back to me at once. I cursed Ed, everybody laughed, and I got over all the heartbreak in a gulp.

But as the morning crept up, I remembered other things, too, about that flat. I had spent some of my worst moments here, experienced my truest loss of identity, and I remembered then, how I used to think that my culture and education, my strength and great ability, would one day soon bring me back out of that dirty industry again – but nothing like that had actually happened.

That morning after work, we walked to the tube station together, like the three graces: three young women with long dark hair, enticing stature, nicely done faces, and glinting jewels, clearing through dawn on the Old Brompton Road, that grand parade of false appearances. A great disillusionment gripped me, my knees went soft and the injustices that gnawed at our three lives came welling up in my throat, an anger of despair and humiliation spread through me, the shocking, rotten absurdity of the whole situation and the infectious smear of baby oil, sperm and

[314]

cheap perfume. The sickening aura of depravity in the red-lit rooms, the memory of smells, all of a sudden wanted to asphyxiate my every hope for a better future.

All of London seemed to me a ruinous fortress of mindlessness and greed for gain, with an underground of cold fear and vacuous addictions. I suppose that I felt that which is so often said that whores feel, a sort of psychological destruction by the mental image of unwashable dirt and stains, the bitter pill to remind me that 'you must never come back here'.

I woke up that week twice bathed in sweat, remembering the U.S.A. and mental hospital. The streets I lived in, the house, and the green, all suddenly had a host of resemblances with my old place in the States. Now the power of involuntary memory was not limited to linoleum hospital floors, but even street signs, IKEA kitchen cupboards, the shape of my built-in wardrobe, the traffic sounds around the square, the police sirens, anything could catapult me back.

At times, I was convinced to have returned to that past, and found myself laying on the bed trembling, gritting my teeth, crying and screaming out of fear. The ghost of my American trauma lay over the streets of London for a few days like a big spiderweb, and in the silence of this strange loneliness I eventually understood I was living deep in the desert, in nimrod, where my soul was sketched and flattened, and my hopes and dreams, those butterflies, lay outstretched motionless with a needle in their heart, on a collector's board.

The silence in the dusty noon of summer sent me on a long and erratic, reflective walk around town.

There had been autumn nights many years ago, when as an undergraduate in London, walking up through Chancery Lane and Bloomsbury, a low and dry fog condensed on the

[315]

facades like pearls of perspiration. Warm light in pub windows and calm suits in smoothly run legal offices, would raise itself off the ground and rise to meet the street lamps, forming a circle around their heads, bending like flowers. As I walked past velvet curtain windows, red bricks, marble, chessboard floors in entrances and spearpoint iron fences, dead leaves hissing before my feet, the smokey chill wrapped about my coat and scarf.

The echo of my steps in these half-deserted evening roads would call up to life lines of great poets, novelists, historians and philosophers that I had read at the library, where the winds used to howl and sing to the reading room. and a male choir of learned mutterings would set in, in my mind. I would pass the British Museum, that stood erect before the mast of Senate House, which seemed like a flagship, then, a grand cruising flagship.

I walked across Bedford Square that day, again. By then, many times past were resonating in the crossing of that square that is always silent and empty, its beautiful park always locked, its delicately grand buildings shut, and unmarked. Many times I'd wondered about the park, who it was being kept so nice for, what it must look like from the windows above, with its lush ivies and stylish hedges. One building especially caught my eye. When I was closer and could read the gold plate at the front, involuntarily, I took a small step back, looked inside through the window. It was a blast from the past, the brown framed photographs, the letter weights I saw, the university logo.

I went back to the libraries much more, started going to the cinema more, to see blockbusters, read the Evening Standard... I joined Harvard, Yale and Penn club evenings in London. I was able to show my face again, I thought, to all those wholesome young people I knew in London, whom I had meticulously avoided until then. The world I

[316]

had once shared with them was a world of good schools, good jobs, and good hair.

I'd already got the wardrobe for the city job, that dull uniform of the ghosts in Moorgate. yes, yes, I was coming back into normality.

As a clerk in Moorgate, in another September many years before then, T.S. Eliot's words began to detatch themselves from the ground, about the death of the soul at Bank station. So rightly he says, citing Dante, 'a crowd flowed over London Bridge, so many, I did not think Death had undone so many', and 'My feet are at Moorgate and my heart is under my feet'.

I walked down King William Street in memory of the poem, I even visited St. Mary Woolnoth, and read the ten commandments there carved in wood. Continuing down to St. Paul's, the ancient trees with their laden green crowns were bending against the white marble beauty of the cathedral and its ancient glass windows.

I stood outside, about to meet Ed for a drink. We went for our drink, and then for a walk. It was the first time we met since the regrettable afternoon by these very same steps. The London riots had happened in between, this had been the feeble pretext for renewed contact.

We kissed in a doorway, he said he had missed me, and we went, hand in hand, to my old shabby bedsit. That night, I saw a kind of curtain fall before all the spectacle of unfulfilled dreams and fancy, every mystery, all the passion and the chance events that had come to me through him. Now that I knew the answer, he suddenly seemed nothing more than a young man with good looks, a city boy bitten by the relentless pursuit of self-interest and moral paralysis. He was lovely to look at, but the depths I'd formerly sought to explore through the translucency of his watery brown eyes had receded into that Sesame I

[317]

knew I would never open. It used to lay there half-open to me, and let glint a few stray gems, but it was now so closed and dark that I began to wonder how I had ever imagined there would be any gold in the ground.

The tone of his voice had not much now of a dream, it touched nothing and was only his plain, parsimonious, and reserved speech in a male-formed accent. Nothing chimed there surrepticiously between the lines that I could pull on, as if it were a glowing fabric to a secret scene behind a double door. There was only that dull grey the eye perceives in complete darkness.

He was not even easy to converse with, and his monosyllabic replies difficult to find inspiration in. Everything that once had been, seemed to have fallen to the ground, like a satin robe falls off a mannequin leaving nothing but an armless, faceless, flaxen bust to stare at.

Is this falling out of love? I thought to myself. I could not give moral lessons to anyone. Disloyal of me, I thought, to reject him, who had accepted me under any weather. Disloyal of me, and guilty of my own lie to have said 'I will always love you', when clearly that was not so.

My heartbreak had been at times unbearable in the weeks before, but here he was, standing obnoxious like a naughty schoolboy, and I had no hard feelings, only a smiling forgiveness of a minor fault, more than having anything to reprehend, I was looking at us both, thinking to myself what foolish children we were, children of the city...

The Ghosts at Moorgate

I was working the dullest city job in mobile telecoms. I had managed to turn from the rock'n'roll despair monger that I was, into one of those affairs in suit and make-up that get on the tube at rush hour, haunt the Moorgate by day, the pub between eight and eleven with assorted locals, only to stumble into a bed, somewhere quiet and a bit musty, in the calmer parts of town.

I had lied my way through the recruitment companies just so I could get a job, pretending to have had experience in sales and customer service. At the outset, I had to improvise a little, as I had never been in corporate environments, and had not been in any way normal for the longest time.

I soon had a reputation of being a boring, but efficient worker, who was somehow always late, but never got in trouble for it. I enjoyed being someone normal, see-through, with a simple life story. And I was surprised how easily I could fool myself, too, and get myself to blank out everything else.

By October, I was sitting quite well in it. Impersonating the cliché of the uptight commuter whose life means nothing, and I knew well that what I was doing, what I was living, did indeed have no significance at all. Sometimes, it felt as if I was once again trapped in a sort of Hotel California setting, from which there was no escape. I would have to put on Herculean efforts to levy myself out of this grey and modest everyday life again.

I joined swing dance socials with Andrea, my truest companion through the good times and the bad, and took to leisurely and deliberative walks in Holland Park with Annis, an actress I had met outside the Royal Courts after Julian Assange's hearing. Her boyfriend, an English punkrock musician, invited me to indie nights, to which I invited my old friends: Rob, a War Studies undergraduate I had met on the streets at night the same evening I met Louis, the tall German I had shared a dorm floor with in the States, now a London banker, and whom I introduced, together with his Italian girlfriend who was studying political science, to an high school friend, who was now also living in London and working at the banks. She had a boyfriend, a Polish lawyer whom she had met in New York.

Florian showed his face more often again, that old Etonian who had been in my Greek play years ago, whom I had seen in New York, lost his contact, written him a note once on a blue night of coincidence whilst sat on a train to New York.

He was still stuck in it, every now and then emerging on my doorstep to discuss the problem of addiction, then disappearing again. Underneath all the destruction and degradation of his body brought on by crack, the Florian I had known, the great adventurer, seemed to be drown and to transform into a squalid ghost, rattling in chains and crying out for help in vain. He disappeared again, for a time, then he returned, and we would talk about the shipwrecks of life, about *1984*, and the cold wind in this big, bad city.

The insufferable office job, the various disillusionments of love and happiness, was shared by my new flatmates, who soon became friends : a pair of brothers from Scotland, who had come to London to escape the North's economic depression, with less than satisfactory success, and an Italian photographer, who was finding it hard to get work

[320]

commissioned and bruising his ego on the exclusivity of London's art institutions.

We were all single, young, and under-employed, living in small and run-down bedsits, which were shamelessly overpriced. Our communion in this disastrous situation, our shared sarcasm, disappointment and burning desire for magic, inspired us to form a hip hop group and we began recording a song and video clip with the modest means of the house.

The photographer's cousin came for a visit, an out-of-control, chain smoking rock'n'roll nanny from southern Italy who was always looking for troule and getting outrageously drunk on week-ends. We all had a big pasta night at our house, and she cooked, and delighted everybody with her salmon vodka sauce.

My young friends and I were in a sort of big cruiseship together, it seemed, a ship of half-truths and good looks, amusement over unbelievable life events, impressions and personality clashes, immigration stories, and as if London had become a grand new American Dream, we wined, dined, discussed all the facts and un-facts of life, tinkering in the London vibe and bathing everything in that gentle humour and the nonchalance of large cities. Ed didn't make himself too rare any more, showing up often with bottles of wine, or to take me out, always moaning under the load of his job in the legal offices.

I had met a colleague at the office whom I went for drinks with on a chance, and as it turned out she had been in the half world for a while as well, and in mental hospitals before then. We were a terrible duo, if we went out on those evenings in autumn, and had endless drunken confessions and laughs together.

It was a running gag amongst colleagues and friends that I was under-employed and should really find something more substantial to further my career. I was walking in a perpetual chorus echoing 'you're a genius, you could be rich, why are you even doing this'... I was grateful for it, because it told me that I was recovered and ready to go.

I started slowly: trainee curator in a museum. The work was new to me, but made me very happy. I had to polish exhibits, create catalogues, investigate missing labels, dust boxes in the basement and unpack collections that had been slumbering for decades, digitize card catalogues, research the history of things, much as I was learning simply by reading label after label, card after card. Those hours spent in a glass cupboarded room full of mystifying jars, arched over handwritten catalogue cards from the 1960s, were an almost spiritual experience, as they restored quiet and focus, and let the madness of life and the times whirl around itself, with the leaves in the wind outside.

One autumn evening, it was a Monday, I didn't go to my (newly) local pub. For reasons unknown, I went to Soho and sat down in the O-Bar. I sat by the window, listening to the 1990s r&b they play in there. Some songs I had not heard again since I'd last sat in there, nor had I been in an incensed cocktail bar full of mirrors and lustre since then.

I sat there alone on the white leather sofa by the window and gazed out for a long time. And there was everyone: hooded figures with dark grin smirking from doorways, passing small wrapped balls from hand to hand, faking walks at the arms of washed-down women, whose longing eyes were bending and twisting their bodies in an eternal dance with death in the arms of their coarse-tongued givers.

There were boys with shorn head and grey down jackets, staring in a daze, against the wall. A couple of old gals with greasy hair and scrunched faces, and over wood-pannelled windows and crumbling facades of flashy paint

[322]

and punched-in neon letters, paper notices were fluttering in the wind. Behind some windows, the familiar red light was shining through white lace curtain and skirts rushed by the handrail on the stairs. Long-haired characters in worn-out suits and modest ties were pacing the block, plastic bag in hand, and teenagers in emo styles and shades stood casually about the place. A girl in wedding dress rode by on a bike. And a small traffic warden walked down the road with fixed gaze hugging his elbows, as if he was cold.

I saw a girl sink to the ground, scraping the wall, opening her mouth as in moaning, but silent, closing her eyes and hugging herself on the ground, then, once it had kicked in, opening her eyes again and blinking as though she just woke up in a cornfield, one quiet summer afternoon. A brown coat hushed by, coughed. And another young man was fainting under the influence, in his dirty trackies and trainers, his mouth gaping open, slightly downturned, and he tumbled on. Somebody hurled something at him. Two old drag queens paraded by. The notices were still fluttering about, brown with rain and smoke, cheap paint was chipping off the closed strip bar doors, and the Windmill had the lights off.

The evil of this drug, the evil of a cheap world like that, acrylic underpants with ribbon and ruffle, cheap perfume in shuttered, red lit bedrooms full of stains on the bed, and the kaleidoscopic memory of a disco ball, burst as a mirror in a thousand pieces, it was as though I heard a glass smash on the floor. And suddenly, a crack grew through the landscape, the house fronts seemed to form rifts. A cry was heard, a terrible cry of pain, anger and disaster, of fear and sure death, and my heart tore in a flash.

Too much here, I knew all too well. On the corner of the road, Louis, the great net-thrower, was wearing fur and showing well cared-for skin. It wasn't the first time I'd run

[323]

into him again. I saw everything in a flash of memory, the falling birds, the wet smell, the downturned mouths, the scraped walls, the dead ends of addiction.

I was starting to feel troubled. A blind heartache was making itself known, and I knew of course what it was: it was the truth. My life, now, was a lie.

I looked in my phone for the next best NA meeting, and found St. Giles. So slowly and pensively, regretting that I had even come to Soho, I walked up to St. Giles. I was a little early and at the entrance, a man in black suit and black fur-lined jacket, with black hat, was just stepping out of a black merc. I looked toward him from the corner, unsure whether I'd recognized the man I thought he was – yes, it was him – Zach.

'Hi', I said, walking towards him. Briefly I'd thought I should perhaps ignore him and let him notice me during the meeting, but I was too curious about the reaction. He looked at me quizzically.

'You don't remember me, I guess. I remember you. I just wanted to say hi'

'I recognize you.' There was a pause, then he said: 'Did I know your name?'

'I would have told you Louise, but that's not my name'

'So why would you have told me that?'

'Because I was working'.

'And where was that?'

'Knightsbridge', I said.

His eyes lit up, and a visceral 'Hah!' escaped him.

'Yes', I said.

'Wow'.

'I'm glad to see you here', I said, 'are you going to go in?'

After the meeting, he gravitated toward me, asked for my phone number, and if we could go for coffee. We sat down at Emm cafe, had cappuccinos, and talked about life and

[324]

feelings, real things. My heart was skipping a few beats. I'd just seen one I had known, intimately, all too intimately. And it was doubly anonymous now, perhaps doubly vulnerable, and doubly intense. But we both saw the interest of having a sober talk, now, by day.

He remembered everything. The time I had taken him out to his car, and about the AA booklet on the car seat. He remembered more than I thought he would, the simple bond we had formed back then. We reminisced, looked each other in the eyes, and looked into the void, during a long talk that we had in that café. There was curiosity, and there was a feeling of joy and relief to see another roaming soul had found the way out of Hades, and to meet him at this rather utilitarian crossroads on the long maze of life. We talked, and talked, and talked.

He offered a ride home. It was still a Merc he drove, but not the same one. Now it was a very slick, brand new black SL thing. He told me he had crashed the old one. Talked about driving on crack, and about the times in the flat with all the hookers. He had come a few times, he said, looking for me, but never found me again.

'I remember you were quite chilled. Honestly, I thought you were cool. A lot of those girls you could just tell they hated their job, they hated me, they hated everything. And who can blame them. But you were pretty cool'.

Ah! Well... I didn't need to think of anything to say to this, because already, he was continuing to speak. He talked a little about the chaos he had been in, at the time when we first met. And about what he really got out of those improbably long coked-up S&M sessions, which he described to be a sort of fourth dimension on himself, the rockstar, the edgy, the insane, the artist.

He asked if I would hold his hand, that he was feeling fragile. He asked where he could find my street, and I said

[325]

it was diffiult to find it, as it was in a one-way system, but that he could drop me off nearby if he wanted to.

'No, I don't want to do that', he said.

We continued driving, talking about the real things. Guilt, shame, disaster, self. That spending more time with me could perhaps help him heal, if we could talk about that time we had, together. Because I had been there to see it – the disaster, his disaster – he could talk about it, now.

When we got to my place, in a hot mess that day, he looked around, closed his eyes, said 'first things first', and we got going, tearing off my office clothes, his black and studded things... It was a truthful, deep embrace we stayed in for a long time.

October, 2011.

A feeling of letting go gripped me briefly, letting go of my normal person disguise, I shook it off there and then. But later through the week, something started opening up within me, all that I had barred behind the black cross of denial, and the brick walls of pretending started crumbling. The deeper and quieter ills, that are normally suffered calmly and hidden away, rose up from their murky waters.

I had re-arranged my entire life so as to avoid hearing or seeing these things, renewing circles of friends, jumping out of one hoop after the other like a snake changing skins. Ever since I've stopped thinking and talking about it, this story's been devolving in darkness. This darkest chime I had so wanted to forget – here it is again, resounding awesomely, like a dark organ.

Denial had been comfortable. Monday promised to shake stuff out of place. Just when I had started to believe that none of these strange things had ever really happened, believing it was something that I'd dreamed...

I've imperceptibly chromed back to normal – back into the darkness and the sulking, my black and bitter mood that is so familiar, it is almost a comfort.

I have been seeing more of Zach now. He's inspired, and inspiring. When he speaks about blues and soul, and the blues, and the soul, it pulls out all the thoughts I buried to be a day girl, but cased in velvet and glam. Spending time with Zach has helped me rethink myself. The edges that used to be rough are a little blunter now, and the angular shape of my past is softly gleaming in what seems a blissful, eternally granted and continually extending distance.

Zach said his girlfriend, who was already with him even when we met back in the KB, is anorexic and that is why he could do with someone else besides her. He was about to start explaining how she hates her body and won't even get changed in front of him. I told him he needn't explain it further: I have been that woman.

I know well enough what it's like when anorexia creeps up to haunt you, brings dark and clouds into the home. Now I know the strain it puts on men, what an infernal machinery anorexia really gets going. By turning yourself into the sick one, you make it seem monstrous of those around you to leave you. At the same time you engender an outward pressure. The truth is, you've already left them yourself and are far removed from caring for the troubles of others, having focused everything on yourself. And yet, those around you, then, often without knowing so, begin to want to get away. They can hardly bear it. Often, they leave without leaving. They cheat. They leave in secret, just as the anorexic dies, in secret.

The tides of this woman who lives with the man in my bed rise to meet me, in the form of my past, and the inverse of my past.

[327]

I walked around Soho and Fitzrovia, past the old pub where I had first met Ed, and phoned him. I met up with him later, at a pub near Trafalgar Square. He showed up shattered like rarely before. He said he had not eaten yet that day, and was feeling low. We went for a stroll in Soho, settling for the velvet lined W-hotel bar and drank old-fashioneds.

He was distraught, held my hand on the road, and took my arm whilst I carried his backpack. At my house, he soon fell asleep, and in the morning, he was in no rush to leave.

A melancholy anxiety gripped me, a dull forethought that this could be going on forever, or could be the last time I ever saw him. He was like the moon to me, again. Clouds swept over his head, and his face, which he held so close to me, seemed distant and withdrawn.

I got drawn to Ed, drawn away from him again, as by moontide, mysteriously, quietly, splashing sea water in parts with laughter, in parts with anger – in this love story, the tide washed me forward, arched me back, I swayed with it like a flower in the breeze, until eventually I decided to leave town.

This town was finished for me. Zach started dropping in and out just like Ed had done, taking me for dining sprees in his slick SL, to the Soho Hotel, to Pizza Express, Denmark Street, to the 100 Club, to Chelsea and Mayfair. Andrea was dating wildly around the place and we were going shopping together, and drinking out a lot.

I went to see one film by myself: *Dreams of a Life*, about a young woman who was found in her bedsit, with her television still on, after she had been lying there dead for three years; no-one had missed her, though everyone had loved her. The film was chilling, and I felt unsafe, as if that woman's fate lay in store for me, too. There was a sadness

[328]

in the ease and shallowness of all my new friendships and flighty loves. Nobody really needed me, everybody loved me though...

There was Timothy, a lawyer-historian whom I had met through English Billy from America, who tagged on to my nights with friends, and we had a brief fling. A chic Oxonian with a flat smack in King's Road, he was sharp, knowledgeable, and brilliant, orderly and aspirational, but somehow a misogynist, not only catholic but bigoted, the socially awkward product of English boys schools, a great drunk dialler... All my friends loved him, but I could not stay with him. Everybody was being awfully sweet to me, but I had to get away.

In the first days of a harsh February, I was ready to leave London. My friends all said they would miss me, but I was so loosely integrated in this circle of friends it didn't matter to me, although I had, inadvertently, become the centre of it.
I knew well it didn't matter what people did, the key was the make-believe, in this hypocritical society that I was growing into, that I briefly had left, and regained in the end, for the comfort, for the simplicity, for the quiet in deceit, the safety and wholesomeness it promised. And I could see in my dear friends the traits of the bourgeoisie draw unseemly lines, distort their honesty and chip at everyone's happiness.

Children were born in London, house moves, parties and projects happened, that I wasn't there to see, but I received many visits. By a strange chance Berlin had, in the ten years that I had been away, become so fashionable and vibrant that Londoners were coming there on their city breaks.

[329]

There were caviar and champagne evenings at my Berlin house, I took friends to oyster bars, to skyline bars, and glamrock bars. I sat with them on their starchy and white hotel room bedsheets, talking all night long about the way our lives were going, and the ways of the metropolis. I led nearly the life of an expat, though in my own home town, showing people around, meeting them at airports, lunching out in famous restaurants.

I felt, for a while, as if I were in a gondola swinging over mountaintops. The world was passing by me, I only had news from friends and the life, my old life, via phone and web. Sometimes, Florian would ring up to tell me about his dreams and we would sit on the phone, analysing. I had a lot to do: ancient Greek studies were again writ large on my day-to-day life plan, and I could sit in the brand new library with a view on the museum island.

Slowly, I got to know the habitual drinkers of Berlin nighttime cafes. I met the playwrights, the poets, photographers and philosophers stranded there, and had a good long swim in this smoky, late aquarium of broken dreams that I had always so much dreaded to get stuck in. In the old-fashioned and bohemian, creative limbo that has no age, where stories trickle down an insatiable drain of whiskeys and urban romance pinned somewhere between extravagant nightclubs, ice cold winters and furs, hot lips, earnest sex, and soulful, blue confessions. All this fascination and this real freak fashion show seems flat and cheap to me now.

I dangled above things in a vacuum, as though an invisible hand carried me through. To-do's that I'd pushed off for a long time, started ticking themselves off the list as by magic, and I became a writer.

[330]

I don't really think everything that I've done is good. But this is not the end.

The production of this book would not have been possible without the creative input, practical help and moral support of Bob Slayer, Clifford Slapper, Dave Kelso-Mitchell, Debra Shulkes, Eszter Galfalvi, Joe Palermo Noir and Sabrina Andresen. Thank you so much x

Its publication was funded thanks to the generous support of Anonymous * Anonymous * Anonymous * Anonymous * Anonymous * Anonymous * Anonymous * Anonymous * Anonymous * Anonymous * Anonymous * Mary Newton * Viv Walker * Caleb Selah * Caroline Fries * Jill Gray Savarese * Tim Arthur * Clifford Slapper * Kevin Zakresky * Allegra Shock * Bob Slayer * Bryanne Melville * Cecilia Lundqvist * Cristina Hanganu-Bresch * Darby Penney * Eleanor Longden * Jonathan Kemp * Joseph Warwick * Kermit Cole * Kevin D * Kirsty Kennedy * Nina Forbes * Oliver Raison * Rich Flannagan * Anke Tietz * Andreas Meinhardt * Anthony McGowan * Debra Shulkes * Isabel de Vasconcellos * Jim Owen * John C * Jupiter John * Mark Thomas * Matthew Cohen * Paul Jerome * Sorabji * Sarah Burnautzki * Susan Ensley * Tomas Aquinas * Tracey Cannon * Alexis Fancher * Cat Jones * Carla Jones * Dylan Willoughby * Grzegorz Olszowka * Mia Morris * Seth Osborne * Silver Office * Stellalink Books.

Thank you very much indeed x

Printed in Great Britain
by Amazon.co.uk, Ltd.,
Marston Gate.